OTHER WORKS

The Twice-Cursed Serpent
The Twice-Cursed Serpent
The Shattered Star
The Burning Hand
The Twisted Sword—A Twice-Cursed Serpent Collection

Twisted Worlds
Within the Darkening Woods (2024)

THE
BURNING
HAND

Copyright © 2023 by Scarlett D. Vine.

All rights reserved.

No part of this publication may be reproduced, distributed, or transmitted in any form or by any means, including photocopying, recording, or other electronic or mechanical methods, without the prior written permission of the publisher, except as permitted by U.S. copyright law.

The story, all names, characters, and incidents portrayed in this production are fictitious. No identification with actual persons (living or deceased), places, buildings, and products is intended or should be inferred.

Cover by Beautiful Bookcovers by Ivy.

Map by Dewi Hargreaves.

Promotional Art by @nox.benedicta.art, @mariamarcelw, @avoccatt_art, @jessamyart, and @bookishaveril

First edition 2023

To Samantha

Thank you for coming along with me on this journey.

Author's Content Note

Much like the first two books in *The Twice-Cursed Serpent Series*, *The Burning Hand* is an adult novel meant for those over the age of 18. In addition to graphic consensual sexual content and harsh language, there is additional content readers may want to consider before proceeding. This includes—but is very likely not limited to—gore and death, including self-harm. Really, there is a lot of death, and everyone in the story is at risk. Torture, imprisonment, and abuse—both physical and emotional—are depicted, including in the context of a relationship. Sexual assault is referred to in non-graphic detail. There are also references to cannibalism and some rather disturbing things involving eyeballs and other body parts, including tooth consumption (not Bethrian's finest moment).

However, any cats or dogs depicted in the novel live long and happy lives.

The Burning Hand
Scarlett D. Vine

Parker & Wilson Press, LLC

Prologue
Liuva

The first sensation I ever felt was pain.

I was not born of my divine mother's body, or so she always told me. But that didn't mean she didn't labor for me. That I wasn't any less treasured as a result. Instead, she brought me into this world piece by piece, forging flesh and bone from other mortals together with her own essence, crafting me strand by strand. Limb by limb.

I was still her child.

The awareness she granted me, a gift from her own soul, awoke at the very moment she fused my first bones together. Those tiny bones were merely a piece of what would become my finger. Unfortunately, even that little bit of connection was enough for me to wake in agony. I existed, and yet I was unmade. Incomplete.

I don't know how long I existed in that state of agony. Of burning. Of a sense of being bent and twisted, pushed to the point of breaking.

All I remember was that the pain grew as more and more pieces were added to me, and thus gave me more places through which I could suffer. Did suffer. Those unlucky humans she harvested the pieces from were dead and beyond feeling any pain. But not me. Never me. There was no relief.

And then the pain was gone.

And then there was her. Shirla. My mother.

My mother was perfect. Golden. She never said as much to me, she just was. She was my maker—my mother. I was not made into a child's body, but I saw the world with a pure innocence. I had a mature body with a child's experience, and the experience of daily life constantly shattered my reality and reforged it. Seeing each animal, tree, and flower was new, each emotion was something I had not experienced before. And my dear mother—my goddess—taught me about each and every thing we encountered.

"Where are they going?" I asked my mother, watching little brown birds dart amongst the trees.

She caressed my shoulder from where she was braiding my long brown hair and took a moment to answer. In those days, gods took their time, because that was one thing they had in abundance. Time. And power. She may have taken a few minutes to answer me. Maybe an hour. It was impossible to know. "Looking for food, my sweet one," she finally said to me. "Maybe looking for a new place to build a home."

"Could we find a new home?" I asked. "If we need one." Even in this idyllic world, I heard rumors that there were creatures and gods that were not our friends. That they would hurt me if they could. I did not understand, but I remembered the pain I endured before. I always feared the pain's return.

"Do not worry," Mother said, seemingly reading my mind. "Your home will always be with me. And I will always be with you. I will keep you safe."

I do not know how long I spent like that, as a child but not a child. My appearance was that of a young human woman, fully grown and in the prime of health. But my inner thoughts were as slow to shift as the cliffs on a shore that were worn away by the tides. How long did it take for me to change, to be complete and mature? Decades? Centuries? Slowly—so slowly—my mind grew until it matched my body.

And through everything Shirla was there, the goddess who was my mother, but not my mother. In those days her relationship to me didn't matter—I had her love. I had her. *The world was a place for me to explore and experience, and I delighted in everything. I played with young gods and sang with the stars, their chorus audible through the clear night. Life in the goddess's care was a perpetual summer.*

And my summer ended the day I met Lyritan.

Chapter 1

Caes

For a god, Lyritan oddly loved humming.

As he rode, walked, ate, and dozed off, the same series of little upbeat tunes emanated from him, like he was perpetually surrounded by bees.

How did Caes know that gods were not normally hummers? Because she had her memories back. All of them. Unfortunately—or fortunately—she wasn't able to access them at will. Finding the right memory took concentration and time, like digging through a long book for the answer to an obscure question. A book that was disorganized and possibly missing pages. Though things were better now than when she first awoke—thanks to Alair, she was able to focus and not lose herself in the who-what-why that otherwise flitted through her very tired head. She remembered what Lyritan liked—human food and songs, especially ones that involved clapping. And dislikes—he had an intense sense of smell and despised false praise. She needed to remember how to handle Lyritan, for their survival depended on it. For now, she had to ignore that he—and the two goddesses—had neglected to mention that she was likely going to die as a result of their schemes.

With the safety of herself and her friends at stake, she was able to mostly ignore the unwilling jolts of lust and fury from Liuva towards Lyritan and focus on the task at hand. She was going to go to the Burning Hand, make one god very happy, save the world from the impending chaos, and try to survive.

Emphasis on *try*.

"Tell me more," Lyritan said from where he rode on his horse through the forest, pushing his long blond hair out of his angular face. After centuries of knowing him as a curly-haired golden warrior—and even more recently in her dreams—hearing his cadences coming out of a much slimmer body was unexpected. Granted it had only been around sixteen hours, but it was still an adjustment.

"You know it all," Caes said from where she rode in front of him, shoving aside the rush of anger she carried from Liuva. She needed to focus. When he traveled from Reyvern, Lyritan had brought an extra horse for her, but instead, he insisted that she ride with him, her hands being too injured from her divine fire to handle reins. Of course, Caes would be one to have divine power and be unable to use it. With Caes occupied, Bethrian rode Caes's horse—as a human, he would have slowed them down if he was forced to go on foot. Lucky Bethrian.

"I don't know everything." He gave her a wide smile that sent a stab of pleasure into her, one even Liuva's anger didn't dim. What Alair did to her new memories—sending them to a place in her mind so that her time as Liuva felt merely like a long and detailed dream—tempered her physical response. However, it was still there, built into her very nature as one created by the divine. Those crafted by the divine—like Soul Carvers and herself—craved the ones who made them. Even when that craving was extremely inconvenient. "I know you assumed my curse and broke it," Lyritan said. "But that was merely a year. Only one year in a mortal life. Surely, more happened."

"What do you want to know?"

"Everything. I want everything from when you assumed my curse up until last night."

"That is a lot." She shyly smiled, even though she had turned away and he couldn't see. Facial expressions affected words.

"Regardless, I want it all. Every detail."

"You've heard it. Seen a lot of it."

"Not from you." His hot breath tickled her neck.

Cylis snorted from behind her, walking on foot through the woods. They had stolen horses from Fyrie, but the poor things were exhausted, so they attempted to spare them the extra weight. Caes ignored Cylis and the other men and women plodding and riding behind them, both Lyritan's men and the rescued Soul Carvers. And Bethrian. One couldn't forget Bethrian.

"All right," she said. "I'll try. Do you really want the details of my research?"

"That isn't necessary," the god said. Cylis snorted again.

Miraculously, with no further interruptions from Cylis or anyone else, Caes told Lyritan what had happened to her since she was taken to Malithia as a hostage and assumed the curse. From how she studied everything about curses and gods she could think of, spending countless hours in a dark library with only Soul Carvers for company, to how she earned the ire of Princess Seda, who had tried to murder her—but maybe Seda didn't try to murder her, since at least one of those attempts was up for debate. Caes left out the details about how Flyntinia was potentially behind the murders and instead blamed jealous courtiers—why bother the god with mere suspicions?

So, her tale continued. She regaled the god with how she went to Lord Bethrian's estate and found the words of the curse, but then Bethrian tried to kill her—again, that apparently wasn't what happened. Bethrian enthusiastically shook his head during that part, but remained silent while the god glared. Caes assured the god that Bethrian was entirely safe to stay in her company—she didn't want him dead—and instead went on to the rest of the story.

Regardless of the murder attempt at the estate, Caes explained how she had to flee into the woods with Cylis, of all people. There, she met up with Alair and eventually made her way back to Glynnith, Malithia's capital, in time to break the curse. Which she did, by taking her own life.

But then she came back from the dead—the god remembered that part—and was promptly challenged by Seda to a battle for her life. Unfortunately, she won, so she ended up becoming a princess, revealed to everyone that her eyes were not exactly human, and set herself up for a lifetime of courtly misery. That was a long day. The night with Alair that followed was delightful, but that part she left out of the story.

After this, Caes's attempt to summarize things became even more complicated, since the story veered too close to her dealings with gods. Dealings she didn't feel like disclosing yet. So, she kept to mundane affairs.

I can't trust him. He wanted to betray me. He would have killed me.

Quiet, she told herself. Liuva's—*her*—hurt feelings wouldn't help matters, despite how the urges and thoughts from who she had used to be had become harder to ignore in recent hours. Granted "hurt" was a bit of an understatement for what Liuva felt, but Caes had more pressing concerns. Like finishing the damn story.

Instead of telling Lyritan just how much Liuva/she hated him, Caes explained how she and Althain, the emperor's son, went to Ardinan to allegedly put down a rebellion. This included a short summary of how she was engaged to Althain—again, Caes left out that Althain's mother, Flyntinia, likely wanted to kill her. Arranged romance aside, Caes's story veered to how, once back in Ardinan, Desmin, her former betrothed, betrayed her once again by killing Althain and imprisoning her. Though Caes hadn't remained imprisoned for long, since she escaped Shirla's/Karima's temple and into Fyrie by pretending to be contrite, where she was rescued by her Soul Carvers. Once they were on the city streets, the Soul Carvers found her, and they all escaped and defeated some sort of monsters that Desmin had sent after them. Sure, in defeating the monsters Caes accidentally-on-purpose accessed her latent divine power and burned her hands as effectively as if she had rubbed them over an oven. But they lived. That was the important part.

And now, after all that, they were on their way to the Burning Hand for Caes to try to put this whole sordid divine mess behind her. If such a thing was even possible.

When Caes was done with her tale, Lyritan looked at her, one eyebrow raised. "You've left something out."

"What do you mean?" Caes gripped the saddle's pommel, ignoring how her blisters stinged.

"There's something you didn't mention, that is, *someone*." Lyritan gestured to behind them, where Alair walked beside Cylis, his face as expressionless as the entire time they were in Malithia. A light sheen of sweat was on his face from the exertion, yet he carried himself as composed as a statue. Even now, her heart leapt to see him. Here. So close to her. But her joy was tinged with fear of what Lyritan meant.

Lyritan watched her, watched the torrent of words and plans that no doubt showed on her face. His own expression was unreadable. Did he want her to confess their love? Did he want her to apologize? Maybe it was something else? The horse's pace underneath them made her struggle to keep her balance at the angle she was in, even as her mind fought for a solution.

"The Mind Melder," Lyritan finally said. "I know how you feel about him."

"I don't—do you—" Shit. Caes paled. Alair had agreed with her plan in the woods just last night—they were going to tell Lyritan about their relationship, but not like this. Information like this needed to be delivered carefully. One couldn't just tell a god that the woman he pursued over the ages was irrevocably in love with another.

Instead of smiting her, Lyritan smiled indulgently. "You've lived a mortal life, Caesonia. Surely, I cannot expect that you would not have formed other attachments. Would you prefer I call you Caesonia? I assume Liuva would be too strange for you."

Caes nodded, at loss for further words. "Caes is fine," was all she managed to say.

"How could I be upset that you experienced what pleasures you could? Besides, what is a mortal compared to me? Especially when we have the history of centuries between us." Lyritan smirked, and Caes caught herself staring at him for too long. Couldn't Lyritan have possessed someone a little less striking?

"Indeed," Caes said. How could this be? He was...alright with their relationship? Lyritan was contained in a mortal body, but only a fool would assume that he didn't have his divine power. The gold light of his divinity sporadically seeped out of his eyes, his fingers, and the little cut on his cheek. There had to be more. If the gods were good at anything, it was destroying what she loved.

She turned to face forward once more, pretending to admire the deep forest they wandered through while a flock of geese flew overhead. The leaves were marked with red and gold, for fall and winter would come especially quickly as they went further north. Unfortunately, Caes could not dwell on bucolic daydreams. She had to placate a god.

Pulling from her memories of when she was Liuva—and Lyritan's lover—she gave in to the physical feelings he stirred in her. Liuva was angry, but she was definitely still attracted to him. Still loved him, despite the hurt. Not that Caes could blame her...not entirely. She reached for Lyritan's hand, gently holding it through the bandage that encased her own. Lyritan's breath caught, such a human reaction for someone who was anything but. "Nothing like that could change this," she said softly. "Us." Secretly she apologized to Alair, both for saying such a thing, and worse, meaning it. To Liuva, Lyritan was...complicated. He was her safety from Shirla, her mother who wanted to use her. Who made her just to kill her in order to gain power. But Lyritan was just as crafty as the other gods. Long ago, he had told Liuva that he had a way for her to be safe, to free herself from the goddesses, and be with him forever.

What Lyritan did not—and presumably still didn't—know, was that Liuva/Caes knew better. She now knew he had lied. There was no possibility that she could grant anyone any of the power she contained without sacrificing her life in the Burning Hand. It was—as far as she knew—impossible for anyone to enter the Burning Hand and leave again. He claimed to love her, only to be prepared to betray her when it suited him.

So, yes, Lyritan was complicated. Caes was furious, terrified, and still very much in love with him.

Luckily the part of Caes that was in love with Lyritan was easy to ignore, thanks to Alair. But that didn't stop the memories and urges that broke through when near him. With him sitting behind her, his muscular thighs pressed against hers, an arm protectively around her waist, pieces of the part-goddess she used to be rushed to the surface. Bitterly, she pushed those thoughts aside. Liuva was the one who had loved him. Liuva was dead.

Lyritan gestured towards Alair, whose expression was somehow still impassive. "Soul Carver, don't worry. Carry on as you wish." Lyritan gave Caes a large smile. "I have never been able to deny my love a single thing."

Divine he was, but Lyritan still traveled like a mortal and had a mortal's needs, meaning that all of them had to continue their journey to Reyvern on horseback or on foot. Reyvern was a kingdom in the mountains, and that fact was impossible to ignore as they approached the range looming in the distance.

"So, you feel pain?" Caes asked Lyritan, half to pass the time and half to understand exactly what they traveled with. She needed to figure out his limitations—if he had any.

"The prince's body is my body," Lyritan said. "He gave it to me entirely. But yes, as a result, I feel what he feels. Pleasure and pain." His voice lingered on the word "pleasure" a bit longer than necessary.

"Are you like Soul Carvers, then? They have mortal bodies. But they're stronger."

"No. Prince Phelan was nothing but a mortal and so is this body. Before you become too disappointed, understand it's out of necessity—I don't know if this body would survive what would happen to it if I attempted to meld my divine nature with his flesh in the manner of the Soul Carvers."

"What do you mean?"

Lyritan shrugged. "Some bodies don't survive. It's an unnatural process. His body housing me is enough for my needs, while forcing every bit of his being to become one with my power would likely kill him." And then Lyritan would no longer have his host. Were gods able to possess people against their will? Probably not, otherwise she would likely have read other myths of it.

"Wait," Cylis loudly interrupted, "so Karima doesn't choose whether or not she brings us back to life?" The other Soul Carvers glanced at each other.

"Is that what she told you?" Lyritan asked and let out a curt laugh. "She has about as much control over the process as a rooster over the sun. But, of course, she would have you believe differently." Grumbling broke out amongst the Soul Carvers. Caes strained her ears to eavesdrop, catching only vulgar expletives and mutterings about what Karima's temples charged to "buy" her favor while a loved one underwent a Soul Carver's trials, until Lyritan spoke again. "We need to keep riding."

Caes nodded, not bothering to answer. She would've only said something all of them already knew. They weren't out of danger—Desmin could've easily sent more of those twisted soldiers after them. Or worse. As they traveled, the Soul Carvers kept close to Caes, watching and listening for any threat.

Regardless, Caes's heart raced—she needed to speak to Alair. This was...this was all so much. She needed his help to handle Lyritan and the course he was bringing them on. But she couldn't, not unless she wanted dozens to listen. The two of them had managed to steal a few moments to themselves in the chaos after defeating Desmin's soldiers—but it was useless to believe that they'd be able to keep having secret conversations uninterrupted. Instead, she reminded herself to be grateful that her feet were now bandaged, and that her arms—which were still burned from using her magic to save Cylis—were taken care of. And that she got to ride a horse instead of walk. What was a little more romping through the woods and trying to understand this god? If Lyritan was going to harm them, it wouldn't be anytime soon. He needed Caes. He would keep her happy. For now.

"What will happen to us in Reyvern?" Caes asked, just as they came to a much thicker part of the forest. Here the bushes made it next to impossible to see more than a few yards in any direction. Critters chirped and scampered at their progress, otherwise invisible in the thicket. Night was falling—they needed to stop if they wanted to set up any sort of camp. Did Lyritan know where they were going? Did anyone?

Caes turned and saw a broad smile break across Lyritan's face. "We're not merely going to Reyvern—we're going to Gilar. And, in due course, we shall go to the Burning Hand."

"Due course?"

"We've waited a thousand years for this moment, my love. You will take your place at my side and see the dawn of the world you fought to create before we bring it to fruition." A comforting hand gripped her shoulder, rubbing her skin through the fabric. Heat ran over her at his touch and her breath caught. "Every moment you've lived and every choice you've made has pushed you towards this. Savor it. It's yours."

Caes swallowed. Hard. "We...the king and queen will allow that? You—well, Prince Phelan—are the heir. And I'm—me. Both Malithia and Ardinan want me in chains. I'm the last person they'd want associated with their heir."

"Are you implying that you're not royal?"

"I'm not. Not by their standards."

Lyritan flicked his wrist. "No matter. Why would I wish to fraternize with a mortal princess, when I have you?" With a single finger he lifted her chin to look at him, his eyes heavy with emotion. Caes couldn't help but notice the way the light filtered through the trees and illuminated the cut of his jaw, the masculine lines of Phelan's face highlighted by the burning intensity of Lyritan's gaze peering out through the mortal's eyes. She hated the way that his sheer proximity made her ache, the leather-and-woodsmoke scent of him going straight to her core, the width and breadth of his body sheltering her from the rest of the forest. A part of her wanted to fold herself under his arm and tuck herself away, safe from everything. But Caes knew better.

"Do the king and queen know about you?" Caes asked and looked directly ahead, not wanting to give away her skepticism. "That you're...you."

"Of course. They were honored that I chose their son as the means to reenter this world."

Was the royal family honored? Or were they terrified to tell the god differently?

"I heard that Reyvern worshipped Karima," Caes broached warily.

"Yes. But long ago they worshipped me. I was bound to that land, and I took it back as easily as summoning a dog."

"And the people? Do they know about your return?"

"Of course. Once I reminded them of what I did—*can*—do for them, they were more than happy to welcome me." After seeing the chaos that resulted from the change of worship in Fyrie, Caes doubted it was as simple as Lyritan was making it sound. An almost-forgotten god had possessed the crown prince and announced that the kingdom was now his. Surely, some people weren't happy about this. Caes's stomach twisted. In addition to being politically complicated, she was going to have to contend with a people who were likely disturbed at the very least at Lyritan's presence, and furious at the worst. Would they take any anger out on her and the Soul Carvers?

Whatever the circumstances, things weren't going to be as simple as Lyritan made them seem.

"We need to find shelter," Alair suddenly said, the first words he had spoken in some time.

"Is something wrong?" Caes asked. Yes, night was fast approaching, but that did not explain the urgency in his voice.

"A storm is coming."

Caes looked around her, listening as hard as she could. There was nothing but the silence of a dense forest and the hooves and steps from their party intruding upon it. "Are you sure?"

"We can hear it, Caes," Cylis said. "We aren't fortune tellers."

"That is not a tone to take with your queen," Lyritan said, narrowing his eyes at Cylis, gold suddenly flaring behind them. Cylis held his head high in a dare. Idiot. Caes's breath quickened. Would Lyritan harm Cylis? Over something so small?

"Cylis saved my life many times, and we faced many dangers together," Caes quickly said. "I am not offended by such flippancies, my love," she added.

Lyritan relaxed and nodded, and Caes's shoulders slumped while she let out a long breath of relief. "So be it."

Lyritan raised his hand. "Alright, Soul Carver, we shall take your advice and try to find a place to hide from the storm. It's time we stopped for the night regardless. As much as I'm in a hurry to return to Gilar." Lyritan then snapped a few orders to the other men and most of the party fanned out into the woods.

That went about as well as expected—at least Lyritan seemed to be past the issue of Cylis and his, uh, zest. Caes caught Cylis's gaze while Lyritan was distracted and he gave her a quick nod. He seemed to understand—he had to be more careful around the god and watch how he spoke to her. Watch how he acted around the god in general.

It would have been easier to convince a rooster not to crow.

They traveled for another half-turn of an hour, searching for shelter that didn't seem to be forthcoming, before Alair suddenly said, "There are men approaching. On horses."

Lyritan called out to his men, who were still scattered in the woods. Within moments, the men returned to their prince and formed a shield around Caes and Lyritan, while Lyritan pulled out his sword. A soft ripple of golden light emanated from him. The Soul Carvers gathered as close to Caes as the men allowed, their own weapons out, and Bethrian...poor Bethrian was stuck trying to find a place to shield himself behind them all.

Now Caes could hear other shouts and the frantic trodding of horses' hooves. There was going to be a battle. More bloodshed. Caes's heart pounded in her ears, her body tensed, waiting for the fight.

"Wait," Caes said, "are the men Desmin's?"

"Doubt it," Kerensa yelled. "They sound mortal. Probably the landowner's. Too trained to be some village watch."

"Whose lands are these?" Alair asked Caes.

"Ummm..." Shit, she couldn't remember. Where exactly were they? The answer to that could mean the difference between a noble who would pretend they never saw them—and facing an army.

"No matter," Lyritan said. "We fight."

The thundering hooves grew louder. This wasn't a small company—there had to be dozens. They were outnumbered. They had Soul Carvers on their side, but everyone was tired and wounded, and while they had Lyritan, what could he do? Could he defeat this many soldiers?

Lyritan does not accept defeat. No matter the cost.

He would see them all dead rather than lose to a mortal. And for what? His pride?

"Stop!" Caes screamed, just as the first men burst into sight. A frantic hope. A desperate action. But oddly, everyone listened. The soldiers pulled on their reins, jerking the horses to a rough stop. And the men were definitely soldiers, wearing clean metal armor and riding fine warhorses bearing a vaguely familiar green banner. "We are just passing through," Caes called out. "We mean no harm to you or your lord."

The soldiers looked at each other, confusion evident, and then moved aside to let a new horse and rider through. A woman. "Who are you—" the woman said as she rode her way to the front, and then she also abruptly stopped once she caught sight of Caes. The woman was young, not much younger than Caes, and was very familiar. "You," she said.

"Baroness Ossia," Caes said as she gave a nod of respect, the memory of her time in Fyrie rushing forth. Yes, this was the same brown-haired young noble from that disastrous "luncheon" in Fyrie. The one where she reminded the Ardinani courtiers that she remembered who had love diseases.

For a moment Ossia stared at her, eyes wide, and then she sprung into action. "Your Highness," Ossia said, dismounting and bowing her head as she sank into a curtsey. The baroness's men followed suit, dismounting and bowing, placing the tips of their weapons on the ground. "We are at your service."

"You know this woman?" Lyritan asked, voice laden with skepticism.

Caes nodded. "This is Baroness Ossia. I met her in Fyrie." She was the courtier who was in danger of having her estate confiscated, until Caes interfered. After meeting her, Caes determined that the estate was almost stolen by the crown on some debacle between other members of the baroness's family, the temple, and the King of Ardinan. Regardless of whose fault it was, the baroness was not to blame, and Caes had had a very bad day and was glad to do something that would annoy the Ardinani. Sometimes, pettiness could be a good thing.

"'Met,' Your Highness?" Ossia asked. "Saved my lands, more like." She gracefully stood from her curtsey. Now, with the mask of a noble defending her home gone, her face was taken over by worry. To her credit, Ossia only hesitated a moment when she caught sight of Lyritan's golden eyes, and then immediately assumed the role of a good hostess. "In the chaos of everything occurring in the capital, I seem to have been forgotten by the court. I have my home. Thanks to you."

"It was right," Caes said. "I'm glad to have helped."

"How is it you're here?" The baroness asked, looking from one member of their company to another, her attention lingering longer on the Soul Carvers and the god. "The last I heard…there were such horrible rumors about you. I feared the worst."

"Most of them are true, I expect. We are leaving Ardinan."

Baroness Ossia nodded, seemingly expecting as much. "You are close to my estate. You must spend the night here, at least. Rest. You all seem to have need of it. And I don't like the sound of the winds."

"If you trust this woman, I will trust your judgment, my love," Lyritan said softly.

At Lyritan's pronouncement, the rest of the company looked to Caes. Was it wise to accept the baroness's offer? Was she going to murder them in the night? Likely not. If they wanted to murder her, the baroness had brought along more than enough men to do that here, and in a place where they wouldn't destroy her home in the process. Besides, they needed help. Her companions needed care—clean supplies, at any rate. Soul Carvers healed quickly, but they had to make sure their wounds were cleaned and bound.

And there was that storm…

Caes smiled. "We will be glad to accept your offer, Baroness."

Chapter 2

Cylis

Few things in life were better than a soft bed. Granted it was best when that soft bed was one's own—preferably with a pretty partner in it—but Cylis wasn't that picky. He gladly accepted all the quilts and goose-down mattresses life wanted to give him.

But not everything was sunshine and fluffy pillows to Cylis. The fact that his current quilt was bestowed by some Ardinani courtier Cylis didn't remember...he didn't like that so much. But Caes insisted that this baroness was to be trusted, and no one asked Cylis.

The baroness's estate was humbler than anticipated considering she was a noble, and consisted of a stone structure that had seen better years and was in desperate need of a new roof. How had she obtained so many men-at-arms? The ones she brought with her must have been a large portion of her retainers. But then again, this kingdom was at war, and no one asked Cylis.

When were people going to start asking Cylis?

Regardless, they were all offered baths, a healer's services, food, and beds. After being checked over by a healer for essentially nothing, Cylis was in the middle of a rather delicious meal. He was dining like a wood tick in summer on potatoes covered with black peppercorn gravy littered with pieces of shredded beef, served with fresh rye bread and creamy butter, when Alair strode into the room and sat at the table with the Soul Carvers. Lyritan's men were in a different dining area, while Caes, Lyritan, and Bethrian—accompanied by Marva—were dining with their host. Because they were special. And royal. Well, Fuckwit was up for debate.

"You look cheery," Cylis said to Alair.

Alair fixed him with a stare, his dark hair in need of a cut—it was getting long. "Have I ever looked cheery?"

"No, but normally you aren't quite so...rigid."

Alair helped himself to a plate and began filling it with an impressive amount of potatoes. "Well, things aren't quite as I wish," Alair said with a sternness that made the air vibrate. Alright, Alair was pissed. Most Soul Carvers couldn't make the air tremble, but most Soul Carvers weren't Alair. For which everyone was very grateful.

Fer the Soul Carver coughed, tossing his flatware on his nearly-empty plate. "I'm going to, uh, leave."

Janell nodded, following suit, along with Jarmilla and Erasmus, the other Soul Carvers rescued from Fyrie.

"Cowards," Cylis said, while the Soul Carvers all but ran out of the room. "Not you, Ker?"

Kerensa snorted from her place at the table. "He's not mad at us." Kerensa frowned. "I think."

"No." Alair sighed. "It isn't you."

Kerensa gave Cylis a look as if to ask, "what crawled into his pudding and died?" but Cylis spoke before she could voice such feelings. "If I had to guess, our dear Soul Carver's ire all stems from the god who decided that he is still in love with Caes, even though that was a thousand years ago, and it's not entirely clear that she doesn't have some remnant feelings."

Alair's eyes narrowed. "More like Lyritan decided to cast me aside when this is not the place to do so. I should be guarding them tonight. What if this is a trap? What if this woman poisons them?"

"Considering I'm on my third helping of everything and feel fine, I wouldn't worry." Cylis took a big bite of beef for emphasis. "Look," he said, chewing as he spoke, "what idiot would poison them and leave the rest of us intact? It would be like at Bethrian's, but worse. Besides, Caes isn't an idiot." Cylis maneuvered his bread in the gravy, preparing it to become his next bite. "If she didn't contradict

Lord Golden Taint in his choice of Soul Carver for the evening, she has a good reason."

"Lord Golden Taint?" Kerensa interrupted, wiping drops of wine off her mouth with the back of her hand. "No. Pick a different name."

"Why? It fits."

"It's annoying. And maybe pick something that won't make him smite you if he overhears. Which he will."

"Fine. Goldie. How's that?"

Kerensa nodded reluctantly. "Sounds like a dog's name, but it's a little better."

Matter of naming the god settled, Cylis lowered his voice. "Alair, you know she would rather have you there. And Marv will take care of her. Marv isn't weak."

"I know."

"And you can't blame Caes too much," Kerensa said briskly. "Lyritan is a god. You can't pretend you haven't felt it."

"What?" Cylis asked. "You mean the urge to ask him to remove his tunic so I can bask in his godly glory?" That was a slight exaggeration, but not by much. Yes, something about the god irritated Cylis in a way that was eerily reminiscent of socks that were too tight, but there was no denying that the man/god had a certain divine aura.

"Yes." Kerensa smiled. "That one."

"I know what she is feeling," Alair said. "Or at least I can imagine it. It's just not what I expected."

"Well, I didn't expect you to come back from the dead," Cylis said, helping himself to more wine. "Things change."

"Yes," Alair said. "That." Alair then picked at his food, though at least the air around him stopped trembling. That was good. That was very good. The three of them talked for a bit about the accommodations and how much longer they were going to have to travel before they were out of Ardinan and into Reyvern's relative safety. They guessed the journey would likely take several days, at least, before they crossed the border.

Oh, goody.

Alair was nearly done conquering his mountain of potatoes when he changed the conversation, his face somehow becoming even more solemn. "Cylis, it occurred to me when I was dead—this last time—that with me gone you had no means of contacting your...friend. You should consider changing that."

His "friend." By that, Alair was referring to Cecilia, Cylis's sister. The one Alair had freed from Karima's temple and hid so thoroughly that even Cylis didn't know where she was. And as the temple had asked Cylis that exact question after she had disappeared, it was very good that they took that precaution. Cylis was very good at blustering his way through conversations, but he wasn't the best at outright lying, especially to the head of Karima's order. Cecilia...it had been years since Cylis had seen her or had even heard anything other than that she was "doing well."

"It's too dangerous," Cylis said, shaking his head. "I can't know where she is. We've discussed this. The temple will never forget."

"I put her in a safe place," Alair said, "but if I'm gone, you need to be able to find her. But the choice is yours, regardless."

"Have him tell you," Kerensa said to Cylis, tearing into her bread with abandon. "We aren't going back to Malithia—at least, not like how we were before. And I doubt we will at all. You should know where she is. Maybe you can pay a visit when this is all done," she said sadly. Was Kerensa thinking of her own sister, the one she hadn't seen since the day she swore to Karima's service? Cylis wasn't the only one who had lost family due to the empire's inherent cruelty.

Should he ask Alair? Once he learned where Cecilia was, Cylis couldn't unlearn that information. If the temple found her because of him, the punishment Cecilia would then face for abandoning Karima's order would be horrific, and involved flaying. But then again, what would happen to her if Alair was no longer there to check on her safety and provide funds for her upkeep? And she had disappeared so long ago now, that surely with everything else that was occurring in the empire—like the succession crisis and the looming rebellion—the temple had other concerns. Yeah, the temple was irritated because priestesses-to-be weren't allowed to escape, but even the temple had to give up sometime. Right?

"Alright," Cylis whispered. "Tell me."

Chapter 3

Bethrian

The storm that Alair had predicted roared outside the manor, but the thick walls and their host's generosity allowed Bethrian to change into something dry and a bit more presentable—though not nearly as well-tailored as anything he owned in Malithia. Though, what could he expect? He was in rural Ardinan. He would wear the outdated borrowed silk, and he would like it, dammit.

Somehow, much like how the estate and its windows managed to hold back the storm, Bethrian kept calm while the outside world thrashed against him. Once Bethrian was shown to his room, he dressed and then darted through the halls like a chicken looking for a prize worm—he needed to talk to Caes, both to warn her, and make sure he wasn't about to be murdered by a god. Or anyone else.

"May I speak to you in private, Your Highness?" Bethrian asked Caes with a little bow. It was mere luck that Bethrian found her relatively unattended in the manor hallway, with only Lyritan and Marva for company. He didn't need an audience for this. Especially Cylis.

"If Your Majesty permits," Bethrian added to Lyritan, the potential executioner in question. Bethrian had been through far too much to question why there was a god possessing a prince or even why a god was here. Caes was involved, and that was enough of an answer.

An eyebrow flicker was all that Caes showed to indicate her curiosity. "Yes, Lord Bethrian." She gripped the god's hand with her bandaged palm. "I'll be alright," she said to Lyritan. "I have Marva with me. And I will see you soon." Caes smiled, which the god reciprocated with a look Bethrian had seen old men give to beloved stallions. How...delightfully nauseating.

"Alright, my dearest," Lyritan said, kissing her hand. "I will see you at the dinner."

The three of them waited until they were alone in the hall before Caes asked, "Here, or in my room?"

"Your room, please," Bethrian said, giving the Soul Carver a nervous glance. A Soul Carver who looked Bethrian up and down and smirked like she knew just how uncomfortable he was. Marva hadn't done anything to threaten him, but considering she could pluck off all his limbs like a chef processing a chicken, having a case of anxious nerves was just good sense.

Caes led them to one of the rooms near Bethrian's own, a modest space that was comfortable and clean. A draped bed rested in the corner, covered with thick quilts. A lit fireplace was against the opposite wall, giving off much-needed heat in the night. While the floor was made of rough stone, it was covered with sturdy—if worn—rugs that further fought the chill. Candles flickered in sconces along the ceiling, letting Bethrian get a good look at Caes, who seemed like she desperately needed a nap. Here, away from Lyritan and their strange hostess, she let the exhaustion show. And could he blame her? In less than a week she went from living on Fyrie's streets to escaping demonic soldiers to now contending with a god. And she didn't have Bethrian's facial hair to help hide said exhaustion.

At Caes's invitation, Bethrian made himself as comfortable as possible on one of the three wooden chairs arranged around a small table in the corner. Thunder rumbled outside, followed by a harsh gust of wind. Ominous. Again, fitting for delivering bad news.

"What do you want?" Caes asked, taking her own seat. Marva remained standing near the door, watching the exchange. If Marva killed him, would she use her magic or a weapon? Which one would hurt more?

Best to get this over with, and hopefully not find out. "I want to apologize," Bethrian said. "I'm sorry."

"For cutting my arm?"

"Yes." Bethrian groaned and rubbed his face. "And everything else. I should have done something to stop Desmin. Anything."

She hesitated, and then said, "There's nothing you could have done. Once Desmin decides to do something, it's nearly impossible to stop him."

"True. But that doesn't mean I don't wish it was otherwise."

Caes nodded but didn't give any other reply. At least she seemed to accept his apology and wasn't in any rush to have her Soul Carver remove him. Permanently.

"But that isn't the only reason I wanted to speak with you," Bethrian said. Caes cocked her head. "I have something to tell you."

"Yes, Cylis mentioned as much." She crossed her arms and leaned back against the chair. Watching him.

How was he to say this? How to even start to tell her...oh, well.

"Caes" –Bethrian took a deep breath– "your father is alive."

All coloring left her face as she stared at him. Then she blinked several times. "Sorry, I'm more tired than I thought. I thought you said—"

"I did. He's alive."

"Bethrian—look, I understand that you don't think of me as a friend, but for you to lie about something like this—"

"I'm not—"

"Truly. Of all the things you could say and do." Caes's eyes narrowed and her nostrils flared. Marva shifted, taking a few steps closer. "This is disgusting. How could you—"

"I saw him," Bethrian rushed out. As he hoped, his words made both women stop. "In Fyrie. I saw him."

Caes remained motionless, though tears welled in her eyes. Now Bethrian saw her as she truly was—a young woman, one who had been forced into a struggle between vast powers at far too young an age. And worse, she had been born to none of it. Bethrian, at least, had known his entire life that he would take his father's place as lord one day. But Caes...

"He's truly alive?" she asked.

"Yes."

"Then I need to rescue him. Bethrian, why didn't you tell me earlier? When we were in Fyrie. I could've done something. We could've—"

"Are you alright?" Marva asked. "Want me to get Alair?"

"No. Not yet." Caes wiped her eyes. "Where is he? How? Is he alright?"

Shit. She really had no idea. Bethrian's stomach dropped and his lungs felt as if they were in a vice. Slowly, Bethrian held up a hand and she stopped to let him speak. Her eyes sparkled. Hope. Well, that wasn't going to last long. He coughed. "That's...oh, fuck, Caes, I don't know how to say this. He is—I mean, he isn't—he's—"

"Tell her," Marva said.

"He's working for Shirla. And Desmin."

Caes's hands dropped from her face and a shadow went over her expression. "I don't understand."

Bit by bit, Bethrian told Caes where he had seen her father in Fyrie with the queen, and how her father had changed—a likely understatement—and was now serving Desmin and Ardinan. How her father seemed to be devoted to Shirla above everything, even his daughter. How *he* was the Penitent lurking in Fyrie, just beyond the notice of the Malithian occupiers.

"That doesn't make sense," she said. "The Penitent is a ceremonial position. They don't have power. They aren't blessed. Anyone can become one."

"Maybe they made an exception for him?" Bethrian offered. "They made it seem like he was something special. Regardless, I thought you should know."

"Yes." Caes covered her eyes, resting her elbows on the table. "Do you mind going to your room? I need a moment."

"Of course." Anyone would need a moment alone after getting news like that. Bethrian stood and let himself out of Caes's room and made his way back to his own sleeping quarters, his steps echoing through the stone hall. There were few servants in this estate, matching the sparseness of the accommodations, though today that was a good thing. He didn't need prying eyes.

Poor Caes. If Bethrian had found out that his own father was alive and trying to kill him...alright, Bethrian wouldn't have been that surprised. He and his father had a contentious relationship due to what was essentially a fundamental personality difference. Bethrian enjoyed life, while his father saw it as a burden to be endured until the sweet release of death. But to most people, finding out that one's father wasn't dead and was instead working towards their demise would be unexpected. And with everything else Caes was enduring...

It made Bethrian very glad that all he had to do in this mess was stay alive and make it back to Malithia and his rightful place as a lord.

Somehow.

Chapter 4

Caes

"Are you sure you don't want me to find Alair?" Marva asked Caes once Bethrian shut the door behind him. "Or Cylis?"

"Oh, no." Caes coughed back her tears. "Definitely not Cylis." She shook her head, trying to steady her trembling hands. "I just need a minute to compose myself."

"Do you want me to go?"

She gave Marva an apologetic look. "If you don't mind."

"I'm not the one whose father returned from the dead. You take the time you need. But I'll be right outside the door if you need anything."

"Thank you."

Marva left the room, leaving Caes alone with her thoughts.

I finally get a father, and this is what he does. To think I ever dreamed of having one.

"Fuck." Caes sobbed. For once, she and Liuva were in complete agreement.

In the prison in Ardinan—the first time—she had imagined this moment thousands of times, each one a perfect echo of her heart's yearnings. Her father, returned to her, alive. Shirla's Chosen, victorious. He would prove all of the Ardinani wrong and save her, punish everyone who hurt her, and then he would take her back home to their farm. Where she would be safe and all of this merely a bad dream.

But to have him returned to her like *this*?

If she was being honest with herself, she couldn't be too surprised that her father was Shirla's acolyte, apparently working dark magic on the goddess's behalf. She remembered the change that had come over her father shortly after the

Sword of Might was discovered, how having even that little bit of magic changed him. Overnight, the two of them had all they could need, he was so powerful. So confident. But that was before she discovered what true magic was capable of. Was her father ever really her father? Or was he gone as soon as he came into contact with the sword, corrupted by the barest hint of power? Or worse, did Shirla affect some change on him, something that sent him—and consequently, her—through the chaos that was her life?

Though, she never would've expected him to help Desmin try to kill her...

Her.

Her heart wrenched and she shook. *You're my precious darling*, he had whispered to her when she cried as a child. *No more tears*, he had said when he wrapped her scraped knee. *The nightmares will never come for you*, he had promised.

He lied. Tears, pain, and nightmares were all she had known.

Luckily for her, she knew how to manage being betrayed by a parent. This wasn't the first time it had happened to her.

I've survived worse. I will survive this.

That was true—Liuva knew all too well what betrayal from a parent tasted like. She was made by Shirla, after all.

A knock at the door interrupted her. She wiped her eyes. "Yes?"

"I'm sorry to bother you," Marva said, "but the baroness has sent word that dinner is prepared."

Chapter 5

Bethrian

The baroness's dining hall was respectable, but Bethrian had seen grander. The walls were patched with chipped plaster, for one, and covered by muted tapestries that attempted to hide areas that needed further repair. Cracking his neck, Bethrian admired the ceiling, and how there were cobwebs from spiders who dared to make their homes at such drastic heights. A fire blazed at the end of the hall, doing its very best to warm them. The storm raged outside, and wooden shutters were the only things valiantly protecting them from the deluge. Good. Bethrian's hair was damp enough as it was.

Moreover, Bethrian wanted nothing to distract him from the delights spread out on the table. Oh, what a meal. A gift from the culinary gods. Something warm. Something fresh. While Caes, Lyritan, and the baroness chatted and exchanged pleasantries, Bethrian enjoyed his roasted pork loin and turnips, served with a sweet cranberry sauce, followed by spiced carrot and leek soup with sweet baked apples. They could keep talking all night for all he cared. It wasn't like they needed him for anything. He would be ignored just like Marva, who stood guard against the wall, her expression borderline bored. While he ate he watched Caes, who somehow showed no sign that she had received devastating news less than an hour prior. No wonder she did so well at court...

Suddenly, the baroness abruptly lowered her steaming cup of some sort of herbal tea, setting it to rest on the wooden table. "Caesonia, I'm afraid we have to speak on a delicate matter. In private. It concerns your father."

Caes looked at Bethrian, who was tugged to the present by the baroness's words. Quickly, Caes turned her attention to their host and shrugged. "I'm afraid I know what you're going to say, and Lord Bethrian knows all." She smiled at

Lyritan and grabbed his hand gently. "And there's nothing I will hide from my love."

Love? Was that true? Was Caes really in love with the god/prince? But she was in love with Alair...right? Granted, Bethrian was surprised to learn about her relationship with Alair, but he would've been more surprised to learn that she abandoned the Soul Carver so seamlessly. Or was this a tactic of hers? Caes was very good at surviving, and nothing good came from angering a god, if half the myths and warnings from Karima's temple were to be believed. Plagues. Fiery deaths. Smiting. A legend ran of two lovers, who, in the midst of matrimonial adventures, forgot to leave their customary offerings for Karima—those two were now allegedly granite pillars on Bethrian's lands that people rubbed when they wanted good luck. Gods were like temperamental geese with endless power, and woe be to the one who found himself on the foul side of fowl.

The baroness's young face creased with worry at Caes's words and her little non-verbal exchange with Bethrian. The baroness wasn't the most beautiful woman he had ever seen, but she was striking, with a complexion most women had to resort to paint to obtain. Was the baroness married? It had been some time since Bethrian had dallied with a noblewoman and thus gained more inspiration for his novels in the process. Maybe Bethrian could...no. He was full. With food. He was sated. With food. He wouldn't make trouble for himself. He wanted more food. Food had less complications.

"Alright," the baroness said, "if you insist, Your Highness. If you trust them, I can do no less." At Caes's answering nod the baroness waved to her servants, sending them from the room. Once the five of them were alone, the baroness said, "I received word from Melonie this morning. Princess Melonie, I mean."

"Melonie?" Caes lifted her silverware to cut into the roast, her bandaged hands deftly using the instruments despite the likely pain. Bethrian recognized the gesture for what it was—an attempt to focus so that she didn't accidentally give something away. "What does she—I mean—"

"I know you're here because of her," the baroness said. "I know she helped you."

"Why?" Caes asked lightly, as if she was asking when the storm was going to pass. "Why did she help us? How do you know her? I never saw you at court before."

"Because I rarely went to court," the baroness said. "And with the conflict in my family, I had to attend to my own affairs." Wait, it was her family who had caused the baroness so much grief in managing the estate? Where were those family members now? Was Bethrian's bed over the graves of troublesome relatives? That would be a delightful story twist. No matter. Bethrian would eat his roast, keep silent, and listen. "But Melonie would travel to our lands—these lands—and hunt when she was younger. We formed a friendship that we kept close to our hearts."

"Close?" Caes's mouth dropped open slightly. "I'm sorry, I didn't realize..."

"Oh, banish whatever sweet thoughts you're envisioning," the baroness said gently. "It was a friendship of convenience and the realization we could help each other with our various aims. She was a princess in that poisonous family of hers, and I had my own situation—but you'd be surprised who is able to help you and when, where politics are concerned."

"You mortals and your plots," Lyritan said, sipping the wine and watching the whole exchange like they were performing a play.

They all ignored him and the baroness continued, "Regardless, Melonie had kept me up to date with the events that were occurring at court—secretly, of course. It was harder to help each other if too many people became aware of our connection. Over the years we've gotten quite efficient at communication, mostly smuggling letters through trusted servants." The baroness frowned. "But this time she sent me a message by bird. A desperate one that was worth the risk of using that method."

"What?"

"Most of the message was for me and me alone, but there was a clear warning I can share with you—Melonie's family is desperate."

"What else is new?" Bethrian couldn't help but quip.

"Ignore him," Caes said. "Tell me."

"You know as well as I that the goddesses have power. Well, the royal family has given into the dark magics. Desmin and your father are following you. Powered by whatever Shirla has gifted them."

Bethrian dropped his silverware. Following? Powered? Bethrian didn't like the sound of any of that.

"I know about my father," Caes said slowly.

"Following?" Bethrian asked. "We already defeated them."

The baroness shook her head. "There's more. Since Melonie mentioned their prior defeat, I can only imagine that there is more to come. All I know is that they are following you," the baroness said sternly, "and that they embraced the darkness that Melonie has long feared would overtake her family. They are coming for you. Hunting you."

Well, that was unfortunate. Until rather recently, Bethrian had no experience with the gods' magics, except for Soul Carvers. Too bad it didn't stay that way.

Shadows came over Caes's expression. That poor woman. After everything, her own father was hunting her. It was one thing to know that he was helping Desmin, but actively pursuing her by his own will? "Divine power is impossible to resist," Lyritan said softly. Comforting. "Mortals crave it, though it will bring their ruin."

"I don't understand why," Caes said, her voice breaking the tiniest bit. "Power is pain. It destroys everything."

"And it allows you to turn the world into what you want it to be." Lyritan spoke gently, yet Caes squirmed.

"Power is one thing, but what can you tell us to help us avoid our hunters?" Bethrian said briskly, turning everyone's attention to him. Caes eyed him gratefully. "We need to get out of the kingdom. Preferably in one piece."

"I will give you fresh steeds, and protection while on my lands," the baroness said. "But after that, all I can offer are provisions and directions."

"We need both," Bethrian said. "And" –Bethrian coughed– "I'm a little confused by all of Melonie's involvement, I admit. But then again, Melonie didn't seem the sort to contradict her family, free political prisoners, and send secret messages."

"She is doing so at great risk to herself," the baroness insisted. "Were you her friend? Can you claim to know her?"

"She freed you from prison, Bethrian," Caes said. "That should be proof enough."

"True. I'm just trying to reconcile what I saw at court with *this*." Melonie was a vain, foppish creature. Hardly the image of a political mastermind.

"That is court," Caes said. "You should know, Bethrian, that one is never who they truly are."

Chapter 6

Cylis

"For fuck's sake, Cylis. Stop fidgeting," Kerensa growled from her cot.

"I can't sleep," Cylis said.

"Since when?"

"Since we're in a stranger's home and facing the possibility of either our host, or the god, or Piggy, or anything else chasing and killing us."

Kerensa sat up and snapped her fingers, calling fire to her hand. Acting as a human candle, Kerensa made sure Cylis took in her scowl and, incidentally, the modest room around them. The baroness gave them shelter for the night, but it wasn't what he considered luxurious. A single shuttered window was their only view of the outside if they wanted one, and the walls were made of rough stone that would be an awful surface to make love against, if one wanted to keep their skin. But the walls and lack of view weren't as bad as the straw bed and dirt floors. Rural homes, even noble ones, weren't known for their comforts. At least the baroness gave them a change of clothes so that he was wearing something that hadn't made the journey from an Ardinani prison. Even if the pants were a little snug.

"Talk," Kerensa snapped.

"Why? You know everything."

"No, I don't."

Cylis crossed his legs, trying not to cough at the scent of burning meat that tended to emerge whenever Kerensa used her magic. It was difficult to ignore in such small quarters. "Well, well, well," he said. "Looks like I wasn't the only one who was doing too much thinking to sleep."

"Thinking? Whatever you want to call it, I guess." Kerensa took a deep breath.

"What is it?" Cylis asked. "Is it one of the Reyverni guards? The baroness's men? Or the baroness? What is weighing on your mischievous little mind?"

Kerensa narrowed her eyes, which illuminated like embers. "I found Ilia."

Cylis blinked. Then blinked harder. "Ilia? Why didn't you tell me sooner? Wait, why are you still here? Caes would—"

Kerensa shook her head. "I know she would, but this could involve the end of the world. My sister is safe, and she won't be if Caes doesn't settle this conflict with the gods. Ilia can wait."

"You know Caes would make you go to her if she knew."

"Yeah. She would. And that's why you're not telling her. Now, do you want the story or not?"

Cylis was stunned into silence as Kerensa relayed the successful final attempt to find her younger sister, an effort that had consumed Kerensa's attention ever since she became a Soul Carver. A sister who was sold into bondage by their greedy father, her life and body no longer hers. Kerensa had narrowly escaped that fate herself and chose a Soul Carver's life instead, which was its own sort of bondage.

"Ker..."

"I mean it, Cylis. I know Caes would tell me to go, but I won't. I can't." She let the fire die, sending them back into darkness, her eyes and fingers still glowing like embers that took their time fading. "Not yet."

"Wow. Um, alright." Cylis laid back down on the squeaky cot. If Kerensa decided she wanted to be here and race to the end of the world with Caes, that was her business. Few people knew what Kerensa had gone through to find Ilia. But he did. He knew everything.

"Are you ready to sleep now?" Kerensa asked.

Cylis snorted. "Hardly. And I doubt I will for a long time. What does Caes have planned next, do you think?"

"I don't think her plans matter overmuch anymore. We have a god with us—I have a feeling he'll decide everything."

"Have you met Caes? I doubt even a god can tell her what to do."

"What are you talking about? She was a perfectly behaved hostage."

"Are we forgetting the part where she canoodled with Alair and then dethroned Seda?"

Kerensa coughed out a laugh. "Alright. Maybe she does have a knack for survival. But who doesn't?"

"Seda, apparently."

Kerensa laughed louder. "That's true." When the laughter faded she let out a long sigh. "Have you shown Caes the hilt yet? The one you almost killed yourself stealing from Fyrie?"

"No chance. I doubt we want an audience."

"And have you figured out what Bethrian is planning on doing?"

"...No chance. And why should I care about Fuckwit?"

A rustling came from Kerensa's cot as she rolled over, the mattress groaning in protest. "Go to sleep, Cylis. Seems like we have a lot of chatting to do tomorrow. With a lot of people."

Chapter 7

Alair

Alair huffed on his fingers, watching his breath fog in the air. The storm had passed, leaving most surfaces slick with ice. He had stayed awake to hear from Caes after that dinner, but until he did, he had little to do other than think. He wasn't going to rest until he knew she was safe. So, instead of lurking in the halls, he walked outside to clear his mind. Little good that did. Everything just made his thoughts deeper and darker.

Winter was coming quickly. Too quickly. And they had to go further north, beyond Reyvern, where it would be an even harsher climate. Mountains. No civilization. How was Caes going to handle it? She had survived in the brutal Malithian winter after fleeing Bethrian's estate, but survival wasn't thriving. And the idea of her suffering wasn't something he could tolerate. He had wanted to take her to a home—with him—and instead he would be escorting her to her death.

"What are you doing?" Cylis asked, suddenly appearing from around the corner. "I thought you'd be with Caes."

"You're supposed to be sleeping."

"Well, I failed. And I asked first."

Alair rubbed his arms. "They're still dining. And talking."

"Still?"

"You're free to go to the hall and see for yourself. I'm sure they'd love to see you."

"No thanks." Cylis approached and braced himself against the stone wall. Cylis's shirt was unbuttoned at the top, letting anyone who cared get a glimpse of his pale skin marred with dark purple. The Soul Carver was fortunate to never be cold. Though, that wasn't exactly true. Cylis had told him he was plenty cold, it was just that being in cold didn't make him any more miserable than normal. Usually. Then again, Soul Carvers could be very creative when describing their powers.

"Alair?"

"Yes?"

"Stop looking. You're scaring me."

"Hmm." Alair moved next to Cylis and braced himself next to him. He took a few even breaths, enjoying the silence while it lasted.

"Can I ask you something?" Cylis asked.

Alair nodded. And so much for the silence lasting.

"Where are you in the royal line of succession?"

"The what?"

"For the Malithian throne."

"What are you talking about? I'm not." Alair pushed his hair behind his ears. As far as Cylis was concerned, that was the only answer.

Cylis smirked. His knowing smirk. Great, he wasn't going to drop the subject. "Stop," Cylis said. "Don't give me that. I know that your father was the king's son. Back when Malithia just had kings and all and not emperors."

"He was the fourth oldest," Alair clarified.

"And you were your father's oldest boy."

"Third."

Cylis flicked his wrist. "Doesn't matter. We both know that that king's direct line died out eventually, due to various shit. And that your older brothers either died childless or left only girls. Which meant that the line of succession was eventually picked up with your...nephew?"

"Something like that. My younger brother's descendants." Alair grimaced. "When did you become such a student of history?"

"While Caes had me stuck in the library. Anyway. What I'm wondering is what does that make you?" Cylis looked at him expectantly.

"...I have a feeling you're going to tell me."

"Oh, I wouldn't think about it. *Your Augustness.*"

Alair stared at Cylis. What was he thinking? If anyone heard him—

"Don't worry," Cylis said, still smirking, "I know better than to say that at court. Though I'm surprised no one else put it together."

"I think they did," Alair said softly. No point in hiding it. Cylis—*Cylis*, of all people—had figured out one of Alair's most closely-guarded secrets. "I also think they realized very quickly I wasn't about to act on it. And they were prepared to remove me if I tried." They *did* remove him once he became too much of an inconvenience. They would've had no problem doing it sooner if necessary.

"And what a wasted opportunity—Emperor Alair. The Soul Carver Emperor. You and Caes could've ruled the empire. You as emperor, her as...whatever she is."

"Well, I am sorry to disappoint, but we both know that's a pointless dream. I have no interest in ruling. Never have, and never will."

"Who said anything about a dream? I'm merely pointing out the missed opportunity. Think of the stories that would've been written. But, regardless, at least I distracted you from whatever the hells it is you're thinking."

Alair wrapped his arms around himself. Cylis may not have been cold, but Alair was not Cylis. And thank all the powers in the world for that.

"We have a long journey ahead of us," Alair merely said.

"No shit. What else is it?" Dammit, Cylis wanted more. And again, Cylis wasn't going to let this go. He never did.

"The god," Alair said. "Can we trust him?"

"Trust Goldie? Alair, I'm the funny one. Not you." Cylis sighed and said, "There are only four people in this whole world that I trust. And I'm standing next to one of them."

Chapter 8

Caes

A steady knock at the door interrupted Caes in her borrowed room, where she was taking a moment to herself after dinner. She was going to find Alair—gods and goddesses knew she needed to speak to him—but she needed a moment to herself to think about...everything. Quickly, she wiped the tears off her face and said, "Come in."

The door opened, revealing Lyritan, whose brow wrinkled as he took in Caes's expression. "What happened?" He rushed to her, kneeling at her feet and taking her bandaged hands in his. Concern was wrought over his beautiful face, which was framed by his brilliant hair. "Tell me, my love."

That bastard...as if he cares about me.

She wanted Alair so badly she ached. She'd find him later, once Lyritan was gone. She wanted—needed—him to leave, but she couldn't let him realize that.

"My father." She swallowed. "He's alive."

"The Chosen." Lyritan's gaze darkened. "I know, my love. I wish our host had found another way to tell you about him, but I don't have the means to command all mortals yet."

Yet? Command? What was he talking about?

"I'm just letting myself think. To settle my mind."

"Ah. I understand." He let go of Caes's hands. "I forget that such things are difficult for mortals to manage."

Caes dried her eyes with her sleeve. Hopefully the baroness didn't expect Caes to give the wool gown back to her—it was surely stained with all sorts of tears by now. "Did you know about my father?" she asked. "I mean, I understand if you didn't want to tell me sooner..."

"Caesonia" –the god's lips pursed– "you know as well as I that our ability to see in this world is limited." His voice lowered. "At least with me nearby, Karima and Shirla won't be able to watch as they would otherwise." How much of his divine powers *did* Lyritan still have? When the gods walked the earth, things had been different. Very different. Lyritan didn't need someone else's body before, for instance. What else had changed? What other limitations did he have? "No," he added, "I didn't know. I would have told you."

A small consolation.

"So, if you're able to hide us from the goddesses, you're able to hide us from my father?" Caes cursed herself at the hope that tinged her voice.

"That I don't know, my love." Lyritan stood and moved next to Caes, placing a consoling hand on her shoulder. "There are all sorts of things that gods could choose to do to a mortal's body. Cursed things. Whether I can hide you is going to depend on what she did to the Chosen One."

"Cursed things?"

"Don't worry now. You have other pain weighing on your heart, do you not? Just trust that if I can, I will protect you. From everything."

What about from yourself?

She nodded, deciding to believe him. For now. He *did* need her for the Burning Hand, after all. "There's more," she said, thinking that the god expected her to keep talking. "With how he is helping Shirla, it just...it stings."

"Oh, my love," Lyritan said, leaning towards her. He was so close she could smell him, fresh soap and leather and something sweet that made her want to move closer. "I know this must be unearthing old wounds. This is why you cannot trust in mortals—they will do whatever it takes to obtain their goals. Goals that do not matter."

"And what about you?" Caes whispered before she could think. "I heard you talking to the nymph." Caes's heart leapt. Fuck—why? *Why* would she mention that?

"What?" A shadow crossed Lyritan's face. "When?"

"How can you not remember?" Caes asked, overcome with a wave of scattered memories. Before she could stop herself, the words burst forth, as if Liuva took over her voice. "Was it just that once? Or did you make it a habit to discuss me—and how you were going to use me—with other dainty women with night-black hair?"

No. She had to stop.

Caes slammed her mouth shut. What had she done? Caes watched the god. What was he going to do? She didn't mean to reveal why she no longer trusted him—but it seemed Liuva had a slight issue with impulse control. And from what she regained of her memories, that seemed to be a rather entrenched character defect.

"That's why you have been so distant with me," he finally said, running his hand through his hair. "You think, that is, all this time, you thought—"

She nodded.

"Liuva," he said, his face contorting in grief. "No. Never." He shook his head slowly. "No. I only—I didn't want Shirla to suspect what I had planned. If she knew how much I loved you, how I had a plan to save you *and* fulfill our goals, she would've done so much worse. I lied to the nymph. I had to."

Caes's lip quivered. He *didn't* betray her? She was wrong this entire time? "I thought that you—"

"If you doubt me still" –he gripped her hand gently– "consider that I have nothing to gain from sacrificing you in such a manner. Any sacrifices made in the Burning Hand have to be willing. So, my love, I couldn't have done that to you even if I tried. I will *not* lose you again. I have a plan—you will not lose your life at that mountain. I promise."

Was that true? Caes searched her memories. Possibly. Once, she had loved Shirla enough that she could've been convinced to do such a thing. But was Shirla merely trying to gain her cooperation so that it would be easier to accomplish her task, or was a willing sacrifice actually a requirement of using the Burning Hand, as Lyritan said? She didn't know. No—she saw the desperation in his eyes. He was telling the truth. But the truth often buried the best lies.

"Know this," Lyritan said, "I have loved you longer than any being on this earth, and I always will."

Slowly, Lyritan pulled her closer and brushed his lips against hers. She opened her mouth, letting him in. Her body—her very soul—rejoiced at his touch, set on fire by being near him.

My love. You didn't betray me. I love you. Until our end and ruin.

And then, when she was so close to giving in to him completely, she broke away and caught her breath.

No.

No.

"I can't," Caes whispered, forcing herself to stop. Now, broken away from the kiss, she banished Liuva's ghost from her mind. Liuva was very much obsessed with Lyritan once more, but Caes had a lifetime of well-earned skepticism fueling her.

Lyritan's eyes widened. "My love—"

"I don't know you," she said. When he frowned, she quickly added, "I mean, I don't know you in this body."

"Is this body not pleasing to you?"

"That's not what I meant."

It wasn't.

Caes let her eyes trail up Phelan's form. It was hard not to admire his physique, which must have been honed through hours of wielding a sword. His black leather breeches clung to thighs strong enough that Caes could see the muscles move as he shifted on his feet under her considered gaze. A tapered waist hidden under the padding of his jacket gave way to a chest that was practically begging for Caes to run her hands over the firm planes of it. His shoulders were broad, his arms muscular yet ending in long, graceful fingers. And then his face...his features were bold, sculpted, the hollows of his cheeks and the curve of his mouth were stunning, and she could get lost in the rich brown of his eyes. She wanted to tangle her fingers through the length of his white-blond hair, drawing closer to him so that she could feel his strength...

"I need time," she whispered. "I need time."

"I understand, my love," Lyritan said with a little bow of his head.

"But, Phelan...is he...how does he feel about me? About us?"

Lyritan smiled. "He gave himself to me, utterly. My joy is his."

"Is he still...here?"

Lyritan shrugged. "In a way. But I can't hear him, if that's your meaning." He grinned. "The little prince gave me a gift—I won't abuse it. I may be a god, but I am not one to harm those who have done such great things for me."

Caes nodded. "Alright."

"And no matter." Lyritan stepped away and stopped, staring at the fire. "Once you are my queen, we will have all the time in eternity to enjoy each other."

"I'm sorry?"

Queen? What?

Lyritan turned to face her. "Of course. What—did you think I was going to live without you again?"

"But you're the crown prince. Of Reyvern," Caes insisted. "What does the royal family think? And me? And you're going to rule?"

"Oh, don't worry. I'm not going to just rule Reyvern." A golden glow illuminated Lyritan's eyes as he said, "My love, once we are done at the Burning Hand, we are going to rule the world." The grin faded. "Don't you remember?"

"The world," Caes said in disbelief. "I don't remember this."

"Oh, my dearest." He shook his head again. "You've forgotten everything. Why we were together. Our dreams. Our plans."

"Dreams," Caes echoed, scrambling through her memories. This would've been an excellent time for Liuva to remind her what had happened. There was so much she didn't understand. Hells, she needed time to *think*. "And I wanted you to rule the world because..."

"What better alternative is there?" Lyritan asked. "Shirla? Karima? The other cruel gods and goddesses that gained dominance on this earth? Trust me, Caesonia. Once we're in Reyvern I will remind you once more of why you chose me, and of the things we are going to do to make this world everything we dreamed of."

Caes let her current situation sink in.

The god who swore to love her, who was her only alternative to Karima and Shirla, had announced that his plan was nothing short of domination. A weight settled onto Caes's chest. This wasn't merely some lord with ambition—this was a god who had thousands-of-years' worth of power and cunning motivating him. And as she stared into Lyritan's golden eyes, something told her that he'd do anything to get what he wanted.

Chapter 9

Alair

Finally—*finally*—a servant came and announced that Caes was ready to see him, if he was willing. And, oh, Alair was willing. It wasn't just that he had enough of Cylis calling him "Your Augustness" to last for one lifetime, but he wanted *her*. The sound of her voice. Her embrace. Her comforting words reminding him of why the suffering he had endured was worth it.

Her.

And when his first sight of her room was of her sitting with her face buried in her hands, what he found was not what he wanted.

"Caes, what's wrong?" Alair asked, shutting the door behind him. "What happened?" He ran towards her, scooping her into his arms, inhaling her unique scent that was now mixed with lavender from the soap she had used to wash her hair. Her eyes were puffy and red and her skin sallow. She had been crying. A lot.

"Oh, Alair," she said, moving from the table and pulling him toward the bed where they could both fit. The bed was surprisingly small considering the number of pillows shoved on it. The baroness must've been trying to impress them. Careful not to touch Caes's injured hands more than necessary, he grasped her fingers with his and sat next to her, positioning himself so their bodies molded together. She rubbed her eyes. "Everything is..."

"Tell me," Alair said. "All of it." He bit his lip. Would he rip someone's mind apart tonight? Gladly.

Trembling, she asked, "Where to start?"

"Was it Lyritan?"

"No." Caes blinked hard. "I mean, not in the way you're thinking."

"Tell me. From the start."

"The start. Right." Caes took a steadying breath. "Well, there's the baroness. She told me she received word from Melonie." Quickly, she told Alair that her father and Desmin were working together. Hunting her.

Caes's father. And Desmin.

Alair clenched his fist, wishing that his gifts could extend across kingdoms and into two particular heads. Caes didn't deserve this. She deserved none of it. After everything she had been through, why did the fates toy with her? They gave her back her father, only to tear him away again. And it seemed they weren't close to being done.

And then Caes told him about Lyritan, enough that Alair bit his lip so hard he tasted blood. He knew that there was no trusting the gods, but to hear Lyritan's plans so plainly...

"He expected you to want him as a ruler?" Alair asked.

Caes nodded. "He seemed to think that having him as both emperor and god was what I wanted."

"And he wants you to rule with him?"

"Apparently." She squirmed. "Alair, what could he do, if he put his mind to it? If he managed to obtain more power? Could he actually be an emperor god?"

Alair groaned. This was all so much easier when the god was in that damn statue. "I'm not sure. But I do know that whatever he did would be enough to send the kingdoms and empire into chaos. A god walking amongst us and conquering? It wouldn't go unnoticed." He turned his gaze away, as if he could see before him the disaster the god would bring. "There are enough people who would be compelled to swear to him for the sole reason that a god is here. And with the kingdoms already weakened after being conquered by Malithia, I'm not sure there would be much resistance. And Malithia is unstable as it is." There was a true succession crisis now that the emperor had no more children, there were natural disasters from the goddesses' feud, and there were also kingdoms itching to cast off their conqueror while Malithia was spread too thin. It would be chaos soon, if it wasn't already.

One complication after another, each more dangerous than the last. Lyritan was potentially the worst complication of them all, but there was only so much they could do about it tonight. In fact, there was nothing Alair could do now other than comfort the woman who had placed so much trust in his ability to protect her. And he *would* protect her, even if it meant getting cleaved from this world again and facing the hells. He would.

"I will keep you safe," he promised, once her tale was done and a soft sob escaped her lips. He rubbed her shoulders, fingering the wool of her gown and thinking of the soft skin that was underneath.

"You will try," she said. "There's nothing that can be done."

"No." He placed a finger on her cheek and turned her so that she looked straight into his eyes. Her beautiful green and gold eyes locked on his, all her trust and love visible. "I will. No matter what, I am yours. Until the end."

"Yours. I am. But what am I going to do about Lyritan?"

"Well" –Alair grinned– "what do you want to do?"

"This isn't funny."

"No." He trailed a finger down the side of her face, enjoying how she shivered under his touch. His Soul Carver senses noted her racing breath, the way her muscles tensed under her clothes. Clothes that were increasingly getting in the way. "It certainly is not. Do you love me?"

"More than anything," she whispered. "And anyone."

"Caes, I understand. Everything."

The look she gave him, the absolute hope and trust, made his heart break. He restrained himself from taking her in his arms, from holding her so tight that she never had reason to doubt that she was loved again.

And he loved her. All of her.

How was he to convey to her that he understood? He was a man who had suffered for centuries, tearing apart his own mind, and who had to slowly piece it back together. And he did—largely because of the perfect woman sitting next to him. If anyone could understand what it was like to have memories inside of memories, lives stacked on each other so that desires and fears rolled like waves on a shore, it was him. Iva, his first love, was the innocence and passion of youth, while Caes mirrored his very self. In her, he saw strength, intelligence, and loyalty. Everything he wished he could be.

There was Caes's before. And there was her now. And her now was with him.

"I love all of you," he simply said. "Who you were before made you what you are. And if you find yourself wanting to enjoy the god, why" –he leaned down to whisper in her ear– "I'll do everything I can to change your mind."

A little gasp was all the reward he needed. She was pulled to the god, her divine nature responding to his call. His own body was much the same, yearning to be in the god's presence and seek his affection and love. It was the same as when he was around Karima. But Alair had a lot of practice denying his mind. He could ignore such things. And he was more than happy for this chance to take advantage of what the god had started.

"In the meantime," Alair said, "never doubt this—you're mine."

He prepared to leaned towards her, but before he could move, she reached for him, claiming him. Her name was the only thing he could utter before she pressed his lips against hers, reminding him of who she really craved. The press of her lips ignited everything he had kept suppressed, leaving him only with the thought of taking her and consuming her. He needed her.

Every last bit.

His cock hardened in his breeches, straining against the fabric and for her touch. In that moment, he forgot everything else. There were no gods, no monsters, and no kings. Only Caes. Her desperate gasp between frantic kisses called to him, begging for more. She climbed on his lap, straddling and resting on him in a way meant for perfect torment. He pressed himself harder against her, but then he broke away, catching his breath and forcing himself to kiss her gently. Tenderly. Sweet kisses were placed on her cheeks and then down her neck and to her collar bone. He had time to devour her as he would. He would take that time.

He ran his hands down her back and grabbed her hips, pulling her body against his, her woolen gown doing a horrible job of concealing all of her angles and curves, the shape of her body that was solely, delightfully, hers.

His heart raced as his hands moved to the front of her garment, where they rested on her breasts, teasing one after another. He grinned at each sigh of Caes's pleasure. He couldn't help it. When she closed her eyes and lost herself in his touch...there was nothing better.

Meanwhile, her hands that were caressing his chest moved down towards his breeches, and he gently grabbed one bandaged hand before it met its goal. As much as it pained him to make her stop.

"No," he said. "Not yet." He couldn't let her touch him like that—he wouldn't last long if she did, and he planned on this taking a while.

Together, laughing softly, they moved towards the center of the bed. Alair tore off his boots and surcoat, leaving him in breeches and a tunic, watching Caes lay down in the center. She smiled at him, face radiant, lit by the fire's soft glow. He could spend eternity looking at her face. Content and awaiting pleasure.

And he was going to provide it.

But she was wearing far too many clothes. They both were.

"What are you waiting for?" she asked as he crouched next to her, his eyes raking over each precious inch.

"Can't I take my time?"

"Not tonight."

Gingerly, he touched her ankle and then her calf, relishing the delicate softness. This was intimate too, in a way. That he could touch everything. Then slowly, bit by bit he moved a hand up and under her gown, pushing the cumbersome fabric out of his way. He rested on her thigh, slowly tracing a finger in a circle on her sensitive skin.

"Please," she gasped.

"Please what?" he asked, moving his hand ever higher. And then stopping.

"Touch me."

"Here?" He moved a little higher.

"More."

When his fingers reached her slick center she let out a whimper, begging him to do more than taunt the outside. Her hips bucked against his hand, prodding him on. Insisting. Goddess, how was he supposed to contain himself? She was going to undo him and he was nowhere near done.

For long moments he contented himself with toying with her entrance, just circling, his fingers lightly tracing the soft heat that awaited him. There was one definite benefit to being a Soul Carver—he could easily hear the little gasps and moans, the racing of her heart, and the little shifts in her body that told him that she liked what he was doing. And he exploited every bit of it.

"You're not doing this to me. Not tonight," Caes said, reaching up and pulling him down to her, his hand still on her. Unfortunately, his body and hers were still clothed.

"Caes—"

"No." She reached for his breeches, palming his member under the fabric. Alair groaned. It was getting harder to think. To resist. "I need *you*," she hissed.

Fuck, he wasn't going to argue with her. Quickly, he pulled off his breeches and tunic and she tugged off her gown and shift, lying naked before him. Utterly bare in every way.

Breathing heavily, he stared at her, even as he yearned to dive into her. To melt into her and consume her and never let go. He took a deep breath. He needed this moment, this precious time that they had together, that they had managed to steal against all the odds.

As always, Alair was struck by the contrast of her body against his—her soft skin where his was rough. Hers curved where his was hard. Though, they had one similarity—scars. She had never been a warrior, but she had survived battles of her own. Her struggles and victories were marked on her skin. Fresh and angry red gashes marred her legs and arms. They would heal, and someday, she would never have to endure such things again.

"You're beautiful," he said. And she was. Beyond her golden and green eyes, beyond her brilliant smile, beyond everything that constituted her body. She was beautiful in more ways than he could count.

And she was his.

His.

"Beautiful?"

"Always."

She flushed in response and reached for him, guiding him—and his member—closer to her entrance. Fuck. It was hot and slick and he didn't bother to bite back the moan of the pleasure that was on him and what was to come. He rubbed himself on her, back and forth, teasing her, until again she bucked her hips against him and pushed him inside, making them both cry out in pleasure. She was perfect—so tight that their first time he feared he was hurting her, but he had since learned that her cries were from anything but pain. Suddenly, she clenched hard around him, both with her core and with her legs, embracing him and consuming him until he could no longer tell her body from his.

They were together, as they would always be.

He helped her sit up, her legs still wrapped around him, and placed her so she rested on his crossed legs. She gripped onto him, pulling him as close to her as she could. Her light brown hair was tousled, delightfully disheveled, a look that was somehow more of a shared secret than many of the things they had done together.

"I love you," Alair said, breathless. "All of you."

"Alair—" Caes's eyes moistened with tears, and then she kissed him. Urgently. Deeply. He ground into her, pushing himself as deep as she could take him, all while kissing her and holding her. There was only her, his movements and her sounds a rhythm he fell into and lost himself utterly. A rhythm he could have enjoyed forever.

They stayed like that for what felt like an eternity, and yet was far too short. Without warning, Caes broke away from the kiss and moved so that she ground on him harder and harder. "Touch me," she ordered.

He didn't need to be told twice. Alair smiled and reached between her legs, rubbing her nub while leaning himself back to allow her to move. "Like this?"

"Yes." She threw her head back, her eyes closed. "Yes, please."

The way her body gyrated, the way she gasped and sought her enjoyment on him and from him, it was more than he could stand. It was all he could do to wait and be patient. To hold back. His time would come while she tormented him so perfectly.

And just when he didn't think he could take another moment of resisting while watching her take her pleasure, she came apart with a cry, her mouth open, her body shaking while she found her release. Then she stilled, panting and resting herself on his still very hard cock.

Slowly, Alair moved her and himself so that he was on top of her. Lost in the afterglow of pleasure, she opened her legs wider, welcoming him in even deeper. Perfect. He thrusted in a steady rhythm until his own pleasure washed over him, leaving every nerve ignited and every thought banished.

Spent, Alair collapsed next to Caes and took her into his arms. She laid her head against him, and then suddenly broke into a wide smile.

"What is it?" he asked.

"This" –she swallowed– "this is the first night we'll be together. In a bed. The entire night and the morning."

Damn. She was right. Being together without fear was a gift that they hadn't had. Something so normal as a bed, something most lovers would never consider, was deprived from them. That, and so many other things.

No longer. That was behind them for good.

"This is just the first night," Alair said. "And there will be many, many more." She let out a sharp breath as his hand reached between her legs, which were freshly wet from him. "And I will be taking you many more times."

This was happiness. This was contentment.

In the darkest pit of his trials, he never imagined a happiness like this. He didn't deserve a happiness like this. But fate had seen fit to grant it to him, and he would seize every drop.

"You sleep so soundly," Iva said. "I never had the chance to see you sleep."

Alair darted awake and sat up, taking in what was before him. The fire had died down to its barest embers, and if not for his Soul Carver eyes, he likely wouldn't have been able to see with the little light that came through the closed shutters. Caes laid next to him, naked under the bedcovers, letting out the even breaths of sleep. She shifted a little at his movements, but otherwise gave no indication that she heard their visitor.

Visitor?

Iva sat on the bed, hands clasped on her lap. Her night-black hair rippled over her shoulders, over the flowing gown gathered at the shoulders that had been in fashion centuries ago. She smiled at him, full of hope and promise. She was young, so young. But then, he had been young, too, when he loved her. And when she died.

"What is this?" Alair whispered. "What foul magic—"

"Foul?" Iva asked. "I think you had better look at yourself." She smirked in a way that indicated just how foolish she thought he was. His heart wrenched. He had pushed himself into the Soul Carver trials for her, and part of him would always love her—but she was dead.

Dead.

Foul magic. It had to be. Dreams weren't this real. He was able to count his fingers. He could count Caes's breaths. This wasn't a dream. A bitter taste entered Alair's mouth. He had been brought back from the dead. Twice. He was made from magic. Could it be...

"You're dead," he said. "This cannot be happening."

Iva's expression was solemn. "You should know better than anyone that the walls between the worlds are liable to break." Iva crossed her legs above her knees. "You've become handsome. Though, you always were. But now you're a man."

What was Alair supposed to say to that? She had died and had barely aged at all. While he was very much alive.

"But why are you here? And now?" he asked.

Iva shrugged. "I wanted to see you. And I found that I could."

"So this means—" The words froze in Alair's mouth as he realized that the bed was empty. Iva was gone. Again. There was no one in the room except for him and Caes. Alair rubbed his face.

Iva had been here. In his soul he knew it. This wasn't some illusion. But why? And how?

Caes shifted in her sleep. "Alair?" she asked with a soft moan.

"Nothing, my love." Alair laid next to Caes, pressing her naked body against his. He kissed her temple and breathed in her scent, relaxing against her comforting presence. "I just had an odd dream."

Yet, Alair found he couldn't sleep. It was not a dream. And if he was indeed seeing the dead, what did Karima bringing him back again do?

Chapter 10

Liuva

Lyritan.

I remember the first day I saw Lyritan as clearly as I remember my first snowfall after experiencing only summer. Both were a sudden thrusting into an experience I had never contemplated. But where snow was cold and brought death to the world, Lyritan was as radiant as the dawn. And he chose to shine on me.

"Who are you?" Lyritan asked me one morning. I was momentarily alone in the forest that was green with the buds of spring, walking aimlessly as I did in those days, taking in the fresh world around me. He was wearing long draping garments that were common amongst mortals, his golden hair catching the morning light. Other beings were with him, a couple young fawns and lovely tree guardians that he sent away with a wave of his arm. They begrudgingly left, giving me envious gazes as they departed. We were alone.

"Liuva," I said. "My name is Liuva." I looked around for my mother in the dense foliage. She was nearby. She had to be—I just saw her moments ago. Or did I wander too far? My breaths were sharp. Who was this strange golden god? He was beautiful, but so much beauty in this world hid danger.

"Liuva," the god whispered, the sound of my name on his tongue sending shivers down my spine. This sensation, too, was new. The way he looked at me...like I was the only thing that mattered to this radiant creature. It was different from the wholesome affection my mother had shown me. It was different than the indulgent glances my companions gave. This was sharp. Invigorating. It made my body stir in places that I did not know were possible.

And I wanted more.

"Would you like to take a walk, sweet one?" Lyritan asked, offering me his arm.

"I...I'm not sure," I said.

Smiling, the god took his arm back. "I understand," he said. "You are wise not to trust someone you came upon in the woods. But I would like to know you, Liuva. May I return tomorrow?"

I nodded, speechless. I wanted to see the god again. Something told me that I should've declined. That I should have made empty excuses. That I should have screamed for my mother. But I found that I didn't want to. I wanted more.

The god waved him arm and issued a light call to his friend. And without another word to me, Lyritan and his band left me in the woods.

Lyritan kept his promise.

He came back to me the next day. And the next. And the next. His clandestine visits rolled into each other until I lost track. How he knew when my mother was not present, how he avoided her coming upon us, I didn't know. I still don't know. Nor did I ask. All I knew was that Lyritan was a secret that I wanted to keep to myself.

A secret. Another experience that I had never had.

And Lyritan showed me so many other things.

Thanks to him, I learned how to tell my way by the path of the stars. I learned how the gods coaxed life from the dying, bringing plants and animals back to health. I met mortals, who were delighted to see me, who gifted me with song and dance. I refused to accept their physical offerings—I had no need of food or drink, for my mother provided for the mortal part of my body. I learned about the pain of life, the pain in birth and in death. There was no escaping the cycle of misery that was foisted upon mortals.

"See what we could do for them?" Lyritan asked me. He had restored a mortal's fields, his face beaming at the adoration he subsequently received. Even now, his name was on the family's tongues. "These mortals will not starve, thanks to me. I can do this for so many."

Using divine power to help mortals was not a foreign concept to me. My mother would do much the same, as she pleased. But she was more recalcitrant, more cautious about who she blessed in this manner. "If we help them for everything, they won't take care of themselves," she had said to me. "Then when they need help and I am nowhere near, what will they do then? They need to show me that they deserve my assistance. I can't change everything."

What was the point of having so much power, if not for doing good in this world? Even as I was, something between a mortal and a god, I understood that my existence was charmed, free from most miseries that plagued mortals and their fragile bodies. Regardless, I didn't like seeing pain when there was something that could be done to fix it.

It was then I realized the limitations of my being. I could not access my divine power, for it burned when I tried, leaving gnarly blisters on my skin that took days to heal. The first time I did so—the only time—Lyritan kissed my fingers and made me promise not to do it again.

My mother, fortunately, was away when I tried. I could only imagine what she would have said or done.

"What are you trying to do?" Lyritan asked. "There's no reason to harm yourself."

"I can help," I said. "Like you. If I could access my power, think of what I could do for mortals. I could change things."

Lyritan smiled and shook his head. "You are too kind for your own good. Banish such thoughts for now. No power is worth your pain, my dearest," he said, kissing me on the forehead. "I understand your yearning, but the time for that isn't now. Trust me." Ripples of pleasure worked through me, even as I chafed against Lyritan's urging to be patient. He was right. I couldn't do anything now. And instead, I was here with him. He was so close to me, close enough to touch. He was my present. My reality. My world.

I parted my mouth and leaned towards him, wishing, yearning—

But he stepped away, leaving me craving more.

Always more.

Chapter 11

Caes

A knock at the door jerked Caes from her sleep in her warm cocoon of blankets and Alair, a sleep she could've rested in forever. Groaning, she rubbed her eyes. Who was it and what did they want? They needed to go away. She needed sleep. Alair was up before she could register anything else, speaking to the man at the door in hushed tones.

"Truly?" Alair asked.

"The baroness is certain," the man said. "Go. I'm letting the others know."

The door shut and Alair turned to Caes, his jaw set. A weight settled through her. Something was the matter. Something dire.

"We must leave," Alair said, moving and dressing quickly.

"What? Why?" She asked, now fully awake. She didn't wait for an answer before she began putting on her garments, a shift and a wool travel dress the baroness had given her, along with boots, thick socks, and a cloak. If Alair said they needed to leave, she'd listen. She had been through far too much to second-guess him now.

"It sounds incredulous," Alair said, "but I'm not about to take the chance."

"Of course not."

"There's a mist, Caes."

"What? We're leaving because of mist?"

Alair tugged on his boots, tying them with deft efficiency, his black hair rippling over his shoulders. "It's more than that. It's unnatural. The baroness's man said that it's been forming near the estate and there are things in it. Demons, the man said."

Ridiculous. Demons in a mist arriving in the night?

But her world was past ridiculous.

Caes had been brought back to life by a god, attacked by twisted soldiers, and was surrounded by Soul Carvers, who had been raised from the dead and molded by a goddess to have immense powers. Nothing truly shocked her by this point. She had no reason to doubt the man's word.

They had to flee. Now. Since they didn't know what exactly they were dealing with, fighting was reckless.

Caes and Alair finished dressing and left the room, turning down the hall to the main courtyard. "What about the others?" Caes asked.

"The man said that they'd be waiting for us. Along with our horses."

"Just ours?" Alair nodded and Caes's heart sank. There were not enough horses for all of them, and they were expensive. The baroness wouldn't be able to provide them with any more, besides exchanging what they had for fresher mounts. Worse, the ones from Fyrie were likely in no shape to flee tonight.

"What are we going to do?"

"We're getting *you* out of here," Alair said, his hand on the small of her back. "The rest of us will be fine."

"Alair—"

"No. It's you they want. You leave, the danger leaves."

He was right. She hated it, but he was right.

Once they were outside, Caes was overcome with dread that froze her steps. The first tendrils of the mist were creeping over the manor walls, snarling and coiling like a snake. This wasn't a normal mist, for it was putrid yellow and smelled of decaying meat. Caes covered her mouth and gagged, forcing the contents of her stomach to stay put. Magic sometimes carried a unique scent, but not this. Never this.

"What is this?" she asked.

"Someone is making this happen." Alair frowned. "Or something. This is old magic. A curse."

Lyritan burst into the courtyard and ran towards Caes, his golden eyes shining in the dark. "My love," he called out, "we need to go." He nodded to Alair once he reached them. "Soul Carver, we'll take the main road north until the sun rises, and wait for you there. Can I trust you to handle this?"

"Can I trust you to keep her safe?" Alair asked.

The god frowned. "Don't insult me, mortal." He gently grabbed Caes's arm and led her towards the horses, where the other Soul Carvers and Lyritan's men gathered. Caes gave Alair a backwards glance, only to find him nodding, urging her along. He may not have liked the god, but he counted on him to get her away from here.

"What about the baroness?" Caes asked Lyritan.

"This is hunting us," the god said. "When we leave, it will follow." Alright—that was two votes that the mist was going to leave. But how long would it take? What would it do in the meantime?

"What about my friends?" Caes watched Cylis talk to Fer and Erasmus, two of the other Soul Carvers. They huddled together, occasionally sending concerned looks at the wall. The others hurried through the courtyard, conferring and preparing for battle.

"I told them how to destroy what lurks within," Lyritan said. "They'll be alright. But we need to go." With that, the god helped her onto a horse and mounted behind her, pressing her against him. Despite everything, his closeness sent a wave of relief over her. Of safety.

He will protect me.

For now.

She gripped the pommel as best she could with her injured hands, her heart racing into her throat. What was in that mist?

Bethrian mounted his own horse, following them closely as Lyritan led his men on horseback to the manor gate. Good. Bethrian was mortal—he would have no chance against something such as this.

"When we go," Lyritan said in her ear while they waited for the gate to open, "they're going to fight."

"I can't leave them," Caes said, struggling in Lyritan's arms. As Lyritan's men—and Bethrian—positioned themselves around them, the Soul Carvers stood at the gate, weapons out and magic called. Alair's face was expressionless and hard, blood dripping from his ear, once again the emotionless man she had known in Malithia. Cylis's face was purple and bloated, his skin coated in ice and frost. Rigid bleeding lines worked their way across Marva's face. Every Soul Carver showed the misery their magic wrought. Would she see her friends again?

"Stop struggling," Lyritan said, holding her steady. "You know they want you to go. I promised your Soul Carver I'd protect you, and I will." Lyritan then ordered the doors to open.

They did.

The old rusted hinges creaked, revealing the yellow mist waiting outside, and the monster that lurked within. A dark shadow approached, turning more solid with each movement. Caes stilled, all thoughts of struggling against Lyritan banished. What approached was nothing human, nothing like any creature that had walked the earth for thousands of years. Yet, Caes's memory stirred—she had known of such horrors. Thanks to Karima.

The creature was the size of a bull, its bottom half like a thick, long snake that moved on the ground, slithering towards them, while from the waist up the creature was a human skeleton. Or, at least, it was human-*like*. It had ribs, and a spine, and a skull, but the mouth was filled with sharp teeth as long as fingers, and nails like bone hunting knives. Though that wasn't the most terrifying part. Although the skull bore no skin, eyes, or a nose, it possessed a long, thick tongue, forked at the end. And dripping from its mouth was a dark liquid like ink. Caes didn't want to know what the liquid was, but she knew it wasn't good.

Caes didn't have to sit frozen with fear for long, for Lyritan urged the horse to run. Before she could cry out, they had galloped into the putrid mist.

"Try to hold your breath," the god said, pushing them through the yellow haze. Behind them, the shouts and the clang of battle rang out. The Soul Carvers were fighting that *thing*. Would they be ok? Not for the first time, she cursed her uselessness, that there was nothing she could do to help. "We'll escape it," Lyritan said. "Hold on."

She wasn't the one she was worried about. But maybe she should've worried a little.

The cursed mist stung her skin. Burned her eyes. She closed them tightly, trusting Lyritan to shelter her. Protect her. They fled into the night, leaving the monster and its poison behind them.

But what was *Karima's* creature doing here? Wasn't Shirla the one working foul magic with her father and Desmin?

A shiver worked down Caes's body as an idea struck her—the two goddesses. What if they were working together?

Lyritan was right—it didn't take long to flee the mist, though it felt like an eternity. Painful moments passed and then the air cleared, the purest thing Caes had ever felt. Clean air. Beautiful air. She took deep breaths, the wind working through her lungs, cleansing everything it touched.

With the pain gone, her mind whirled. Where was Alair? Cylis? Marva? Janell? Where were they? Were they alright? What about the others? Could they kill that thing? Caes frantically searched her memories, and realized she didn't know if Soul Carvers could destroy something made by gods.

They are made of Karima, as that monster was. They have better odds than most things on this earth.

"We need to help them," Caes yelled once they were free of the mist. "They could be dying. You're a god—help them!"

Not Lyritan. He's too precious to risk.

"Help them," she begged, ignoring the part of her that urged otherwise.

"No, my dearest," Lyritan said, her pleas causing no more than a wrinkle on his brow. "We must move on."

Despite her cries, they didn't stop riding. Lyritan pushed his men—and Bethrian—hard, traveling on the main road until morning. Once the sun was over the tree line, the god raised his hand, ordering them to come to a halt, just like he had told Alair.

The place they stopped was nothing like the scene they had left, the estate that was covered in a ghastly fog. A cool breeze shook the trees, sending a few yellow leaves scattering to the ground. Caes wrapped her cloak tighter around her and looked at the path they had traveled. The dust from their horses still hovered in the air. She stared at it, willing it to produce the ones she had been forced to leave behind.

Lyritan dismounted, pulling her from her thoughts and then helping her to the ground. She landed with a soft thud and leaned against him to catch her balance. "You need to rest and eat," Lyritan said, gently guiding her to a clear spot next to a tree. His men and Bethrian did the same, pulling supplies out of their sacks. At least the baroness had supplied them well. They must have packed everything immediately upon their arrival, expecting their guests to leave as soon as possible. Oh, gods below, was the baroness alright? If she survived that monster, would the Ardinani discover how she had helped them?

"He's right, Caes," Bethrian said, dropping on the ground near her. "They all are okay." He took a bite out of a stuffed pastry and visibly worked hard at chewing. After a valiant effort, he swallowed and said, "They'll come. They'll be fine."

"How do you know?" she asked.

"Because Cylis isn't going to do me the courtesy of leaving me in peace." He smiled, and she rewarded his attempt at levity with a little smirk.

As there was nothing else to do, she gave into Lyritan's demands and rested and ate. It would do no good to be hungry. They needed her not to be more of a burden than she was already. If Alair were here, he would insist she take care of herself and be angry if she didn't. So, somewhat full and comfortable, she rested. And waited.

The sun was nothing more than an orange haze on the horizon when familiar voices announced what she had spent the day fidgeting and waiting for. Lyritan shifted, looking down the road. He had stayed near her all day and yet barely spoke. Was he worried for the Soul Carvers too? Or was he worried that they'd fail and then he'd have to face that creature without them? But the voices—the jubilant calls—made every bit of her body spring to life, urging her towards the sounds.

They were here. Here.

"Alair!" Caes cried, throwing off the extra cloak she was using as a blanket and running towards him. He was alive. He seemed exhausted, his gait sluggish and shoulders bowed. He had dried cuts on his cheek and hand, but he was alive.

And Kerensa. And Cylis. And Marva. They were battered and worn, but alive.

She threw herself against Alair, kissing his face, his neck, his hands—his poor, blood-covered hands—every bit of him. Her tears blurred her vision as she took in her Soul Carver, with his mirrored eyes reflecting the last of the fading sun. He was alive. Nothing else mattered.

It was then she noticed that two people were missing.

"Where's Erasmus? Jarmilla?" Caes asked, looking behind them and counting the remaining Soul Carvers. Lyritan and his men approached the Soul Carvers, welcoming them back. For his part, Lyritan seemed unbothered by how she greeted Alair, and frankly, Lyritan was the last thing on her mind. He claimed he didn't mind her relationship with Alair, and now it was time to prove it.

Janell shook her head, her clothes covered in what was likely her blood as her skin was still a horrid mess from having used her magic. She had been flayed alive in Karima's realm. "They saved us," Janell said. "And paid for it."

"Dead?" Caes whispered. Downcast eyes were the only response she received.

Dead. Two more people dead. For her.

Caes trembled, letting the tears flow, even as Alair wrapped a comforting arm around her. Somehow, she knew that this was only the start of the pain to come.

Chapter 12

Cylis

Leaving the baroness's home was leaving a warm bed. Literally.

Cylis had been pulled awake in the middle of the night, tossed into the woods, and made to fight for his life against something whose smell he would never forget. Nor would he forget Jarmilla and Erasmus, who had both melted like they didn't have any bones when the *thing* broke past their defenses.

Poor bastards. Normally, he'd stoically whisper some prayer or Soul Carver incantation asking that they "be safe in Karima's bosom," but he knew that was a lie. No matter what, alive or dead, Soul Carvers were miserable. The afterlife that awaited Soul Carvers wasn't the best to begin with, but Soul Carvers who had traveled and protected the person who was working to destroy Karima? Yeah, probably not a good time. Erasmus was decent enough in the few dealings they'd had, Jarmilla was also decent enough, and neither of them deserved being stuck with Karima. None of them did. Erasmus and Jarmilla had been good friends, having gone through the trials close to the same time, and rumor was that they were more. At least they weren't alone, whatever Karima was doing to them.

Unfortunately, while the rest of the Soul Carvers weren't dead, they weren't out of danger, and thus had to journey onward. On foot—always on foot—they traveled through the Ardinani north, avoiding most people and doing a very good job of not engaging with those they encountered. And the few that they did engage with got Alair's wonderful distraction treatment. It was either have Alair handle them, or kill them, and frankly, none of their stomachs could take the second option this soon after what had happened to the Soul Carvers.

Other than that, what was there to say? They woke, traveled, and slept. Bethrian wisely kept to himself, Alair kept to himself, and Caes looked behind her so often Cylis half-expected her head to pop off like what happened to his sister's doll when she played with it too much. Did Cylis find her another one? Yes. Because Cylis was a good brother.

At least he had Kerensa, the one sensible mind here.

Once they had been on the road for close to two weeks, they crossed into Reyvern. Two weeks of his sensitive skin burning and chafing from the constant friction and dryness. Two weeks of mediocre meals that got worse as the supplies ran low, until they were forced to make soup out of dried meat. Two weeks of wishing for some moisture and then getting rained on, leaving everything smelling of mildew.

Good times.

After they crossed into Reyvern, Lyritan's men looked visibly relieved. It was hard to understand why—it looked exactly the same as Ardinan. It wasn't like the trees magically changed color once they crossed the little gorge that marked the border. Though the trees *should* have changed color. It would have made this journey a smidge more whimsical, and he needed some whimsy.

Now that they were out of imminent danger from Ardinan, Cylis decided it was time to pull Caes away from whatever god-filled reverie she was having and focus on something much more important—his accomplishments.

"Your Highness," Cylis said to Caes as he jogged up to her horse, "may I speak with you?" It was difficult to keep his expression even and humble as Lyritan looked down his nose. But Cylis did. Because he had a healthy fear of the god. And while Cylis may have physically admired that god more than he did any other man—an unpleasant side effect of his divine-ish nature—it was admiration buried under a healthy layer of fear.

"It can wait until we stop for midday," Lyritan said.

"Actually, would it be alright if we stopped now?" Caes asked. "I could use a moment to rest."

Lyritan nodded and raised his hand, and the company went about dismounting, stretching, and doing whatever they needed that couldn't be done from horseback. The trees in this part of Reyvern had lost their leaves at a far more rapid pace than they had in Fyrie, and most of them had been replaced by various types of pine. The distance was dotted with various mountains, and from the way Cylis's thighs ached, they probably had already climbed a few.

"Yes," Caes said to Cylis, "what is it?" Her hands gripped her horse's reins, now free of their bandages, though healing scars still dotted her fingers. At least having some scars was better than having a sliced hand. Probably. He owed her for that one. She dismounted, noticeably smoother at doing so than she was when they had left Malithia. Lyritan dismounted and approached the two of them, hands on his hips, watching Cylis. He really didn't want to do this with an audience, but he couldn't wait any longer.

It was time to see if what Cylis risked everything for was worth it.

Cylis fumbled through his bag and then pulled out the hilt he stole from Fyrie, presenting it to Caes like a trophy. The hilt was bulbous, with a mermaid tail at the bottom and faces of grotesque women lining the side. It was one of the ugliest decorations Cylis had ever seen—that it was magic had to have been the only reason the Ardinani displayed it. What other reason could someone have for keeping the thing?

"What is that?" Caes asked, eyebrow creeping upwards. Alair moved to stand behind Lyritan, watching the exchange with his signature lack of expression.

"The hilt." Cylis smiled, ignoring the unease that crept through him at Caes's confusion. "For the Sword of Might." He paused. "From Ardinan."

"Cylis," Caes said, "that's not the Sword of Might's hilt."

Cylis felt like a horse sat on his chest. "What?" A couple Soul Carvers—and probably Bethrian—snickered from behind him. "This is the hilt."

"No. I'm sorry, it's not." Caes didn't mock him. Worse, she visibly pitied him. "Where did you get this?"

"From the statue in the courtyard in Fyrie. This has to be it. There's no other reason for something to be this ugly."

Caes tried to hide a sigh. And failed. "That hilt has been there for decades. The statue was a gift from a noble family in Cyvid. Cylis...that's not it. That's not from the sword."

Seriously? Was she politely telling him that he risked his life—everyone's lives—for nothing more than a decoration? An ugly decoration? Cylis bit his lip to keep from saying what he really felt.

He was about to take his ugly hilt and stride off and do something unpleasant to it when Lyritan stepped closer and held out his hand. "Give it to me," he said. His blond hair shone in the sunlight, making him glow in a very god-like way that had nothing to do with his eyes. Phelan was admittedly an attractive man, but with the god possessing him, he was *more*.

Reluctantly, Cylis gave the god the item that he had almost died for, biting a protest. That awful, ugly thing. Since Cylis was the one who had struggled so hard to get it, he should've had the privilege of defiling the damn thing.

Hand clasped around the base, Lyritan turned the hilt over, inspecting the deplorable craftsmanship. "No," Lyritan said, "this hilt is not from the Sword of Might. Though this has a distinctive enough design you can be forgiven for thinking so." That was the nicest thing Lyritan had said to him this entire journey, and the nicest thing anyone could say about the item. Suddenly the god grasped the hilt and gestured with it, like it had a blade attached and he was parrying some invisible foe. "But it is a fine weapon. Or it could be."

"How so?" Caes asked. "It was ornamental."

Cylis bit his tongue. Hard.

"This metal—it is from a meteorite, is it not?" Lyritan asked.

Caes shrugged. "I don't know. I just know that it was a gift, and one that was too important for Viessa to get rid of. Why?"

"Not all metals and substances interact the same way with magic from the gods." Lyritan smiled at Caes in a way that made Cylis throw up in his mouth a little. "Plain iron is from the earth, but meteorites are from the heavens. And something from the heavens allows me to do this." The god closed his eyes and gripped the hilt so hard that the skin over his knuckles went white. A moment later, white and then golden ooze seeped from under his nails, and wrapped around the hilt in a brilliant web. The hilt itself glowed golden, and then faded.

What the...

"Lyritan..." Caes said, a note of worry in her voice. Alair moved closer, seemingly ready to dart between Lyritan and Caes. "What are you doing?"

The god's eyes opened, revealing an unnatural golden glow, even compared to his normal gaze, that slowly faded. "There," he said, accomplished. He offered the sword hilt back to Cylis. "A gift."

Slowly, Cylis reached out and touched the hilt, and then grasped it when he realized that the white webby things weren't going to re-appear, wrap around his hand, and then strangle his fingers off. Whatever Cylis thought of Lyritan's attractiveness, he wanted nothing to do with anything that could be considered a white product of his.

"...Thank you," Cylis said.

"You're very welcome."

Cylis coughed. "Um, what did you do?" Granted, Cylis's plans to defile the hilt weren't exactly wholesome, but what Lyritan did was oddly disturbing and—if he was honest—gross.

"Oh." Lyritan grinned and placed a hand on his hip. "That sword is now yours. Yours alone. Fashion a blade to it in Reyvern and you'll have a weapon that will make you a true adversary. My gift, for all you have done for my betrothed."

Betrothed? Oh, not that again. Sure, Cylis had heard about Lyritan's grand plans to make Caes some sort of empress goddess before now, and each time he promptly forgot because it sounded like an awful plan. As if Caes was going to go along with that—did Lyritan even know Caes? Cylis caught a glimpse of Alair, his face still impassive. How did Alair feel about Lyritan's little announcement? Though, from Alair's even expression and untensed jaw, it seemed they had come to some sort of agreement regarding Caes.

Nope, the little vein in his throat was bulging. Yep, he was truly pissed.

"So, uh" –Cylis shifted on his feet– "just so we're clear, what have I done for Caes?"

Caes shook her head in faux bewilderment while Lyritan's brow furrowed. "Cylis, now you're just seeking compliments," Caes said.

"He's good at that," Kerensa said, grabbing Cylis's arm and leading him away from the god. She likely thought she was saving him from saying or doing something worse. She was probably right.

"Well," Bethrian said, "at least something good came from your little adventure."

"It's not too late to put you back in a prison, Fuckwit."

"Nah, you'd miss me. Though you need to learn to listen to me. You'd be much better off if you did. Admit it."

Cylis bit his tongue.

Don't annoy the god, don't annoy the god, don't annoy the god, Kerensa had warned him every moment they were alone. *In other words, don't be yourself.* As much as he hated to admit it, Kerensa was usually a very good guide for his behavior.

And Bethrian was very lucky that he had to be on good behavior.

Chapter 13

Bethrian

Bethrian was well traveled—by Malithian standards. He had been to Tithra once as a child, Artonia twice, and Cyvid three times. But a voyage through Adrinan's northern forests and Reyvern's mountains—that was new. Unfortunately, he regretted every moment of it. And it wasn't necessarily because an ass as perfect as his wasn't suited to banging against cured leather for weeks on end.

"How long are you going to stay with us? Once we get to Reyvern, I mean." Caes asked him during dinner, a rare time that he was seated directly next to her. Lyritan was off discussing something with his men. They hadn't encountered much in the way of Reyverni other than patrols that resupplied them and gave them fresh horses, but that could change at any time. Lyritan said they were avoiding settlements so that they wouldn't be slowed down, but roads did have people. Regardless of the reasons, the "coveted" spot next to her highness was vacant. There was a good chance he had ended up here due to Caes's design—if Lyritan wasn't there, Kerensa and Cylis had a tendency to swoop in like cats fighting over a sunbeam. Even Alair was off somewhere, for once. Yes, she very likely planned this.

"Where else would I go?" Bethrian asked, nibbling on a rather bland traveler's stew.

"Another kingdom," she suggested. "Back to Malithia."

"I'm not going back to Malithia until it's determined whether or not I'm set to be executed. I'm still a lord, and I still angered the emperor." Bethrian picked out something from the stew that was either a bug or a malformed bean—regardless, it wasn't going into his stomach.

"He'd kill you without a trial?"

"I never said that. It's more like any trial would be very short."

Caes took a stately bite of her own stew, swallowed, and then said, "The emperor never liked your family much, did he?"

Bethrian coughed. "That's an understatement."

"Why?"

"I told you before—we have good lands."

"It can't be just because of your estate. Yours isn't the only prosperous one in the empire. His actions are personal. Why you?"

"Caes…" Bethrian stirred a piece of meat that floated to the top in his tiny metal bowl. What animal was he consuming? Best not to ask questions. The last time he did he didn't like the answer.

"Humor me," Caes said. "It's not like I'm going to tell him."

"The answer is complicated."

"Try me."

"Fine." Bethrian took a deep breath. How was he supposed to explain something that was so delightfully Malithian? "Well, let's start with me. He never liked me. Ever. And my association with Seda didn't help."

"…Did the emperor make a point to like young noblemen?"

"Not like that. Caes—you were a Malithian princess. You had to have seen his attendants."

"I did."

He kept staring at her. "And what were their names?"

"Oh. So, those young men were lords. Actual lords." Caes frowned. "For some reason I thought it was just a courtesy title."

"You're not that foolish."

Caes's frown deepened. "But when I asked my tutor, Lady Dethria, who her family was—"

"That's different. That's a teacher."

"…So, in some circumstances they're noble and in others, it's a courtesy."

"Yes. Now you're getting it."

Caes took a deep breath. "Let me guess—you never received an offer to be the emperor's chamber pot emptier."

"Exactly." Now it was Bethrian's turn to frown. "Though you're making it sound like that's a good thing."

Caes laughed softly. "Glad to help."

Bethrian bobbed his head. "What else to tell you...yes, that was just me. He never liked me. And as for my father, sure, he had his religious views and unique political ideas, but if rumor is to be believed, the real reason the emperor didn't like us was because of my mother."

"Your mother?"

"Yes. I guess the emperor wanted to marry her once upon a time, and she chose my father instead."

"Ah." She frowned. "You don't believe it?"

"I'm more inclined to think that my father forgot to properly bow once and old Barlas never forgets a slight, but it's possible. My mother was a beauty in her time."

"She's still beautiful."

Bethrian nodded. Yes, his mother was. When she wasn't lecturing him. Though Bethrian's explanation to Caes left out a lot of history, the little rivalries and exchanges between his grandfather, father, and then him, with the emperor, which culminated with Bethrian's father spouting heresy. "My mother never mentioned the emperor, and I think she would have brought such a thing up at every opportunity if it was true."

"She'd say such things to your father?"

Bethrian snorted. "There's little she wouldn't have said to him."

That was enough family history for the Ardinani lady. Caes didn't need to know everything. She already knew too much, and Bethrian had a lot of things he'd rather not talk about now, or ever. For instance, the last thing she needed to know was that he had swallowed Seda's tooth. Bethrian had done eccentric things in his time, but that...but that...Caes would either think he was ill and get him a physician, decide he had lost his mind and cast him from their group, or decide he was possessed and ask Cylis to get rid of him. Alright, maybe there was a wide variety in Caes's possible reactions, but none of them were pleasant.

While seemingly mulling over Bethrian's words, Caes stirred her stew. "You don't have to stay with us, you know. You're not a prisoner."

"No. Not by you."

"If I asked him to let you leave, Lyritan would let you go."

"That's kind, but I'll be staying."

"Why?"

"Other than I have nowhere else to go?" Bethrian smiled. "I'm a lord and I belong at a court."

"Do you think someone there will petition the emperor on your behalf?"

"I doubt it. But what am I going to do? Leave and be some nameless wanderer? A merchant?" Bethrian shuddered. "I'd rather wear homespun wood."

"That's not being entirely fair," Caes teased. "I can think of several professions you'd excel in."

Shit—did she discover his identity as Lady Peony Passionflower? Were the papers of his discarded novel discovered in Ardinan and given to her? He wasn't ready to explain this...

"Teacher, auctioneer, actor, herald," Caes said instead, counting off professions with her fingers.

Bethrian let out a tiny sigh of relief. "Those are all occupations that require theatrics or yelling."

"Exactly."

Bethrian laughed and took another bite. When he swallowed, he wiped his mouth and said, "If the other reasons for me staying aren't enough for you, think of this—the fate of our world is in your hands. And I never miss a good story."

Chapter 14

Cylis

Cylis had seen all of the trees. All of them. There wasn't a single one in the world that escaped his notice. Fir, Tuncer fir, cedar, blessed cedar, Malithian pole thorn, birch, pine, empire pine, spruce, and far too many more that he didn't know the names of. But he saw them. All of them. He'd be happy if he never saw another tree again.

From his place riding a few paces behind Caes, Alair, and the god—they had acquired even more steeds from a Reveryni outpost they visited—Cylis hopped off his horse as soon as the company decided to take some rest. Once the horse was situated and happily munching on the sparse fall grass that was a rare sight in this cursed rocky kingdom, Cylis went to the woods to take care of some more delicate matters. Private ones. But upon his return to the camp, just when he was almost within sight of the company, his privacy was ruined.

"I was hoping to find you," Marva said, her eyes glinting in the afternoon sun. She adjusted her black cape—a gift from the baroness—around her shoulders. She hadn't complained nearly as much as the others on this journey, meeting everything with the same pleasant expression she always did. How she managed it, Cylis didn't know. He wasn't used to pleasant people.

"Why?" Cylis asked, crossing his arms. "You see me all day."

"Oh, stop that," Marva said, sighing and walking past him to a nearby log. She swatted off some wet leaves and then took a seat. "I know you."

"Oh" –the corner of Cylis's mouth quirked up- "you do?"

"Yes. So, stop pretending to be pissed and talk to me." She patted the spot next to her for emphasis, giving him a coy smile.

Who said he was *pretending* to be pissed? He was annoyed. His stomach was empty, and it was time to refill it. The others were likely passing around the afternoon biscuits and dried apples, a little something to tide them over until dinner.

Yet the snarky retort died on his lips. Marva grinned, her arms resting behind her. Daring him to argue.

Not worth the effort.

Cylis shrugged and sat where she indicated. "What's so important?"

"What are you going to do with that?" Marva asked, nodding towards the hilt tied to a sheath and resting around Cylis's waist. Currently it laid there—useless—next to his actual weapon.

Cylis looked down at the stupid thing. "No idea."

"You have a weapon from a god."

"I have a doorstop."

"Don't listen to Kerensa," Marva said. "She isn't right about everything."

"That's an understatement. But she's right about this being—again—a doorstop."

A pause settled between them. The leaf-bearing trees were bare, so they were surrounded by rows and rows gray gnarly branches. Once in awhile a frigid blast came through that made Marva tug her cloak closer around her. Cylis didn't need to bother with that. It wasn't necessarily that he couldn't be cold, it was more that he was already in perpetual pain from it and it wasn't going to kill him—so why let it bother him? Even now his fingers were numb, his skin seized with a tautness that came only from severe cold. Kerensa and Cylis compared their gifts over the years and she seemed to have a similar issue—being thrown into a fire wouldn't kill her, but she blistered and felt every bit of pain. The only difference was that the fire wouldn't result in permanent injury or death. Lucky them.

"It wasn't a waste," Marva said, "grabbing the hilt."

"No one said it was."

"Cylis," she said, her voice lowered in warning, "stop that."

"What do you want me to say? We could've died." Cylis kicked the dirt with his heel. "Stel did. I decided to run off and look what happened to him."

"I was there—Stel would've died anyway."

"You don't know that."

"No. But you don't know that going straight for the gate would've saved him. Think—what if by going right to the gate something else happened instead? You could've died. Any of us could've." She let out a long breath. "There's no point thinking about it. It happened, and you have to trust that this was how it was supposed to be."

"Supposed to be? Says who? And trust what? We have a god walking with us, and you mean to tell me that he is arranging our lives? All he cares about is seducing Caes." Cylis grimaced. Thank fuck he wasn't Alair—Cylis wouldn't have been able to watch his lover with someone else that way, even if it was pretend. Though, Caes and Alair could manage themselves.

"I mean something beyond them. Beyond the people here."

Cylis slowly shook his head. She had to be talking about the belief that there was something beyond the gods who was really in control. Oh, well, whatever helped her keep that serene, confident expression she always seemed to have. Cylis had no such thing. Because he was smart.

Marva's eyes crept up and down his body. Normally, Cylis would've wished he had on a better shirt, but he was too annoyed to dwell on his appearance. "There's something else," Marva said slowly. "Tell me."

"You seem to be awfully good at reading me."

Marva smiled. "It isn't easy. But thanks for confirming that I'm right. What is it?"

"Nope."

After a groan, Marva said, "Look at it this way—either you tell me and I talk sense into you, or you keep quiet and then say or do the worst thing possible."

"How do you—"

"It's *you*, Cylis. I've known you for years."

"And yet we barely spoke."

"And whose fault is that?"

Cylis frowned. "You wanted to talk to me?"

Marva flicked her wrist. "No matter. Now, is it Alair?"

"No."

"Caes?"

Cylis didn't answer.

"Caes. Hmmm…"

"Fuck, this is irritating," Cylis muttered, and Marva unfortunately smiled in victory. "It's that damn god."

"Ah. And what about the 'damn god?'"

How was he supposed to explain? Say that the god gave him nightmares? That he was pretty sure the god had imagined all the Soul Carvers skewed on stakes at some point? That he was also pretty sure Caes had no idea how the god stared at her when she wasn't looking? Cylis had seen starving dogs with less desperate expressions.

"I don't trust him," Cylis said simply.

Marva pursed her lips and took some time answering, staring at a pine tree for most of it. "None of us do. And we shouldn't. That's a god." Her shoulders slumped. "But that doesn't change that he's our best chance of surviving this." Unfortunately, she had a point. Karima would for sure make them suffer. Shirla, too. But Lyritan? He probably liked them a little bit better than that.

"We need to find the sword," Cylis said, desperate to change the subject. Well, nudge it in a different direction. "The real one." Caes wouldn't be able to destroy any deity without it.

"Yes. We need to talk to Caes about it, when we get a chance. She might have an idea of where to look. Remember that her father was in Reyvern—that was the last place he was seen with it."

"Allegedly."

Marva shrugged. "It's better than nothing. Maybe it is in Reyvern."

"What, hiding in a store of used wares?"

"Someone may have heard something, even if the sword isn't there anymore. I can't imagine no one recognized it or had a hint of what it was."

"How? How did you come to that conclusion?"

"I'm guessing, Cylis. That's what people do when they have no idea how to find mythical weapons. They give it their best guess."

"Also, remember that it was apparently shattered?" Cylis pointed out. "What could shatter a weapon designed to kill gods? It's supposed to stab *gods*. Which are supposed to be unstabbable." When Marva didn't answer, Cylis groaned. "Caes may be acting like she doesn't have a care in the world, but trust me, she knows better than all of us that things are about to get very complicated."

Chapter 15

Caes

Another journey through forests and mountains, and, at the end, another court. Caes was sick of courts. Sick of the games. Sick of having to navigate webs of intrigue and blatant selfishness and stupidity. Sick of having to remember names, positions, and histories.

Yet, here she was, at another one.

She once believed she belonged at court. She believed that being at court would make her happy. At that time she was young and foolish and didn't understand the depths to which the world could hurt her. She was wrong. So very wrong, about so many things. Titles weren't protection and there wasn't a single gem or fine dress that desired you in return.

She belonged with Alair. Nothing else mattered. She didn't need anything else.

"What are you thinking?" Lyritan asked, wrapping an arm protectively around her shoulders, guiding her through the woodland trail. They had dismounted from their horses, since Lyritan insisted that this part was best done on foot for safety, since the trail approached cliff edges. The party's feet crunched fallen twigs and leaves, the shrubbery mostly bare of foliage. Lyritan's warmth spread through Caes's clothing, heating her in this brisk fall weather.

I'm so lucky.

Her heart fluttered at Lyritan's touch. Good gods below, this was torture. She wanted the god. Missed him. Her traitorous heart and the piece of her that was Liuva craved him. Yet, what did Lyritan do to her in the past? What was he going to do with her now? And everything he had planned for the mortal world...

He had so many plans, and each one roiled Caes's stomach.

Alair turned back at Lyritan's question and then looked away, his face impassive. They had discussed this, planned this, yet doing this to Alair broke her heart.

Lyritan will make this world a better place. Some will suffer. Some will lose. But that is the cost of great change.

By whose standards? Liuva's? Caes was slowly getting the impression that this life wasn't the first time she had been a naïve fool.

Caes gently caressed Lyritan's hand, buying herself a few moments to answer. "I'm thinking I don't know anyone at this court. I barely know who anyone is," Caes finally said, instinctively glancing backward to make sure all of their company was still behind them and weren't lost in the never-ending forest. "I'm afraid I won't make a good impression at court. Especially as I'm to wed Reyvern's crown prince."

Lyritan scoffed, but there was only kindness in the action. "Do not worry about that, my love. I have chosen you, and that is enough."

"You and I both know it takes more than that to placate courtiers."

"Maybe to mortals, but none are going to challenge *me*."

A dozen steps later and they came to a bend that curved around the jutting stones of the mountainside. In the distance lurked more mountains, and one towered over the others. Was that the Burning Hand? A weight pressed on Caes's chest, her eyes drawn to the mountain with uneasy familiarity. She *had* seen it before. But any desire to stare at the mountain that held her fate was pulled away by Lyritan, who guided her around the stone outcropping. "A few steps more," Lyritan said, "and you'll see your new home."

A new home.

Home?

Caes had heard stories of Gilar, Reyvern's capital city, which was tucked between the mountains. Nothing prepared her for what awaited her once she turned the corner. The ancient city was built into the sides of a mountain and its surrounding hills, the tall stone buildings and narrow, winding streets and tunnels wrapped into and around the mountain itself. The city wasn't merely on the mountain—it was part of it. Gilar was surrounded by towering peaks, and its only access was a single road—which famously made it difficult for any kingdom to conquer. Despite difficulty in accessing it, merchants and commoners darted along the cobblestone road hundreds of feet below their party like ants going to a hive, the city being the center of commerce in this isolated realm.

The kingdom was so isolated that Caes knew little of what awaited her within. What would these people think of her? How would they be treated? How would the Soul Carvers be treated? The Reyverni guards and travelers they had encountered so far since the Ardinani border were awed by Lyritan/Phelan, and the only reception they had received was a mix of deference and curiosity. But without Lyritan next to her, who knew what would happen? It'd be foolish to think he could protect her from everything.

"Come, my love," Lyritan said, gently nudging her towards the switchback path that led to the main road below. Her legs ached, hardened by weeks of travel, and her feet were mounds of blisters and callouses. The prospect of the arduous journey being almost done made a smile rise to Caes's face, despite the circumstances.

Gilar was nothing like Caes expected—it was vibrant and devoted to art. She expected stone. Gray. Hardness. Instead, this was a city devoted to making every inch a prayer to beauty. Sculptures, carvings, and murals—of flowers, animals, and scenery—were everywhere that could hold them. The people mostly wore gray and brown clothes—that was to be expected, considering the cost of dyes and finer fabrics—but jewelry, seemingly of copper and silver, was worn by everyone. Rings, necklaces, earrings…everyone had some adornment celebrating Reyvern's numerous mines.

"Cylis, be happy," Kerensa muttered from behind Caes. Caes and Lyritan led their group through the streets, Lyritan's soldiers spread around them in a small guard.

Cylis grunted in response.

"What's wrong?" Kerensa asked, her voice teasing. "Too pretty?"

The silence that followed could only mean that Cylis was giving Kerensa his notorious glare. No matter. A Cylis without a scowl was like a skunk without a stripe.

"Is it what you expected?" Lyritan asked Caes.

"No," she said. "I never imagined anything like this. I heard that Reyvern is small and dark."

"I hope to make you speechless with pleasure in more than one way before this is done." Suddenly, before Caes had an opportunity comprehend what he said, Lyritan turned to look behind them. "Soul Carver, walk next to us," Lyritan said to Alair.

"What?" She was being introduced to the city as Phelan's/Lyritan's bride. What were the people going to think? For a royal, approval meant safety. But Lyritan was a god. He obviously didn't care about such trivial things, or he thought he could handle whatever came his way. Maybe he could—Karima had been worshipped in Reyvern prior to this, and they weren't set upon by pitchforks and flames immediately upon entering Gilar. Somehow, he had gained a measure of approval.

Alair obeyed, stepping next to Caes and giving her a reassuring smile. He didn't take her hand—not here—but his presence, so close that he brushed her arm, was comforting in a way a thousand words could never be.

For his part, Lyritan was obviously recognized. He strutted through the crowd, relishing the adoration heaped upon him. The crowds parted as they walked, the people making way for their prince, who had returned home. Shouts of joy rang out through the city, horns blasted, and people cried out for Prince Phelan. More than a few collapsed to the ground, singing divine praises for the god who walked amongst them. And a similar number stood back, eyes narrowed, watching the scene with barely disguised distrust. For all Lyritan had rarely used his divine power, there was no doubt he still had some—his eyes were the clue to that. The extent and cost, however, were something to be determined.

"They certainly admire their prince," Bethrian said to one of the Soul Carvers, and Caes couldn't hear any response. "Admire" was an understatement.

This is what we wanted. And he accomplished it.

"What's going on here?" Caes whispered, knowing Alair's sensitive ears would hear. "A prince safe and welcomed in a crowd, in the city streets? Accepting him as a god?" Everyone obviously knew that their prince was possessed, and it seemed that many were thrilled. But what about the royal family? Did they want their son and heir returned, or were they pleased with having a god instead?

"First impressions are just that," was all Alair said. That was all he could say without someone overhearing. It was enough for her to pick up on his meaning—he was just as confused and wary as she was.

As they made their way through the city—and the adoring populace—Caes could see the castle looming in the distance. It wasn't tall so much as it was wedged into a cliff, a creation that fused with the mountain. Even from within the city, accessing the castle wouldn't be easy for anyone who wasn't invited. Indeed, it was difficult enough for Caes's tired legs to make the trek through the streets, and she had to resist leaning on Alair to steady her. The road to the castle itself was a narrow winding mess through the city, until the sides of the road gave way to gullies that had likely claimed more than a few unfortunate travelers, judging by the weathered remains of wagons strewn at the bottom.

But even as the road became treacherous to Caes's untrained gait, Lyritan strode along with ease. He and his men were the only ones of their company to do so—everyone else stayed as close as possible to the center.

The gate to the castle was made of iron lattice, guarded by several guards who bowed low upon seeing Lyritan. Lyritan's soldiers exchanged greetings with the men, a happy homecoming for some. With broad smiles on their faces, the guards opened the gate.

And thus, Caes entered yet another court.

After a few hushed conversations with stewards they were corralled off to the castle's side corridors, managing to seemingly avoid all nobles until they made it to the great hall. None of them spoke—not even Cylis—leaving all conversations for Lyritan. Cylis seemed to have sense when he needed it. Their guards went to their own destinations, leaving Caes and Bethrian alone with the Soul Carvers and Lyritan. She'd trust Lyritan to handle this. She had no choice.

The hall where the king and queen of Reyvern greeted their son's divinely-occupied body was unlike any other audience hall Caes had ever seen. Though, at least this one was empty, except for a few attendants and guards. While walking to the thrones, Caes took in the hall itself, which carried the beauty that echoed through the rest of the castle. The walls were made of brilliant gray stone and were decorated with ornate tapestries depicting scenes of men and women at work in mines and fields. The vaulted ceiling was supported by massive stone pillars that were carved with filigree images of hammers. The effect was oddly phallic, though it was likely meant to be anything but. The floor itself was made of polished white marble, inlaid with precious stones such as lapis and garnet, and it glimmered in the light from the silver sconces mounted evenly along the walls.

And then she came before the king and queen, the people who would possibly decide her fate. She couldn't go to the Burning Hand if she didn't leave this court alive and wasn't provided means. Supplies for the journey had to come from somewhere.

King Stinbehd of Reyvern was an older man, whose years were etched onto his pale skin. His hair was gray and white and thinning at the top, while his short beard was well-groomed with little remaining color. Despite his age, King Stinbehd carried himself as a man of far fewer years, with a rigid posture more fitting for a scarecrow than a man. His spine could've been used as a ruler.

As for Queen Silvay, she was decades younger than her husband. Phelan's stepmother, Caes recalled, who had married the king after the last queen died from the pox. Or was it the flux? It was something deadly with an "ux." This queen was Cyvidian, and she had married the king before her former kingdom was conquered by Malithia. Despite the age difference between them, the queen echoed her husband's regal bearing, her black hair resting high upon her head.

Her expression wasn't unpleasant, yet it was solemn, her light brown complexion showing no sign of discomfort, despite the company before them.

What a sight they must've been—six Soul Carvers, a former princess, a lord—and a god.

From their dark wooden thrones, the king and queen watched the newcomers. What were they thinking? They gripped the thrones' arms, their faces placid. However, Caes noted that they stared at the god/Phelan more than anyone else, their lips twitching the tiniest bit as they did so. Though she had stood before kings and queens, emperors and princesses, priests and gods, Caes still trembled before these rulers. Because she had good reason to be afraid. Despite Lyritan's presence, she was a pariah—a princess wanted by two different kingdoms, and someone the Reyverni likely didn't want in their lands for the trouble she could bring. If the king and queen wanted, they could make her life difficult—or non-existent. Lyritan couldn't protect her from everything. Caes bowed her head and gave a deep curtsey, respecting those who ruled over the hall.

Lyritan, however, made no move to bow, and instead tugged on Caes so that she stood upright. "You do not bow to anyone," he said softly. "The world will prostrate itself before you."

And how did he plan to accomplish that?

Blood and death.

Caes gave him a small smile. "Of course, my lord." Lyritan met her smile with an approving nod before turning his attention back to the king and queen.

"You have returned, my lord," the king said to Lyritan. There was no mirth in his voice, though there was a sensible amount of respect. "And my son's body is intact."

"Unharmed, as I promised," Lyritan said, resting a hand on his hip. Ah—that explained matters some. How much of this deferential treatment was because they wanted to keep Phelan safe? Were they hoping to get rid of the god and keep the crown prince? Was that even possible?

But any questions Caes had were pushed aside as Lyritan turned to her, placing a possessive hand on her lower back. "Your Majesties, I told you I was to retrieve the one who will save the world, and here she is—Caesonia. The Princess of Malithia and Ardinan. Daughter of Shirla. Prophetess of Karima. Lady of the Never-Ending Dawn. And my beloved." Well, he certainly took some liberties with her titles. And added a new one.

Again, Caes bowed her head to the royals. "Thank you for receiving us. I am honored, Your Majesties, and thrilled to be able to see your beautiful kingdom for myself." From the king's and queen's expressions, they didn't share the feeling.

"What do you intend to do next?" the queen asked, ignoring Caes. Odd—the king and queen seemingly refused to address Lyritan by name. The king's use of "my lord" was a begrudging title, a minimal courtesy. Then again, how *was* one supposed to address a god? Mortals of yore called Lyritan "father," "blessed," and "divine," but there wasn't an official honorific. And the king probably didn't want to call the god anything polite.

The severity of the situation washed over Caes. Oh, hells. What did Lyritan do in Reyvern before he came to find her? The king and queen were acting like Phelan was being held prisoner—was he? Did Lyritan take him willingly? How had this happened? Caes had to find out more about the prince. And soon. It would help her understand the god, and she needed every bit of help she could get.

I know him better than I know my own heart.

No one knows their own heart. Not until it's too late.

"We're to rest here," Lyritan said to the queen with a satisfied smile, "and I will further my work for the future."

"Work?" the king asked. "What are you speaking of?"

Lyritan raised his hand like one would to a child. "I forgive you your ignorance, mortal, for I understand such grand plans are beyond your ambition." While Lyritan spoke, Caes fought to keep her face straight. No king would appreciate this. "Reyvern is the beginning of what will be a new empire, and a new order." New empire? New order? And…what were his plans for those who didn't want those things? "And then," Lyritan continued, wrapping an arm around Caes and moving her closer to him, "we shall go to the Burning Hand, as I told you. We will defeat Karima and Shirla—and as thanks, Reyvern will prosper. As I promised."

"It's winter," the queen said. "Phelan will not be able to handle the blistering cold of the range. Surely, you're not—"

Lyritan raised a hand, cutting off her protest. "We will do what needs to be done. But for now, we need to rest."

Rest. Lyritan's idea of rest consisted of rushing Caes away from their companions and into private chambers, and then having servants bathe and oil every inch of her, while feeding her cheesy breads and savory meats. Alright, this part of "rest" wasn't that bad.

When she was done, Lyritan was waiting for her in the sitting room in chambers the queen and king had begrudgingly provided for her. She had been unwelcome at courts before, but this was the first one where she felt like a relative who had overstayed their welcome—and she hadn't even been here one night. Everyone was polite, but no one engaged with her any more than was necessary. No one smiled at her when Lyritan wasn't paying attention. No one asked if she needed anything unless Lyritan was next to her. It was safe to assume that her companions were receiving similar treatment, if not worse.

The sitting room was filled with furniture meant for comfort and contained ample quilted blankets and a roaring fire. From the size and amenities, Caes guessed that these rooms were meant for minor members of the royal family. Again, this wasn't bad, considering. Thick blankets made up for all sorts of bad manners.

When she was done, dressed in soft robes of silk and wool and a cloak lined with fur, she stepped into the sitting room.

"My love," Lyritan said, brushing his long blond hair behind his ears. He reached up to pull his hair into a tail, fastening it behind his head with a leather strap. The motion drew attention to the way his biceps bulged through the padding of his jacket. His face, without the curtain of hair, was as honed and deadly as a blade.

And he's mine.

"Lyr," Caes said, giving into the urge to call him by a name she had used so many centuries before. His face broke into a broad smile at her familiar greeting, one Liuva had sometimes favored in times of intimacy. Whatever happened at this court, she needed Lyritan to protect her, and that was more likely if she acted as smitten with him as he was with her. What would Reyvern do with her otherwise? Having her here embroiled them in conflict with both Malithia and Ardinan. Word would spread fast—it was likely the kingdoms knew where she was, or would soon. It was probably out of courtesy—or fear of Lyritan—that they didn't address her political circumstance sooner. But they would. They had to.

"Come." Lyritan guided her to the velvet-covered couch and helped her sit down gently, looking over her hands, which were now covered with faded burns. Her skin tingled where he touched with his calloused fingers, making her shiver. "You are healing well."

"It feels much better."

"Good. That pleases me." His expression became grim. "But, Caesonia, you cannot risk yourself like that. You are divine, but your body—especially after what Shirla might've done to it..."

"What do you mean?"

"You're aging. You've never aged before." He watched her, like he was waiting to see if a dropped glass was going to shatter.

"Oh." Caes let out a soft laugh. "That's no matter. I never thought I'd live forever."

"I cannot bear that outcome. It is unacceptable."

"I lived and was a mortal infant. Why wouldn't I expect to die someday?"

"We will find a solution," he concluded with a grim nod, ignoring her protest. He leaned forward, resting his head on his hands and his elbows on his legs. The firelight caught the lines of his face and his golden eyes, making her tremble under the intensity of his attention. Heat pooled in her core. What would it feel like to be touched by those hands? Kissed by those lips?

But Caes knew better than to let her body's urgings take over her mind. She would use it, and it wouldn't use her. Not again.

"Lyr, what are we going to do now?"

He crossed his arms. "You need to rest. I know that your body is almost mortal, and you've been through so much. It will take time for you to heal. But soon, once our supplies are assembled and we're ready, we will go to the Burning Hand."

"The queen brought up a valid point, though. It's winter. And I will be cold."

Lyritan huffed and frowned. "And we can't wait. If we wait until spring, who knows what Karima and Shirla will have planned for us? I'm sorry, my love, but we don't have a choice. I want to delay until spring. I want you to understand my goals and dreams once more. I want you to share in them again, with your heart as committed as it once was. And for that I need *time*. But time is a gift we do not have." A burning log popped and Lyritan looked over at the fireplace, watching the flames dance. "It will be too dangerous for us to stay here. You saw only the beginning of what the goddesses can do."

Lyritan was right. It was too likely that Desmin or her father or the goddesses would concoct a plan if they stayed in one place for too long.

Though while she had his attention, she would use it. "I've been meaning to ask you," Caes said, "have you heard anything about my father? If he did come here, to Reyvern? The last thing I heard in Malithia was that his sword was found here, shattered, and he was gone. There was no body."

Lyritan slowly nodded. "Yes. He passed beyond Reyvern's borders. And his camp was discovered by hunters."

"What about the sword?" Hope rose in Caes's chest with her heartbeat. "They found it?" Then she cursed herself. Mentioning it twice was too likely to raise the god's suspicion, and she didn't want him to know that they were looking for it, even after Cylis's mishap. Not yet. For now, she needed her own plan for dealing with the gods.

One that didn't rely on Lyritan.

"No." Lyritan clenched and unclenched his fists. "They found nothing. They only knew it was his camp because one of your father's companions was there, dying. He succumbed to his wounds shortly thereafter."

"What will we do without the weapon?" Caes asked. "Won't I need it in the Burning Hand?"

"You will need something to use in the Burning Hand," Lyritan begrudgingly acknowledged. "But we're going to the place where our world is linked to what is beyond. The area around the mountain is...different. Touched. We will find something there. Do not worry. I will not send you anywhere without everything you need. And I have a plan, my love. I will protect you. I did not go through centuries of suffering just to lose you now."

With his words, her hope fell. If her father did indeed have the Sword of Might and lost it in Reyvern, it was gone. Yet, something seemed off about Lyritan's tale, a crucial piece of information unaccounted for. Was he lying? No, she didn't think so. He had no reason to. However, magic god-smiting swords didn't just disappear. *Someone* knew where it was.

What if that someone had lied to Lyritan? What if Lyritan himself didn't know the full truth of what had happened to her father and the weapon? Caes had long ago learned not to assume that people were competent—what if Prince Phelan himself was never told about the weapon? Did the people of Reyvern somehow successfully lie to their prince? How long had the prince been acting bizarre—untrustworthy—before Lyritan possessed him, if he had a personality change at all? Reyvern had been Karima's domain until very recently—Phelan interacting with the god was unusual at best. Caes searched her memory. Rumors about the prince being different—and suddenly partaking in inter-kingdom politics—had reached her even in Malithia. If word reached her there, Lyritan must've already been working on him by that point. How long was the prince under Lyritan's thrall? Was it when she was first in Malithia?

Caes immediately banished that idea.

Lyritan was trapped in stone when her father disappeared. Lyritan couldn't have influenced Phelan and Reyvern's potential decision not to tell him everything about her father and the Sword of Might. Did Reyvern have doubts about their crown prince before Lyritan possessed him? That seemed more likely.

Was it possible that Reyvern *did* have the sword and just never told their crown prince about it, fearing what he would do with that weapon and knowledge?

Reyvern's succession politics didn't concern her. But the fact that they may have known more about her father—and the sword—certainly did. Though, that was something she wasn't going to tell Lyritan now. Or ever. The god may have been their best chance of surviving Karima and Shirla, but that didn't mean she trusted him. Not even close.

"So, we're to stay here, in Gilar?" Caes asked. "The queen doesn't want me here. And the king would be a fool if he did." Caes took a deep breath. "No one wants me to stay here. I endanger everyone."

A crease marred Lyritan's forehead. "Explain your concerns."

"Concerns? I'm a former Malithian heir and, well, I told you what happened in Ardinan. Both kingdoms want me. The moment word reaches Malithia and Ardinan that I'm here, Reyvern is going to be placed under immense pressure to return me. The empire is already planning on conquering Reyvern."

"I decree that you will stay, and that is it."

"Is it so simple?"

"It is for me. Once I am done, the empire won't be a concern to anyone." The god's eyes darkened. "And I will repay a thousand times what they did to you in Ardinan. The kingdom will be razed to the ground. The only thing to sate their thirst will be blood, and the bones of their children their only food. Fear not, my dearest one. The little powers of this earth are nothing compared to what is to come."

Well, that was certainly a happy thought.

Caes swallowed. "So, what am I to do? Hide in my chambers and wait to leave?"

Lyritan smiled. "The opposite. Embrace your court. Relish it. While I need the mortals to keep things intact while we settle matters at the Burning Hand, someday, this throne will be yours. I promise."

Chapter 16

Bethrian

A knock at Bethrian's chamber door pulled him from sleep, in a chamber that was little more than a closet with a bed. Beggars couldn't be choosers, and Bethrian was not about to protest sleeping on the first mattress that graced his back in weeks. At least he didn't have to share a room with a Soul Carver.

Groaning, Bethrian pushed himself upright and rubbed his eyes. "What?"

"You're wanted," Marva said, her voice muffled through the door. "Caes."

"Now?" Bethrian blinked. "Doesn't she know people sleep?"

"Yes, now. Come quietly."

Hells and deeper hells. What did Caes want with him at this time of night? Bethrian brushed his hair out of his face and attempted to make it passable. He would shovel manure for an entire day if only he was allowed one full night of uninterrupted sleep in a bed.

After donning his plain gray woolen doublet—a "gift" from someone in this palace—Bethrian followed Marva silently through the halls, her glinting eyes catching the torch light like fireflies in the near darkness. At this hour, no one was near, no one witnessed him dressed like some dour grandfather. Any guards that were on duty were either posted elsewhere or distracted with whatever petty crimes that occurred this late at night. Unsurprisingly, there weren't any servants—even servants needed to sleep. Like Bethrian did.

When they reached and entered Caes's chambers—even the carved wooden door indicated that her accommodations far surpassed his—Bethrian was a smidge surprised to see that she had assembled a midnight menagerie of Soul Carvers. Alair, Cylis, and Janell raised their heads from their muffled conversation when he entered, and from their lack of reaction they expected him. Cylis and

Janell stood, while Alair sat on the couch next to Caes, rubbing her hand gently. Where was Kerensa? Then again, clandestine meetings were likely best done with as few attendants as possible.

"What is it?" Bethrian asked, slumping onto one of the brocade-covered chairs. Undignified, but most of this party had seen him imprisoned and do unspeakable things into a bucket. His posture wasn't going to scandalize them. "Don't tell me we're escaping."

"No," Caes said. "Not yet." She sighed and looked to Alair, who nodded, before turning her attention back to him. "We have a problem. And, Bethrian, I think you might be the only one who can help us."

If they were still in Malithia, Bethrian would have preened if Caes and Soul Carvers begged for his assistance. But they weren't in Malithia, and Bethrian was in no position to bestow easy favors. "With what?" he asked wryly. "I have a feeling it isn't going to be bedding pretty servants."

"It might," Caes said as Cylis rolled his eyes.

"Oh?" Bethrian sat up straighter. This was getting interesting.

"As you know, I will need the Sword of Might in the Burning Hand."

"Can you remind me of why? Just to make sure I'm understanding everything."

"Caes," Cylis said, "I told you Fuckwit wasn't going to be helpful."

"There you are wrong, my shiny-eyed friend," Bethrian said, and was rewarded with Cylis's scowl. "Only a fool wanders into these things unprepared. And as I haven't been a party to all our conversations with our new divine ally, I want to know what I've been missing. Why isn't he here? Why isn't he helping with this?"

Caes suddenly looked like she swallowed glass. "We...aren't telling Lyritan. Yet."

"Never," Cylis said.

"Ah. I assumed as much. Why?"

"Can we leave it at that I'd like my own plan, just in case?" Oh, she didn't want to tell Bethrian every last detail? Understandable. Now, Bethrian wasn't a complete dunce—between smatterings of conversations and his own astute eyes, he had guessed that they didn't entirely trust the god, and likely for a good reason. Bethrian nodded, urging Caes to continue. "If I'm to destroy the goddesses on my own," Caes said, "I need a weapon. There are only certain weapons in this world that can destroy a deity in the Burning Hand, and the Sword of Might is one. My father was the last man known to have had it, but he is inaccessible. For obvious reasons. And his sword, last I heard, was shattered. And no one has heard of it since."

"What can shatter a weapon that can kill gods? Are you sure the sword isn't intact somewhere else? Like some noble's library?"

"No. I'm not." Caes lowered her gaze for a moment, and then looked back at Bethrian. "I have reason to think that Reyvern might know more about the sword than they're admitting, and that Prince Phelan and Lyritan don't know everything. Lyritan seems to think the weapon is lost. I think someone in Reyvern knows where it is."

"What reasons?"

"Nothing concrete. A hunch." Caes tilted her head.

"So, you think the Reyverni *do* have the Sword of Might, and they just didn't tell Prince Phelan or Lyritan."

Caes grimaced sheepishly. "Pretty much."

Bethrian rubbed his beard, making a note to get a trim and a haircut as soon as possible. "I admit, I'm skeptical, but you've been right too many times before—who am I to say you're wrong now?" "Skeptical" was an understatement—the organization behind such a scheme as Caes proposed would've been impressive, to say the least. However, Bethrian wasn't about to voice his doubts, for the reason he admitted to Caes—she did have a tendency to sniff out answers. And she was also his only chance of having any position at this court. A smart man never irritated his patroness.

Caes's expression softened, pacified at his words, though the Soul Carvers seemed as grumpy as ever. "What do you know of Prince Phelan?" she asked. "What he was like before this?"

Bethrian placed his hand on his lap and thought. He had never met the prince, Malithia being on a conquering rampage and all. "Nothing awful, but little good. Common consensus was that it'd be good for Malithia once he became king."

"He's a fool?" Cylis asked.

Bethrian shrugged. "Possibly. Or given to indulging in...various things. I can't say I spent much time noting gossip on the Reyverni court. Why?" he asked Caes.

"Like I said, I think Reyvern may not have told its own crown prince the truth about what happened to my father. If Phelan was a fool—or worse—before this, it's possible they wouldn't want him to know what happened to the weapon that can kill gods."

"Fool enough not to know about a divine weapon, yet still left in Reyvern's succession?"

"Foolish kings are nothing new," Alair said. "Kingdoms endure that curse all the time."

Bethrian thought he heard Cylis mutter "Your Augustness" but decided he had something stuck in his throat because Cylis coughed. "We're also trying to figure out what happened in general, Fuckwit," Cylis said. "Basically, we think something happened to Caes's father. He took off, lost the sword, and Reyvern found the pieces."

"You don't think he just...ran away?" Bethrian asked. That rumor swirled in Malithia for some time—that the Chosen One had turned craven. "I'm sorry, but sometimes the simplest answer is the truth."

Caes seemed to ponder his words. "I don't know," she finally admitted. "It's possible. Anything is possible. But after what my father was capable of, *something* had to have happened. And I don't think that something is as easily explained as 'he lost Shirla's favor.'"

"He did magic. True magic, correct?" Alair asked.

"Yes." Caes frowned. "I think so. Even now, I know it was no stage trick. Was it an effect of having the sword? Possibly. Probably. I've never seen magic like his before or since. And it gave him the ability to fight as well. But this has caused more questions than ever."

"There is a cost to power," Janell said. "Even power channeled through a weapon."

"You don't know that. Like there's other magic swords we can compare this to," Cylis said to Janell. "You're guessing."

"And I'm likely right."

Bethrian cleared his throat. "Then sorry for begging the obvious, but what does this have to do with me?"

Cylis's face devolved into a scowl that was impressive even by Cylis's standards, while Caes met his gaze. "That's just it—Bethrian, you want to help me. Us. Right?"

"I want what keeps me alive. And if that's helping you, I will run through the streets wearing only a necklace of feathers and screech your name, if that's what it takes."

"We can trust Fuckwit on that," Cylis said. "He likes living."

"I do," Bethrian agreed. "I truly do." Janell rolled her eyes while Alair watched, amused. This entire time, Alair's gaze had softened when he looked at Caes, lingering on her more than anything else in the room. And then she would give him these small smiles that were entirely out of place, like the two of them were in their own little world. Damn. It was enough to make Bethrian jealous.

"I think the Reyverni know more than what they're saying," Caes said, "and we need to know more before we act. But I'm watched, far too closely. Anything I say will be discussed. Analyzed. But you" –her eyes sparkled– "I know you can be quite charming. When you feel like it."

Cylis let out a hearty guffaw that ended when Marva elbowed him in the ribs. Bethrian ignored him. "So," Bethrian said, "you want me to see what I can find out from the Reyverni courtiers."

"And servants. Whoever may know."

Bethrian picked at his beard. "Alright. I'll do it. Sounds easy enough."

Caes nodded, having apparently anticipated his answer. "I'd also like Cylis to help you."

"What?" both men asked, one louder than the other. Caes wanted him to work with *Cylis*? The man had no subtlety. No tact. Cylis and Bethrian exchanged disdainful glares, until Cylis looked back at Caes in indignation. Alair covered his mouth, doing a piss-poor job of hiding a smile.

"You want me to help *that*?" Cylis asked, pointing at Bethrian.

"Caes," Bethrian said, eyeing Cylis and his rather tense muscular limbs, "I'm not sure this is the best—"

"I'm not saying you need to be joined at the hip," Caes explained. "Hells below, I'm not that much of an idiot. What I want is the two of you to talk and compare results."

"Be allies," Marva said, smirking.

"You'll be spending a lot of time together," Janell said, sharing a conspiratorial look with Marva. By this point, none of the other Soul Carvers were bothering to hide their amusement.

Fuck. The gods were truly punishing him for not taking religion more seriously in his life. It had to be. Oh, hells, was this a punishment for sneaking sweets instead of observing Karima's fast days? Was it because he dressed too well? Goddesses didn't like it when mortals looked better than them. This would be Bethrian's punishment—Cylis.

"Stop," Caes turned and said to the Soul Carvers, before giving her attention back to Bethrian and Cylis. "The two of you—together—have the best chance of this working. You and him will have access to different people. With different methods. Bethrian is delicate while you, Cylis—"

"—are a hammer," Alair helpfully finished.

"Caes has a point," Marva said to Cylis. "Guards may talk to you, but it's unlikely they'd talk to Bethrian. This city used to belong to Karima."

"Why not you?" Bethrian asked Marva. "Why can't you be paired with me? You seem nice." Marva smiled at him in response and brushed a dark curl behind her ear. Soul Carvers were too damn beautiful for their own good.

"I thought of that," Caes admitted, "but then realized as one of the Soul Carvers who was with me when I broke the curse, Cylis would have a better chance of getting information. Religious-minded people will trust him more."

"Ker was with you too," Cylis said, obviously as thrilled about this turn of events as Bethrian.

"I need Kerensa to be one of my guards," Caes said. "I'm at a strange court. While Lyritan may be more...open-minded than most when it comes to propriety, it would be best if I kept women with me while I'm in my private chambers." Caes sighed. "It needs to be you. You're the only one I trust who can do this."

Cylis crossed his arms and hung his head. "Fine."

One by one, Bethrian cracked his knuckles. It was good Caes needed him—that meant he had some sort of security at this unfamiliar court. Though, that meant he had to work with Cylis—*Cylis*—to find out where the sword was. Was the sword even here? How was he going to talk about a magic weapon without anyone getting suspicious? And what was Caes going to do with this information in the unlikely event they found something? Oh, this was going to be interesting.

Too interesting.

Too bad Bethrian loved all things that were interesting.

"Alright," Bethrian said. "When do we start?"

Chapter 17

Cylis

"It's not that bad," Marva said to Cylis. It was the following morning after Caes announced that he had to partner with Fuckwit. Marva and Cylis took their simple breakfast of weak tea and bread, butter, and jam in one of the rooms that had been set aside for the Soul Carvers, three to a chamber. He shared this one with Fer, whose dislike of Cylis was mutual, and thus he was never around. There was an extra bed that was presumably meant for Alair, but he spent the night with Caes. There would be no small bumpy mattresses for that bastard, even though he was in the rooms with them this morning, happily munching on toast. No, these weren't awful accommodations, but they could've been better. A lot of things could've been better.

"Bad?" Cylis asked. "Easy for you to say. You don't have to work with a fuckwit."

Marva picked at her nails. "You forget I have to work with *you*."

Alair laughed from his bed, covering a mouthful of breakfast with his fist. He shook his head, watching them. Cylis ignored them both. They were enjoying this far too much.

Marva. Her ethereal features were highlighted by her long black curls, which were still unbound. Like most Malithians, her hair was ink black, like a night without stars. And as with all Soul Carvers, her skin was a smooth, unnatural white, like flesh that had never seen the sun. But her mirrored eyes sparkled, squinting at him with blatant amusement, her elegant jaw and rosy curved lips bearing a smirk. Today she wore a dark red wool dress that hugged her figure, the skirts loose and hovering just above the ground.

He'd get back at her for that comment later. And ignore how much he wanted to stare at her.

Alair cleared his throat. "What do you fine people plan on doing, then, while I'm serving Caes?"

"Serving?" Cylis rolled his eyes. "Is that what we're calling it now?"

Alair deadpanned. "I can make this very uncomfortable, and you know it." The blood left Cylis's face. Whether Alair was threatening to either use his magic, or start telling stories, Cylis didn't want to know.

Marva shrugged. "You're guarding her, right, Alair? This court isn't friendly."

Cylis snorted. "That's an understatement."

"I'm not a guard," Alair said with a slight frown. "Not technically."

"So, what's exactly going on with the three of you? Goldie the god is keeping you as her...lover?" Cylis asked. "While he's planning on marrying her?"

"Apparently," Alair answered, picking off another piece of toast. "Caes doesn't like it and neither do I—too much attention on us. We were tired of hiding our relationship but this" –Alair waved his arm– "wasn't what I planned."

"None of us could have planned this, or wanted to," Marva said. "Caes thought she was going to the Burning Hand to die. And now she is becoming an empress? For a different empire?"

Alair nodded. "Lyritan says he has a plan to avoid her death and kill the goddesses, but we think he may be bluffing to keep her calm and go to the mountain willingly. If he had such a plan, why would he need her to go to the mountain at all?" Alair sighed. "No, I think he has some other goal."

"Fuck..." Cylis mumbled while the others fell into a depressed silence. Marva seemed unsurprised at Alair's musings. Then again, none of the information surrounding Caes was a secret. And Caes talked. To Soul Carvers, at least.

"She's attending a formal midday meal today as Lyritan's guest," Alair suddenly said, speaking up for the first time in about a dozen bites. The bread was now depleted. "Might not be a bad time for you to explore the palace." He nodded towards Cylis. "See what you can learn."

"See how long I can go without murdering Fuckwit, more like," Cylis muttered.

"People will know you're new and it won't seem strange if you ask questions," Alair said.

"He's right," Marva said. "People will be expecting it. You can't waste this chance."

Waste this chance. There shouldn't be a "chance." Cylis was a Soul Carver, not a spy. He was, without a doubt, the worst person Caes could've asked to do this. Except Fer. Fer would've been worse.

With Marva and Alair's chipper encouragement in his ear, an hour later found Cylis standing against the wall near the palace's more social occupants, huddled and chatting with Fuckwit like they were illicit lovers instead of...whatever they were. Around the corner, the court was fluttering over some princess or duchess or something, their conversation a throbbing din in Cylis's ears.

It was too early for him to deal with Fuckwit, but it couldn't be helped. They needed to be seen together now so that later it wouldn't be noted as strange. Or so Marva had said and Bethrian agreed.

And they needed to come up with a plan, so, two birds, one stone.

"I'm not happy about this either," Bethrian said to Cylis, peering over Cylis's shoulder at something behind him. Cylis resisted the urge to see what he was looking at. "It's not like you're going to be useful to me. You might be the least friendly person I've ever encountered."

Cylis squinted. "No shit. But this is what Caes wants, and I'm not about to tell her no."

"Unfortunately, I can relate." Bethrian braced his forearm against the rough stone, which had minimal lines showing where the bricks were fused. Cylis was starting to think that part of this palace was carved directly from the mountain. Though, now that he thought about it, that should've been obvious. It had been a long year—he wasn't at his brightest.

"So," Cylis asked, "what's your plan for the day?"

"The normal. I'm going to attend the meal with Caes and see what I can learn about the court," Bethrian said, nodding towards the room of chattering nobles. "I'll start there."

Cylis squirmed. "You're not expecting me to go with you—"

"Hells, no. Our relationship is one of exchanging information. We don't want..." Bethrian's voice trailed off when a young woman approached them. She was pretty enough—certainly wore enough jewelry—and her gait reminded Cylis of his grandmother's small dog, which was an oddly chipper thing that moved constantly and never seemed to get very far.

"Excuse me," the woman said, her wide eyes looking at Cylis. Looking for far too long.

"Yes, my lady?" Bethrian asked while Cylis crossed his arms as hard as he could.

"I...I..." the lady kept staring at Cylis.

"What is it?" Cylis snapped.

"What my friend here meant to say," Bethrian said, giving Cylis a warning glance, "is that we're at your service. Please, tell us how we may assist you."

"You're a Soul Carver." The woman batted her eyes. Oh, dead and cursed gods, what was this?

"Yeah, I am."

"Are you...by any chance...like Fenrick? You have his coloring."

"What?" Cylis asked. Bethrian's face took on an unusual shade of gray, even as he trembled, likely stifling laughter. "What is it?" Cylis asked Bethrian. "What's a Fenrick?"

Bethrian took a deep breath and straightened. "I can assure you, my lady, that my friend Cylis is nothing like Fenrick. So much a pity." One of Bethrian's fleshy masculine hands patted Cylis on the back like he was burping an infant. Fuckwit was very lucky Caes needed him alive.

"Oh, that's too bad," the woman said, still staring at Cylis. "Lady Peony Passionflower made such an amazing character that I hoped..." She leaned forward and whispered, "It's so rude but I may never have another chance to ask—is it true? Do you have a knot?"

Bethrian turned a very corpse-like shade of white as Cylis said, "Um, maybe a little one in my neck. Slept funny."

"No." The woman smiled and giggled playfully. "I meant a *knot*."

"A not...what?"

"I'm afraid Lady Passionflower created such things for literary purposes," Bethrian said.

"Will someone please tell me what a Fenrick and Passionflower is?" Cylis asked. The not/knot mystery would have to wait.

"You haven't heard of them?" the woman asked. "Why, it's Malithia's greatest literary achievement—*One Night with a Soul Carver*."

"One...night..." Quickly the pieces assembled in Cylis's head. "That sounds like a romance novel." Bethrian nodded and Cylis gulped. Something in Cylis's expression made the woman suddenly turn shy and excused herself, right as he realized what that woman had asked. Did he just get solicited for...*that*...because of...

"Bethrian," Cylis asked, tapping his foot on the stone, "is there really a romance novel featuring a Soul Carver?"

"Several. I'm surprised you haven't heard of them."

"And I look like one of the characters?"

"You all tend to look alike, so, yes."

"So, these court women think that I'm this...Fenrick." Cylis curled his lip. Hard.

"Probably. Though you don't have their sparkling skin."

"*What?*"

Bethrian smiled. "In Lady Passionflower's lore, Soul Carvers have skin that sparkles like a thousand shattered suns."

Cylis blinked several times. "How do you know so much about this?"

"I know a lot of things. I made it a point to do so." True—Fuckwit did tend to make his way around the Malithian court, so it wasn't surprising he had heard about this...flower.

"Fuck," Cylis muttered. "If I ever meet this Peony, I'm going to have words. Lots of words."

Bethrian looked like he wanted to say something more, but then wisely thought better of it. Cylis wasn't in the mood. "And what about today?" Bethrian cautiously asked. "What's your plan for our little adventure?"

Cylis paused before answering. "I think I'm going for a walk. Stretch my legs. See if anyone approaches me and what they'll tell me on their own. Yes, yes, I can be subtle if I need to."

"Hmm, not a bad option." Bethrian seemed impressed. "And you're right, it's too early to be asking questions. And if your little adventure gets me a name or two, so much the better."

Chapter 18

Caes

One thing in Lyritan's favor, the god knew how to make an entrance. But then again, he always did, even thousands of years before. Though, this wasn't a forest somewhere in the untouched Malithian wilds—this was a court of stone, and full of nobles who wouldn't hesitate to seek his blood.

They wouldn't dare hurt him. He's too powerful.

Caes pushed Liuva's remnant naïve musings aside. The current Caes would never underestimate what the fearful and desperate were capable of. And with their crown prince held hostage, Reyvern was both. The air practically reeked of it.

After a leisurely morning in her chambers spent dressing and gleaning what she could from her maids—it was mostly a futile endeavor since the poor girls seemed terrified of her—Lyritan sent word about meeting him for a midday meal. Lyritan also included a dress with a note saying that it would please him if she wore it. Alright. She wasn't about refuse him something so simple.

Lyritan strode into the dining hall where the court waited, head held high, with Caes's hand clasped and raised between the two of them. His smile was dazzling, to the point it was unclear whether his expression or his glowing eyes shone brighter. At her. He wore a dark blue jerkin with a black undershirt and black wool breeches and matching calf-skin boots. The light and the dark, the god and the human. Her love and her damnation.

Caes returned Lyritan's smile, using her free hand to adjust her long skirts. She couldn't trip and fall. Not now.

It was hard not to. The dress Lyritan gifted her was a marvel among court dresses, designed to constrain the wearer like a cocoon. The gown was made of a flowing dark blue velvet, accented with black embroidery of a phoenix, and a low-cut neckline that retained a couple tasteful inches to prevent a failure of modesty. The garment's symbolism was apparent—these were Reyvern's colors and symbol. There was no train—thankfully—since the skirts were so full that it would've been too much for her to handle. A silver circlet rested on her forehead. Simple, and yet it proclaimed that she was royalty. Or was supposed to be treated as such.

They stepped into the hall, ignoring the customary hush. No one announced them. No one needed to. Besides, this was supposed to be a relatively small court meal, not a formal audience. Though, *some* sort of announcement was expected. Yet, Lyritan seemed unbothered by the apparent slight. Did he know that court etiquette normally required an announcement? Did he care?

Lyritan never concerned himself with the formalities of mortals.

With this, she was in complete agreement with Liuva—some things hadn't changed.

To Caes, this slight was another sign that the court was merely tolerating Lyritan, hoping that their crown prince would be returned. Did Prince Phelan have younger brothers or a competent sister? Hopefully, or the kingdom was likely facing a frightful succession dispute, and it couldn't afford one with the threat from Malithia. Though, this was one dispute Caes was certainly staying out of. If she was dragged into an *Idici Sors* again, she'd forfeit and flee.

Caes's entourage followed behind her—except for Cylis, Janell, and Fer—dressed mostly like they did in Malithia, except a smidge nicer and in garments borrowed or gifted from the royal family. Kerensa glittered in a dark crimson velvet dress that had—luckily for her—few layers compared to Caes's own. Bethrian glinted in a dark green doublet and snug breeches, earning him more than a few admirers. Alair strode immediately behind her, wearing a long black surcoat, and Caes could only imagine the dour expression he gave to gawking courtiers. Lyritan had been sincere—he wasn't going to interfere with their relationship. It seemed he was more than content to introduce Alair to the court as his betrothed's mistress. Mister? Master? What did one call a princess's openly-acknowledged lover?

The Reyverni court was similar to its Ardinani and Malithian sisters, except the halls were made of carved stone, accented by what Caes suspected was a natural waterfall against one wall. Her maid from this morning mentioned that there was a larger one in the royal bedchamber, which was considered one of the most impressive sites in the city, for those privileged enough to witness it. Between the unexpected humidity and the chill from the altitude, Caes was glad of the excessive layers, for once. She would've been miserable without them.

As for the people, the expressions weren't as hostile as those in Ardinan, but they were difficult to read. There were few frowns and even fewer smiles, and those smiles came from young men and women who likely didn't have enough sense not to lust after a god. A sign that few courtiers, if any, were pleased. The common people of Gilar had seemed thrilled by Prince Phelan/Lyritan, though that was easily explained by the court pretending that everything was fine, in order to keep the commoners from worrying. Here, it was a different matter entirely.

By this point, Caes was used to walking through crowds without a single familiar face and full of hostile glances, which was why her heart leapt into her throat when she saw Sabine.

Sabine.

Here? In Gilar?

Sabine had dark circles under her eyes that hadn't been there before, and she was wearing something that was more like an upside-down tulip blossom than a dress, but it was her friend. Someone Caes never expected to see again.

And next to her was none other than Lady Flyntinia, Althain's mother. The older woman was as kempt as ever and dressed as regally as a princess, though new lines marred her face. No wonder—she had lost her son. Caes managed to look at them for a few more seconds before she had to turn away, lest she call attention to them. Sabine didn't need to be hounded by courtiers, and Caes needed to compose herself. And in those few seconds, she found a smattering of familiar Malithians in the crowd. No one overly important, but still.

Why were Malithians here?

And now?

Soon they came to the long head table where Caes—after all the proper formalities—took her place next to Lyritan facing the crowd with the rest of the royal family. The royal family in this case consisted of the king and queen, royal descendants, and a dowager relative or two. No one introduced themselves to Caes and she didn't dare make the introductions if no one else was going to. If Lyritan wasn't bothered enough to say anything, she certainly wasn't. The rest of her company dined below with the court. Her Soul Carvers—and Bethrian—sat at a table near them, close enough that Caes could've tossed a biscuit and hit Bethrian's head. She didn't.

But this was a court—there would be some sort of ceremony before they were permitted to eat, and Caes found she was right. One relative after another took their turn engaging in what Caes could only describe as "creative verbalizing." Once homages to the king and queen were done, and a short round of speeches welcoming Phelan and the god back to Reyvern—and politely referring to Caes as his guest—were concluded, the meal commenced.

The soup course, a spiced blended squash served with hearty steaming bread, passed with little incident. Parties politely inquired about Caes's journey and how she found Gilar. She had to credit everyone's restraint in not pressing her on matters and keeping their expressions serene. It was impossible to tell what they were thinking. Lyritan seemed to be having the same experience, the royal family talking with him like it was normal that a god was possessing their prince and then decided to come to a meal.

The fish course similarly passed without incident, and she was able to dine on a filet poached in butter with garlic and dill in peace. Her immediate dining companion was Phelan's older sister, Saryn, who was married to a lord who wasn't important enough to sit at the table. She did an excellent job introducing Caes to who was who at this court. Again, she had to admire Saryn's restraint in treating Caes like she was a visiting princess on a diplomatic visit. Though, it was possible that Saryn didn't like her brother and considered Lyritan an improvement. Stranger things happened in families.

It wasn't until the meat course, consisting of an array of mountain birds cooked and then tucked back into their own feathers for serving, that Saryn lowered her voice and said, "You're not the only Malithian we have at this time."

"I thought I saw a few familiar faces," Caes said, taking a small sip of the too-sweet wine. She had to keep her wits with her. "I wasn't aware that the emperor sent more on his behalf."

"No, I'm afraid they weren't sent by the emperor," Saryn said, deftly slicing into the slender wing of some unfortunate creature. "They arrived almost a week ago, exhausted, claiming to have ridden from Glynnith at the first news of the bastard's death." Althain's death, she meant. Caes gripped her goblet's stem at Saryn's callousness about her friend.

That was a mere couple weeks ago...how did Flyntinia and Sabine learn about what happened to Althain so quickly?

"So, they aren't here as ambassadors?"

Saryn let out a polite scoff. "No. Lady Flyntinia claimed to have a message from the goddess and that she needed to be here—in Gilar—when Prince Phelan returned. And we weren't inclined to ignore her."

"Understandable." And it was, in a way.

Karima used to be worshiped in Reyvern, until very recently. Lyritan seemed to have effectively stolen the kingdom from her, though he had mentioned there were people in the rural areas that never stopped worshipping him. What was Saryn not saying about Flyntinia? A lot, most likely. Who knew what the royal family had told Flyntinia about Lyritan? Did Flyntinia know that Caes was returning here with him? Caes remained silent, listening to Lyritan speak with the king about road conditions into Reyvern and bridge maintenance, something obscenely mundane for a god.

Saryn had apparently noted who she was listening to. "He's made a few changes, you know. The god."

"Oh? Such as what?"

Saryn shrugged. "The public funds. The ones that aid the needy. He ordered that all the nobles provide a large...gift. Stated that there was only so much a mortal body needed to survive."

"That was very kind of him. How do the nobles feel about such generosity?"

"I think you can imagine, Your Highness," Saryn said with a grin. "They were about as happy with that as they are at the prospect of my son being king, at all of three years of age."

"You wouldn't inherit?"

A long sigh escaped Saryn's lips. "Thanks to my marriage, no. It was explicitly written into the marriage contract in order to get approval from the Black Council."

"Black Council?"

"Ink is typically black, no?" Saryn took another bite of the animal. Once she swallowed, she said, "Those men and women do quite a bit of writing, with issuing laws and all."

"Oh. That's not as ominous as I imagined."

"I expect not. But regardless, I cannot inherit so my son is next in line, and he is far too young to rule."

Caes resisted the urge to look up from her meal and inspect Saryn's countenance. Was Saryn pleased with Phelan being possessed because it meant that her son would be king, and she would be regent for a long time? No wonder she seemed happy Caes was here. This was getting more complicated by the moment.

"Her Majesty and I would like to speak with you," Saryn said softly. "Once you have a some time to spare."

"Of course. I'm at your disposal." Like she could say anything else.

Whatever Caes had stepped into at this court, this was only the start.

Chapter 19

Alair

It was amazing how little courts changed through distance and centuries. If Alair closed his eyes—and ignored the Reyverni accents—he could almost pretend that he was a very young man again, barely more than a child, nervously fidgeting at a court dinner. His oldest brother, Aeron, would be boasting about whatever exploits would get him the most attention from his dinner companions and Taren, the next youngest, would be watching Aeron with badly concealed admiration. His youngest brother and two little sisters wouldn't be at such dinners, as they were still confined to the nursery. One of his sisters wouldn't live to be ten and the other was taken by a pox when she was nearing the age to court, but there was no way Alair could've known such things then. Instead, Alair would've been trying to find his place in the world, wondering what he was going to do to gain the respect and position that was so critical to life, and yet, next to impossible for a younger son such as him.

If only Aeron could see him now, one of the most feared Soul Carvers of his generation. Then again, with how Alair seemed to be attracting the dead, maybe wishing for his brother to see him wasn't a smart idea.

Alair ate his dinner, resuming the muted expression and mannerisms that he utilized in Malithia, at first unwillingly as he was haunted by his Soul Carver trials, and then, as years passed, by choice. It was easy to pretend that he was numb to the world, and it allowed him to focus on observing. Life was easier when one didn't have to maintain vapid conversation with idiots. Not that that stopped people from trying.

"What do you do for the Lady Caesonia?" A man of around fifty years of age asked him. The man wore a dark red overcoat that was lined with braided gold embroidery, which highlighted the man's splotchy red complexion. Whether it was from drink, a life in the blistery cold winds, or plain bad luck, Alair couldn't say. And Alair couldn't have cared less. Alair gave the man a blank look and went back to eating his fish. It was overcooked and rubbery, but at least the taste was there.

"She seems to favor you," the man's companion, a woman of near the same age, asked. Likely his spouse. Her skin was even and clear, and she seemed to have been spared her husband's ruddiness. "It's not hard to tell that she seeks your approval."

Alair gave her another blank stare, blinked hard, and went back to his fish. They would learn nothing from him.

"Is he a mute?" the man asked his wife.

"Ignore our sullen friend," Bethrian called out from the other end of the table. "His Soul Carver trials have left him unappreciative of fine conversation." It was a good thing Cylis wasn't at this meal—he would've had something to say about that comment. Bethrian coughed. "If you'd like to hear about the Malithian court and our fine princess's heroic exploits there, you're welcome to join us." Bethrian held up a goblet for emphasis and his dining companions, a gaggle of young men and women, turned towards the couple with smiles written across their faces. Whatever Bethrian was telling them, it was no doubt more dramatic than anything that actually occurred and somehow also empty of the truth. It was perfect. The couple nodded their heads and focused on Bethrian, who then regaled them with the tale of Caes and the Stone God's curse. Nothing everyone in Malithia didn't already know. Though, Bethrian had improvised a rather dramatic speech of her accepting the curse that Alair didn't remember—because Caes didn't do dramatic speeches.

Caes. Slowly, he turned his head towards her, where she was sitting at the table on the dais with the rest of the royals, her every mannerism that of a queen's. He had been watching her this entire meal, while doing his best to hide that he was doing so.

Gods, Caes was beautiful. Her sharp eyes roamed the court, speaking to the intelligence that lurked within. As much as she hated courts, she was good at handling them. There was no doubt she was fighting a battle of words through this entire meal, but to all appearances she was a beautiful princess relaxing and being hosted by royals who were lucky to have her. That dress…it was made of several more layers than Alair preferred, but it hugged her curves, and the color was flattering. She didn't need silks and finery, but she wore them well when she did. All such trappings did was highlight what was already there. A princess.

Alair had met many princesses, from courts now lost to dust. Some were beautiful, most were not, but none were Caes. He grieved his first love, the one who had been his reason for pursuing the trials—still missed her bitterly, as seeing her reminded him—but fate had given him Caes, and he could never regret what had led him to her. All the centuries of suffering were worth it.

"This isn't good," Kerensa muttered from next to him. The others were distracted and missed her hushed words. She cut into her slice of spiced bread drizzled with a sugar glaze. A simple dessert, but it was an excellent finish after the meal's richness.

"What isn't?" Alair asked, staring off into the distance.

"You saw that Flyntinia's here. And Sabine. Why? Why now? Why at all?"

Indeed. Alair had sometimes wondered how much of his life was fate, in the control of some power beyond the gods. To what pushed him into the Soul Carver trials, to selecting that very trial that made him inadvertently survive through centuries, to how he happened to be at the point in time to find Caes. To how, right before her fight with Seda, he happened to use the phrase "blessings of Kaj," which told her that her father's prophecy was in truth hers. "Kaj" so that it rhymed with barrage, wasn't even the correct pronunciation—it had been twisted over the years. If Alair had just happened to use the original version, would that have changed Caes fate? Such a small thing could have altered everything.

So, no. He didn't think that it was anything in the realm of coincidence that brought Flyntinia and Sabine here. He was no longer a believer in coincidences, if he ever was at all.

Sabine being in Reyvern was one thing. She was devious, but she seemed to have a genuine affection for Caes.

Flyntinia, however, was another matter. In the years Alair had been acquainted with her, she had genuine affection for only one person. And after Althain's death...

"I don't like it," Alair said softly.

"Me neither," Kerensa said. "But what else can we do but watch? I mean, we could roast her."

"That might be a bit rash."

"Alright, no roasting," Kerensa agreed and then frowned. "Not unless Caes tells us to."

"No, as much as I hate it, we have to wait and see what she has planned for this court."

Chapter 20

Cylis

Good goddess, nothing in this maze of a castle made sense.

Normal castles had wings—where people lived—and halls—where people ate—and parlors—where people socialized. And normal castles also had outer areas, consisting of courtyards and barracks, where the strong and brave fighting men lived and fought strongly and bravely. But in what world were these three things broken into chunks and scattered within and outside a mountain? Cylis had already been turned away by one peeved servant, who had informed him that he was too close to the royal chambers, then he found an empty rampart, and then he came across more chambers. That wasn't even counting how he had encountered some sort of indoor training ring, an alcove with beds behind a waterfall, and a doorway that led to stairs overlooking a small canyon that were in desperate need of a railing. Or a warning placard.

This was ridiculous and surprisingly dangerous. He would've been better off attending that meal with the others. At least then he'd have a full stomach.

More turns. More halls. More stairs—fucking stairs. And then Cylis came to a room off a wide corridor that seemed recently abandoned. Half-burnt candles rested in alcoves and rows of benches circled an empty altar. Odd. The walls were painted with elaborate designs and inlaid with tiger's eye and jasper. This wasn't some cast-off closet—this was a place of worship. Besides, what closet had space for fifty muscular men?

"Her children always call to her," an old man said, tottering towards him from the shadows. The man fit the stereotypical description of someone lurking at an abandoned place of worship. Voluminous brown robes. Wrinkled, saggy skin.

Eyes heavy with wisdom. Little hair on the top of his head, leaving his shiny scalp to reflect the light as efficiently as Cylis's eyes.

Cylis crossed his arms and opened his mouth to give some retort about not being anyone's child, but then remembered he was supposed to be useful. Instead, he asked, "This was Karima's temple?"

The man nodded slowly, gesturing at the desolate space. "A chapel, consecrated to her at the insistence of our king's first wife. A gift, upon the birth of Prince Phelan. I was its priest, until recently."

That explained a lot.

"Why's it empty?" Cylis asked. He knew the answer—Lyritan took Karima's place. But he wanted to know what the priest would say.

The priest's eyes narrowed. "We have a new deity in residence. Once who has declared Reyvern for himself. And he has asked for worship in person—and in daily actions. Not temples."

"He can do that?"

The priest nodded. "Somehow, he was already bound to this place, long ago. He stated he merely reclaimed what is his. But I don't think I need to tell you what a travesty this is, Child of Karima." Nope, he didn't. Travesty, schmavesty, Cylis needed answers, not ramblings. But this priest could probably be poked into giving Cylis what he needed.

"But you're still here," Cylis observed.

"I am." The priest's jaw clenched. "I swore off Karima's worship and the queen promised that this...blasphemy is temporary. The god seems content to let me be, so long as I don't wander from here." Considering what happened when Malithia took over temples, Karima's priest was very lucky.

"How did the prince manage to do this? I didn't know gods could possess humans. Karima doesn't."

The priest bowed before Cylis. "May I take your hand?"

"Ummm...sure?" Cylis held out a hand and the priest took it, clutching it between his own. His touch was chilly, even to Cylis's frosty skin.

"Long have I yearned to touch one who has touched Karima. Drank her very essence."

"Yes, yes, it's an honor to have been chosen by her."

The priest's eyes darkened. "Phelan knew nothing of such worth, of such devotion. He was devoted to pursuing his passions, but then something whispered to him, pushing him to seek power even beyond a throne. Promises of glory that would ring through the world." The priest's gaze went downcast. "I know not how it happened, *this*"—the priest waved his arm around the room—"it was all so fast. Phelan would've done anything in the pursuit of power. No matter the cost. He was always a boy who sought his pleasures. He demanded respect. But he was never one to respect the goddess."

Voices echoed in the corridor. Both Cylis and the priest turned their attention to the open door and watched two guards walk by, chattering about being moved to a different shift. Nothing Cylis cared about. When they were gone, Cylis said, "He was the crown prince. Sounds powerful enough to me. You're telling me this all started because he was greedy?"

"More than that. If only it was as simple as greed. He was afraid."

"Don't tell me I stepped into a murder mystery."

"No. Nothing quite like that." If the priest was surprised by Cylis's callousness, he gave no indication. "If there was another option—another son of the king—another prince would've been chosen as heir. The eldest is typically chosen, but that's usually out of convenience as opposed to right. People die young, and kings are no exception. No one wants a child on the throne. For some time, once Phelan's lack of respect for his position became more evident and showed no signs of maturing with age, there was talk of giving the title to Phelan's sister. But her husband—no, that match already caused too many conflicts in the court. But with the princess's marriage the king acted first, regretted later, and thus it is."

The priest went on for a bit, rambling about the court's power struggles, and how Phelan had a few mistresses who were banished from court once Lyritan took over. Cylis probably should've listened, but he didn't care. Caes would care, but if Caes wanted details she could prance down here herself. What Cylis knew from talking to the priest was that Phelan had apparently been a bit of a half-assed donkey before this, and Lyritan likely enticed him with promises of greatness. And while it seemed the court wasn't thrilled that Lyritan was here, it was a brave or dumb person—arguably both—who insulted a god when that god was right in front of them.

That solved the mystery of Phelan, at least enough for Cylis's taste. Now, what about the sword?

"I'm traveling with Karima's Prophet," Cylis ventured, cutting off the priest's diatribe about which of the king's younger sisters was the most devout.

The priest's eyes widened. "Her—oh, I cannot wait to see her. To have died and been resurrected in the very service of Karima herself. And her divine son." Poor guy—Cylis wasn't about to correct him.

"Yep, her. As you might know, her father was the cursed hero of Ardinan." Cylis held up a hand and staunched the priest's protests. "I know. She knows. She regrets his stupidity. But he was her father, and she wants word about what happened to him. Gentle heart and all."

"Oh, I suppose any child would want to know the fate of their parent. Even one as misguided as him." The priest paced a few steps away, looking at the empty space where Karima's statue used to be. From this short encounter with the priest, Cylis suspected that the man slept next to the statue, hugging it like a child hugged a doll. Finally, the priest turned to Cylis and said, "It was carnage, at the camp where he was last. Her father wasn't there once our men discovered it, only his supplies remained. His companions, as far as I know, died there or soon after."

"What sort of carnage? Battle?"

"No. Word amongst the other priests was that he encountered one of the creatures from the mountain. I'm more inclined to think they were attacked by wolves."

Wolves or mystical creatures. Neither sounded pleasant.

"Creatures? Mountain?"

The priest's mouth dropped open for a moment before he spoke. "I forget you're one of the southern folk. Here, we are close to the Burning Hand and live in its shadow." The priest took a deep breath. "There are lots of rumors about the mountain, many tales of its origin and purpose. I won't bore you with them, unless you'd like me to?"

"No. No need to bore me." *More than you already are*, Cylis left unsaid. He widened his eyes and hoped he reminded the priest of an enrapt student.

The priest seemed encouraged by Cylis's expression and continued, "Well, one thing is for certain—things are strange near the mountain. It's surrounded by creatures that shouldn't be part of our world and things left over from the days the world was formed."

"So, monsters."

"Yes. Terrors and nightmares. They typically stay near the mountain itself, but sometimes they venture further south." The priest made some odd gesture involving his forehead, likely a northern warding symbol. "There's a reason that none but the most faithful or desperate travel northwest of here—too many don't return."

And it seemed they'd have to contend with these creatures on the way to the Burning Hand. Just wonderful. After the nightmare that was whatever Damek and Desmin did, Cylis had hoped that was the end of mysterious creatures for the remainder of his life. Apparently, he was not that lucky.

"Do you happen to know who found their camp?" Cylis asked. "Caesonia remembers some of her father's companions. She'd like to know their fates." Cylis had no idea if Caes knew them, but he'd take the whole "gentle heart" thing as far as the priest would let him.

"They were discovered by hunters, and then the king sent out Lord Dyvith's men once the hunters returned to Gilar and reported what they found."

"He sent a lord's men? Not his own?"

"No. If something needs to be done, usually Lord Dyvith is the one who volunteers—and funds the activity. He didn't become the king's favorite for no reason."

Cylis didn't want to raise the priest's suspicions by asking too many questions about Lord Dyvith so soon, so he decided that this was a good time to wrap up this conversation. And he was hungry.

"Thank you," Cylis said, bowing his head. "I will make sure Caesonia knows how you have aided her. It's bad news I have to convey, but she will appreciate the knowledge."

"Any other use I can be, please let me know."

"Before I go, may I pray?" Cylis forced an innocent smile.

The priest's eyes lit and motioned Cylis to the front of the benches.

Pray? Ha. Cylis just wanted a quiet place to collect his thoughts and it was important to leave with a good impression. And, oh, was Caes going to be pleased. She had to be, for he had a name of where they should look next. If the priest was right, if the sword *was* found along with Damek's camp, then this Lord Dyvith had the answer.

Chapter 21

Bethrian

"Typically, my nighttime visitors are more...comely than you," Bethrian said, letting Cylis into his room. While Cylis wasn't an ugly man by any means—no Soul Carver was—he could've paid a smidge more attention to his attire. And Cylis wasn't a beautiful woman with sensible, yet voluminous breasts. That was the first mark against him.

"Rough evening?" Bethrian asked, pointing at Cylis's black woolen shirt that had misaligned buttons near the top. Cylis looked down at his chest and scowled and fixed the garment. There. At least now he wasn't quite so slovenly.

Though, it wasn't likely Bethrian was any better at that moment. Bethrian was wearing his loose cotton and linen tunic and breeches—his sleeping clothes. Because it was night. And he was supposed to be asleep. Some men preferred nightgowns, but some men didn't care if their garments rode up and exposed their nethers. Might as well sleep naked in that case. And, unfortunately, he had only been sleeping, as much as he desired another activity. Oh, he had a proposition given to him at dinner—some lady who was enticed at the idea of sampling a Malithian courtier—but he didn't need to make a name for himself quite yet. Yes, he was going to help Caes, but if he could help himself by endearing himself physically to the correct noblewoman, so much the better.

"You know," Bethrian said, "we could arrange for you to get a mirror."

"Shut up." Cylis strode over to Bethrian's bed and sat, crossing one leg over another. "What in the hells is this?" Cylis pet the fur draped over Bethrian's bed like it was a beloved animal companion.

"Beaver. I think."

"Why?"

"If you actually managed to get cold, you'd understand. I asked for another blanket and they gave me this. I wasn't about to complain."

Cylis sneered. "I'm more surprised you're deigning to sleep with a carcass."

"Desperate times."

Bethrian placed his hands on his hips and watched Cylis make himself comfortable on his bed, the one place in this entire palace that Bethrian could indulge in solitude. The Soul Carver's scrunched face took in his meagre surroundings, weighing each object with a glare Bethrian's mother would've appreciated. But they both likely knew this wasn't a social call.

"Since we don't want to attract attention by talking much in public, I'm going to guess you have something to say," Bethrian ventured. "Something that couldn't wait until morning, apparently."

Cylis raised his head, as if daring Bethrian to challenge him. "Don't you like to sleep on information? Dream about gossip or something? I can come back later."

"No, no. You're already here." Dear dead and cursed gods, what was Caes doing making him work with this man? It was punishment, revenge for what he did to her in Fyrie. It had to be. "Tell me. You obviously found something. Unless you *want* to be around me."

"Hardly." Cylis's fingers worked their way into the beaver fur in a way that was oddly...thorough. "I found a chatty priest," Cylis said. "He's pissed that Karima got evicted. Anyway, he mentioned that the king sent someone named Lord Dyvith to see what happened to Caes's father. Made it sound like hunters found the camp and then the king wanted it investigated."

"Dyvith, Dyvith," Bethrian muttered, pacing the room. "Shit. You're sure?"

"No."

"Cylis—"

Cylis shrugged. "What? That's what the priest told me. Not my fault if he was wrong." Cylis's features somehow scrunched even closer together, oddly reminiscent of a fleshy paper fan. "Why the 'shit'? You know him?"

A long sigh escaped Bethrian's mouth as he rubbed his face. "Only by reputation. Desmin mentioned him once while he was in Malithia, saying that Lord Dyvith's family has lands in Ardinan through his grandmother."

"So?"

"So" –Bethrian lowered his hands– "I think it's possible we just found out how it was that Desmin, a Prince of Ardinan, knew so much about Reyvern's activities." Bethrian tugged on his silky hair. Not hard, though. He didn't want to risk becoming bald a moment sooner than nature demanded. "Which means, damn, he probably won't talk to me. There's a decent chance he's Desmin's ally."

"Well" –Cylis slapped his thighs and stood– "not my problem. Good luck, Bethy."

Bethrian froze. "You're leaving?"

"What? I did my job. I found a name, which is more than what we had this morning. Now you have to dazzle or whatever shit you're good at. Not that I ever understood it." Cylis said the last part in a low mumble that Bethrian decided to ignore.

Without waiting for a reply, Cylis left the room, closing the door behind him and leaving Bethrian alone with this new dilemma.

Cylis. Some partner he was—he didn't ask or care what Bethrian had been up to that night. Or offer to help with the next steps. Or even ask how Bethrian was doing. No matter. At least Cylis gave him a point of direction to work on next.

Bethrian dramatically collapsed on his beaver skin and gripped it like much like Cylis had. It *was* oddly soothing. And it let Bethrian sort out his thoughts. What else had he heard about the noble?

Lord Dyvith. He was old. Military commander. Didn't have a reputation for being friendly. Bethrian finding and endearing himself to him was probably going to go as well as trying to wear the beaver skin on his bed and getting adopted into an active dam. So, befriending the man anytime before the next century was likely impossible.

Let's see...what did Bethrian learn this evening while he frolicked through the court? He had heard a little about Lord Dyvith, along with several other lords.

Lord Dyvith was married, but his wife was at a country estate, so seducing her wasn't an option.

But Lord Dyvith *did* have three daughters, one of which was at court. She was primed to be married off, as it was finally her turn after dealing with all the attention given to her now-married siblings.

So, right now, at this court, there was very likely a young woman who was desperate for attention and compliments. And that was perfect, because Bethrian was excellent at both of those things.

Chapter 22

Caes

"Welcome back to court, my lord," a woman said to Lyritan with a graceful curtsey, her head downcast. The streaks of gray in her hair shone in the candlelight, along with the myriad of jewels around her face. Even as a fawning supplicant, the woman didn't resist stealing glances at Caes. And Alair. "I have anxiously awaited your return."

"Have you truly?" Lyritan asked, his arm entwined with Caes's. "And why is that, Countess?"

"You will be the glory of Reyvern—and the world," the woman replied. Whether the woman meant it, or was merely trying to placate the god was impossible to say. What Caes *did* know was that this was around the fiftieth version of this encounter they'd had with various nobles so far tonight. While one would think that being paraded through a strange court at a god's side would be exciting, it was—for the first ten times. After that, the novelty diminished fast.

Lyritan accepted the countess's answer with a magnanimous nod. He was handling this miraculously well—Caes found nothing in her memories indicating that Lyritan was such a skilled politician. Maybe the time he spent in stone taught him some patience. Or maybe, for the time being, he needed the court more than he wanted to admit. "May I introduce to you Princess Caesonia, my betrothed."

The woman's eyes widened. They shouldn't have—the entire court knew of their engagement. "Betrothed? Does this mean you intend on staying with us, my divine lord?"

Lyritan's brow furrowed. Caes straightened. *This* conversation was new.

"What do you mean by that?" Lyritan asked calmly.

"N-nothing, my lord. I only meant—"

"Are you asking if I plan on forsaking everything?"

"No."

"Whether I will be *leaving*?" Lyritan all but spat out the last word. He gripped Caes's arm tighter. A soft step behind her was the only indication Alair had come even closer. She wanted nothing more than to leave this encounter between Lyritan and the noble and hide behind Alair, but she couldn't. She had to stay still and watch.

"Phel—I mean, after being so close to you, I was worried that we'd be forced to be without your presence," the woman rushed out. "You have done so much for the kingdom."

"Is that so?" Lyritan asked.

"Yes."

"Well, in that case, I thought I had made my feelings about such" –the god gestured to the woman's jewels– "displays of wealth known. Or did I forget?" Lyritan's eyes flashed gold.

"No, my lord." The woman took off her earrings. "I shall gift them to the public fund tomorrow."

"Do it tonight."

"Of course, my lord."

Lyritan nodded. "Oh, did I introduce Alair?" Lyritan nodded towards the Soul Carver. Caes's heart leapt a little at seeing him. If only he was the one at her side. "He is my betrothed's companion." This evening Alair had been introduced as Caes's "friend," "champion," "guardian," and "companion" depending on Lyritan's mood. And the amount of scandalization that showed on the nobles' faces varied greatly. This woman, however, had the facial composure of an iron statue. Alair and the woman exchanged greetings, and just like that the conversation returned to the familiar pattern of so many before it and so many yet to come.

So, so many yet to come.

"I thought that would never end," Caes said, leaning back against her headboard and relishing the feeling of shoe-less feet against the bedcovers. Her first day at court was done, and now she was gifted the reward of rest for a few hours before morning. She put in the effort to open her eyes and saw Alair laying on her—their—bed, draped out like a magnificent god.

Their bed.

Never did she expect that they'd have that luxury. In a castle, no less. Lyritan had respectfully let her keep her own room with Alair, making good on his promise that he'd give her time to adjust to the new "him." That didn't stop Lyritan from making whispered promises that made her breath catch and heat pool in her core when they had a few moments between courtiers. That didn't stop her from remembering who he was and what he had done to her.

I'm overthinking it. Lyritan wants me to be happy.

Ha, Caes told herself. Maybe he did want her to be happy. But he wanted himself to be happy first. Maybe there would come a time when she and Alair would have to face Lyritan expecting more from her. But that wasn't today. And who cared if people at court spoke ill of her virtue, of being entangled with more than one man? She was worried about a few things at this court, but not that. Her reputation at the Reyverni court wasn't going to last long, one way or another. She had too much to survive before her ordeals with the goddesses were done, and it was likely she'd die in the Burning Hand before spring. In the meantime, she was going to enjoy the life of a woman of ill repute. Enjoy the man on her bed.

Alair sat up, his linen breeches low on his hips, revealing his sculpted chest and arms. The muscles were deep rivets, and she traced them. Tension wound within her, though she was still tender from their prior lovemaking. She had been with him so many times and yet she couldn't help but daydream what it would be like for him to touch her now. She bit her lip as his hand reached for the band of his breeches—and adjusted it higher. He noticed her watching and was unable to hide his satisfaction at her obvious disappointment.

"I'll let you have the big pillow if you tell me what you're thinking," he teased, a grin plastered on his face.

"Is that a euphemism?" Caes joked back. Alair chuckled while Caes grabbed the bed's largest pillow and wrapped it in her arms. "You're going to have to pry this from me. By force."

"Hmm...promise?" They stared at each other, and Caes reflected on how this was the same Soul Carver who had greeted her on the snowy steps of the Ardinani palace a lifetime ago. The Soul Carver who had fascinated her from the start, no matter how much others held him in a distant awe. For so long they had been in each other's company, but could do nothing beyond mere formalities. In that time, knowingly or unknowingly, she had memorized every part of him. How his eyes creased when he was amused. The way he slowly rubbed his pinky and thumb together when he was concentrating. To the faint scar on the inside of the third finger of his left hand, now little more than a white blotch. Every little piece of him was ingrained in her mind.

And now she didn't have to pretend around him, not about what she felt or thought, hoped or dreamed. She was bare before him, in a way that was truly intimate.

"I'm still not used to this," she said. "Us. Here. Like this. Alone."

He took her hands in his. His calloused thumbs rubbed against the back of her hands. Caes let out a deep breath. Did he know how he was torturing her? Probably. "Then I suggest you become accustomed to it," Alair said. "I promised I'd never leave your side. I meant it. Though" –he looked at the sea of quilts and pillows surrounding them– "I can't promise that every bed will be so accommodating."

Caes moved towards Alair and he took her in his arms, kissing her deeply. His stubble rubbed her face as he placed a few soft kisses on her forehead. She leaned against his chest and took a deep breath, her heartbeat echoing his own. They had already enjoyed each other once this night, and likely would again before dawn. But not now. Now, she wanted to delight in the feel of his skin pressing against hers over her nightgown, his strong hands gripping her back and shifting her so she nestled onto his lap. She gently caressed his face. She admired every inch, every curve of his jaw, down to the tiniest wrinkles just starting to form around his eyes.

"You're scaring me," Alair said, yet his jovial tone belied his words.

"Hardly." Caes said. "Now, how did I get so lucky as to find you?"

"I've asked myself that question every day," Alair said. "How *did* you get so lucky as to find me?" They laughed, but then his expression turned serious. "The things that aligned for the both of us to find each other, it is a gift I didn't expect or deserve."

"Deserve?" Caes frowned. "What do you mean?"

"I was the emperor's executioner. And worse."

"Obeying the emperor wasn't your fault."

"That's a weak excuse, and you know it." Caes tensed and Alair sighed. "I'm sorry." He rubbed her back gently. "I didn't mean to be curt. I'm just angry at myself for how I fell into the easiest path available after I awoke. And that path was obeying the emperor and taking his coin. No matter what he ordered."

Caes relaxed. She knew the feeling all too well. "We both did things we regret. That doesn't mean you don't deserve happiness."

"You didn't hurt people."

"Not on purpose. But I caused many to be hurt anyway." Caes heart twisted at the memory of the murdered Malithians who had accompanied her to Ardinan. And that was only some of the people who had suffered because of her.

Alair scoffed, though there was no harshness in the action. "I wish you could've seen what I was like, back before I became a Soul Carver. I thought I was better than my brothers. They were older, and I told myself that was the only reason they were the heirs. I trained to fight. I was decent, yes, but not nearly as good as I thought I was. The things I dreamed of…no wonder I chose the trial I did. I was Alair. I was the best—no matter that others couldn't see it. I would accomplish the best." His face fell. "I never got to say goodbye."

"To who?"

"Everyone. They knew I was going to attempt to join the Soul Carvers, because the temple had to get approval from the king because I was so close to the throne. But my departure was set to be an event on the full moon with a farewell party and everything. But then I got in the way."

"What?"

"Around a week before I was to go, I got into a fight with my older brother, something stupid that started with him saying I was going to be a coward and run. And fool I was, I couldn't ignore him. Instead, I ran into the trials that night, pushed my way into Karima's realm. I never got to tell my mother goodbye, and she never wanted me to go. Or my father. Or Iva."

Caes hugged Alair close, letting his head rest on her chest. "We can say goodbye to them, if you'd like. Find a quiet place, if we cannot find their graves. You can talk to them. They'll hear you."

"They're long gone."

"You don't know that."

Alair shrugged. "Enough about sadness. Tell me something about you. Something I don't know."

"Um...I like squirrels."

"...What?"

"Squirrels." Caes smiled. "I used to feed the ones near my house whenever possible. My father even built me a little feeding table. I love watching them."

"They're rodents."

"They're adorable."

"They're rats with tails."

"Fluffy tails," Caes corrected.

"This is *not* quite what I had in mind," Alair said, holding back a chuckle. "But it works. I wanted something that isn't sad."

"Oh, it still is. Our neighbor boys used to hunt and eat them. They thanked me for making them 'marbled.'" Caes shrugged.

Alair's lips curled. "That's awful."

"Is it?"

Alair nodded and Caes laughed awkwardly. How much did her divine nature affect her ability to feel? But then again...

"It was a hard life," Caes explained. "I enjoyed the squirrels while I could, but I knew better than to get attached to anything."

"Surely, you had friends. You mentioned someone, Tirana?"

Caes nodded. "Our neighbor's daughter. Not the ones who—" Caes gestured to her back, where there was now a patch of barely-healed flesh that used to be burns from a farmer's wife. Until Desmin sliced it from her. "She was friendly, yes. But most children avoided me. We lived out in the countryside—not many people around—and few wanted to be near me. Or my father."

"Was he unfriendly?"

"No. Not at all. People just never went out of their way to visit us. Just...part of me wonders if they sensed that there was something different about me. Something that told them to stay away."

"Their loss," Alair said, squeezing her hand. "Here." He tugged her back down to the bed, rolling her in a cocoon of blankets and laying close beside her. His breath heated her neck and his hands rested on her front, holding her close.

"Is your plan to cuddle me into submission?"

"I don't need to resort to such measures." He tickled her, just long enough to make her squeal. Laughing, she lost herself in the simple moment, the idyllic lie of what they'd never have.

Here, with him, it was easy to forget everything that awaited them.

Everything that would be waiting come morn.

Chapter 23

Caes

The morning came far too soon.

Maids entered Caes and Alair's chambers at dawn, opening the drapes and stoking the fire, keeping their eyes downcast as Alair sat up, blankets tucked around his waist. It was obvious the two of them had spent the night together.

"Your Highness," a maid, a pretty girl with braided black hair, said, "the queen has requested that you break your fast with her this morning." Ordered, she meant.

"What do you plan to do?" Caes asked Alair, trying not to admire how his tousled hair made him look devilishly undone.

"Her Majesty Queen Silvay has requested just you, Your Highness." The maid blushed. "Meanwhile, our god-blessed prince has suggested that Lord Alair would like to visit the armory, since his equipment has been misplaced. The other Soul Carvers will be there as well."

"Misplaced?" Alair whispered. "That's one way to say 'dead.'" He said it with such a smirk that Caes couldn't help but giggle, though the memory of her grief at losing him still haunted her. The maid's eyes darted at Alair and then back to the ground. Poor girl—this was likely her first encounter with a Soul Carver, and she was certainly getting an experience.

"Go," Caes said to Alair. "I'll be fine."

"You need someone with you," Alair insisted. "If only to walk the halls."

"The Soul Carver Janell has volunteered to assist her highness as needed this morning," the maid said. "The god-blessed prince has arranged everything."

"See?" Caes said to Alair. "I'll be fine."

"Alright. But don't get into any trouble without me." Alair winked.

After dressing in a simple dark blue velvet gown—this one without voluminous layers—Caes met the queen in a small room. However, the room's minute size didn't diminish its grandeur. The walls were covered in rich, dark blue tapestries woven with gold thread and depicting scenes of creatures that hadn't been seen in thousands of years. Unicorns, walking trees, people with butterfly wings…Caes would've doubted they had ever existed at all, but she had seen them for herself, back when she was Liuva. They had existed and lived as every other animal, before they were hunted to extinction once the gods left. The ceiling was painted white and adorned with intricate wood carvings—more hammers—and gilded gold moldings inlaid with garnets, while the floor was covered with thick rugs. A roaring fire burned in the fireplace, a necessity in this early winter weather.

The table display was meant for a queen. Made of an almost pitch-black wood, the table was far longer than necessary for three breakfast guests. Three place settings of engraved silver were set near each other along with perfectly polished cutlery, leaving most of the space unoccupied. A floral arrangement rested in the center, made of evergreen boughs and tulips. Where had the queen gotten tulips at this time of year?

Saryn, Prince Phelan's sister, and Queen Silvay, the king's second wife, sat at the table waiting for her, though only the princess stood to greet her. Again, another courtesy she didn't expect. Caes curtsied to the queen and princess. "I hope you weren't waiting for me long," Caes said upon rising and after giving the proper greetings.

"No, not at all," the queen said. "We were just enjoying our tea. Sit." The queen motioned to the seat to her right, which was directly across from the princess. While Caes positioned herself, Janell did as well, setting herself next to the door, near the queen's own guards. She placed her hands on her hips, watching them with feigned disinterest.

"How are your accommodations suiting?" Saryn asked. "Are they adequate?"

"More than adequate," Caes said, sitting back and letting a servant pour her a cup of tea. "Very comfortable."

"Good," the queen said.

And thus they passed a surprisingly pleasant breakfast consisting of pastries filled with honeyed fruit, fresh apples, and spiced porridge. Simple as royal meals went, but delicious. Caes helped herself to a third pastry with abandon. While conversing with the queen and Saryn she learned a lot about Reyvern, at least regarding the general beat of commerce in Gilar for this time of year. She also learned that Saryn was fond of needlework with beads and...Lady Peony Passionflower. Saryn asked if Caes had met the Malithian author. Caes hadn't, though that would've been an interesting meeting, since Passionflower was popular for a reason. However, Saryn seemed quite disappointed that Caes didn't know if there was to be another book of hers chronicling some Soul Carver. Based on what Caes had read from Passionflower so far, she didn't want to ask any further questions.

Finally, once they had broken their fast and were sitting and drinking yet another cup of tea, the queen said, "I would like to speak with you privately, if you would be amenable," she said to Caes.

"Of course."

"Your Majesty—" Saryn said and was interrupted by the queen.

"You too, Saryn," the queen said. "I'm afraid I have some rather personal questions for her highness." Saryn's jaw set in a line, but she nodded, obeying the queen.

The honey in Caes's stomach soured. As much as she didn't want to face the monarch alone, it was better to see what the queen wanted. She gave Janell a nod, and the Soul Carver obeyed by leaving the room with the queen's guards and the princess. Janell wouldn't go far—she'd stay close enough to barge in at an instant if necessary. Besides, Caes highly doubted that the queen would be foolish enough to harm her, though she had *that* mistaken thought before.

Once the door shut behind Saryn, the queen said, "I won't ask why you're here, because if half the stories are true you had little say in the matter. What I am wondering, however, is what you plan on doing next."

"In regard to what, Your Majesty?" Caes rested her hands on her lap, fidgeting with the gold ring she was wearing.

"Anything. Everything. You can't pretend you haven't noticed that Phelan's change was unexpected on our part. They say you're clever."

"For once they're too kind. But yes, I did notice that it seemed some were…surprised at the turn of events."

"Well?" The queen cocked her head. "Is that your plan? To marry my possessed stepson and become the Queen of Reyvern?" The queen was older than Caes, but not by that much, and at that moment Caes was struck by how she was far too young for the lines around her eyes, likely the mark of recent sleepless nights.

Caes let out a long sigh and tossed her napkin on the table, earning her an upraised eyebrow from the queen. Fuck this.

"I don't know what Lyritan told you, but no. I'm done. I'm not ruling kingdoms or empires. I've been a princess of both Ardinan and Malithia, and both kingdoms can burn for all I care. I'm going to the Burning Hand and I'm finishing the shit that's tormented me my entire life. Long before that, if we're being candid. And then, when this is done, I don't know. I'll sail on a ship and leave this land and never look back."

The queen nodded, watching her rant. "I'm inclined to believe you."

"Once I wanted to rule." She scoffed and shook her head. "That day is long behind me."

Was it a risk being so candid to the queen? Yes. If Lyritan heard of this conversation he wouldn't be thrilled, with Caes apparently being his chosen empress and all. But Caes was counting on one very distinct fact—the queen didn't like Lyritan, either. It behooved Caes to keep the queen happy at this moment and worry about pacifying Lyritan later, if necessary.

Besides, she was done being diplomatic. If she was less diplomatic when she was first brought to the Ardinani court—like, maybe if she told a few royal aunts what she really thought of them, for instance—then maybe she would've found herself shipped to a temple after her father left on his quest instead of being entrenched with Desmin. Diplomacy was for someone who gave a damn, and that someone wasn't Caes.

"I see," the queen said, searching Caes's expression. "So, are you going to take the prince with you to this mountain?"

"I don't know if I have a choice," Caes said. "Unfortunately, without Lyritan's help, I'm not sure we'd survive." They wouldn't. They needed him to ensure they were provisioned, to hide and protect them from the goddesses, and even give them directions. They needed the god. But Caes wasn't about to tell the queen that. Instead, she gave the queen the most sympathetic look she could muster. "I regret that we cannot take the god without the prince, for what it's worth. And I regret that this happened to him of all people. Small comfort it must be to you."

The queen tapped her fingers on the table. "You seem to know things about the gods. I've heard the rumors—and there's your eyes. Is there hope for Phelan?" The queen clenched her hand. That the queen dared ask such a thing spoke to her desperation.

"I don't know," Caes said honestly. "My knowledge of the gods is from an era that was long before such an ability was needed." Caes thought for a moment. "I'd be willing to say that getting Lyritan to leave without his cooperation would be next to impossible. His essence is entwined with every part of Phelan's. That's not easily undone."

"I feared as much." The queen sighed. "As much as we fear what the god will do." The queen's eyes darted to Caes's, as if remembering too late who she was speaking to.

"There's no need to worry about telling me such things," Caes said. "My concern is what must be done at the Burning Hand. Beyond his purpose there, I have no other aim for Lyritan. Certainly not ruling the mortal lands."

"He's told you that, then."

"More or less."

"He's spoken of what will be done at the mountain—slaying the goddesses. But why not remove him too? Save us the trouble?"

"I can't," Caes said. "Trust me when I say we've considered all other options. Karima and Shirla will eventually devastate the world if left in place. Lyritan isn't perfect, but he's better than the alternative."

"And what's that?" The queen's brow furrowed.

"A foreign god. Because one *will* come. And their aims are entirely unknown. It can always be worse where gods are concerned. Sometimes it's best to play with the god you are dealt."

"Even if that god is stirring your kingdom to war?"

Caes's eyebrow quirked up. "He is?"

The queen nodded. "We've been as noncommittal as possible—Reyvern is in no position to attack outside our borders—but Lyritan is agitating the common folk. Many believe that he's here to bless us. That Reyvern will rule the world with him at its helm." The queen huffed. "Fools."

"So, people will follow him? Already?"

"People will follow anything if they think it will be to their benefit."

Caes paused. The queen and king were in a difficult situation. As a god, even in a mortal's body, Lyritan was likely far too powerful to just ignore and offend. And they didn't want to risk harming their prince and heir. And they didn't want to wage a war they couldn't win.

"I can't fix your problem, but I can buy you time," Caes said. "We'll be at the Burning Hand. It will take weeks, if not months, for us to be done. That will give you a chance to act, maybe negate his influence."

"But our prince will be with you."

"Unfortunately."

The queen's lips pursed. "Well, we must deal with what we are dealt, as you said. And we will. Reyvern has survived four civil wars and five invasions over the last several hundred years. We will survive this." Caes nodded in what she hoped was an encouraging manner.

"If you're not able to directly help us, then humor me one other question," the queen said.

"Anything."

"Do you think Malithia will attack us?"

Caes paused. A question and a test in one. The queen was curious if Caes would divulge information that could work against the emperor, to see if she was still Malithia's creature. A fair concern, considering every one of her companions was Malithian and she had been named the empire's heir.

"If you had asked me this even three weeks ago my answer would've been yes," Caes said. "Barlas is under a lot of pressure from his nobles to expand the empire—not that that's new—but it's something of an embarrassment that Reyvern is still an independent island amidst the conquered lands. But my answer has changed." The queen's eyes widened with interest. "With Althain dead, the emperor is facing another succession dispute since he has no direct heirs. He's also too old to wait for another one to be born and grow to adulthood. And after Ardinan's rebellion, I wouldn't be surprised if other kingdoms—or parts of them—follow suit, if they haven't already. And that's not to mention the various disasters that have struck the kingdoms. No, I think the emperor is far too busy staying alive in his own court to bother to attack. That's one less thing for you to fear, at least." The queen nodded, her shoulders slumping the tiniest bit.

Then conversation lapsed, the queen seemingly lost in her own thoughts, until Caes asked, "Lady Flyntinia. How is it that she's here?"

"You know her?"

"Yes. She was the mother of my...second betrothed." Three betrothals and no marriage. There had to be a joke or parable in there somewhere.

"Yes, the emperor's son. Althain." The queen sipped on her tea, setting down the cup with a light clang. "What happened to him? Besides his being dead."

"Murdered by Ardinan." There was a question in the queen's eyes, but she didn't press the issue any further.

"And not by you?"

"No. He was my friend." Caes looked at her plate. "He was murdered the same night as the rest those who accompanied me to Ardinan."

"I'm sorry." The queen's tone was surprisingly kind, but that kindness faded as the conversation shifted back to Caes's question. "Lady Flyntinia arrived one night with her small entourage, claiming that Karima sent her. Since we didn't want to offend Karima or the emperor, we welcomed her. For now."

"I see. And the Lady Sabine?"

"The one from Cyvid?"

"Yes."

The queen nodded. "You know her well?"

"Yes."

"How well?"

That was...an oddly intense question. Sabine was her friend. Sabine saved her life. But how well did she really know Sabine?

"We were companions at the Malithian court," Caes said. "The emperor instructed her to assist me, and we found ourselves compatible."

"And now she is here, with the mother of the emperor's slain bastard." The queen took a deep breath. "I left Cyvid before it was conquered by Malithia. Have you ever seen a conquered city?"

"No. I can't say I have. Not while the brutality was occurring, at any rate." Most of the horrors Caes had directly witnessed in her life had been done to her, and not others. In an odd way, that may have been a good thing.

"Neither have I, if I'm being truthful," the queen said, "but I heard stories, and the things my family said in their letters....haunt me. Men used as target practice. Women violated. Elderly beaten. And I'm speaking gently. My family didn't have nearly as much concern when they wrote to me."

"I'm sorry," Caes said. "Fyrie was conquered by Malithia while I was inside, but I was aware of nothing."

"Sorry to be callous, but how is that possible?"

"I was Ardinan's prisoner. At that point I was kept underground. Alone." Alone and trapped with nothing but rats to keep her company, unsure of whether it was even day or night. Unsure of whether each half-rotten meal was going to be her last.

"Ah. So you were unaware of everything outside, yes?"

Caes nodded.

"I assumed as much. But I do not say this to shame you—it is a warning. Lady Sabine was reportedly present when her city fell. The things she likely saw, the stories she heard...be careful, Caesonia. If she has that position at the Malithian court, she has a gift for self-preservation. I doubt she will hesitate to use it."

The queen went back to her tea, sipping on it one more time before shifting the conversation to the more pleasant topic of court events before she rang a bell to call the servants back in. While Caes played along, she mulled over their conversation.

What was the queen really trying to say about Flyntinia and Sabine? More importantly, was there something she knew that Caes had missed?

Chapter 24

Liuva

One winter morning, I greeted my mother with the dawn, her golden hair splayed around her like a halo. She smiled when she saw me, her arms open wide. "My child," she said, calling me to her. I obeyed, running and then cherishing her warm embrace once I reached my destination. Her arms. My home. "My darling," she said, moving so that she could take in my face, "do you wish to walk with me this morning? It has been some time since we have done so."

I nodded enthusiastically. My mother had been distracted as of late, gone for weeks or even months at a time on some errand or another. She was a goddess. I did not question it. Monsters, men, or gods, her affairs made no difference. Seasons were like the changing hours of a day to me, for all they blended together. Shirla could be gone from early spring to late summer, and I would barely notice. Why would I? I had forever. We had forever.

I don't recall how long Lyritan had been my friend at that time. Since I did not age, and I was almost never around those who did, time was nearly impossible for me to note. By that point, our friendship was such that when I did not see him, I noticed his absence as keenly as a missing heartbeat. Our friendship was nothing more than gentle platonic touches and burning looks, but still, his presence ignited something in me. Stirred me awake in a way that I had never felt before or since. My dreams, both waking and asleep, were of him. Each time someone approached, I turned, hoping it would be him. I could barely remember a time when thoughts of him were not a constant presence.

The winter was fierce that morning, with frigid winds and deep snows, but we were divine. We could appreciate nature's beauty and none of its bitterness. The cold did not bother us, not when my mother's arms were wrapped around me, not when the clothing crafted by her maidens graced my back. I was not entirely divine, but in her presence, with her love, I may as well have been. We stepped over the snow without sinking, and smiled as the cold air whipped our faces. It wasn't until much later that I realized how I had once thought nothing of how nature itself would bend to please gods. Soft breezes, gentle snows, smooth paths—anything that could please the goddess was done.

"I love the winter," Shirla said, her voice as light and gentle as the snows themselves. "It is so quiet."

"I miss the birds," I said. "The little ones that dance."

Shirla smiled, the corners of her golden eyes creased. "You always loved the small things. And fear not, for they will return with the spring. Such is life." She said nothing else and merely stared at the clouds floating against the brilliant blue sky.

"What is it, Mother?"

"Nothing, my little one." She turned to me, wrapped me in her arms, and then whispered, "I found a way to save us both."

I frowned. "I don't understand. Save us? From what? Karima's monsters?"

Shirla pushed the hair out of my face and placed kisses on my cheeks. "My dear child. I did not want to worry you. I cannot worry you. But I found a god who will save us. One who loves me and promised to keep us safe."

"Save us from what?" I looked around, as if I could see what she was talking about. "Are there monsters here?"

"Oh, no, my darling. Never worry about such things."

"Who? Who is helping us?" I asked, though my heart stirred. There weren't many gods in our area of the world, not ones who would make my mother so happy, at any rate. My mother protected her lands.

"Lyritan."

I don't know how I restrained my face, but I did. When she looked for a reaction, I gave her happiness and relief. She deftly evaded my questions, and I stopped asking, letting her think I was a child still and happy merely because she was. I held back my tears, stilled my shaking arms, and made it home. And waited.

And waited.

My mother soon left me, as she often did. While she was gone, her maidens tended to me. Sang to me. Gave me everything I could want and need. Yet, I could not stop the unease flitting in my core. Did someone tell her that Lyritan had met me? Befriended me? Should I have told her about my new companion? She would have expected, even demanded, that I told her I met a god, for both my safety and hers. Yet every time I had thought of speaking his name my tongue froze and would not utter a word.

Then one morning, as the snows melted and the first hints of color broke into the world, Lyritan found me in the wood. The maidens were not nearby, not bothering to watch me ardently this close to where we slept. None would have made it to me without being detected. None other than him.

"Liuva," he said, joy wrought on his face. Joy at me? Or joy at seducing my mother? It never occurred to me that he could harm her. I never thought him possible of such things.

"I'm surprised you came to see me," I said. "Though, I shouldn't have..." I couldn't help it. I choked back sobs, hot tears that glowed and faded like sparks in the night.

"Don't cry," Lyritan said, wrapping me in his arms and rubbing his hands on my back, consoling me. His muscles were taut under his tunic and he smelled of the forest, rich moss and fresh dirt, and something sweet that was distinctively divine. Him holding me, like I was a treasure to be protected, completed a part of me that I never knew was missing until that moment. He leaned down to whisper in my ear, and his warm breath tickled my neck and stirred new parts of me. More. I wanted m ore.

But I could not lose myself in my wishes.

"You are in love with my mother," I said accusingly, but my hurt and longing staunched some of the bitterness of my words.

Confusion darted across his features, and then understanding. "No. I am doing everything—everything—to protect you. All for you."

"What?"

"How much do you know of why you are here? With Shirla."

"She wanted a child. One that was only hers."

Slowly, Lyritan shook his head, his golden curls rippling. "Unfortunately, that is only part of the story." It was then that Lyritan told me the truth of how I was made, and my world shattered. That I was a font of power that the gods could access at the Burning Hand. That he was attempting to join with my mother to complete her power so that she'd be free of her sister, Karima, the specter that haunted our lives. All so that my mother would not have to sacrifice me.

Me.

For those who entered the Burning Hand never emerged. For power to be taken, the vessel needed to be broken.

"No," I cried out softly. "She wouldn't do that to me. She loves me."

Lyritan's eyes were heavy. "What is love when one could have the ability to live without fear? You know the gods. Tell me what your heart is telling you."

My heart? My heart. That traitorous thing raced in my chest at the sight of Lyritan and hadn't stopped. And it broke at the thought of my mother destroying me.

My mother.

She was supposed to love me.

But she created me in pain. It was only fitting that she would end me in the same manner.

"I don't know what to do," I said, shaking in Lyritan's arms.

"I will protect you," Lyritan said, "until the world breaks."

Then he kissed me.

Chapter 25

Bethrian

Dyvith. Lord Dyvith.

Why couldn't the potential keeper of secrets be a young woman who had an infatuation with brown-haired Malithians who were witty with the pen and had the ability to juggle? Hells, he would've been able to make do with any woman who liked men. Nope, instead the keeper of said secrets was a curmudgeonly old lord who wouldn't be susceptible to Bethrian's amorous wiles. At least, Bethrian hoped not. Regardless, Bethrian wasn't going to find out.

Bethrian spent the morning striding about the court, joining nobles as they listened to musicians, drank far too much wine, and followed various royalty and aspiring royalty. As a seasoned courtier, he spent the morning dangling bits of information to his eager companions, who wanted to know everything about the Malithian princess and their god-blessed prince. Was Prince Phelan's occupied state an instance of divine fortune upon Reyvern? A sign of blessings to come? Or a curse? Regardless, Bethrian soon realized that the young nobles—or at least the ones who frolicked around him—shared little of the apprehension that affected the staider courtiers.

Bethrian gave all of them vague and dramatic answers, speculating about Caes's mysticism when it suited him, and pretending to be a devout worshiper of Karima when that course was better. He even dropped a few hints that he thought the Reyverni court was superior to Malithia's—in truth, there was no comparison. But his conversational skills worked, since more and more people warmed to him. Damn, he was good at this.

That was how, after a few hours, he found himself chatting in a secluded corner with a young noblewoman named Clarima, named after Karima and who insisted on going by "Clar." She wasn't a great beauty, but she was pleasant company, and more than happy to let Bethrian direct the conversation. The other nobles were similarly frolicking about, passing the time before night fell and the true amusements could commence.

"You don't know anyone here, do you?" Clar asked coyly, twirling a strand of brown hair around her finger. They had been talking long enough for Bethrian to learn that Clar was promised to a rather well-connected lord, so any interaction between them was merely a veneer of flattery and faux love.

"I know you." Bethrian smiled, sipping on the little silver flask he had acquired. A court fashion, one he admired. "Are you implying that more than your acquaintance is needed?"

"Oh, Lord Bethrian" –Clar giggled– "I am just one little piece of wood, floating around this court." She waved her arm for dramatic effect, not caring that it attracted a few confused glances.

"You and I both know that's not true." Bethrian winked and was rewarded by yet another giggle. Bethrian leaned back and positioned himself against the wall, Clar settling next to him. This was going to be the tricky part—he had to get information, but not let her know that he was trying to do so. "So, who do I *need* to know here?"

"Oh, you think I'm going to just oblige you?" The corner of her mouth turned up in a grin.

"You would leave me, a poor foolish foreigner, ignorant and afraid?"

"Oh, Lord Bethrian, you're anything but ignorant or afraid."

"I note you didn't disagree with foolish."

"Well, do you want me to lie?" Clar asked teasingly.

Clar spent the next twenty minutes or so pointing out various nobles and sharing little quips. Unfortunately, Bethrian and Clar didn't share the same opinion of what constituted good character and fine manners, so Bethrian had to restrain himself from antagonizing her. So, the Duke of Henlin found himself deep in his cups and with a new mistress every week? Sounded like a delightful companion, though Clar's comments about the duke veered to downright condemnation.

Meanwhile, Clar conveyed that the Lady Yulina, daughter of an earl, spent her days in dedicated meditation while knitting socks for the poor. Clar didn't try to force the admiration from her voice, while to Bethrian, Yulina sounded like someone to avoid at all costs. And after this, it would probably be best if Bethrian avoided Clar—she wouldn't care for him if she knew him better, and he needed people to care for him.

Bethrian was just about to excuse himself in search of a more obliging companion, but then the conversation turned to Lord Dyvith.

Dyvith.

"I know his name, but I'm afraid I know nothing else," Bethrian said.

Clar preened, seemingly pleased to be distributing more information. "Be glad he isn't here."

"Why?"

"He's sour. The court gets dreadful when he's here."

"How does he manage to have that effect?"

Clar shrugged. "The king cares what he thinks. So, we care. Dyvith can make things...dull." If Clar considered this man dull, he was probably as exciting as a pair of dice with no dots.

"Does he stay at court often?" Bethrian took another sip.

"No. But when he does, he goes to his rooms and rarely comes out. Yet somehow" –Clar frowned– "he's able to make the whole place miserable."

"Impressive." Bethrian screwed the cap back onto his flask. "Have you met him?" he asked, trying very hard to make it sound like a casual curiosity.

"Of course. I live here." Clar smiled, but it wasn't happy.

Clar's expression gave nothing more away. Why would she lead with that and then stop as soon as the conversation became interesting? "Sorry, I just haven't encountered many nobles who create such strong feelings. And I was at the court of the Malithian emperor."

"If that perplexes you, then you *are* new." Clar sighed. "It's hard to explain. He creates strong feelings, both politically and otherwise." When Bethrian's eyebrow crept upwards she continued, "He's too friendly with Ardinan, too friendly with our king, and he hates everything that's fun in life." How could this lord be both friendly and miserable? Dear goddess, what did that man do for the royals that he was able to be this...entity? That was the only explanation—he did them favors, so he did what he wanted.

"I heard he has daughters," Bethrian ventured. "Are they the same as he?" The daughters. His one chance to crack the fortress of Lord Dyvith.

"Yes. And no." Clar grinned, as if reading his mind. "Careful, my lord. They won't like you. Their loss, for I find your company quite enjoyable." She eyed Bethrian's flask. "Even if your habits are a bit too crass for my taste. But you're Malithian, so some excuses must be made."

"Oh? And what is Malithia's reputation here?" Bethrian teased.

"Well, for one, there is quite the scandalous book circling the court...."

"A book?"

Clar lowered her voice. "It's about Soul Carvers. As lovers."

Oh. Oh, this was too good. Bethrian swallowed hard. "I heard another woman speak of it. Is it truly that popular here?" *One Night With a Soul Carver* wasn't his most popular work in Glynnith, but it did seem to have devoted readers.

"Shamefully so," Clar replied. "And with Soul Carvers here, you should hear the things I have been told—"

"I can imagine, my lady. No need to force yourself to speak of such matters to me." Bethrian stifled laughter. He hadn't meant to write a main character that could have been Cylis, but after some introspection, he realized Fenrick *was* Cylis. The physical descriptions were the same. And Fenrick was a cranky braggart that women inexplicably lusted after. Yep, Bethrian had accidentally made Cylis the star of a romance novel featuring Soul Carvers. Oops.

Any further questions Bethrian had about novels or Dyvith were quieted by a sudden hush in the halls, followed by what could only be the steps of people entering the room. Only important people quieted crowds. As one, the mass of nobles bowed.

And then Bethrian realized who had caused the fuss—Reyvern's queen had arrived at the head of a parade of even more nobles.

"Rise," she said to the assembly. Her expression carried a slight smile as she turned her head about the room. "Let us rest. Enjoy our peace before dinner." As if on some invisible cue, the musicians in the corner started playing and the courtiers went back to talking. Bethrian expected a spirited song on violins and instead they were serenaded with something involving cellos and a flute—an oddly mysterious tune for what was otherwise a pleasant day.

With all the grace stemming from a lifetime of perfecting manners, the queen took her place on a chair in the corner, naturally forming a fawning court around her. Bethrian was familiar with that magnetic circle—Bethrian had called it "Seda's Cyclone." Oh Seda...but this wasn't the time or place for sad memories. Now that everyone was in their places, Bethrian had a chance to look at those who came with the queen—the fawning men and women bumbling for a prime place.

And Caes.

Caes.

"Are you going to talk to her?" Clar asked, mouth slightly agape.

"What?"

"Have you met her? Wait, you're her companion, correct?"

"Caesonia?"

"Who else?"

Meet her? Talk to her? Bethrian had slit Caes's arm open. What did that make them? Slicing sisters? Cutting companions? Bleeding brothers? Those all sounded like bad villains from one of his novels.

"I will engage with her highness," Bethrian said, "but not now. She's meeting this court as well and has her own engagements."

"But her eyes—they say she can see the gods."

"She has."

"That she can read a man's soul."

"Well—"

"So, it's true?"

"With Caesonia, it's best to assume that whatever you think she can accomplish, she can do even more."

Clar fell silent and Bethrian smoothed his hair, watching Caes at her courtly work. Bethrian had admired her before, but she was good at this—it was like watching an artist paint a masterpiece. She had the right smile, the right posture, and that way she seemed to make people think they were important. That was a skill that was nearly impossible to teach, but essential for a courtier. Caes was born a peasant, but here, now, she was a queen.

Though, there was one thing that got overlooked in the sheer bizarreness of the situation that was Caes—Caes's eyes were difficult to behold. Not to look at, exactly, but they marked her as other, and her emotions were tricky things to read. Was she enjoying meeting one courtier after another? Was she tired? It was hard to tell, unless one knew her well. And Bethrian did. She wasn't tired.

She was pissed.

Well, maybe not pissed. But to Bethrian, she seemed more than done with the court, for all she carried a smile and polite word.

It was then that Bethrian noted that Sabine had entered the room, along with Lady Flyntinia. Ah, Sabine. That crafty woman. That wasn't an insult—quite the opposite—but it meant that Bethrian would watch her. She was another who was far too good at navigating the Malithian court, though admittedly their interests collided most of the time. Bethrian was more than capable of admitting he had his biases. However, while Bethrian was merely biased as far as Sabine was concerned, he *knew* that Flyntinia was dangerous. Sabine had been Caes's friend, while Flyntinia never loved anyone other than herself and her now-dead child. How much blame for the situation did Flyntinia lay at Caes's feet? Likely much more than was warranted.

Sabine and Flyntinia drifted towards Caes, circling like logs in a whirlpool, though they made no move to directly approach. Oh, that was going to be a difficult conversation. Would Flyntinia manage to restrain herself? Good thing Bethrian wasn't Caes, and good thing that Bethrian hadn't caught the attention of any of the Malithians. He was all but invisible. Though Caes was hardly alone. Here and there through the room were the Soul Carvers, their glinting eyes unmistakable, and each focused on her, no matter who tried to distract them.

Alair strode towards Caes, parting the crowd, until he stood by her side, staring at anyone who dared to meet his gaze, his body positioned possessively close to her.

That was...bold. Huh, they really *were* done being subtle, weren't they?

Forget keeping Clar happy, he had more important things to watch. Bethrian finished off his flask. Maybe it was the alcohol, but at that moment, Bethrian realized that Caes had nothing to lose by acknowledging Alair as her lover. Did Caes really plan on coming back here to rule alongside Lyritan after being done with the Burning Hand? Doubtful. Lyritan and all his quirks aside, she didn't seem to enjoy the finer points of ruling—such as telling others what to do. While Bethrian, why, he had no issue admitting he enjoyed it. All of it. That moment of doubt that flashed behind a servant's gaze when they heard his order, the hesitant movements as they moved to obey. The bowed head that followed when the servant finished giving him the demanded third helping of potatoes...it was marvelous.

But then Bethrian noted another woman among the queen's retinue, one who also seemed to have a court of her own. She was tall, far taller than what was considered average in the Malithian court, with a rosebud mouth, a gently curved jaw, striking brown eyes, and a crafted posture. She was dressed in a snug brocade gown that eschewed the voluminous skirts and fabrics that seemed to be an epidemic at this court, but it was obvious that was on purpose. This woman made fashion—she didn't follow it. Instead, she relied on a thick cape trimmed with sable fur to keep herself warm.

"Who's that?" Bethrian asked. One of the king's nieces? A visiting princess from Tamsen, perhaps?

"That," Clar said, "is Relyntis. Youngest daughter of Lord Dyvith."

"That?"

"Yup," Clar said, biting back a smile. "But she hates her name. Everyone calls her Rella."

No wonder Clar had said that Rella wouldn't like Bethrian—this was a woman who had no shortage of attention, despite being a younger daughter. This wasn't a woman who could be charmed with flattery and an enjoyable evening. Successfully working his wiles on Rella would take time. Time Bethrian didn't have.

Shit, what was he going to do now?

Chapter 26

Cylis

"How long do you think she's going to want to stay here?" Kerensa asked Cylis and Marva.

They had been at the latest court gathering for over an hour, and Cylis found himself shifting from one foot to another in an attempt to amuse himself. Yes, things had become that sad. What else was he supposed to do? He was bored. Caes was just talking to people while some sort of butterfly funeral music played in the background. Even Fuckwit, who was supposed to be finding out how to get that stupid sword, wasn't able to keep the consternation off his face.

"No idea," Cylis said. "Not soon enough. You could always ask her yourself."

"I'm not interrupting *that*." Kerensa nodded at the flock of courtiers around Caes. They seemingly couldn't get enough of her. The feeling wasn't mutual. There were dark circles under Caes's eyes hidden under makeup, and the lines around her eyes were deeper than normal. No one else likely noticed, but Cylis had a Soul Carver's senses and excellent powers of observation.

"I think there's enough of us here," Marva said to Kerensa. "You should probably get some rest if you need it."

Kerensa nodded. "If you're sure…"

"Go," Marva said. "I'm here, and so are Cylis and Alair. Not to mention I saw Janell and Fer wandering around earlier. They can't be far."

Kerensa's face contorted. "What if some sort of decomposed monster attacks us again?"

"You heard Caes and Lyritan—we're safe in the city," Marva replied.

"You believe them?"

"As much as I can believe anything."

"Get some rest, Ker," Cylis said. "You've earned it. And if we do get eaten by monsters, consider yourself lucky that you weren't here."

"Well, if you insist..." Kerensa flashed a smile and then left Cylis and Marva alone. Well, as alone as one could be in a crowded room. Cylis watched Kerensa leave, wishing he could follow her. Whatever Kerensa was doing, it had to be better than being here. Cylis wasn't meant for court—at least, not serving at one. He was meant to eat court food, though.

"You always do that," Marva said to Cylis.

"What?"

"Rub your nose when you're uncomfortable."

"And why would I be?"

"I don't know" –Marva sighed– "maybe it's that you hate nobles. Maybe your nose runs when you're nervous. Or you're not sure what to expect from your new sword."

"Way to change the topic."

Marva shrugged. "It's not like we've had much chance to discuss it. So? How's the weapon?"

"You tell me. I haven't gotten it back yet."

"I know. But I figured you've gone to see the progress."

The royal blacksmith had taken Cylis's hilt, the one imbued by the god, and announced he had just the thing for it. Whatever that "thing" was was a mystery that would have to wait. But at least he wasn't burdened with the reminder of his shame any longer. And hopefully, once it was given back to him, it wouldn't look the same. He didn't need a permanent reminder of his stupidity. Maybe, once they were done with Lyritan, Cylis could trade the sword for something he had use for. Like a bed.

"You seem to have watched me very closely," Cylis said, crossing his arms.

"Well, why wouldn't I?" Marva grinned, her eyes sparkling.

"You apparently don't have enough to do."

"What if I don't want to do anything else?"

What the...? She was antagonizing him on purpose. She had to be. "Maybe *you're* the one who needs a nap," Cylis said.

Marva smiled, but didn't answer. "How's your friendship with Lord Bethrian coming along?" she asked instead.

"Fuckwit?" Cylis groaned. "I've never met someone so full of himself. You'd think he thought he was the best thing to walk this earth. He's thinks he's smart. And that he's always right. And—"

Marva covered her mouth with her hand.

"What? What is it now?"

"Nothing." Marva blinked. Hard. "Forget I asked. And let's focus on something else." Luckily, Marva didn't ask why or how Cylis had to field constant subtle and not-so-subtle questions about Fenrick the Sensual Soul Carver, especially since a group of three young noblewomen had been constantly staring at Cylis and tittering. They kept asking him about knots and he was still confused. At this point, he was going to keep some string in his pocket and hand it to them when they asked. Maybe that would get them to shut up. "What are you doing this evening?" Marva asked, pulling Cylis from his stewing and calculating how many knots he needed to make.

"Um...sleeping?"

"Other than that."

"Probably wash my hair."

Marva groaned. "Other than that, Cylis. I'm not trying to discuss your sleep rituals."

"You're the one who asked."

"And I'm regretting it by the moment. Now answer the question—what are you doing this evening, once we are done with Caes but before you engage in the act of going to bed?"

"Uh, I probably should talk to Fuckwit and see what he learned, but that can wait. Why?"

"Want to go to the city?" Marva's eyes glinted with mischief.

"Why would we do that?"

"Why not? I've never been here, and I'm sure you haven't either." Yes, that was true, for a reason—Reyvern was difficult to get to. "Come now" —Marva tugged on his sleeve— "let's do it."

"Just the two of us?"

"Unless you'd rather invite Bethrian, too."

"Hells, no. And fine." Cylis glanced back at Caes, who was talking to yet another noble couple, Alair lurking over her, ever the imposing guardian. "If *she* doesn't need us, why not? At least it will get me away from these idiots."

Chapter 27

Caes

Reyvern was a small kingdom—how was it there were so many people at this court?

In truth, the number of Reyverni courtiers at hand was far less than what surrounded Malithian royalty at any semi-public outing, but Caes's limbs felt like melting into her chair and her ears hummed with the constant chatter. Like sitting in a henhouse. Caes had enough of this banality, and, unfortunately, she wouldn't be free from it for some time.

In between greetings and light discussions about nonsense, Caes couldn't take her attention away from two people who lurked at the crowd's edges—Flyntinia and Sabine. They watched her, their faces inscrutable, until they approached her.

"I can send them away," Alair whispered in her ear. "They won't even know they're doing it."

"No." Caes gritted her teeth. "Best to get this over with. And in public. With witnesses. Let me handle this."

"As you prefer," Alair muttered, moving back a step.

"Your Highness," Sabine and Flyntinia said together, dipping into a deep curtsey, before paying a similar respect to the queen, who watched the exchange from her seat a short distance away. The two of them were dressed in a very Malithian version of the Reyverni style, with Sabine wearing a bright red gown and Flyntinia a black velvet one trimmed with black fur. Their sleeves and skirts hugged their bodies tighter than the Reyverni fashion, though Caes had come to appreciate that voluminous skirts meant the ability to conceal more warm layers. How had they happened to possess such fine winter attire so soon? It was unlikely they bought them here, due to the style. Then again, this was Sabine and Flyntinia—they both had a pastime of ordering excess garments.

"Lady Flyntinia." Caes stood, showing respect to the lady. Courtiers surrounding them murmured, and even the queen paused her conversation. Althain had been Caes's betrothed, and this sign of public deference was the least she could do. "Lady Sabine." She gave her friend a genuine smile, with Sabine's earlier warning about Flyntinia's desperation and ambition ringing in her mind. Did Flyntinia blame Caes for Althain's death? It wasn't Caes's fault, but that was small comfort to a grieving mother. A mother who couldn't even have a proper funeral for her son or obtain his body—Ardinan had no doubt burned it with the rest of the Malithians.

"I am sorry about your loss, my lady," Caes said sincerely to Flyntinia. "Althain was a true prince. I can't fully express the outrage I feel at what befell him."

"Your sentiment is appreciated, but you seem to have recovered well enough," Flyntinia said, sending Alair a sideways glance.

Caes swallowed. More people had stopped speaking, leaving an uneasy quiet. "I pray daily that the Ardinani who betrayed him will be brought to justice." Slowly, she took her seat once more.

"I pray for the same, Your Highness," Flyntinia said. "Justice is all that anyone can hope for at such times, though it seems to be the most elusive gift."

"Althain is how we came to be here, Your Highness," Sabine said, gently redirecting the topic in a way that wouldn't anger Flyntinia. Probably. "We received word that we were needed here. That we'd receive the answers we so desperately need."

"Needed by who?" the queen asked.

"By both our kingdoms," Sabine said without hesitation, "in order to maintain peace." Was it true? It didn't matter. It seemingly sounded good enough to the queen, who accepted the answer with a polite nod.

Caes echoed the queen's gesture and said, "I will share everything with you that I can about Althain's final hours. It is my dearest hope that the emperor will seek vengeance on his behalf."

"But not you?" Flyntinia asked. "Don't you wish to see such betrayal repaid, and take care of it yourself?"

Caes spread her hands in supplication. "I am but a woman. And as my story will reveal, it was hardly by my own volition that I am here. Not that it was unwelcome—but it was unexpected." Her eyes roamed the room. Where was Lyritan? If she ever could've used the god to overpower a conversation, it was now. Damn, she should've let Alair interfere and make Flyntinia leave. This conversation was getting uncomfortable. Fast.

Flyntinia smiled. It wasn't kind. "You should know better than anyone that women are masters of their own stories."

"Yet a god decided mine."

"For now." Flyntinia still held the smile.

The two women stared at each other, taking each other's measure. What *was* Flyntinia doing here? Did she really travel all this way to learn the circumstances of Althain's death? How did she *know* to come here? Karima? If it was so easy for gods to speak to mortals, why didn't they do it more often? Though, maybe they did, and the listener ignored them. If so, that was probably for the best. In the meantime, what would Lyritan do if—when—he learned that Flyntinia was here at Karima's behest? Caes relaxed—she didn't have to worry about Althain's mother. Flyntinia was in a foreign court while Caes had Lyritan. Flyntinia could do little to her here. Oh, Caes wouldn't be lulled into believing the woman harmless, but she didn't need to worry about being attacked at a public ball. Again.

Suddenly, the queen flicked her wrist, calling their attention, and the two visiting women curtsied deeply once again and exchanged the proper formalities.

"How long will you be staying with us?" the queen asked Flyntinia, tapping her finger on the arm of her throne. "I forget."

"Not much longer, Your Majesty," Flyntinia said. "We would like to return to Malithia before the snows overtake us."

The queen nodded, visibly relieved. Caes felt much the same. Despite what she told herself, she knew better than to underestimate Flyntinia.

That evening, once she was free from court, Caes had Sabine summoned to her chambers. In doing so, she asked Alair to leave for a few moments so that the meeting could be private, for Sabine's sake. He left, agreeing to visit the other Soul Carvers, but made her promise not to leave her chambers, even though Fer was taking his turn to watch her. Caes readily agreed. The only plans she had after this meeting were with her bed for a nap before dinner.

It was difficult for Caes's young maids to find her Malithian friend, but necessary. Apparently, Sabine hadn't lost her old habits of spending every moment possible talking to courtiers and seeking what inroads she could. Well, Sabine's social crops had to wait to be planted, since Caes had to know what Flyntinia wanted.

But then Bethrian arrived instead. That man always did have a talent for theatrical timing.

"Your Highness," Bethrian said, bowing dramatically deep to Caes once the door was shut behind him.

"We're alone," she said. "No need to bother with that." They were alone—she had sent Fer to wait outside in the hall along with a maid who was in the process of refilling the candy jars in her room. Even banished, the Soul Carver was close enough to probably hear the entire conversation, especially with their hearing. Oh, well. There was little the Soul Carvers didn't know anyway.

"I'll bother with it," Bethrian said, grinning, "if only because you seem singularly unhappy with the situation."

Caes flushed but wasn't about to indulge him. "Do you have any news for me? I'm going to guess you didn't come here for my company."

"Don't lower yourself like that," Bethrian said. "You were plenty amusing, even as a mortal captive."

"There's no need to flatter me."

"No. But it never hurts."

Caes couldn't help but grin. "So, you learned something?"

"A little—about a lord I need to investigate. I have a name, at least." Bethrian frowned. "Names."

"So, you don't know if the sword is even here."

"No. Sorry, Caes. But I need more time. I know we're in a hurry, but if I start asking everyone I meet about the sword, that conversation is going to be ended very quickly. *I'll* be ended quickly. I just wanted you to know that I'm not wandering aimlessly. I have a goal—and I have hope it will work."

"I understand." She did. Only idiots wandered a new court and asked about mystical weapons that were likely a royal secret. But at the same time, she felt their upcoming departure to the Burning Hand rushing towards her like a flash flood after a drought. She was going to leave for that mountain and face whatever lay between her and the god and goddesses. Face her past. Her past and future were going to collide, and there was no guarantee she'd survive unscathed. No, she probably wasn't going to survive, no matter what Lyritan promised. Gods would say anything to win a heart. Lies were a small price to pay for adoration.

Unfortunately, if she was going to have any chance of accomplishing her goal, she needed that sword. In her heart she knew she needed something at the Burning Hand if she was going to kill a god—and they couldn't rely on Lyritan providing something for them. She couldn't rely on Lyritan for anything at all.

I can rely on his love.

No. Nothing at all.

"The Sword of Might was fastened with the blood of the first god," Caes suddenly said, unsure of where that knowledge came from. Bethrian's eyes widened. "I need it, Bethrian."

"The first god is real?"

"As real as anything else in this twisted world." Caes scoffed. Liuva certainly hadn't met the first god and knew only what had been told to her, stories of the first divine footsteps on a dark and rocky world. A god who was later destroyed by his own creations and whose shape could even now be seen among the stars. "Regardless," she said, "we need it. If we go there without it, we may as well not go at all and continue letting the gods play this foolish game of theirs and destroy what they want in the process."

Bethrian's expression turned morose. "Do we truly matter so little to the gods?"

"I don't think you want the answer to that."

Bethrian's normal joviality fled his handsome face. "I'll do what I can. I promise. There's no point in being a lord if my lands are buried under an avalanche. I have reason to help you."

A knock sounded at the door, followed by Fer calling out from the other side, "Sabine's here. Your Highness."

"Send her in," Caes said, giving Bethrian a nod of dismissal. Bethrian bowed and moved to leave at the same moment Fer opened the door and ushered her friend inside. Sabine and Bethrian acknowledged each other with polite, if reserved greetings, their posture stilted in surprise at encountering the other.

"Sabine," Caes said once they were alone, letting out the largest smile she'd made all day. "I'm so happy to see you. You look well."

She did. Sabine's light brown skin was bright and carried a hint of a blush, her green eyes clear and sharp. Her hair was wrapped into a tight bun accented with a silver comb, and she was still wearing the quasi- Reyverni style of dress. She was uniquely Sabine, with her little deer antler pendant and all.

"Caes," Sabine said, rushing forward to give her a hug, which Caes enthusiastically returned. "I missed you. What happened?"

"Later." Caes ushered her towards the sofa. "First, what happened to you? How did you come to be here?"

"Oh, so, so much."

"Start at the beginning."

Sabine's eyes focused on the closed door that led back to the hall.

"Don't worry," Caes said. "Fer won't say anything, even if he's listening."

"Oh, is that his name?"

"...Yes?"

Sabine's faced reddened a little further and then she cleared her throat and then started her tale, not giving Caes time to think about what that little exchange meant. "After you left…" With that, Sabine rushed into an explanation of how things at the Malithian court were initially peaceful after Caes left for Ardinan. The emperor was debating building a new palace, Sabine's husband was debating buying a summer home in the country, and Ferlie, Seda's former favorite lady, had married and absconded far from court.

But then news came of Ardinan's betrayal, and overnight the empire was thrown into chaos. The emperor's various relatives reared their heads, each one poised to go to war and fill the void Althain had left. It didn't matter that Caes was alive, other than as a complication for whoever would take the throne. Sabine candidly explained matters, though Caes wasn't surprised to hear that she'd never be safe in the empire again. If she wasn't about to face her death in the wilderness, Caes would have been more upset. As it was now, she found it a minor annoyance. "It's horrible," Sabine said when she was finished with her tale. "There's rumors that more of the provinces will follow in rebellion, and there's going to be war. I just know it. The empire is going to fall to ruin." Provinces—referring to the once independent kingdoms as "provinces" was an indication of how far Sabine had taken to Malithia's authority.

"To ruin?" Caes asked, frowning.

"Ruin," Sabine repeated. "When kingdoms fall, cities burn, and death follows." Tears welled in her suddenly red eyes.

"Sabine…"

"You don't understand, the last time I saw it…"

"What happened?" Caes asked softly, now comprehending, thanks to the queen, why her friend was so tormented. "I know you were in Cyvid, when Malithia conquered it. That you were in a city that was taken…"

"Taken." Sabine said grimly. "Makes it sound like it was merely a child snatching a toy. I'd do anything—*anything*—to never see that again. To keep my family safe. Do you know what burning human flesh smells like?"

Caes nodded. Thanks to Kerensa, she did. It made it difficult to eat certain types of roasted meats.

Sabine wiped her eyes. "The smell was in my nose for days. My clothes. My hair. Even now, sometimes I dream that I am waking in the smell. And the screams..." A sob choked in Sabine's throat and Caes wrapped her arms around her. Her friend leaned her head against her chest and let out little sobs.

"It's alright."

Sabine let out a full cry.

Seeing her friend so undone shattered her heart like it was glass. Poor Sabine...

People spoke so casually about war, of moving armies and conquered cities. But those bare descriptions left out the trail of misery that followed. It always followed. Conquered cities were restored on the bones of the dead.

"You are safe," Caes said. "I promise."

"You can't protect me." Sabine corrected her posture. She had left tear stains on Caes's dress, and those same tears were now streaked wildly over her face. "Unless you go back to Malithia and become a princess again," Sabine offered lightly.

Caes's lip quirked. "I can't. Even if they'd accept me after everything, I can't. I'm sorry, Sabine, but I will not be returning to Malithia. Or likely any part of the empire." Caes took the chance to explain to Sabine in general terms what they had to do at the Burning Hand. She left out the details about her relationship with Lyritan and her fears about her father and Desmin—some things were better not to burden her friend with, but she told her everything else. About Althain, his murder, her subsequent torture and escape. Anything the Reyverni or Ardinani courts knew, she told Sabine.

The sword. She also didn't tell Sabine about the sword. She trusted her friend, but the less people who knew about their goal, the better.

"So, when this is done," Sabine said, "I probably won't see you again."

Sabine may as well have slapped her. Caes's realization that she was spending her last days with her friend washed over her, jarring and unwelcome as a winter wind. "Don't say that," Caes protested. "Besides, we have some time yet before we leave."

"Hardly."

Caes reached over and took Sabine's hand. "I cannot promise to protect you forever, but I can promise you now. Don't let yourself worry, my friend. If it's in my power, I will keep you safe. I promise."

Chapter 28

Caes

Mercifully, Caes was able to take dinner that night in private. She had an invitation to dine with the royal family, but she was informed that she could decline. And, oh, she declined. In some courts it was almost mandatory for the royal or ruling family to eat every meal in public. Fortunately, Reyvern wasn't one of them. Though, it was possible that the royal family ended that tradition in order to keep Lyritan away as much as possible.

Being excused from the formal dinner didn't mean she was dining alone—Lyritan invited her for a meal, and she was in no position to decline that invitation. Maybe it was for the best. The more she could learn about the god, the better.

Thus, she found herself with Lyritan in his—Phelan's—rooms, and he did nothing to minimize the luxury of the experience. They ate quail glazed with honey and served with leeks in a mustard sauce, and dessert consisted of a flaky fruit tart, not to mention the delightful little cheese platters Lyritan insisted on feeding her.

Regarding decor, Phelan apparently wasn't one to spare expense—blue silk draperies and brocades lined every surface that called for fabric. Portraits of long-dead kings lined the walls, along with marble busts of various men and women—some of them more than a little suggestive due to creative arm placements and bulges. A lit fireplace crackled, letting Caes discard her cloak. There was a table in the corner against the wall covered with open books and stacks of parchment—was that Phelan's research, or Lyritan's?

She didn't have time to wonder, for the god stared at her with his golden eyes, like she was a rare bird threatening to fly away. It was hard not to do the same. The god's shirt was open at the top, revealing a layer of taut muscle. The light caught on his skin, marking each perfect curve and angle of his face. He was both desire and doom, a yearning her body urged to embrace, despite the threat of betrayal.

Caes took a sharp breath. Her desire was just the effect of the god making Phelan seem better than he was. That's all it was. It wasn't real.

He is real. It's all real.

A real pain.

"I'm sorry I have been neglecting you," Lyritan said, his familiar cadence marking each word.

"You haven't been." Caes reached out a hand, taking Lyritan's into her own. She gently leaned into the feelings that surged from Liuva and used them to guide her. "You have responsibilities. Duties. I understand."

Lyritan smiled proudly. "You've always put the good of others first."

He came back to me. He came back. He came back.

Caes moved as if to reach towards him, but she quashed the desire. She needed what she could glean from Liuva, but such urges were harder to contain in Lyritan's presence. A part of her still loved the god and believed in him against all reason, but Caes now knew better than to trust him. What would Lyritan do if he realized that Caes wasn't committed to his plans? Would he kill her? Would he kill Alair? Or everyone else she cared about? It was hard to know. He may be merciful, but he had killed his own son to save himself. There was no doubt Lyritan wouldn't hesitate to do the same to those she loved.

"What is it?" Lyritan asked.

"Nothing. It's just, I feel like I haven't gotten to know you. Not as much as I'd like."

Lyritan's grin made her heart flutter. "You will. We have forever."

"You said before that I'm mortal." Caes motioned towards her chest, where her heart raced. "I have a mortal's body. I will die."

Lyritan flicked his wrist. "Such things can be dealt with. Do not worry, my love. I failed you before, but I will not do so again." Each word was said with sincerity. He meant it.

But he had meant it before.

"What's going to happen to Reyvern, once we are done with the mountain?" Caes asked. "Are you truly preparing for war?"

"Of course. I am the best option for this empire—and unfortunately, mortals sometimes need a reminder of what is best for them." Lyritan let go of her hand and leaned back, watching her reaction. His eyes pulsated gold, reminding Caes that she was dealing with a god. Not that she needed the reminder.

"We planned for this for so long," Lyritan said, and then his lips set in a line. "Or do you not remember?"

What did she remember? Furtive touches and frantic breaths. Promises of today and eternity. A desire to shape the world, to allow all to live without fear. Lyritan could do it. If any god could guide the world to peace, it would be him.

But such a peace wouldn't come without blood.

"Are you going to give kingdoms a chance to accept you, before invading them?" Caes asked.

"No need. Once we are done at the Burning Hand, knowledge of me will spread. That is plenty of opportunity." Lyritan clasped his hands and set them on the table. "Do not fear, Caesonia. I remember your pleadings from so long ago, even if you do not. I will care for the mortal lives, and your heart is not meant for such harsh things. Put your fears from your mind and let me take care of the rest. For now, I will have you join me in holding court. Soon. Then you will understand that I am the best option for this world. Kings and emperors die and diminish—but I will be there. Always."

So, he seemed to think that her reluctance was from a lack of memory rather than disgust at a god waging war on the mortal realm and ruling it forever. She was alright with that.

"When are we leaving for the Burning Hand, then?" Caes asked, returning her attention to her fruit tart. Sugar was always a good distraction.

"Are you in a hurry to leave?" Lyritan raised an eyebrow.

"No." She peeled apart the pastry. "Yes. The longer we wait, the more time Father and Desmin have to prepare. The more time the goddesses have to prepare. The more they could do to us."

"And we will defeat them again. We'll leave before they are able to manage much."

"You're not worried?"

The god shrugged. "I've been thinking of little else than those two goddesses for the last thousand years. Even if they manage to send an *Ocul d'carn,* I have no fear of such things."

"A what?"

"A rather gruesome monster. I'd tell you more, but I don't want to spoil your dessert."

Caes kept eating, appreciating that Lyritan didn't steal her joy.

"It will be cold in the mountains," the god said while she ate. "Your mortal body will struggle."

"I've been through worse."

"And we will make sure you're well-equipped this time." Lyritan took a long drink of wine and then wiped his mouth and said, "I've already been assembling supplies. We will have everything we need. I am aware of the struggles this body has with things like cold."

"Do you…feel pain?"

"I feel everything."

Lyritan paused for a moment, tapping the base of his goblet, and then said, "And there's things near the mountains. Monsters and myths. We need to make sure we have the right companions. That they are prepared—"

Suddenly the door opened, revealing a young manservant who bowed. The man's short hair was slicked far too close to his head, his face clean shaven, bearing the tell-tale signs of losing an encounter with a razor. His posture was rigid, to the point Caes expected him to snap when he bowed from his waist. "Alair the Soul Carver is here," the servant said.

"Send him in," Lyritan said, pushing back his chair. His golden eyes shone brighter with each word, sending Caes's heart to her throat.

"What is it?" Caes asked. "Why—"

"A small favor," Lyritan said. "You will humor me, my love. Won't you?"

Then Alair strode into the room and bowed deeply to Lyritan, his movements smooth and practiced. His sword was at his side, leaving no doubt that what had walked into the room was a deadly weapon, crafted by a goddess and honed through suffering. Caes's heart leapt again at the sight of him, wishing she could greet him as she pleased. Wishing that the two of them were anywhere but here.

"My lord," Alair said. "Your Highness." Alair was nothing like Lyritan—where Alair's coloring was dark, Lyritan's was light. Where Alair was solemn, Lyritan was smirking at some joke that no one else heard. Alair had come back from the dead for her, while Lyritan...

Caes clenched her fists under the table, digging her nails into her palm. "I don't understand—"

"Thank you for coming here, Soul Carver," Lyritan said. "I summoned you here to do me a favor."

"A favor?" Alair asked.

"Kiss her."

"What?" Caes asked, frantically looking back and forth between Alair and the god. He knew about them—encouraged it—but this was...what game was this?

Alair's face was a perfect unreadable mask, but the muscles quivering in his neck gave away that this wasn't what he expected. None of them expected this.

"You're too formal around me," Lyritan said. "That needs to change. Both of you. Come now, Caesonia, surely part of you remembers what I expect."

He's hurt at how I'm treating him as little more than a stranger.

He *was* a stranger. Even now he stared at her with his golden eyes, the hints of gold leaking through his fingernails. The air around him seemed to shimmer, dancing to his whim. It was easy to forget his power, to become complacent around it, for he contained himself so well. But at moments like this...

No help for it. She would have to placate the god.

"If you insist." With that, Caes stood from the table, moved over to Alair, and took the Soul Carver into her arms, pressing his muscular body against hers. This didn't spur on her pleasure—this was survival.

"It's alright," he whispered under his breath.

If Lyritan wanted a show, he'd get one. Caes didn't just give Alair a small peck, she devoured him, savoring the taste of him in her mouth, each breath on her lips. After a moment's hesitation he followed suit, his lips on hers, echoing her movements with his own. Out of the corner of her eye she watched the god, who laid back, watching with contentment and something else...desire? Yet his being there stirred something in her, something unfamiliar that she yearned to explore. Something that needed to go away.

He has been through so much. And he loves me.

They broke away from the kiss, and arms still around each other they faced Lyritan.

He smiled. "That's better."

Caes nodded, gripping Alair's hand. The air around Alair trembled, a sign he was dancing on the edges of his power. He would fight to the end to protect her, no matter their foe.

What did the god *want*?

More importantly, what would he do next?

Do? He laughed. Shaking with mirth, the god poured himself more wine, filling Caes's goblet in turn. "You mortals are so tense. So staid." He held up his goblet. "Come, now. We have a long evening to fill, hmmm? I don't know about you, but I'm in the mood for music."

Chapter 29

Cylis

"Hasn't this damn city heard of a ramp?" Cylis snapped, his boots thudding on the carved stone steps. At least his Soul Carver vision let him see well in the muted light, as the sun had set hours ago. "Or railings? Railings would be nice."

Cylis and Marva walked down yet another set of stairs, attempting to get to something resembling a market so that they could buy something resembling dinner. But, apparently, getting somewhere without burning your ass off in this city wasn't a possibility. And Cylis was a Soul Carver—his posterior was in perfect form.

As was Marva's.

Cylis tried not to stare—he really did—but she wore a lovely pair of breeches that hugged her curves. Oh, it was modest, especially coupled with a doublet and cloak, but Cylis knew what to look for. And when. Was she truly in a relationship with Fer, that sorry excuse for a Soul Carver? Caes had mentioned it, and Cylis hoped that Caes was wrong. Fer didn't deserve someone like Marva. He deserved a rock.

"There's more noise this way," Marva said, gesturing down a street. A middle-aged man and woman gave Marva a curious glance as they walked by, but otherwise ignored them. "I think we'll find food there."

"I hope it's edible."

"Please. I've seen you put tomato sauce on baked potatoes."

"So?"

"You don't get an opinion." Marva winked at him and Cylis flushed. Damn, the stairs really were starting to get to him. No, the altitude. It was the altitude. Something—anything—was why he was so flustered. It definitely wasn't Marva.

As for Cylis, he was wearing a thin cloak for appearances. It was cold enough that most people needed thick cloaks and more, but Cylis *was* the cold. His skin was already embraced by the frigid wind, his fingers constantly battling the familiar numbness and burn. Surely the dark purple that was always on his chest was spreading, welcoming the frost that created it, the winter calling forth his magic. There was no point in fighting it.

Gilar, Reyvern's capital, was a maze of a city—no wonder it was something that the empire didn't want to invade. The terrain was treacherous and narrow, even within the city walls. Only a small contingent could work its way through the city, due to its tunnels and sudden cliffs—and only some roads permitted people to walk more than six abreast. Sure, that sounded plenty wide, but that wasn't considering the carts, vendors, animals, and various organic matter than filled the sides of the street. In practicality, it meant travelers had to expect to travel single file with their companions. Beyond that, the locals knew this maze. They knew the mountains, the tunnels—everything. They could survive a long siege, and quite possibly escape. If the empire actually did invade...damn. The empire would prevail, eventually, but the cost would be high for such a small kingdom.

Considering the late hour—well, it felt late because night came early during this season—the city was still bustling. Music rang out from multiple directions along with shouts and songs. Though, good luck finding where a particular sound came from. Hearing a noise and finding the source were two very different things in this city. Cecilia would have loved to see this place. Maybe he would take his sister here, once this was all—

No. He couldn't see her. It was one thing for Alair to visit her. But for him? He could be discovered, and the temple would never forgive being cheated of a life.

Just when Cylis was going to demand they return to the castle to have a decent meal, they came to a market square that emitted mouth-watering scents. Roasted meats. Heady spices. Was that cinnamon? They must've been in a well-off market—cinnamon had to be imported from warmer climates. A quick glance confirmed his suspicions—they were in a decent part of the city. Sure, there were the urchins and lurkers dressed in patched rags, but they were outnumbered by people in tidy garments, speckled here and there by someone wearing far too many gems.

"This seems promising," Marva said, slowing to a stop. She looked over the crowd. "There–" she pointed at a small shop with a serving window "–let's go there."

Cylis crossed his arms. "Fine."

Marva quirked her lip. "You really are always like this, aren't you?" she asked with sarcastic awe.

"Like what?" The arm crossing deepened.

Marva sighed. "Come on. Let's get something to eat."

That "something" ended up being a pastry stuffed with spiced potatoes and some sort of earthy meat, possibly goat. Possibly venison. Possibly something he didn't want the answer to. The pastry was surprisingly good, considering that the man who served it had such bushy eyebrows it was a miracle he could see.

Food in hand, they sat on a nearby stone bench and watched the crowd. It was...uninspiring. Cylis had been in dozens of markets, so what was there to say about this market? That women talked, men talked, and children...also talked? So what that they did it in a different accent and environment? It was all the same. Any market worth the name had scents, music, and people.

"What's wrong?" Marva asked.

"Nothing." Cylis watched a plump dog wander through the crowd and be fed little morsels wherever it went. Huh—people seemed to like street dogs here.

"I thought you'd be happy to get away from court."

Cylis picked off a piece of the pastry and dunked it in its gravy innards. "Sure. I am. But this is hardly a holiday." He popped the piece of bread into his mouth, chewed, and swallowed. "And we both know things are going to be changing for both of us. Soon."

"How so?"

Slowly, Cylis stretched his arms. "We're about to leave for a journey to the most epic of epic mountains. You mean to tell me that isn't bothering you? What waits for us once we leave this city?"

"Caes seems to be handling this all rather well—"

"Caes is a fucking professional by this point." Cylis cracked his neck, realizing he couldn't see the stars through the city lights. "She's already died once—maybe technically twice. I doubt she's losing much sleep over the prospect of the third time."

"You mean she's more worried about accomplishing her goal than death?"

"Probably. That's Caes. More worried about everyone else than her. Except me, for some reason. She matched me with Fuckwit."

Marva reached out a hand and patted him on the back, finishing her gesture with a slow rub. That...should not have felt as good as it did. She was lucky Cylis couldn't muster the energy to glare. The moment was ruined when Marva said, "Don't worry. I'll take care of you. I'll protect you at the Burning Hand."

At her words, the men, who had been sitting nearby on their own bench, perked up like sparrows tossed seed. Younger than Cylis's father, they both wore sensible quilted jackets dyed a deep red and purple respectively. Like some Reyverni, little gems were sewn along the seams, making the men resemble fish scales in the moonlight. He guessed that they were well-off, gaudy merchants. One man had hair the color of harsh mustard and the other reminded Cylis of a ferret—he had a rather pointy nose. The men's mouths dropped open once they realized who—or what—sat near them. Figured their anonymity wouldn't last. Damn, and they had been all-but ignored up until this point. No, that wasn't true. People knew what they were instantly. It was just that everyone else was likely too intimidated to engage with them.

As was right.

"Blessed Soul Carvers." The men bowed their heads. Alright. Maybe this city had its perks. "Children of the goddess. We are honored."

Marva gave them a kind smile and nod. "The honor is ours. Your city is lovely."

"Yeah." Cylis coughed. "Lovely." Marva elbowed Cylis in the ribs. The men's proclamations attracted more attention, causing several citizens to stare and more than a few to bow. Alright, this city really did have its perks.

"Blessedness," the mustard man said, "did we hear correctly that you are going to the Burning Hand?"

"You did," Marva replied. Should she really have been telling them this? Oh, well. What did it matter? Lyritan wasn't exactly subtle with his intentions. "Why?" she asked.

Mustard man's face creased in a frown. "Blessed one, do not go. It is too dangerous."

"So we've heard," Cylis said. "We know. It's a mountain. A magic one."

"It's more than that," the mustard man said, exchanging concerned glances with his companion. Others in the crowd nodded in agreement, some making superstitious warding gestures. "People here don't travel that path, not beyond the second peak."

"Even going that far has its dangers," the ferret man added. "Only the most devoted go."

"Go...where?" Cylis asked.

Mustard man answered. "The path to the mountain is the path to the holiest of the divine. Judge not others for yearning for its embrace."

"...Alright," Cylis said. People wanted to cross a mountain to stare at another mountain? Everyone had their quirks.

"We can see the Burning Hand from here?" Marva asked. "I guess I never thought to ask." Cylis couldn't tell if Marva was serious or just humoring them to make conversation.

"Yes," the ferret man said, "it's that close. If it were just a matter of distance the mountain could be reached in under a week. But none except the most determined leave the valley on that path."

"Let me guess," Cylis said, "because they never return."

"They come back missing pieces," the mustard man answered solemnly. "If they come back at all."

It was Cylis's and Marva's turn to perk up. "We've heard rumors of what awaits us," Marva ventured. "Can you tell us more?"

"Everyone can," the mustard man said. "The mountain is linked to the realms beyond. And as such, nothing is as it should be near there."

"What?" Marva asked.

"Talk about vague," Cylis muttered, and received another elbow from Marva.

"The ground itself is as glass," the mustard man said. "The plants poison. The air dust and rot. And the creatures…such monsters were slain in legend, but near the Hand they walk still."

"What monsters?" Cylis asked. "Like dragons?" He snorted. This was all a bunch of folk tales. Sure, there were likely some gnarly things in the mountain, but of course there were—it was a wilderness.

"If only." That caught Cylis's attention. More than the men did already. Mustard man cleared his throat. "Things that should be dead. Things that were left over from the creation of the world."

"That sounds ominous," Cylis muttered.

"Thank you," Marva said. Cylis wanted to pester them for more information, but deferred to Marva's judgment. "We will keep your warning in mind."

"I would rather you not go, Blessed One," the mustard man said, "but if the goddess commands you, then you must obey."

"Indeed."

Conversation with the men ended and most of the assembled crowd went their separate ways. Yet a few stayed behind and lurked. Were they looking for an evening's entertainment? If so, they were about to be disappointed. It seemed like Marva and Cylis's evening of adventure was over—there would be no more blending in here.

Marva leaned toward Cylis and said, "Well, looks like we get to tell Caes that whatever she expected, she should probably add living nightmares to the list."

Chapter 30

Alair

Alair couldn't sleep.

This wasn't an uncommon situation, especially when they were in a place that wasn't safe. And they certainly weren't safe in this castle. Despite the god's assurances, it would take a lot more than words before he'd dare to relax here.

Instead, he sat up in bed and watched Caes rest, her even breaths moving the blankets in a steady rhythm. Caes, who would soon be facing her death a second time. Alair worried a button on his tunic. Her light brown hair framed her beautiful face, and he had to resist brushing it aside so that he could see more. He wasn't sure what he was going to do at the Burning Hand—what he *could* do—since so much and so many depended on her destroying the corrupt goddesses, no matter the cost to herself, and him. Yet, he would find a way to save her. He wasn't going to stand aside while she died. Again.

Besides what awaited her at the Hand, Caes had enough to worry about in Gilar. She had to placate Lyritan, navigate a court that wasn't happy that Phelan was gone, and also Lady Flyntinia, of all people. If it wasn't for their Reyverni hosts—who Alair didn't want to shove into a difficult diplomatic situation—Alair would've killed Flyntinia and been done with it. Nothing good for Caes was going to happen with the emperor's former mistress around. What had happened to Althain was a tragedy and not Caes's fault. But Flyntinia was hardly an innocent grieving mother—she had done more than her part to ensure that other mothers lost their children when she helped her son remove the competition to the throne.

Alair took a deep breath. Maybe it wouldn't be the worst thing if he killed her. He could make Lady Flyntinia walk off a balcony and make it look like an accident...

No. Caes wouldn't want him to interfere like that. Not yet. Lady Flyntinia was merely a mortal woman, who Alair could easily remove if needed, and there was time to deal with her.

Unlike what awaited them at the mountain.

Marva and Cylis had returned earlier with tales about what lurked near the Burning Hand. Mere rumors from common folk, but at this point, it was better to prepare for the worst. Alair had already heard as much about monsters and chaos—the Burning Hand used to feature heavily in children's stories—but from how they were telling it, those stories were tame. His stomach twisted at the thought. Monsters? Actual monsters, besides whatever Desmin and Damek sent after them? Alair whispered a curse. Caes had already been through so much—her healed blisters told the story of the last time she was injured. That was just the last time. And soon she was going to be forced into even more danger.

But he would be with her this time. He would keep her safe.

No matter what.

"Alair," his mother said from near the window. She stood next to the glass and looked outside, dressed in the simple cream robes she favored so much. Robes that had not been in style for centuries.

"Mother?" What was this? A hallucination? A ghost? Alair got out of bed and walked to the window. He wanted to touch her, but would that make her disappear? "This is a dream."

"No." She smiled sadly. Her face was lined with more wrinkles since he had seen her last, and with a pang Alair remembered reading that she had died around ten years after he had entered the trials. From a lingering sickness, described as "malaise of the lungs."

"I don't understand."

"You were always so impatient." She looked him over, seemingly pleased at what she saw. Instinctively, Alair stood taller under her gaze. "You have grown."

"I have learned patience."

"Yes," she said. "I imagine so."

What if this wasn't a dream, but it was something so much worse? Was he devolving back into madness again? His past and present had mixed to an indiscernible degree when he emerged from the trials. And now it was happening again. But he never had his hallucinations talk so...coherently.

"You're dead," he said.

"Am I?"

"What is this? Is this a trick from *her*?" Alair didn't want to speak Karima's name. She still bound his soul, who knew what she might be doing to him?

"You called me. Thus, I came."

"I have no such gifts." No one did, unless they delved in practices that were anathema to the rules of nature. But then again, *he* was against the rules of nature. He had died and came back to this world. Twice. Being pulled twice from death would not leave a soul unmarked. It changed him. Somehow, it changed him. His chest felt as if he swallowed ice. What had happened to him? This had to be a trick. Some twist from Karima to make him doubt his sanity. She brought him back as a part of a bargain with Caes for her own reasons. There was no possibility it was done purely out of generosity. Especially now that Karima knew that Caes had no intention of keeping her side of the bargain.

And his mother...

His mother watched him with a coy smile. "Yet you did. You called me. I came. It was you."

"Mother—"

"You look different."

"I aged."

"No." She shook her head, her expression suddenly mournful. "It is far more than that. Careful, my dearest boy. Please be careful. Your soul is not your own."

Then his mother was gone and Alair was still standing and staring at the empty window.

"Who are you talking to?" Caes asked groggily. She rolled, tucking the covers around her.

"Nothing. No one." Alair went back to the bed and laid next to Caes and was rewarded when her body molded next to his. "It was just an odd dream."

Chapter 31

Bethrian

Damn, Bethrian was good. Well, that was a given, but it was truly amazing how varied his skills were. Horses, grilling vegetables, styling clothing, gambling, fine literature, and—of course—women.

"That was—that was—" a young woman named Trelia gasped. "Amazing. It really is true what they say about Malithian men." She was laying on her back, her black curly hair spread over the pillow and her bare chest moving with each breath. The rest of her was haphazardly covered with a blanket, thrown over once they were done. A pity—and a bit pointless since he had seen that and much more besides. But who was Bethrian to judge when one wanted a blanket's shelter?

"Oh?" Bethrian rested his head on his hand and propped it up with his elbow as he laid on the bed. He didn't bother to restrain the satisfied grin spreading across his face. Nor did he bother to cover his manhood. "And what do they say?"

A giggle was the maid's answer.

It took a few days of navigating the thicket of the Reyverni court, but Bethrian eventually found success in the little task Caes had given him—of course he did. The success in question consisted of a weakness in the fortress that was Lady Rella, the daughter of Lord Dyvith and suspected keeper of the Sword of Might—a pretty maid. It was surprisingly easy to seduce the maid, but then again, Malithian men were something of a fashion at the moment. Bethrian was careful not to promise the maid more than what he was willing to give—he never found the need to resort to such base measures—and she had all but thrown herself into his arms.

There had already been a night in his chambers, a rushed encounter in a linen closet, an engagement in the garden, and back to his chambers—at this rate

Bethrian was going to be a desiccated sponge before she was done with him. And he still hadn't gotten what he needed.

"Do you need to return to your duties?" Bethrian asked, tracing a finger over her stomach.

"No. I am done for the night," Trelia said, and Bethrian breathed a sigh of relief, couched in the countenance of an enamored lover. Good. Plenty of time for a leisurely conversation. And to finally get to the point of this whole endeavor. Trelia was pleasant, but Bethrian had things to do.

Thus, with the skill of a conductor guiding an orchestra, Bethrian coaxed Trelia's life story from her. The whole thing. From her quasi-humble beginnings as a wool merchant's daughter, to a lady's maid for a minor noble, to a lady's maid for that noble's mother, to—finally—Lady Rella. Bethrian had heard worse stories, but he had also heard a lot better. The good thing about Trelia's tale was that it gave him inspiration for a novel, something about a maid who seduces her way through court…yes, his audience would love that. And Bethrian would love the money that came with it. And this time, he wouldn't accidentally make Cylis the hero.

"Have you encountered Lord Dyvith often?" Bethrian asked. When Trelia grimaced, he continued, "I heard some interesting tales."

"Fortunately, no. The lady doesn't see her father overmuch."

"That's surprising." He paused, letting her guide the conversation.

The maid shrugged. "Maybe. But she isn't his heir. The lord has his own obligations. And I wouldn't be surprised if she managed to convey that she wasn't going to be pushed into any marriage she didn't want."

"Doesn't every noblewoman say the same? Yet, they all end up at the altar one way or another."

"Not Lady Rella. She's like her father. I think even he knows that it's better to leave her to her own devices."

"I heard he serves the king." Bethrian rolled on his back and looked at the ceiling. It was easier to seem nonchalant if he wasn't looking someone in the eyes.

Though Trelia's hands creeping towards his member didn't help with focus. "I mean, by doing him special favors."

"What?" Trelia shifted. "No, they're not lovers."

"I didn't—I meant that he does tasks for the king."

The maid relaxed and a little laugh escaped. Bethrian relaxed. Clumsy conversation certainly had its uses—such as putting people at ease. "Oh, that's a given," Trelia said and then chuckled grimly. "I've heard a fair amount from his servants, when he happens to come to court."

"Oh? Sorry." Trelia's hand resumed its journey to Bethrian's manly manliness. "I just heard some things that can't possibly be true."

"Like what?"

And then the hand found its destination. Bethrian took a deep breath. He had to focus. Caes. Magic. Goddesses.

Trelia did a jerking motion that she was accomplished at.

Focus.

Cylis. Oh, Cylis worked. Yes, he would think of Cylis.

Bethrian rushed out his answer. "That Lord Dyvith found a secret shrine to Karima in the forest. And sacrificed seven goats."

The maid laughed, and her movements blessedly stopped. "No, but..."

"But what?"

"I shouldn't."

"It's alright." Bethrian rolled to his side and faced the maid, giving her his winsome smile. Painfully ignoring Trelia's lingering ministrations. "I promise I won't say anything."

"It's nothing, it probably isn't even true..."

"Oh, come now. Those are the best stories."

Trelia's eyes twinkled with mischief. "I heard that he once found a Soul Carver in the woods and seduced her," she said. "That the Soul Carver is the mother of Lady Rella."

"What?" Bethrian's mouth dropped open. That wasn't where he was hoping his seeds would sprout. Time to try another tactic. Before his other head took over again. "If that Soul Carver was anything like the Soul Carvers I've met," Bethrian said, "I highly *highly* doubt they would jump on ol' Lord Dyvith in the woods." Soul Carvers typically didn't frolic with non-Soul Carvers to begin with, much less wrinkly lords.

"I've heard that they're particular," Trelia admitted, "but no one believes that tale. Not anyone who knew Lady Rella's mother, at any rate." The maid's brow furrowed. "But I did hear something that seems a bit more truthful—I heard he found a weapon in the woods."

"Oh?" Bethrian's dinner threatened to leap into his mouth. Calm. He had to stay calm. He didn't care what Trelia said, not even a little bit. At least Trelia stopped moving her hand, caught in her tale. "Like a bow?"

Nope, he didn't care at all. Bethrian didn't care. Casual. Calm. He had to stay calm.

"No, like a sword." Then Trelia laid back and played with a single black curl from her head, wrapping it around her finger, much like the sweet way she had recently wrapped her fingers around his other body parts. "Some odd thing that was very hush hush—which of course meant everyone knew about it."

"Why? What's so special about it?"

"No idea. Maybe it's magic? But I heard Lady Rella talking about it with another lady—and here's the secret—they said her father found only a small piece of it and everything else was gone."

"I don't understand. Wouldn't the king want all the pieces of a magic sword?"

"He had them destroyed, apparently. Don't ask me how. But it's Lord Dyvith. I wouldn't be at all surprised if he kept some of it for himself."

"There's a rumor," Bethrian ventured cautiously, "that Caesonia's father's sword was found near here. Shattered. Think it was that one?"

"Maybe." The maid gave a dramatic shrug that made her breasts wobble. "I have no way of knowing." She watched Bethrian's lower body, obviously aware of where his masculine attention was, and where his intentions were going.

"Huh. Well" –Bethrian moved to position himself over the maid– "I have a sword that I think you do know a lot about. Would you like to learn even more?" When the maid giggled, any suspicions likely banished, Bethrian grinned.

There were certainly some perks to being Lady Peony Passionflower.

Chapter 32

Caes

More meaningless days at the Reyverni court.

This was a court at which Caes had no intention of spending a moment longer than necessary. There was nothing but pointless titles, ostentatious dresses, and people who wouldn't dream of saying what they actually meant. It was all she could do not to snap at everyone to leave her alone—she wasn't going to rule. She didn't *want* to rule. She wasn't going to marry the crown prince. She didn't want to get married at all—what was the point of swearing love before a goddess? Instead, Caes was going to go to the Burning Hand as soon as she could convince Lyritan to leave, hopefully not die in the process of destroying the goddesses, and then...she didn't know. But whatever waited for her after, it wasn't going to be a court.

I can be with my love. Lyritan promised me, and his promises have come true.
Shut up, Caes snapped at herself.

"Are you alright, Your Highness?" A noblewoman asked. The woman's eyebrow arched dangerously close to a dangling gray curl.

Caes shook herself gently—she had to pay attention. "Yes. I am sorry. What did you say?"

"I was wondering if you are looking forward to the play."

"Play?"

The other women exchanged knowing glances, their expressions heavy with judgment. Wonderful.

Caes and a clowder of noblewomen were sitting in a room designed for lounging, music, needlework, and whatever else the women of the court wished to do. The queen was indisposed this morning and Princess Saryn was off meeting with her steward, so there was apparently no one else for the female courtiers to flock around. Except Caes. Lucky, lucky Caes. The Caes of yore would've been thrilled to be sitting amongst such fashionable ladies who vied for her attention. Caes of the present was ready for a nap.

"Yes," the woman said, managing to contort her face into something respectable. "The winter play—it's tradition. And it's in a couple days."

"I, uh, yes. Of course. It sounds exciting." Every court had its traditions, and the Malithian and Ardinani courts were no strangers to such things. Every spring the Ardinani court had a flower bouquet juggling contest. It was harder than it sounded. "What is this play about?" Caes asked to get the women talking and not focused on her.

The woman adjusted the lace on her sleeve cuff. "Normally it's a lovely dance, where the women and men of the court portray the conquering of summer, the victory of winter, and then its death and triumph by spring." Ah, dancing courtiers and no plot. Again, typical of courts. "But this year, our god-blessed prince has requested something else."

God-blessed prince? Requested?

Oh no.

"What is it?" Caes asked, fearing the answer.

"A play he wrote. It describes how he made your acquaintance thousands of years ago, his entrapment, and then victory." The women stared at Caes, watching her reaction like squirrels waiting for a nut to drop. Caes couldn't blame them. If she was sitting next to someone romanced by an ancient god, she would've been staring too.

"The prince wrote a play? About us?" Lyritan had mentioned he had a surprise for her, but where would the god have found the time or patience for crafting a play?

"He did indeed," the woman said.

"I'm sure it will be a delight to watch," Caes tactfully said. Kerensa chuckled in the background, which was quickly covered by a coughing fit. Slowly, Caes reached out and tapped the arm of her chair in an uneven rhythm. Well, at least she could talk to Kerensa about it later and complain.

"Your Highness," Kerensa said, approaching and bowing, "as requested, a reminder that you have an appointment with the seamstress."

Caes had no appointment—she had a Kerensa, which was much better.

Caes stood and the other women followed suit, bowing to her as she made her apologies to them and left the room. She barely made it out the door before the buzz of gossip broke out behind her. No matter—this court wasn't going to be her problem for long.

"Thank you," Caes whispered to Kerensa. "You're amazing." At least the stone hall was excellent for dampening sound so that Caes was able to shove the noblewomen out of her mind.

"I know." Kerensa grinned. "You lasted longer with them than I expected."

"Too long." Caes huffed. "Did you see how Phelan's mistress glared at me? I thought he sent them all away."

"Women are stubborn. *You* could have sent her away."

"She was irritating, but I can't blame her." Caes brushed a stand of hair out of her face. "I did end up stealing her lover."

Kerensa grimaced. "Well, I guess the positive side is that she's no worse than Flyntinia."

Caes groaned. "Don't remind me. At least she found other things to do. I wouldn't have been able to keep talking with them if she stayed."

"Why did you?" Kerensa raised an eyebrow. "Stay with the noblewomen, I mean."

"I will be empress someday. It is best to know the court," Caes said, in case someone was listening after all. But the rolling eyes she gave Kerensa told a very different story.

"Ah, yes. Yes, you will be a fine empress. Finest of them all."

"Too far," Caes whispered.

"Sorry."

They turned down one hall after another, keeping up the appearance of princess and escort in front of the servants and courtiers until they made it back to Caes's rooms. Once the door was shut and the lurking servants banished, Caes threw herself onto a padded chair and moaned. "We need to leave." She rubbed her temples. Her golden eyes and apparently divine powers did nothing to save her from the headache that grew stronger by the moment.

"I know." Kerensa helped herself to a chair and sprawled. "What's Lyritan waiting for? Winter is just going to get worse—we need to go."

"I don't know. Don't ask me. Supplies? Men? For the stars to align?"

"The culmination of his plans to conquer the world?"

"Don't remind me."

They lapsed into silence, and then Kerensa ventured, "What are you even going to do at the Burning Hand?"

Caes raised her head to look at her friend. "Ker, you more than anyone should know I have no fucking clue. Karima and Shirla aren't stupid—they know I'm not helping them. And at this point leaving one of them in charge would be as good as jumping off a cliff. Not to mention what they would do to their new territories." Caes sighed. "But Lyritan…"

"There've been worse gods."

"And just how many had a corporeal body to conquer the world with?"

"More than you'd think." Kerensa frowned. "But they all died and a good city or two was destroyed with them."

"Wonderful." Caes had long heard stories of mortals possessed by gods, but she had thought it was just that—stories.

Caes noted the wine decanter on the table and popped off the top, taking a heavy drink straight from the bottle. "Meanwhile, my father and Desmin are planning their next attack, and I'm stuck here, playing court." Caes offered the bottle to Kerensa, who took it and helped herself.

"Shit," Kerensa suddenly said, wiping her mouth with her sleeve.

"What now?"

"Well, I wasn't looking forward to telling you, but now that I have you alone, I can't put it off."

"Ker..."

"I heard some women talking earlier today. Melonie was killed."

"What?" A jolt worked its way through Caes's body. "How? Killed? In Ardinan?"

"Executed for treason." Kerensa set the bottle on the table. "Apparently, she wasn't as good at hiding her plans from her family as she thought."

"Fuck. Oh." Caes closed her eyes for a long moment. Images of the Melonie she had known, the haughty princess, flashed in her memory. "Poor Melonie."

"She was awful to you."

"But she saved Cylis and the others." Caes paused, wishing there was a god she dared whisper a prayer to. "And she also sent the information about my father and Desmin that warned us. She didn't deserve a traitor's death."

"Probably not. But a lot of people who don't deserve them get them anyway."

Kerensa reclined in the chair, her mirrored eyes catching the light from the window. If Caes had been told while she was in the wagon as a Malithian hostage that she would someday be sharing a bottle of wine with the woman who threw piss at her, Caes would've never believed it. But then again, there was very little in Caes's life as it was now that she would have believed.

"In happier news," Kerensa said, "I managed to talk a few guards into telling me what is on the way to the Burning Hand."

"How is that happier? Please say it's better than what Marva and Cylis heard. Will we be attacked by kittens?"

"Close." Kerensa smiled. "If those kittens are large. And undead. And are instead sentient 'eldritch monsters of flesh and bone.'"

"Ker, that's nothing like a kitten."

"No, but it sounded better this way. The acceptance of bad news is all in the delivery."

Caes didn't reply, and instead took another long drink from the wine bottle. Kittens or monsters, they needed to get to the Burning Hand.

All games end, and there was no doubt this one would end in ruin.

"Where are you taking me?" Caes asked Lyritan as they walked with Alair through the castle halls. "It's not time for dinner." The evening meal wouldn't be for a couple hours yet—this court often dined late.

"No," Lyritan said, his hand holding hers. "I promised I would show you what my rule would mean—and I keep my promises." He gave her a secretive smirk, sending an unbidden trill of pleasure through her, despite the nobles and servants watching them pass.

I don't need to worry. He loves me.

Caes knew better than to trust someone who needed something from her.

Caes couldn't relax in her rooms for long with only Kerensa for company. Far too soon, Lyritan had sent word that he wished for her to dress for a formal court event and meet him in a vestibule. She did as bid, wearing a long red velvet gown that hugged her curves, yet still had the voluminous skirts favored in Gilar. Lyritan, however, wore a casaque, a long black garment that was similar to the robes worn by Karima's priests and priestesses, but this was *more*. Elaborate black embroidery depicting runes lined the sleeves, and the front was rimmed with tiny bits of onyx. When Caes had asked why he chose that particular garment, all Lyritan did was beam and take her hand.

At least Alair was dressed like himself, in his black garments and surcoat. Alair, who walked by her side, taking her other hand in his own. Alair, who was her anchor against the onslaught of this court. And Lyritan.

Another turn and they found themselves back in the castle's main hall, the massive cavern where Caes had first met the Reyverni king and queen. This time, the hall was packed with bodies to the point Caes wondered if there were any people left in Gilar. Rich and poor, young and old were pressed into the space, their shoulders all but smashed against each other.

What was this? Caes gripped Alair's hand harder and received a steadying pressure in return.

Lyritan led them through the parted crowd to the pair of empty thrones that waited at the end of the hall. Was he? Fuck...he was. He wanted her to sit on one. Both Alair and Lyritan guided her up the stairs, and Lyritan motioned her to the throne—the one meant for the Reyverni queen.

"Sit, my love," Lyritan said. "Sit."

Caes hesitated, staring at the wooden throne. The arms were worn smooth, the intricate designs faded from years of queens gripping the wood. "I'm not the queen of this kingdom," Caes said. "I cannot." What would their hosts think if they saw her sitting there? At least this way they'd know she protested first.

"You are more than a queen," Lyritan said. "You are my beloved. And this seat is only the first throne I will give you."

Caes forced a smile. It was what Lyritan expected. She smiled for Lyritan, but Alair was the one she looked to, the one who gave her an almost imperceptible nod. The king and queen could make her life in Reyvern difficult, but Caes needed Lyritan to be happy with her. She sat, settling into the throne, ignoring the wave of silence that rushed through the crowd. The thousands of eyes staring at her. Watching her. Alair moved to stand behind her, his shadow blending with hers on the stone floor. She took a deep breath. She wasn't alone. Never alone.

For his part, Lyritan sat on the throne with little ceremony and clapped his hands twice. The hall quieted.

"Reyverni," Lyritan said, "I told you that I would bring blessings upon this kingdom. That I would return a divine rule to these lands—that you would be first among all the lands of this earth." The crowd cheered just enough to not offend Lyritan, but to Caes's experienced ears it lacked enthusiasm. How did he manage to get all of these people to come here?

If Lyritan noted that the cheering could've been more genuine, he gave no sign and merely held up a hand, bobbing his head like an indulgent parent. "The foundation of any competent rule, that of gods or men, is justice. Thus, I am here. Beseech me." He reclined while he watched Caes's reaction. She nodded. She didn't have the capacity for words, and he clearly expected something.

"This is what awaits us," Lyritan said softly to her. "Watch—and be comforted."

The first petitions were surprisingly routine. A property line dispute to be settled once the records were retrieved from the archives. A man who was ordered to repay the cost of a cow after it died while he was using it for his fields, along with two lashes for his cruelty—the man apparently forgot that cows needed water. Normal things. Contract disputes and the like. All in all, Lyritan was surprisingly competent at handling these matters. He knew when it would be best to seek more information and when to pronounce judgment immediately, and he was skilled at coming up with solutions that reeked of compromise. After the seventh petition, Caes relaxed. Maybe having Lyritan ruling the empire wouldn't be so bad. There certainly had been worse kings. Yes, this could've all been a performance for her, but her buried memories of Lyritan hinted that it was likely not—Lyritan loved deference and being obeyed. What was holding a petitioning session but both of those things?

The next petitioner was a young woman, barely into her teenage years. Her brown hair was tucked under a bright blue cap, and tears stained her ruddy cheeks. Next to her stood a man and a woman, older and also dressed in practical, yet sturdy clothing. The girl's parents?

"What brings you before me?" Lyritan asked as the three of them bowed.

"This is our ward, divine one," the man said. "Her parents relinquished her to us four years ago."

"Relinquished?" Caes asked, speaking up for the first time. Lyritan gave her a curious look but didn't bother to interrupt.

"Yes, Your Highness," the man said. "Her parents gave her to us. We were to raise her, and in exchange she would help us in our business. We're merchants, see. Mostly furs, but sometimes silk." The entire time the man spoke, the girl stood silent, watching the ground in front of her. Caes let out a long breath. The man had described a common arrangement among the poorer classes, but something had gone wrong in this case. Otherwise, they wouldn't be here.

"Again, why is she here?" Lyritan asked.

"She stole from us," the woman said. "My mother's hairpin. It's gone. After three silvers the week before that. And a similar theft two weeks before that. Only caught her because she went back a fourth time."

"I didn't—"

"We caught you," the woman said, glaring at the girl. "Don't you dare deny it now."

"I told you" –the girl coughed through her tears– "I was putting it back."

"And you dare blame Tresina for this?" the woman said.

"Who is Tresina?" Lyritan asked.

"Our daughter," the man replied. "She's a year older than *this* one."

Silent, Lyritan stared at each person in turn. Caes's heart raced—was the girl guilty? The explanation she gave was an awful excuse. Too awful. Suspiciously awful. No…Caes had a feeling that there was more to the relationship between Tresina and the accused girl than Master and Mistress Silken Leather were admitting to. At least Lyritan was patient enough to get to the truth of the matter.

"What are you seeking?" Lyritan asked.

"I want her to learn never to steal from us again." The man crossed his arms.

"Alright. Fifty lashes should suffice." Lyritan flicked his wrist. "To be admitted now." Fifty? Caes's heart plummeted. That would likely kill her. The girl screamed, the crowed murmured, and even the man and woman looked at each other, eyes wide. Yet they did nothing to stop the guards from taking the girl away amid her howls.

"Lyr, my love," Caes said softly, "what if the girl was telling the truth?"

Lyritan's narrowed eyes flared gold. "You're questioning my wisdom?"

Caes's mouth went dry. Oh no. Did she push him too far? Would he hurt her? Punish the girl worse? Lyritan never liked to be questioned—especially by someone he considered subservient. A hand pressed on Caes's shoulder. "She has a lot of compassion, my lord," Alair said. "She thinks with her heart instead of her mind."

Like water dousing a candle, Lyritan's expression turned amused. "Oh, that she does. I'm sorry, Caesonia. These mortals tire me, and it has been a long day. Do you mind if we retire?"

Caes swallowed. "Not at all, Your Highness."

"Perfect." Lyritan shouted something at the guards, lowering the sentence to only five lashes, while Caes forced her breath to steady. That was too close. Far too close.

Whatever happened with Lyritan, she was going to have to be very careful indeed. And worse, he was exactly as fit to rule the kingdoms as she feared.

Chapter 33

Bethrian

Once Bethrian extracted himself from Trelia's form-fitting embrace, it was time to meet with his erstwhile companion. His friend for this epic adventure. His partner at delving into the depths of Reyvern.

Cylis.

The Soul Carver braced his back against a wall in Bethrian's room, hands on his hips and scowling while Bethrian sat on the edge of his bed. Bethrian was starting to wonder if Cylis had some sort of persistent rash or needed a better tailor, since he was always frowning with such bad posture. Better not to think about things like Cylis with a rash.

"You know it's for sure here?" Cylis asked. "That stupid sword."

"Yes, I believe so." Slowly, Bethrian told Cylis what Trelia had told him. How Lord Dyvith had apparently found a magical weapon in the woods that sounded suspiciously like the Sword of Might and that Lord Dyvith possibly retained a piece. A piece that could still be in the castle.

"How did you get all of this in only a few days?"

"Talent. Lots of talent." His prophecy that was spoken by the priestess to commemorate his birth had warned him to *beware the hidden heart*. Hidden heart? Ha. A more pressing concern of his was dealing with hostile courtiers. "I've had lots of practice with difficult courts."

"I see. Does that 'talent' have anything to do with why it smells like a brothel in here?"

"Maybe." Damn Soul Carvers and their sensitive noses.

Somehow, Cylis grimaced further. "And you don't think she's lying?"

"I doubt it. Why would she?"

"I can think of a few reasons."

"Cylis, whatever you may think about me, I can assure you women leave me satisfied and with a song on their lips." Bethrian ignored the resulting eye roll. "She brought it up on her own. I merely shifted the conversation to goddesses and woods. She supplied the rest."

"I don't like it. Too simple. What if the lord took it with him?" Cylis picked at his lip. "And more, that still doesn't explain how Ardinan decided that Caes's father faked having the sword and magic. Or how Ardinan ended up with the hilt—if they even have it. Too many puzzles left."

Bethrian shrugged. "I wouldn't be at all surprised if the Ardinani were told what they wanted to hear. Lord Dyvith may have Ardinani connections, but his first priority is likely Reyvern. And Reyvern benefitted from Ardinan in chaos." Brilliant, for a courtier forced to play both sides.

"I guess. Though as long as the sword is here, I'm not about to care how or why."

"That's what I figured. I'm hoping there's more of the sword than what the maid implied. I'm guessing Caes wants more than enough to shave your face."

"Probably."

Bethrian picked at a little scab in his beard—he was never going to go long without a visit to a talented barber again. "The maid heard that the Reyvern royal family ordered the sword destroyed, but I'm not sure that's possible. Can those weapons be destroyed?"

"How would I know? They probably just buried it or threw it in a lake." Cylis shrugged. "That's good enough most of the time. And I don't blame them for not wanting to keep the damn thing, especially if it did to Caes's father what it seems to have done."

"Indeed." Bethrian had never asked Caes what she thought had happened to her father, since by all accounts he had real magic once upon a time. Was it the sword that gave it to him in the first place? Did that magic fade? Did he abandon his quest? Or—and this was seeming more likely—did something stop him? At times like this, Bethrian wished he had paid more attention to the lessons on

Karima he had been forced to endure as a spry little lad. It was possible they would've taught him something useful.

"Well," Cylis said, "so, where is it?"

Bethrian slowly scratched his nose and then crossed his arms as Cylis's glower deepened. He'd never pass up a chance to annoy Cylis by something so simple as taking his time. "The only place I can think to look are Lord Dyvith's chambers in the castle. I've heard more than one person say he has permanent ones here."

"Really? You can't think of anywhere else?"

"We can start elsewhere, if you insist. Where would you like us to go first, Cylis?"

A pause. "Alright. His chambers it is. And where are they?"

"I can find that out easily enough," Bethrian said. "A few comments about how the lord must have the best ones in the castle and someone is sure to mention a detail or two. I can narrow it down from there."

"Clever," Cylis said sarcastically.

"That it is. You'd be amazed what people will say if they think it makes themselves look better—all I have to do is imply someone has inferior ones and they'll practically be crooning where his rooms are."

"...I'll decide to believe that you can find this out. But then what? We can hardly knock on the door and beg to get inside."

"True. Especially since there's no one in there." When Cylis raised a questioning eyebrow, Bethrian continued, "He's not at court. His rooms will be vacant. Anything valuable will be hidden, locked up, or both."

"Yeah, I can't pick locks."

"Neither can I. But I'm betting that you can bust off a doorknob with your Soul Carver abilities."

"My what?"

"Your frosty muscles."

Cylis locked eyes with him. "You are very, *very* lucky Caes wants you alive, Bethy."

"And you are very lucky to have me in your life."

While Cylis paled, taking in that statement, Bethrian said, "The door is one problem, but one thing at a time. We'll worry about anything around the sword, like additional locks, once we find where it is."

"Wait, bust?" Cylis pushed himself off the wall. "You want me to bust the locks," Cylis said in disbelief.

"Yes, with frosty muscles. I thought we settled that."

Cylis shook his head. "Bethy—that's going to be loud. Someone will notice."

"No, they won't. Because we'll look for the sword during the play. That winter celebration thing. The entire court will be there, and probably most of the servants. No one is going to be lurking near a lord's vacant rooms."

Unblinking, Cylis looked at him. "It's probably a good thing you didn't become emperor. We would've ended up joining the Free Kingdoms of Tamsen, and they would've thought it was our idea."

"I'm going to pretend that's a compliment," Bethrian said.

Cylis rolled his eyes—how were they still attached to his head?—but said nothing. For once. "I think we should bring one more person," Cylis said instead.

Bethrian flicked his wrist. "No, not a good idea. The more people involved the harder it will be to explain away, and the easier it will be to be noticed by someone in the first place. Unless it's Alair. He could help us get out of there easily. Wait—could we bring him?"

"Doubtful. Assuming that he'd be willing to leave Caes during this play—and after what happened in Ardinan, good luck—he won't be as much help as you think." Kerensa would probably also insist on staying with Caes, for the same reason.

Bethrian frowned. "He can craft illusions. Manipulate minds—"

"And make people walk off a cliff. I know. I'm the last person who needs an explanation of Alair's 'powers.'" Cylis made air quotes at the last word. "But the problem is that his abilities are temporary—and the person will know that they were fucked with. It may take a bit, maybe a couple days, but their memory will eventually sort itself out. Even if Alair was somehow not seen…" Cylis shook his head. "Trust me. If we were going through the city and we were dealing with people who had never met Alair and would never see him again, that's one thing. They'd probably think they had too much to drink. But people in a court where we're the only thing they've been talking about since we arrived? Trust me. The pieces would be put together fast. Especially since Alair is practically a legend."

"But I've seen Alair leave people insane. For good." Including a chef who made an amazing beef baked in pastry that Bethrian sorely missed—but that was what happened when one tried to poison the emperor.

"I'm assuming Alair won't do that to the people here. And having someone who oddly loses their mind permanently while on guard duty the same night that a doorknob to a lord's apartments was obviously tampered with? Nope. Not good." Cylis shook his head, the effect oddly reminiscent of a dog shaking off water.

Damn, Cylis had the ability to make sense, as far as Alair was concerned.

"Then why do we need someone?" Bethrian asked.

"Haven't you ever stolen something before?"

"Not in person."

"Rich ass." Cylis took a deep breath. "You and I are going to search and possibly break into a safe holding the sword. And someone else will wait by the door to stand guard. Soul Carvers have great hearing, so we'd get a lot of warning before we'd be discovered. And we need warning."

Cylis *did* have another point, as much as it pained Bethrian's soul to admit it. Bethrian couldn't look for the sword alone since Soul Carvers were able to sense divine magic—or something like that, in addition to their other talents. Bethrian wrote off Cylis's failure to detect that the stolen hilt was not divine as an unfortunate mix of panic, desperation, and ignorance. Most Soul Carvers were not like Cylis. Caes was lucky indeed to be essentially taken into their most trusted confidences—he couldn't recall anything like that happening before. But then again, Caes herself was unique—she had access to all their power and she likely never dreamt of using it for her own ends. A pity.

Caes's uncanny ability to engender loyalty aside, the point remained that Cylis would have a much easier time finding the sword than Bethrian. And Bethrian was next to useless compared to a Soul Carver for standing guard. And Bethrian wasn't about to have two Soul Carvers go alone and leave him behind since, well, Bethrian was better at improvisation. And as Cylis was his prize show sheep, he wasn't about to let it wander into the fair alone.

"Alright, I agree," Bethrian said, "we need someone. Now, who do you have in mind?"

"Leave that to me."

Chapter 34

Cylis

"It was nice of you to invite me to visit," Marva said, "but you could've chosen a better hour." Marva looked around Cylis's well-used room, and he felt suddenly aware of the state of the furniture and bedding. Not that the items or condition had anything to do with Cylis or his choices. But Marva was here, and his meagre furnishings in the space he shared with another Soul Carver were hardly worth showing off to company. Especially Marva.

"Sorry," Cylis said, shrugging. "This wasn't my idea of great timing, either."

"Wait. You apologized." Marva's eyes turned into saucers. "You actually apologized. Of your own volition."

"And?" Cylis frowned. He had admitted when he was wrong in the past. Granted it didn't happen very often, but it did. Occasionally. Rarely. Almost never.

"Nothing," Marva said. Still bearing a satisfied grin, Marva sat on Cylis's bed, her hands bracing herself as she leaned back. She looked up at Cylis, who remained standing. "Now, what's the reason you dragged me here at this cursed hour?"

"You were still awake. And walking with Fer."

"So?"

"I would've thought that he'd have been with you. Privately."

"What?" Marva blinked hard. "Oh, damn, Kerensa talks."

"She does. But it was actually Caes."

"She's no better."

Actually, Kerensa had said the same thing as Caes, but it was nice to confuse Marva. It was a good look on her. But Cylis wasn't able to focus on her expression—until it shifted to a giggle.

"No." Marva snorted. "It wasn't for that." Marva giggled more and then was finally unable to hold back laughter.

"What was it then? What did he want?"

"Breathing techniques," Marva said. "I was teaching him some breathing techniques I learned from a pottery merchant when I was in Artonia."

"Breathing. *Fer?* Sounds like that's a code for something."

"No" –Marva stifled a laugh– "it isn't. But what were you thinking, Cylis?" Marva looked at him pointedly.

"You *know*." Cylis awkwardly cocked his head to the side a few times, praying she wasn't going to make him say it. He cursed to himself. Here he was, acting like some foolish youth seeing a woman for the first time.

"No, nothing like that." Now Marva's expression crossed into outright bemused. "The Artonians have different breaths for waking, resting, focusing, cheering up, and so on. I was teaching him some. But he asked that I not say anything, so..."

"And why are you telling me now?"

"Because you asked."

"I—"

"And because I didn't want you to think that I was...with someone. Especially not Fer. And you *are* the one who dragged me here."

Oh. This was awkward. Cylis sat on the bed, focusing on how his weight shifted the mattress. Was she saying what he thought she was saying? "I see."

"No," Marva said, "I don't think you do." She leaned forward and—after hesitating the briefest moment—kissed him. Cylis froze. Was this happening? Wait, it was happening. What was he doing? He needed to do something. Anything. Wait, he knew what to do.

Letting his instincts take over, Cylis pulled Marva closer to him, relishing her little gasp of surprise. Marva shifted her weight so that she sat on Cylis's lap, a knee on each side of his legs, her arms wrapped around him, her lips never leaving his. She was so soft, even softer than he imagined. If she sat any closer to his hips, she was going to notice just how much Cylis was enjoying this.

"Well," he said after they stopped for breath, "I didn't expect that."

"I figured not," Marva said, biting her lip.

"Are you, uh, thinking about staying here?" Cylis nodded to his bed. There was a very important reason he invited Marva, but that didn't matter at the moment.

"Men." Marva rolled her eyes. "I know what we're usually like, but that's not what I have in mind. Not now." Usually like—Soul Carvers weren't nearly as prudish as regular humans in regard to partners. Soul Carvers' lives were hard and often short—why would they deprive themselves of any pleasure? If someone drew a line connecting who had laid with whom amongst the Soul Carvers, it would be like a spider's web.

But...why did Marva want to stop?

"You don't?" Did he do something wrong? Did she not like it? He never had complaints before. "Is something wrong?"

"Not at all." Marva said, brushing a curl behind her ear. Her red lips tempted him, forming words when they should have been forming around other things. "Let's just say I have better plans for us than that."

Cylis frowned. But should he be frowning? Wasn't that a good thing? What was she trying to say?

Marva laughed. "Good goddess, if I didn't know you better by now, I'd be very offended by your reaction."

"What reaction?"

"Frowning. I'm trying to tell you that I *like* you. And that I'm not in the mood for something that lasts a night. Not right now. So" –Marva scooted off him– "I'm going to insist that we wait."

"Wait."

"Yes. It's called delayed gratification. You'll like it." Marva winked and reached for his hand. Wait, she was saying that she liked him...that much? *Him?* Cylis let her take it, his mind at loss of any thought other than how good it felt to have

Marva next to him. He normally wasn't this inept at moments like these—he definitely had had more than his share of partners. But usually they didn't want to talk to him. No, by this point, they'd have been naked and well on their way to doing what Cylis did best.

"Yep," Marva said, jerking him from his thoughts, "you're very lucky I know better."

Cylis coughed. "That wasn't why I called you here."

"No. But I thought this was as good of a time as any to see how you felt. We aren't alone that often."

"So...uh...we're...what are we?"

"Let's call it 'starting a relationship.' Is that alright with you?"

Was it ever...

But Cylis only managed a nod.

Marva smiled, as content as a child with a plate of pie. "Now, tell me what brought me here at this time of night that apparently had nothing to do with 'us.'"

Thought. Cylis needed thoughts. Actual thoughts. "Um...want to help Bethrian and me break into a noble's rooms and steal something?"

Marva's eyes sparkled. "Obviously."

Chapter 35

Cylis

"Well, Fuckwit, you're sure this is it?" Cylis whispered, glancing down the stone hall to make sure they were still alone. It was now two days after the encounter with Marva in his bedroom. Days that passed painfully slow, for various, unrelated reasons.

Marva, Bethrian, and Cylis stood outside of a wooden door in one of the palace halls, in a corridor that took four sets of stairs and a tunnel to get to. As far as doors went, it was alright. It was made of wood and solid and adequately fulfilled its destiny as a door. But it was locked. That wasn't alright.

"Yes," Bethrian said for the third time that night. "Two different nobles mentioned where it was. And it makes sense—his daughter's rooms are just that way." Bethrian pointed down the hall.

"I can't hear anyone inside," Marva said. "I'd assume if the noble was in residence, there'd be at least a few servants present, cleaning and such. Whether there was a play occurring or no."

"Me neither," Cylis agreed. "Unless a servant is sitting and reading."

"How many servants have you seen reading?" Marva asked.

"None," Cylis said. Servants were too busy.

"Marva's right," Bethrian said. "The chambers would never be empty if the lord was here, and we should've discussed this before we left."

"That would have been wise," Marva agreed.

"No point lurking here. Time to get inside." Cylis reached out and touched the metal doorknob and poured his magic into it and the latched padlock, ignoring the agony of ice working its way up his hands, like he had dipped his hand in water and then left it outside in the middle of winter. His breath came out in frozen gusts, and his chest seized with the difficulty of breathing in cold air. The cold warped his mind, pulling all of his senses into a hum of pain. It would pass. It would pass. It always did. Suffering was the cost of his magic, and he paid it willingly.

Once the lock was good and frozen, Cylis tugged, snapping it off and removing the mechanism that held the padlock in place. Some of his skin stuck to the metal and decided to stay there. He shook his hand, biting back a snarl as the metal took a layer of flesh with it.

"You alright?" Marva asked.

"Fine. It's been a while since that happened. I'll heal fast. We always do."

Bethrian winced when he saw Cylis's hand. "Well, this lock will be work to hide," Bethrian pointed at the hunk of metal while Cylis opened the door and led them inside. "Someone probably heard that."

"No one is near," Marva said, moving the busted wooden and metal joints back into the wood so that it looked like the mechanism was still in place. Sort of. Too bad the door didn't have metal screws—that would have been easier to undo. And replace.

"Come on," Cylis said to Bethrian. "We'll hide it later. Or be gone so it won't matter. Let's get this thing and go. If it's even here." The three of them entered the chambers, pausing only to absorb their surroundings before Bethrian and Cylis moved on while Marva stood guard at the entryway, listening for anyone approaching.

What was there to say about the chambers? They were fancy. Expensive. Crowded with gilded furniture and art, most of which was likely handed down from prior generations of Lord Dyviths. The palace in Malithia was full of rooms almost exactly like this, except for the devotion to Reyvern's archaic runes that littered various surfaces. This part of the castle was above ground, and thus was made of both wood and stone, though some of the styling was a seeming attempt to make one forget that fact.

A bigger problem than the lord's gaudy furniture was the light, or lack thereof. The lord's chambers were dark, almost too dark for Cylis to see. Fuckwit was as good as blind, for he knocked into more than one piece of furniture before Cylis grabbed his grubby hand and tugged him along.

"Slow down," Bethrian barked.

"I doubt he hid the damn thing in his living room, so come on."

"I need to *see*."

"Debatable."

"Unless you wanted to get me alone with you in the dark. Is that it?" Bethrian chortled. Cylis shook off Bethrian's hand. Fuckwit could guide himself. "Yes," Bethrian said, "that's it. This was all an elaborate ploy. But fear not—I came prepared." Bethrian passed Cylis a box of matches.

"Where in the hells did you get these?" Cylis asked, inspecting them warily. Matches were rare, a new development from Vergas and likely imported from elsewhere. That Bethrian managed to obtain some…

"I may have found a few other things while I was gathering information."

"I thought you said you didn't steal."

"I didn't." Bethrian winked.

"Argh. Fine." Cylis found an oil lamp and handed it to Bethrian, along with the box of matches. "I'm not ruining these things, so it's up to you to use them. Do you even know how?"

"Oh, Cylis. Your mind is a knowable thing." What? Was that an insult? No matter—what else did one expect from a fuckwit?

Bethrian spent a few minutes fumbling and lighting the lamp while Cylis slowly inspected the room. All of the furniture was covered with sheets, every window clamped shut. It was night and the sky wasn't cooperating, so opening those would've done little for Bethrian's vision. And there was also the small matter that someone might have noticed the shutters opening in "vacant" chambers. Guards tended to only see what was right in front of them, but occasionally some managed to do their job.

Cylis wrinkled his nose. Maybe they should've opened a window—the room smelled. Musty. A hint of some strange smoke. And…wet dogs? Yes, that was indeed dog. How many animals did this lord have that he could smell it so strongly? There were animals at this court as at any other, but they stayed in their masters' and mistresses' rooms. Where they belonged.

A sudden glow illuminated the room. Bethrian stood, taking in the surroundings with his newly-returned vision. "Sense anything...godlike?"

"Nothing. You didn't mention the lord had dogs."

"Yes. He's fond of them."

"You didn't tell me."

Bethrian raised an eyebrow. "Does it matter?" He sniffed. Hard. "Ah. Soul Carver noses. Do you smell everything? Must be unpleasant."

"Mind your own business."

Bethrian shrugged. "Fair enough. Let's keep walking."

They had passed through one room and then another when Cylis felt a tingling in his fingers, like the charged air before a storm. The feeling became stronger with each step. It was different than the pull he felt around Lyritan or Karima. This was...zestier. The sword. It had to be.

"What's wrong?" Bethrian asked.

"This way." Cylis guided them to a room that had to be the lord's personal office, due to the relatively small size and massive dark carved wood desk. Several dozen portraits of dogs adorned the walls, varying in styles from brilliant watercolors to dark oils.

"I like dogs as much as the next person, but where are the portraits of his children?" Bethrian asked.

"I think he likes the dogs more."

Bethrian nodded. "Understandable. Dogs are usually far less of a disappointment. Think these are all his?"

"Considering how old he is and the smell...probably." Cylis's jaw set. He would've liked to have a pet, but being a Soul Carver never gave him the opportunity. He could've had a pet rock, and even that he would've neglected. Bethrian was wrong—dogs were gross and an immense disappointment. He respected pets that were able to manage themselves.

The disconcerting feeling in his hands grew stronger and spread through his arms. "It's in here," Cylis announced. "There." Cylis pointed at a portrait of a particularly rotund hunting dog wearing a lace cape.

"Madame Sweets," Bethrian read from the gold plaque under the portrait. "Did she eat them, or..."

"Come on." Cylis felt around the painting and then took it down, revealing a small safe in the wall. A solid iron safe with a barely-visible seam.

"Fuck," Cylis said. "I can't break into this."

"Well" –Bethrian strode over to the cast iron implements next to the fireplace– "we can improvise."

"What are you—"

Before Cylis could question the wisdom of this plan, Bethrian stabbed the poker into the wall, chiseling around the safe, revealing it wedged into the wood. "Think you can rip it out?"

"Obviously." Cylis gripped the revealed safe and pulled. Hard. Thank the fucking gods that the thing was tiny, no bigger than a few decks of cards placed side by side. Then again, why would the lord have a mythical piece of the sword in a *massive* safe? Obviously, the entire sword was not here—Cylis felt no other indication that it was around. Maybe the king destroyed it. Maybe Dyvith gave pieces to Ardinan. But regardless, something divine was in this box, and this box was going to Caes.

"So, we abandoned subtlety?" Cylis asked, eying the destroyed wall.

"I mean, we'll hang the picture back up." Bethrian looked at the wall and grimaced at the bent nail that had formerly held Madame Sweets. "Or try to."

"Your call. Not mine."

Safe in hand—hands, as it was surprisingly heavy—and covered in chunks of plaster, Bethrian and Cylis brushed themselves off and ran to the door. They couldn't linger. Each moment risked discovery, and they *would* be discovered if anyone came down the hall and bothered to look at the door. Bethrian had clumsily hung the portrait back on the wall—Madame Sweets was lopsided—and that did nothing for the massive pieces of plaster and wood on the ground.

"We're fucked," Cylis said. "They're going to notice."

"Yes, but I don't think the lord wanted people to know he had the sword in the first place. He won't come looking for us. They'll do a quick investigation for a jewelry thief and that's it."

"You're awfully confident."

"A matter of necessity."

"What if there *is* jewelry in the safe?"

"We'll be fine. Trust me. We'll throw it down a refuse shaft or something." Bethrian flashed a wicked smile Cylis didn't trust in the least. No matter—it was time to get out of here.

Once the two of them reached the door, Marva turned to greet them, eyebrows raised expectantly. "We got it," Cylis said, holding out the safe.

"Give it to her," Bethrian said.

Cylis turned to look at him. "Why?"

"Because we still have plaster dust on us. If we get searched, we can't have it. Go," Bethrian said to Marva. "Go back another way—not the way we came. We'll leave separately."

"Alright," Marva said, taking the safe and tucking it under her doublet, holding it in place with her upper arm and bracing it with her other hand. She gave Cylis a grin that made his heart skip. "I'll see you soon."

With the safe safely ensconced in their possession, the three of them went outside the chambers and into the nice and empty halls. With a little wave, Marva went down the north end of the hall while Cylis and Bethrian fumbled the lock into something somewhat presentable. "Somewhat" being a generous term for the dangled metal and busted wood. Their handiwork would be discovered by the next morning, at the latest.

"Let's go," Bethrian said once Marva's steps faded, walking down the hall in the opposite direction.

"What next?" Cylis asked softly. He patted the plaster dust off his shirt. He shouldn't have worn black. That was a poor choice.

"Why, I have missed far too much of this play. I need to change that." Bethrian flashed another winsome smile, as was his wont. Fuckwit. "You should consider attending, too. There will be events all evening, and we should be seen in public."

"Great. Just what I want to watch. A play."

"I'm sure the ladies will be happy to see you…"

"No." If one more person called him "Fenrick" he would show them what being a Soul Carver truly meant. They wouldn't be lusting over him if they witnessed him in the throes of his Soul Carver magic, full of purple skin and icy discharge. Then again…sigh. That could very well just make them want him more. He *did* have that effect on people—the more they saw of Cylis, the more they wanted.

In blissful silence, Cylis and Fuckwit turned down another corner, coming across yet another empty hallway. As much as Cylis hated to admit it, Bethrian did choose the time of their adventure well. No one was around. No one except…

Voices echoed down the hallway. Male voices. With stern steps. Clanging metal.

"Someone's coming," Cylis said. "Guards."

"Shit." Bethrian looked around them. "They're going to wonder why we're here."

The sounds grew louder—once the guards took a few more steps, they'd reach the corner and be discovered. There was nowhere to hide in the hallway. Even the little alcove that held a couple wooden chairs wouldn't conceal them.

Before he could react, Bethrian pushed Cylis into the alcove, slammed him against the wall, and pressed his lips against his.

Cylis thrashed and groaned, yet Bethrian held him in place with surprising strength, his moans of passionate bliss covering Cylis's muffled yelps of protest.

What the fuck? What was Fuckwit doing? No matter Cylis's movements and mangled curses, Bethrian kissed him harder, maneuvering his hands down his back. Bethrian's facial hair rubbed against Cylis's skin, making an unnatural scraping feeling of beard meeting shaved flesh. Bethrian's cologne wafted into his nose, along with his body musk—maybe others, especially women, liked how Bethrian smelled, but Cylis wasn't a woman.

Bethrian had five seconds to stop or he was going to get very hurt.

"What are you doing here?" The guard asked.

Sheepishly, Bethrian and Cylis turned to the guard, the red on Cylis's face very real as Bethrian's plan smashed into Cylis much as Bethrian's lips had done moments before.

"Malithians," the other guard muttered, turning and tugging his companion along the hallway. The other guard followed without so much as a backwards glance, leaving Cylis and Bethrian alone.

That was close. Far too close. And left Cylis feeling far too compromised.

"Let's go," Bethrian said once the guards were gone, holding Cylis a few moments longer than strictly necessary. "We have work to do."

Chapter 36

Caes

Royal plays weren't known for their brevity, and this one was no exception. It was a spectacle of dancing and singing that tried to reenact scenes from a past she only now remembered. And now scarred into her memory was the refrain:

Our goddess, our queen,
The brightest we have seen.
Caesonia the Divine,
The greatest of our time.

Maybe Lyritan liked such platitudes—he was a god, after all—but Caes was left feeling a bit...uncomfortable.

"You're beautiful," Alair whispered in her ear. The play was done, and Lyritan was now mingling with the crowd, people who both were awed and cowed by him in equal measure. As such, Caes was left with Alair, who held her closely as they danced to the music with others of the court. It was just them. Just them.

But I love Lyritan...

A familiar pang echoed through her chest, of loss and desire. Of memory that burned as it comforted. How Lyritan once held her as she cried under the night sky, promising that he would never leave her, that she would never feel the sting of betrayal again. That—together—they would make the world a place where no one had to hunger or fear.

No. Caes couldn't let Liuva distract her.

"I'd hope so," Caes muttered. "These undergarments I've been forced to wear are ridiculous."

"Oh?" Alair asked. "How so?"

"It's..." A shift yet not a shift. The damn thing did its job of protecting her skin against the heavy dark blue gown accented with a silver coronet, yet it was...She gave Alair a wide smile. "You'll see. Later." Lyritan had sent it with the dress she was wearing tonight so she felt obliged to wear it, but *why* did he send it? There was only one reason someone would wear such a thing—Lyritan was likely expecting more from their relationship. Soon. Tonight, even. That was the last thing she wanted to have happen.

Caes leaned forward and breathed in Alair's scent, relishing the hard muscles that were barely concealed under his surcoat. His mirrored eyes sparkled, looking at her. Only her. His hands curved over her back, moving ever lower, pressing her against him. Each finger dug into the brocade fabric, wrenching it, like he wanted to tear it apart. And she wanted him to. Tension coiled in her stomach, spreading an illicit heat through her, despite the audience.

"Later," he said to her. "I know that look."

"What look?"

He leaned towards her ear. "You're thinking about me inside you."

"I'm doing no such thing."

"No? Then tell me why your heart is racing." He looked at her and grinned, satisfied. "I thought so."

"You're insatiable."

"Only with you." He ran a light finger over her lips. "Don't worry—I *will* see this garment you're speaking of." A promise.

A cough from behind interrupted them, making her start like someone dumped cold water on her head. "Your Highness," Bethrian said, "I wanted to pay my respects this evening."

Caes turned and found Bethrian, who was dressed in a shiny crimson doublet and as polished as if he were present all night. Which he was, if anyone were to ask her. "Such formalities are not necessary with us, my lord," she said, giving Bethrian a respectful nod.

"Yes, greater ones are necessary," Alair jested, so low only Caes could hear.

"Still, Your Highness" –Bethrian bowed– "I wanted to make sure you knew that I thought tonight was a great success."

Great success.

"Oh? You enjoyed the play?"

"I enjoyed everything about this night."

They found the sword. They had to have. Bethrian wouldn't have bothered to make such empty platitudes otherwise. Not with her. Caes smiled. "Thank you, my lord. I'm pleased to hear it."

At that moment, Sabine approached, first curtseying to Caes and then to Bethrian. She was dressed in a gray silk gown that set off her gorgeous eyes.

"My," Bethrian said, "if this isn't quite the reunion."

"You're so clever, Lord Bethrian," Sabine said with a coy grin. "You always have the right things to say."

"And you have a tendency to appear right at the most opportune moments," Bethrian retorted.

"Surely, Lady Sabine didn't come here just to banter with you, my lord," Caes interrupted, before their thinly veiled bickering attracted attention. Back in Malithia, Bethrian had supported Seda's succession to the throne, while Sabine supported Flyntinia and Althain. The division was now moot, but old alliances created old habits.

"Indeed," Sabine said. "Your Highness, I was hoping to have a moment with you. In private, after this gathering."

"Of course. Tonight is not an option, for obvious reasons. But I have time tomorrow morning, if that is acceptable. In my sitting room."

"Perfect. I have a tea from Glynnith I'd be happy to share with you."

"Tea?" Bethrian snorted.

Caes ignored him. "That sounds wonderful. I think that—"

"My love," Lyritan said, approaching and banishing all except Alair with an abrupt wave. Bethrian and Sabine watched Lyritan as they left, clearly thinking that the conversation ended too soon, while Alair stayed back a respectful several feet. "Were you pleased with the play?"

"Very much so. I will never forget it." Caes leaned into Liuva's feelings—she *needed* Liuva's feelings—and so she gasped when Lyritan reached for her hands and pressed them against his lips. Her skin burned where he touched, an ignition of desire. Desire that was going to go unanswered.

Lyritan leaned toward her, his long hair brushing against her. His cheeks pressed against hers, his hand resting on her shoulder.

My love...

Caes didn't silence the thought. She echoed it. She leaned into him, and for a moment, Lyritan froze out of surprise, but then he smiled.

"Will you come with me?" Lyritan asked. "Both of you."

"Come with you?" Caes raised an eyebrow. "Leave the party?"

"This party is hardly my priority. Everything I did was all for you. And only you."

The scandalous shift. The invitation. It was too clear what Lyritan wanted.

Luckily, Caes and Alair had prepared for this eventuality.

"My lord," Caes said, "we have guests."

"They can wait."

"I haven't paid my respects to the queen, yet."

"Not necessary. She will understand your absence."

"If you insist, then—"

"Fire!" Voices rang out from the other side of the hall. Bodies thrashed, moving to get away from the blaze and black smoke that suddenly emanated from the other side of the room.

Lyritan looked in the direction of the chaos, frowning. Whatever fire there was wouldn't go far, not in this palace of stone. But depending on what Kerensa ignited, it would certainly cause a mess. And no shortage of chaos.

"Your people need you, my love," Caes said. "Go. I'm not going anywhere."

"No, you're going back to your chambers," Lyritan said. "Until this is settled." With that, Lyritan left to attend to the fire, and the people fleeing.

Alair moved to stand at her side, blood dripping from his ear. "You heard him," Alair said, both of them watching Lyritan snap orders at servants and guards, demanding order—and water. "We need to leave. But I have a different location in mind than your chambers."

"What did Kerensa do?" Caes asked Alair while they walked through the halls. People were darting both toward and away from the fire, leaving them more or less ignored in the disorder. "That was fast."

"I talked to her before the play—she stayed near convenient things all evening," Alair said, wiping the blood from his ear with his sleeve. "Things with candles nearby that will be easy to blame."

"I hope no one gets hurt."

"Doubt it. Kerensa's not cruel. I'm guessing a few tapestries and maybe some buffet tables have served their last day on this earth. The room is stone, so unless someone got unlucky enough to catch on fire, everyone will be fine." Alair squeezed her hand. "Don't worry." Caes wouldn't worry—Kerensa wasn't one to make innocents suffer if she could avoid it.

"Where are you taking me?" Caes asked. "This isn't the way back."

"No. I just figured since Lyritan was so nice to arrange everything for us, it would be a shame to waste."

"Everything?"

"You'll see." Heat pooled in her lower body at his tone of voice, low and seductive. He cocked his head and looked at her sidelong, his pupils wide even in the well-lit hallway. Alair looked like he was starving, and she a feast presented to him to consume.

Caes knew the general direction of where they were headed, but the random hallways yielded no clues to where they were going as Alair dipped a hand to her lower back and guided her forward, his fingers flitting across her spine and making her shiver. She wracked her brain, trying to wonder what he had meant with his reference to Lyritan. Did he mean....

Yes. He did mean *that*. Her heart lurched—she wanted his touch, here and now, in places they couldn't dare with risk of an audience.

"I still don't know where you're taking me." She bit her lip, feeling her cheeks flush at the way that his hand moved down to cup the curve of her rear.

"Sshhh. Let me worry about that," he whispered into her ear, drawing her closer to his side. She leaned into his warmth, relishing the way that she could feel the strength in his coiled muscles even though the layers of his clothes. Her breasts were suddenly sensitive against the shift's gauzy fabric, something that was now in the way.

A few turns and several long halls later, they were passing through large wooden doors that could only be leading to one place.

"Alair, this is the throne room," Caes said, a whisper that echoed in the cavernous hall. The space was nearly dark, as only a few cursory torches were lit in sconces against the walls. The thrones at the end were empty, waiting for their royal owners to return and claim them.

The gleam in Alair's eye was wicked in the low torchlight as he shut the door behind them, the latch thudding into place and echoing in the quiet. He kept pace alongside her, steering her towards a nearby column until her back hit the cool, carved stone. Her hands met the firm planes of his chest as he crowded her in, his hands on either sides of her shoulders as he dipped his head and placed a line of kisses up her neck, making her shiver.

"What if we get discovered? They'll be angry." Despite the barren space, Caes couldn't help but keep her voice low, even as a thrill ran through her. They weren't supposed to be here. It was forbidden. Wrong. To desecrate this space, the center of a foreign court, was almost unthinkable. But as Alair slipped a finger underneath the neck of her dress, teasing it off her shoulder, she shuddered and felt her resolve weaken.

"Yes, probably. But where else would I take you?" He smirked at her, and for a moment she caught sight of what he must've been like as a younger man before the Soul Carver trials twisted him—daring and full of mischief. And Caes...Caes never had a chance to do anything like this. He was offering her pleasure and danger and she was ready to seize both.

Still, she maintained her conviction that this was a terrible idea. Although that was increasingly hard to do as she felt Alair's hard length nudging insistently into her stomach, his bulk trapping her against the pillar. "What if someone sees us?"

"Then I'll make them forget." He moved a hand around the back of her neck, tangling his fingers in her hair, drawing her in for a kiss.

Caes lost herself in the heat of Alair's mouth, his tongue sweeping against hers and making her moan. She moved her hands up to twine her arms around his neck, and it was only when her brain, slow as molasses, caught up to what he'd said that she drew away again, employing every last bit of her willpower.

"I don't want you in pain for something like this." Caes touched a finger to Alair's lip, although she couldn't help but smile as he reached out with his teeth and nipped it. Even though they were excellent at ignoring it—or pretending to—their magic always pained Soul Carvers.

"Caes, there's been very little in my life that I've enjoyed using my gifts for. Let me have this. I promise—you'll have no consequences from this night other than satisfaction."

The hungry look in his eyes, the demanding press of his body, finally shattered what was left of her stoicism. Heat flared in her core, the ache building at the way that Alair was so totally consumed by his need for her that he would risk this—the use of magic, physical agony—just to have her.

She let out a soft sigh that was still loud in the cavernous space. "...Alright."

Alair grinned.

Caes half-expected him to take her right there, to undress her and have her against the pillar, like a noble taking a serving girl. The thought thrilled her in its own right—the passion, the frenzied nature of a coupling like that—so much so that she was almost disappointed when Alair abruptly pulled away. "Where are you going?"

Alair cocked an eyebrow, beckoning her with a crooked finger. "You didn't think I was going to take you against the *wall*, now did you? Not when there's such a more suitable option for a princess."

He caught her hand and tugged her forward, their fingers twisting together. He pulled her further into the room—towards the twin thrones—Caes's heart beating louder with each step. His hand returned to her back, those clever fingers snaking their way further and further down her spine until his hand was cupping her ass.

Trembling, she looked at him, her arousal mingling with fear. All they were doing was walking in an empty room. It was just walking. It was a room. But it was *this* room. Where they weren't supposed to be. And if Lyritan caught them doing *this* after he was interrupted so...

But there was no more time for worrying when they reached the dais. Once at the foot of the thrones, Caes was done thinking. She reached for Alair's head and pressed her lips against his. His hands wrapped around her back, pulling her closer to him. Gods and goddesses, the taste of him was familiar and stirred something deep within her. But as she was about to kiss him even deeper, he pulled his head away.

"Now, let's see this shift you told me so much about." His hands roamed over the front of her dress, his eyes following the movements. When his fingers brushed over the peaks of her breasts, she let out a soft gasp, her hands flying up to his wrists.

"Will you be able to help me get it back on again?"

"I think I can handle some laces." Proving his statement, Alair reached behind her back and tugged at the top lace of her gown, gently undoing it as she worked at the buttons as best she could. "Let me," he said.

She did.

Button by button. Lace by lace. Alair took his time undoing the fastenings, letting it fall down her shoulders and back when he was finished. She was wearing nothing but the shift and the silver coronet, and he stood there, staring at her.

Under his piercing gaze, Caes felt herself shivering with desire and anticipation. Exposed.

"...I think I need to thank Lyritan," was all Alair said.

She let out a short laugh. "Maybe keep that thanks to yourself." The shift in question was made of dark blue gauze, covered with dark blue flower appliques all over her body, yet it showed enough to leave little to the imagination.

He swallowed hard and took her hand, leading her to the king's throne. "You can't mean for me to sit here," she said, looking behind her at an invisible audience.

"I definitely do."

"But I'm not—"

He placed a finger on her lips, covering her protests. She closed her eyes while his finger slowly circled her mouth. "You are not Lyritan's queen, or the queen of any kingdom or empire. But you are mine. And I will worship you."

His dark mirrored eyes shimmered as he looked at her, desire and devotion laying in his gaze.

Slowly, she sat on the throne, placing a hand on each arm. This was the seat of the rulers of Reyvern, and there she sat, her core throbbing in anticipation while Alair bowed before her, placing his hands on her knees. She reached a hand to caress his hair, but he gently guided it out of the way. "Not yet," Alair said.

"You're sure no one will hear us?"

"I'm sure. I can hear if people approach long before you will. Trust me."

She did. He saved her in Malithia. He came back from the dead for her. Time and time again he proved that he deserved her trust. Trusting him in this was a small matter, and easily done.

Readily done.

She smiled, which turned into a moan as his hands slid up her shift, soon teasing at her slick entrance. Biting on her fingers, it was all she could do to stay still for him as she worked the fabric to her waist.

"Alair..."

He sat back and inspected her, all of her, his black hair now past his shoulders. "Hmm...not quite right."

"What do you—"

"Shh," he said, holding a finger to his lips, covering a grin. "Let me." He grabbed her ankle, moving one onto the throne's arm. "Lean back," he commanded. She did. Her weight moved, he grabbed the second ankle and placed her foot on the other arm, leaving her fully displayed. "Much better." To emphasize the point he reached to her, spreading her. What they were doing before was scandalous. This was depraved. She had sat on so many thrones before, had thousands stare at her. The familiarity of the space made it all to easy for her to imagine what it would be like if thousands were watching her now.

Oh hells, she was throbbing, moving herself wider for his touch. She needed it, now.

All her thoughts were pushed aside as he knelt on the ground and took her into his mouth, plunging his fingers deep within her. She writhed against his lips, shaking as his other hand alternated between touching her over the fabric and under. His fingers expertly delved inside her, moving in ways he knew she loved, and that would undo her. He nibbled on that most sensitive part, using his teeth to delicately taunt and tease.

"Alair—"

"Yes?" He lifted his head to look at her, his mouth wet. She panted, gasping for breath. "I thought so." Smirking, he went back to his task, flickering his fingers so that she bucked against his face. Who cared that she was on a throne? She was losing herself in him. Her pleasure built within her, higher and higher—

And then Alair pulled away, right as she was on the precipice.

"Don't you dare," Caes gasped. She needed him. All of him. Now.

"I dare plenty," he said, undoing his breeches. His lips pursed as he pulled out his member, stroking it and standing over Caes, who let a leg dangle over the side of the throne. She couldn't look away from him, from what was waiting for her. He was obviously ready for her, ready to take her. Her legs trembled. She was so close. It wouldn't take long for her to take her pleasure. "I think we should—"

"No." Caes turned over and grabbed the back of the wooden throne, presenting herself to him, moving her ass so that he could see everything. "Like this." Where before she was nervous, now she had no shame. She needed him. All of him. Now.

"Caes," he said reverently, lifting the shift and touching her slick throbbing center with his finger. If he had any argument, it was forgotten. The sensation of his fingers was soon replaced by his manhood. It pushed at her opening for a moment, circling her as he moistened himself with her, and then, slowly, he entered her with a deep sigh. "Gods, you're perfect," he said.

He stretched her, pushing her to her edges until she couldn't take any more. She moaned, biting her lip and gripping the back of the throne. Him within her, a part of her, was an exquisite ecstasy.

And then he started to move.

They both fell silent, voices gone and then replaced by a chorus of sighs and groans of pleasure. He filled her completely, rubbing on her with his rough hands in that perfect way as she gripped the throne's back. His other hand held on to her hip, guiding her over him, again and again. Curious, she turned around to watch him. His body was like sculpted stone, his muscles clenching, focused on his ministrations. Soul Carvers were designed for battle, they devoted themselves to it, and their powerful form was evidence of the results. Carefully, she arched her hips, taking him deeper into her, and far as she could.

Their movements fell into a rhythm, both muffled and all-encompassing. There was only him and her. Him inside her. Him with her. Her pleasure broke over her almost unexpectedly, and his followed, their cries echoing through the staid hall.

Once he was spent he rested against her until his breaths evened, and then he pulled her to sit on his lap while he sat on the throne, still inside her. His skin was damp from sweat, his heart racing so hard she could feel it. Carefully, she wiped her hair from her face and relaxed against him. They would have to figure out how to get her presentable, but that was a problem for later.

"I love you," he said, brushing her hair out of her face. "More than I can express."

She kissed him in answer. "You've proven that to me every day we have been together."

"And there will be many more. Thousands more." He held her hand, gently rubbing it with his thumb and fingers. "I promise." Here she was, on a throne with her lover, a Soul Carver, still inside her. She looked over the empty hall. In a way, it was like she was seeing the dangers that waited for them. It was him and her against everything—and with him, she felt like she had a chance to survive. She had a life of betrayals, but in Alair she had everything she needed.

Some promises were far too uncertain to keep, but Alair obviously meant every single word. For now, that was enough.

Chapter 37

Liuva

My early life with my mother was paradise. It was an existence where I did not have to think—I only had to feel. And be. I knew I was loved in the way that I knew my feet touched the earth's soil.

But all dreams end, and all dreamers wake.

After Lyritan revealed how I was made, and how I was created by my mother to die, my life was irrevocably changed, like how petals once plucked off a flower cannot be replaced. If my mother noticed the change in me, she said nothing, distracted by her own concerns and plots. I thought little of Karima, then, of her monsters, magic, or creations. However, my mother's attention was taken by her sister. Whether she was consumed with the desire for power or revenge or even hated, I could not say. Never mind the thousand other duties that called to her as a goddess.

I was an afterthought for her. Why would I be anything else? I never required more from her before.

As for me, I did as Lyritan bid. I pretended that nothing was wrong, no matter how much my heart burned to utter accusations to my mother. I danced with the same nature spirits as always. I wandered the woods and fields. I visited the mortals from time to time, watching their lives from a distance, and how they aged and died in seemingly little more than the turn of a year. Poor mortals. They barely had time to appreciate the world around them before they were torn from it.

Yet my life had come to be more than this farce. Lyritan still came to me in secret, as he always did, and taught me everything there was to know of love. A real love. One where he gave to me as much as I gave him. A love where he treasured every single moment with me. I had no thought too small, no wish too frivolous, that he would not endeavor to fulfill.

"Why me?" I asked him one night, while we were both sated with our lovemaking. "Why me out of all the other women in this world?"

Why me when you are seducing my mother? *I left unsaid.* By then a nugget of doubt had started to bury into my soul, growing and spreading its roots through me. My mother needed my power, yes. But couldn't Lyritan use it as well? Did Lyritan truly have nothing to gain from me, except for love?

"You have never asked me for anything more than what I can give with my own hands," Lyritan said. "Do you know how rare that is amongst the gods? Even mortals can't stop asking us for favors—it is in their nature to beg for what blessings they can wrench from us."

I did know the rarity. But I could not resist teasing him. "I just asked you for plenty," I said, running a finger over the marbled panes of his chest.

Lyritan pulled me closer, a brilliant smile on his perfect face. His golden eyes stared at me, as full and turbulent as the sun. "That is something I am more than willing to always give."

My head now on his chest, he breathed a few deep breaths into my hair. And then his mood turned solemn, nothing like the lighthearted frolic we had just engaged in. "We cannot continue like this forever," he said.

"I know." As something adjacent to the divine, I had a small taste of what forever truly meant. And Lyritan was right—not even mountains stayed untouched for eternity. How could we hope to hide from a goddess for all time when we had to worry that the very birds and trees could spill our secret?

But a greater fear worked its way into my heart. "Are you saying you no longer wish to see me?" I asked, my heart both desperate for and fearing the answer.

"Never. Even if my heart be turned to stone, it will always love you."

I kissed him, then. Even as I worried about what was to come next, for something *was* going to come. Much as one can sense an approaching storm, the winds of our fates were rushing towards us, a blight from which we could not run.

"I have a plan, Liuva," Lyritan said, stroking my hair. "A way to free you forever. But do you trust me? This won't work unless you absolutely trust me."

I did. I trusted him with everything that was within my heart. I trusted him until I felt my being break with it.

I trusted him until he brought about my ruin.

Chapter 38

Bethrian

The next morning, Bethrian went to visit Cylis to bask in their accomplishments. They had the magical sword. Well, a piece of it. But that piece was apparently enough. And now he had the life experience necessary to write a character in a future Passionflower novel who was a thief. A thief who stole valuable jewels—and maidenheads. A true artist never passed up a chance for inspiration.

So, while Bethrian wouldn't be keen to visit Cylis under normal circumstances, their victory was enough to put a spring in his step after Fer the Soul Carver mumbled Cylis's invitation.

But much like the fantasies he spun as Peony Passionflower, reality was a bit more underwhelming.

"That's it?" Bethrian asked, staring at the metal shard on the rough wooden table. The shard was half the length of a rolling pin, jagged and sharp. That part was obvious—it was a piece of a sword. The surprising part was that other than some weird markings on the metal, it looked the same as every other weapon.

"Yup, that's it," Cylis said, sitting on the chair, arms crossed. Marva sat on Cylis's bed, watching the exchange with her mirrored eyes. Fer had left them alone, telling Cylis to do his own errands next time.

"No chance that this is—"

"No, Fuckwit," Cylis said. "It's the sword."

"It feels…charged to us," Marva said. "Trust us. This isn't a normal piece of metal. Besides, why else would the lord go through the trouble of putting this in a safe?"

"There was nothing else in it?"

Cylis shrugged. "Some rings, some stones. I threw them out the window."

The lord in Bethrian groaned at the lost valuables. "Could have given them to me."

"You were the one who said they'd be looking for a jewelry thief. Better we don't have those jewels if they look our way."

Bethrian wasn't thinking clearly when Cylis was the voice of reason. "So, this is the sword. How's *that* supposed to be of any use?"

Cylis shrugged. "No idea. It's not like we can ask the blacksmiths here to make a hilt for it or anything—too many questions."

That *would* engender too many questions. But to put the shard to use at the mountain, Caes would presumably have to hold the thing, and this thing was sharp. Too sharp. Bethrian sat on the chair, staring at the little piece of metal that had caused them all so much difficulty. Despite knowing what it was, Bethrian felt nothing. No shiver. No tremor. He even tried to embrace his inner Soul Carver and imagined he hated everything—still nothing.

Oh, well. Bethrian was talented at many things, but esoteric sensing wasn't one of them, unfortunately.

"How'd you ever get the safe open?" Bethrian asked. "It was solid."

"Kerensa," Marva said. "She said in her prior life she developed certain…skills."

"I see." Bethrian bit back a smile. It warmed his cold heart to think of the Soul Carver picking open the lord's safe. "Where's Kerensa now?"

"With Caes," Cylis said. "Sabine is visiting and she asked Ker to be her guard while Alair presumably gets some rest."

"Rest from 'guarding.'" Marva said knowingly.

Now Bethrian fully smiled. He had been watching the tension between Caes, Alair, and Lyritan for weeks now, and it was highly amusing to watch Lyritan fail so spectacularly. "I'm guessing Caes had something to do with the fire last night?"

"No. Never," Cylis said. "Caes doesn't start fires."

"Right…Now, what does Sabine want?" Bethrian asked. "Is it just a social call?" A memory flickered. Tea. That was right—Sabine said as much last night. She wanted to give Caes tea.

"No idea," Cylis said. A pause, and then, "What are you thinking, Bethy?"

"Nothing. Just...no. Just old feelings from when Sabine and I were on opposite sides at court."

"That's right," Marva said. "How did the two of you cooperate enough to save Caes? She was poisoned in Glynnith, right?"

"Cooperate? Easy. We may have picked our sides, but we had nothing against each other personally. And we both had our motives for saving Caes." Sabine liked Caes, while Bethrian wanted to use her. At least Caes benefitted from that arrangement.

The three of them fell silent. Bethrian scratched his beard. Sabine was Caes's friend, as much as one could be at court, but her alliance with Flyntinia complicated things. So far, Flyntinia had been on good behavior during her time in Reyvern—despite Althain's murder—but something about this itched Bethrian the wrong way. Sabine had showed up here. Now. With Flyntinia.

Sabine, with her fine manners and somewhat sudden obsession with her husband's deer antler sigil...

"Bethrian?" Marva asked. "What's wrong?"

His prophecy, his *oral* prophecy, told him to "beware the hidden heart."

Heart.

Heart.

Hart.

Hart?

Fuck.

Bethrian's chest tensed. "Come on!" he suddenly yelled at the Soul Carvers, rushing for the door. He didn't stop to see whether the others followed. "Find Caes!"

Chapter 39

Caes

"I'm surprised you're awake this early," Sabine said to Caes, the almond sugar cookies they were snacking on resting on a platter before them. The tea Sabine had brought was sitting in a kettle on the table near the wall, steeping for the exact thirteen minutes that Sabine insisted it required. The tea smelled good, at any rate, bearing a rich citrus and chocolate scent. For this meeting they weren't in Caes's chambers, but were instead in one of the royal sitting rooms, something private, but a little brighter than the dark space Caes and Alair called their own. Caes had changed her mind about the meeting place this morning, wanting a different scenery and to give Alair a chance for better rest.

"I don't sleep well," Caes said truthfully. "There's a lot occurring."

"That is true." Sabine fidgeted with her fingers. "Though you seem to be accepted at this court well enough."

"I think they're just tolerating me and hoping I go away."

"Tolerance turns into acceptance once they get used to you. Trust me—I've been a newcomer at court before."

"Yes, but Malithia never expected you to rule it."

"No, that is true," Sabine agreed.

The conversation lapsed. Sabine smoothed her gray skirts, the deer antler pendant she wore more often than not shining against her skin. Her friend's eyes were red and puffy—was she sleepless too? Poor Sabine. Caes had been so absorbed with her own trials that she barely spared a thought for her friend. Something she would make a point to rectify, while she could.

"I'm hoping to return to Malithia soon," Sabine suddenly said. "I've been away from home long enough."

"You are? I thought Flyntinia—"

"I don't think she wishes to stay here through winter," Sabine said. "This court isn't Malithia."

"The weather is harsher, that is for sure."

Suddenly, Kerensa entered the room. "Good morning, Lady Sabine," Kerensa said, her voice oddly chipper. "Is the tea ready?"

"No," Sabine said. "And I'm afraid I only brought enough for two."

"What? I was looking forward to it."

"I'm sorry."

"Sorry, Ker," Caes echoed. She should've known better than to mention a new luxury to Kerensa. For all Soul Carvers liked to pretend to be contrary and eschew frivolous things, that didn't extend to their stomachs.

"Fine." Kerensa huffed, taking her place against the wall. This morning Kerensa wore a burgundy surcoat over breeches. Alair had often wore the style from his youth at the Malithian court and Kerensa adopted it, claiming that it was much easier to store things in pockets. At the realization she wouldn't be getting the tea, the Soul Carver faked pouted and let out a little breath of smoke, making Caes shake with stifled laughter. Caes would find something good for her to eat later, to make up for this. Ker liked chocolates, and Caes was sure there was a trove somewhere in the kitchens.

"Is it ready?" Caes asked. "I think it's been thirteen minutes."

"Come," Sabine said, standing and ignoring Caes's observation. Kerensa frowned. "I want to see the Burning Hand. It's visible through this window, isn't it?"

"I'm not sure."

"Let's look." Before Caes could stop her, Sabine walked over to a window draped with heavy blue velvet. "Is that it?" Sabine pointed at a large mountain in the distance.

"Yes," Caes said. The mountain towered over the surrounding countryside. There was no snow on it, despite its height, as best as Caes could see. It was strange—it was so close that she could see it, but it may as well have been on the other side of the empire. In certain light, the mountain seemed to shimmer. Whether that was from some twist of the mountain air, an aura around the mountain, or her own imagination was impossible to say.

"I'm glad I have this chance to see you," Sabine said, still looking out the window.

"Same." Caes smiled. "You've done so much for me."

"The honor was mine, my friend." Sabine rubbed her eyes.

"What's wrong?"

"Nothing. Just the start of a headache." Sabine gestured towards the tea. "I think it's time."

"Yeah, that's not happening," Kerensa said. "Not without me tasting it first."

"Ker, what are you doing?" Caes asked, striding towards the Soul Carver. "It's tea."

"Exactly." She placed her hands on her hips. "One sip and you can have the rest."

"Kerensa, are you truly accusing Sabine of what I think you are?" Caes asked.

"Her? Not necessarily. But considering the company she keeps, let me be paranoid."

The blood left Sabine's face. "I wouldn't..."

"I know," Caes said. "Which is why we're going to humor Ker, and then once she's happy we're going to pretend she didn't have such awful manners."

Kerensa smirked. "Do it for Alair. What would he want you to do?"

Caes rubbed her temple. *She* was getting a headache now. All this over a cup of tea—what was Ker thinking? She wanted to taste the damn thing that badly she'd accuse Sabine of poison?

"Fine," Caes said. Kerensa walked over to where the tea was steeping, poured, and took one of the cups—and a long sip. Meanwhile, Sabine stood, frozen. That was strange.

"Are you alright?" Caes asked.

"Fine," Sabine croaked out.

Before she could question her friend further, Caes turned towards Ker, who was loudly smacking her lips. "I guess it's fine," Kerensa said, passing the cup to Caes. "I expected something not so...tart."

"Yes, it's known for that," Sabine squeaked. Sabine's fist was clenched as she took her own cup from Kerensa, who was helpful enough to pour two.

"Come," Caes said, clutching her cup. "Let's sit."

Caes walked over to the couch and raised the cup to her nose. It *was* an oddly tart smelling tea—citrus and...mint? And some berry Caes couldn't place. Caes lifted the cup to her lips.

Suddenly Bethrian darted through the door, followed by Cylis and Marva. "No!" Bethrian screamed, jumping and tackling Sabine. Cylis grabbed Caes and pulled her backward, making her throw the cup towards the ceiling, where tea sprayed in the air and rained over the furniture and rugs.

"What's the meaning of this?" Caes cried out. "Get off her!"

"She's trying to kill you," Bethrian howled. He sat, pulling up Sabine with him. Her friend was shaking, her gaze darting back and forth. "She's trying to kill you," he said again.

"What are you talking about?"

"The tea," Bethrian said. "Admit it, Sabine. The tea."

What? Could her friend really have...

Caes covered her mouth. "Sabine, is this true?"

The look Sabine gave made Caes stop breathing. "Yes," she whispered. "Flyntinia."

"Why?" Caes choked out. "Why?"

"Because" –Sabine swallowed– "I knew I was going to die doing this. But at least my sisters would live."

"Your sisters..." Then Caes remembered—Sabine had been brought to Malithia as a hostage for her family's good behavior. If Malithia changed its mind...if Flyntinia convinced the emperor to change his mind...

"I would've helped you," Caes said. "We would've saved them. We still can."

"You would have tried. But we both know that you have a different path."

Caes shook her head. "None of that. No one died. We have time to—"

"Ker!" Cylis screamed.

Kerensa.

Kerensa was sitting on the floor, blood dripping from her mouth. Her dark eyes were wide, trapped as if seeing some invisible horror. Shaking, she clenched her fists and gasped for breath, her mouth opening and closing in desperation.

"Ker, no. No. No. No. Help her!" Cylis cried. Kerensa collapsed onto Cylis, her head resting on his lap. Gently, he rubbed her hair and patted her face. The icy discharge from his eyes dripped onto her face and on the ground. "Stay here, Ker. No. Fuck, no."

This couldn't be happening. It wasn't happening. Not Ker.

Caes was on the floor next to Cylis. She didn't remember moving. Suddenly, she found herself screaming.

Moments moved like hours, and yet it was not long enough.

With Cylis holding her, pleading for her to live, Kerensa died.

Chapter 40

Caes

D ead.
Dead. Dead. Dead.

Kerensa's empty eyes stared at the ceiling, her mouth open, blood and foam trickling out of the corners. Her pale skin was now purple, declaring the agony her last moments brought her.

"Kerensa..." Caes whispered. And then she sobbed, biting her hands. Ker was going to move. She was going to sit up and laugh and tease them for making such a fuss over her. She was going to...

She had to...

Cylis hovered over Kerensa's body, shaking it. "Come on, Ker. Wake up, dammit. Wake up. Wake up." Tears streamed down Cylis's face. "Wake up..."

This couldn't be happening. No. Not to Kerensa. She was so alive just moments before, annoyed at Sabine about the damn tea.

The tea.

Sabine.

Slowly, Caes rose and faced Sabine, grinding her teeth. Her divine power stirred under her skin, pulsating gold in her veins. Heat gathered on her flesh, swelling and threatening to burst with her budding magic. She could reduce Sabine to ash. She could destroy her in a moment.

No.

Taking deep breaths, Caes forced the power down. Away. She couldn't touch her power for this, not when the cost was far too high. Not when Sabine's death would surely bring Caes's own.

And she didn't need to use her magic to handle this.

Marva stood guard over Sabine, who was still on the floor next to Bethrian. Absentmindedly, Bethrian patted Sabine's back as she sobbed. Bethrian stared straight ahead, lost in his own thoughts.

"I didn't mean to," Sabine said to Caes, lifting her tear-stained face. "I didn't want to. I'm so sorry." She wiped her eyes with her sleeves and sniffled. "I didn't want this. I begged not to have to do this. Please, believe me."

Caes collapsed on the floor, watching her former friend. Sabine's body shook and she wrapped her arms around herself, rocking back and forth. What was Caes supposed to do? One of her friends was dead at the hands of another, through a poison meant for her. What was she supposed to do?

What could she do?

Sabine had saved her life, back in Malithia. A debt was owed.

A debt she didn't know if she had it in her to repay.

"Your Highness?" Marva asked. "We will have company soon." Yes, they would be interrupted. Someone had to have heard. Guards and courtiers would be intruding on their misery.

What should she do? Should she leave Sabine for the court's justice—and Lyritan's? There was no doubt what route that justice would take. If Lyritan was willing to order a girl beaten—if not killed—over an alleged theft, what would he do to someone who tried to kill her? Lyritan wouldn't care that Sabine had little choice in the matter. Flyntinia would've been more than willing to carry out her threats to Sabine's family if she had not done what she wanted. Would Caes have done any differently, to save those she loved?

The cost of love was pain and vulnerability.

"Sabine," Caes asked, "do you want to go home? For good."

Sabine nodded and whispered, "More than anything."

"Take her," Caes said to Marva without looking away from Sabine. Sabine's eyes widened.

"Your Highness?" Marva asked.

"Fer and Janell want to go back to Malithia. They've been patient, but we all know that what's to come needs willing volunteers, and they don't want to be here, in this foreign kingdom, while we're gone." Fer and Janell respected Caes and obeyed her—but they wouldn't undertake such a task for her, and she wasn't about to ask them. "Make sure they take Sabine home first—alive and whole—and then they are discharged from my service," Caes said. "With my gratitude," she added. Fer seemed to like Sabine—hopefully, that would be enough to ensure she made it home safely. Regardless, the two Soul Carvers wouldn't make this a pleasant journey for her. Soul Carvers protected their own.

"What?" Cylis hissed. "What are you doing?"

"Is that an order, Your Highness?" Marva asked, her jaw set.

"Yes. A direct order."

"You can't let her escape," Cylis said. "She killed Ker. Caes, you can't be doing this. She. Killed. Ker."

Caes stood and took a deep breath, brushing her skirts. She straightened her back. "Go," she said to Marva. To Cylis and others, she said, "Sabine saved my life. More than once. I will not take her life. A debt is owed—it is now repaid."

"But—"

"She intended to kill *me*, Cylis. Not Ker. And none of you can claim you would've done differently if Flyntinia had threatened you in the same manner. You all know Flyntinia. You know what she would've done. And you know what Sabine has done for me." Caes blinked back tears. This was a nightmare. It had to be. She would wake and Kerensa would be fine and this was all a dream. Caes swallowed a sob. She had to prepare to manage Lyritan—she couldn't be so lost in her grief now. There was a time to mourn, but that time would come after contending with the god. And his wrath.

Marva and Sabine stole out of the room, Marva yanking her away and down a hall when Sabine paused to give Caes one more pained glance. Then she was gone. Caes stared at the empty spot where Sabine had stood. Somehow, Caes knew she'd never see her former friend again. How could she? Sabine was going to Cyvid, while Caes was likely dying at the Burning Hand. But Sabine...Sabine had helped her navigate the Malithian court, saved her from Seda, and nursed her during the poisoning. Sabine had gained her trust in a way few had. But the two of them were mere players in others' games, and Sabine had been forced to the wrong side.

"We can't let this go," Cylis ranted. "I won't. Caes, how could you?"

"And we're not." Caes felt power stirring under her skin. From the way Cylis jerked she could only imagine how her eyes shone. "There's only one person to blame for this. Flyntinia."

"Caesonia." Lyritan dashed into the room, all but crashing into her at his frantic pace. His golden hair was disheveled, like he had ran from the other side of the castle. He probably had, as his body was slick with sweat under his linen shirt and brown leather jerkin. Was he training before he heard what happened?

Who cared? He was here. Someone who could protect her was here. No matter how she felt about the god, he would protect her from Flyntinia. Flyntinia was only a mortal woman—she was nothing against a god.

"Lyritan," Caes said, melting with relief. Cylis went to get Alair, leaving her with a silent Bethrian for moments that felt too long. Until now, she didn't realize how much Kerensa's death had frightened her, how much tension she held. And so, she gave into the angry sobs she had held back, not caring that it made her appear anything but a princess.

"You're safe, my love," Lyritan whispered, his arms warm and comforting. "I promise." He regarded Kerensa's body. "I will order her to be treated as royalty, for she gave her life for yours."

Caes nodded in gratitude and wiped her eyes. Kerensa would've liked that. She coughed, trying to find words. She had to tell Lyritan what happened, if she wanted justice for Kerensa. "I'll never be safe. Not while the one who caused this is still alive."

"Who?" Gold light flickered behind the god's narrowed eyes. The air danced around the god, shivering with an eldritch energy, like the air itself would bend and twist to the god's will. "Who did this?" he asked, his voice low and rigid. "My love, tell me."

Caes swallowed. She had nothing to fear from him. Not now. "Flyntinia—the lady from Malithia."

"I know of her."

"She sent an assassin to do her work for her. She tried to poison me."

Lyritan looked over the room. "And where's the man?"

"Gone. My Soul Carvers took care of it." Man? Caes would let him believe that Flyntinia sent a man and not Sabine. And the Soul Carvers did, in fact, take care of the assassin. If asked later, she'd claim that grief overwhelmed her.

"Good." Silent, he stood and took Caes upright with him, wrapping an arm protectively around her. Her heart skipped, and she longed to push herself further into his embrace.

He loves me. See?

"Do you want to go to your chambers?" Lyritan asked, rubbing a hand gently on her back. They walked towards the door, to the hall where others had already gathered during the commotion. Nobles and servants alike peered to watch their prince-turned-god. Surely, rumors of Caes's death or worse had spread, so it was no wonder people were curious. "You need to rest," Lyritan said softly. "There's no need for you to be involved further. Alair can stay with you while I take care of this."

"No." Caes shook her head violently and clenched her jaw. "I want to see this through to its end. I don't want to give her a chance to escape."

"As you wish, my love, though I don't recall you ever wishing to witness violence."

"You never saw me lose one of my closest friends." *More than one*, she left unsaid.

"Someday, you will never have to fear losing anything again. Soon."

Once they encountered guards, Lyritan barked out orders that Flyntinia and the rest of her Malithian entourage be summoned to the throne room, his voice no longer that of a comforting lover. Did Sabine make it out of the city already, or at least the palace? Would the Soul Carvers keep their word and take her to Cyvid? Caes could only hope so. She had done what she could for Sabine—she was on her own now.

As for Flyntinia…Flyntinia had a lot to answer for.

The crowds grew thick as the two of them made their way to the throne room, the same place where Alair had taken her just the night before. The ecstasy of their lovemaking now felt like a lifetime ago, crushed under her grief. As he did the last time he was in this room with her, Lyritan placed Caes on the queen's throne, while he took his place on the king's.

Where were the king and queen? It didn't matter.

Ker was dead, Sabine was gone, and Flyntinia was to blame. Caes was beyond caring about propriety.

Several anxious moments passed while throngs pressed into the room, muttering and gawking. Caes could only imagine what she looked like, her divine magic coursing under her skin, bubbling under her hands. It burned, dancing on the edges of pain, but what was pain at a time like this? Meanwhile, Lyritan was leaking gold, which oozed out from his nails, his eyes, and glowed under his skin, like a light lingered under the prince's flesh. What did the mortals think when looking at them, their putative divine emperor and empress on their thrones? Whatever Caes's plan was for their future, she'd embrace this role for now—she would see justice done for her friend.

Suddenly, Alair ran through the crowd, pushing aside whomever he came across, using his gift to make the unwilling get out of his way, sending them careening to the ground. Blood leaked from his ear and was smeared across a cheek. He approached her, ignoring Lyritan. "Are you alright?" he whispered, kneeling before her.

"I am." Now that he was here, she could handle anything.

"I'm sorry," he said, lines marring his forehead. Grabbing her hands, he rubbed them with his fingers, looking her over as if checking that she was, in fact, still alive. "I should've been there."

"You're here, and that's what matters. Stay."

He nodded and took his place behind her. "Always."

More rustling. More chaos. Reyvern's king and queen entered the room, holding their own small court in the corner, watching what was to occur. They didn't try to interfere with the god on the throne, or even utter a hint of protest—Lyritan was a bolt of lightning ready to strike. Only a fool would get in his way. His hands gripped the throne's arms, searing the wood. Phelan's skin smoked, the scent of cooking meat wafting to her.

"My love, justice will come," Caes said gently to Lyritan. She couldn't have Phelan destroyed in his rage—she needed Lyritan alive.

"For doing this to you, they will burn." His eyes were golden orbs, his expression a mask of solid fury.

"They will," she said. "But not yet."

He nodded and stared at the courtiers, as still as if he was stone once more.

Another wave of commotion and the crowd exclaimed as Flyntinia was brought before them, hauled between two guards. Others of the Malithian company stood behind her, their arms restrained. Caes could only imagine what the Reyverni courtiers were thinking. Flyntinia was part of a Malithian delegation—harming her was as good as declaring war.

Too bad—she brought this war upon herself.

Flyntinia, the former jewel of the Malithian court, fell to her knees. Her piercing eyes took in Caes sitting on the throne and sneered. "I should've known," Flyntinia said.

Lyritan raised his hand and the entire room fell silent. Even Flyntinia. "Your name," Lyritan ordered.

Flyntinia did not answer.

"Your name," Lyritan said again, harsher, sending a jolt of light through his body, like he was struck by lightning. The sparks danced on the ground before they faded into nothing.

"Lyr, my love," Caes said softly, "it is not worth burdening yourself for such a trivial matter. I can tell you this myself. This is Lady Flyntinia of Malithia, former mistress of Emperor Barlas Tuncer."

"And mother of his son, Althain," Flyntinia clearly said. "A son I would still have, were it not for you."

"I have told you as much before and I will say it again for all to hear," Caes said. "I regret his death. I regret everything about it. Althain was an admirable man, who would've made an excellent emperor. And he was my friend," she finished softly. Lyritan laid back against the throne, his expression almost...proud?

"'Was,'" Flyntinia said. "If not for you, he would still be here."

"That is true," Caes admitted. "And if not for me, several of us wouldn't be here, including our divine lord who is beside us now." Some muttered in the crowd at that. "But I did not cause Althain's death. You *know* this. He wouldn't have wanted any of this. And you *know* it."

Flyntinia cursed. "You have done it again, haven't you? Except this time, you found an even stronger protector. Sabine, the Soul Carvers, that maid, even Bethrian—you make friends everywhere you go, and they will gladly go to their deaths for you. And they do. They die, and they do it gladly. For you."

Caes's heart stilled. "You speak truer than you know. My friend is dead because of you."

Flyntinia looked up slowly. "What?"

"My Soul Carver drank the tea you sent. She is dead."

At that, a muttering erupted through the room. Attempting to murder a royal was one thing, especially one who wasn't overly welcome to begin with. But murdering a Soul Carver? That was unheard of. Even in Malithia, such a thing would have been considered a crime against Karima akin to murdering a priestess. And for all that Reyvern accepted Lyritan, they still held Karima close to their hearts.

Flyntinia looked downcast—regretful?—but that was quickly shoved behind a mask of defiance. "It should've been you," Flyntinia muttered.

"What?" Caes asked. Was she truly that foolish, saying so in front of the god? But then again, did Flyntinia have anything left to lose? "I am sure I misheard."

"It should've been you," Flyntinia yelled. "Another dead, because of *you*. My little boy...there is nothing in this world that is worth him. *Nothing*. And certainly not some conniving whore."

The air around Lyritan made Caes's hair stand on end, while it also trembled from the distant feeling of Alair restraining his magic.

As for Caes, she was calm. A wave of certainty settled over her, of knowing that a matter was about to be ended once and for all. "You are right," Caes said. "My friend is dead—from saving me. But I am still here. And I will see justice done." Flyntinia would be imprisoned for as long as necessary. She would suffer, and she would regret everything until her grief turned to madness and despair.

Suddenly, Lyritan stood and Caes reached out and touched his bicep, wincing at the charge of power that leaped into her. "Lyr," she said, soft enough only he and Alair could hear, "as much as I want to, killing her will anger Malithia. Reyvern does not want to anger them."

"She tried to kill you," Lyritan said, his voice low and rumbling.

"And there is more at stake than just me. Reyvern does not want a war."

Time stopped while Lyritan smiled, his radiant light beaming from him. He was a god, holding the fate of a mortal in his hands, a life that was worth as little to him as an insect to a spider. "I will decide what Reyvern does and does not want."

No.

There was nothing she could do.

Helpless, Caes watched while Lyritan approached Flyntinia, his power charging around him so that the stones under his feet cracked and shattered and the air whirled. As for Lyritan himself, the body was barely containing the gold light—how was Phelan still intact? His skin burned at the edges. Peeled. Charred. It was never more evident than now how mortals were poor vessels for the power of gods.

Before Caes could utter a word, Lyritan reached down and touched Flyntinia on the head. A sudden blinding burst of light and she fell over, smoke emanating from her body. He killed her with only a single touch and seemingly without a care.

Caes bit her cheek, the blood seeping over her tongue. What was this? She gripped the arms of her throne with shaking hands, and Alair placed a hand on her shoulder. Together, they watched the god and his rage, his power that burned. A legend made flesh.

And then, as quickly as it came, the air calmed, Lyritan's movements returned to normal, and the light faded, leaving raw, angry burns over his neck, arms, and hands, but otherwise seemingly unharmed. Caes's heart raced. What was this magic? Nothing from her time as Liuva prepared her for *this*.

When Lyritan gave her a familiar, almost boyish smile, Caes remembered—she had a part to play, one she had to do to perfection lest she suffer Flyntinia's fate.

Caes stood and ran to him, wrapping her arm gently around him and placing a hand on an uninjured part of his face. "Are you alright?" Caes asked, hoping to calm him. The court didn't need a furious Lyritan any longer.

"I am, my love." Lyritan swallowed. "But I realize now that we need to finish our task. You won't be safe from vile attempts like this until we finish what we need to at the Burning Hand. As soon as you bury your friend" –Lyritan kissed her hand– "we go. We need to end this."

Caes watched Lyritan take his place back on the throne, daring anyone to approach. This wasn't a man, not at all.

This was a god, full of wrath, power, and the promise of doom.

Chapter 41

Cylis

Death was a funny thing. Someone is there one moment, present and whole. And then they're gone.

People don't die just once—they die multiple times to those who loved them. There's the immediate knowledge that the one they loved is gone. And then there's the shifting, the thousand little deaths that come after as the deceased moves from the present to the past, and then slowly fades from memory.

Kerensa loved nesting dolls, the stupid little Malithian things where little carved animals were shoved inside one another. Who knew that about her? Only Cylis. She never owned any—why would a Soul Carver bother? But she loved them. How long would he remember that, before that part of her faded?

And that was just fucking dolls.

Death was a Soul Carver's constant companion, lurking behind their very power. Their pain and suffering were permanent reminders of their deaths. Moreover, it was all too common for them to die young, killed in battle or by their own hands once they couldn't take any more pain. But expecting a loss doesn't make it any easier to bear.

Cylis stared at the lit pyre, which even now was changing Kerensa's fabric-wrapped body to ash. He snorted. The irony. Kerensa had fire as her gift from Karima, and even now it covered her body in flames one final time, sending her away from this life.

Where was Kerensa now? Was she already in Karima's realm? What was Karima doing to her, after helping them so? After disobeying her? Cylis closed his eyes and took deep, calming breaths while a young man sang some mournful song about how death was the fate of all living things. Easy for him to say—he wasn't going to have to face the goddess he betrayed when he died.

Fuck the gods. Fuck this life. Thousands deserved to be burning on the pyre, but not Ker. Even when they first met, when he was already a Soul Carver and she was some desperate urchin, she stood out to him. She had a raw energy that promised she'd fight until the very end. And for her to be taken by something so cowardly as poison...

Caes silently sobbed from the other side of the pyre in the small courtyard, Alair's arms wrapped around her, his chin resting on her head. No, Ker would've been happy to know that she saved her friend, to know that her death meant something. If she hadn't been so reckless, who knew what would have happened to Caes? One of his friends had been saved at the cost of the other. He didn't think about which of the two he would've saved if given the choice. There was no point in an exercise that could only end in bitterness.

Bethrian stood at the back behind the Soul Carvers, watching the proceedings with lowered eyes. Caes—after confirming with Cylis—had requested a small ceremony, one Lyritan excused himself from, claiming the desire to give them privacy. Standing next to him, Marva was the only other person in attendance, since the other Soul Carvers had presumably left with Sabine.

Sabine.

What a waste of a life. Cylis would've killed her—gladly—but Caes made her decision, and as much as it ate at him, he accepted it. She was going to have to be the one to live with her choice.

"Are you alright?" Marva whispered.

"How can I be?" Cylis asked. Kerensa was more than his friend and his erstwhile lover. She was...there wasn't a word. He was the one who found her before she became a Soul Carver, rescuing her from some despicable thugs. He was the one who greeted her when she came out of the trials. She was the one who suggested he ask Alair for help when he was desperate to save Cecilia. Kerensa had been there for most of his Soul Carver existence, and now she was gone.

"She was lucky to have friends such as this." Marva took a deep breath. "That is a gift not given to many."

"Lucky? If she was lucky, it would've been me with them that morning. Not her." Cylis scowled. Caes and Alair briefly looked over at them before turning their tear-stained eyes back to the pyre. "I hate tea. And I would have stopped Sabine before anything happened."

"Kerensa would lecture you for dredging in the what-ifs like this, and you know it."

"No. She'd love it." Cylis wiped his eyes. "She liked making me uncomfortable. She was great at it."

Marva slowly wrapped an arm around him, pulling him closer to her. She was his shelter from grief, the bit of warmth his heart was able to seize. But fucking gods, what he wouldn't give to see Ker again. And after everything she had gone through to find her little sister. Ker had found her only remaining family, and then she was ripped from this world before she could save her from whatever slavery she had been sold into.

I promise, Ker, he silently vowed, *when this is done, I will find your sister. I promise.*

Chapter 42

Caes

Caes was no stranger to death or saying goodbye to those she loved. This time was no different. She wanted to scream and cry, to break everything she could, to let her power destroy whatever it dared. But such things wouldn't bring Kerensa back, and to act out such grief was a luxury she didn't have in this tense court. Loss or no, the goddesses were still there, as was her fate.

What was that fate? They still needed to decide what they were going to do at the Burning Hand—who was she going to destroy and how? And that was if they could even make it there alive.

Long before her grief had a chance to dull it would be time to leave Gilar, and the time to plan before they left was very short. In particular, they had to figure out what they were going to do with the Sword of Might.

Claiming that the stream of people in and out of the god's/prince's chambers would be too much for her to tolerate, Caes had managed to hold on to the room she shared with Alair, no matter how much Lyritan tried to have her stay with him. Yes, it was good not to have to contend with a stream of the curious and favor seekers. It was also good not to have to deal with a god who didn't seem to understand why Caes was so distraught over the loss of a mere Soul Carver, though he acted like he respected it—Lyritan didn't have friends. Worshippers? Yes. Enemies? Yes. Lovers? ...Yes. But true friends were a rare thing for gods.

Though Lyritan had no idea there was another purpose to Caes's desire to stay in place—it was hard to hold secret meetings with an audience.

"What did you tell the maids?" Alair asked, helping Caes bind a jeweled clip in her hair while they faced a mirror. Caes adjusted her sleeves—Alair did a surprisingly good job getting her into her dress this morning, including tying the stays. Though, he did have a lot of practice getting her out of them, so it wasn't too surprising he was skilled at the reverse.

"Same thing as always," Caes said. "I said I needed time to pray. And that I wanted to pray with my Lord Bethrian, who knew Kerensa well."

"And they didn't ask who you're praying to? Your 'god' is currently plotting the empire's downfall."

Caes shrugged. "No. But if asked I'd say I was praying to the Burning Hand for guidance. Vague enough."

Alair raised an eyebrow. "At this rate, you'll be known as Caesonia the Pious."

"No." She laughed. "No more titles. Please." A pain stabbed Caes's heart. Kerensa would've loved that name—Caesonia the Pious. Hells, Kerensa would've probably started using it, just to vex Caes. Caes's stomach twisted. It wasn't fair. Any death Kerensa experienced should have been due to valiantly giving up her life for some worthy cause, in a grand battle. Not poison. Not *Flyntinia's* poison.

Another person she loved was dead because of her, like so many others. Beltina. Althain. Not to mention all the other Malithians who were killed for no other reason than that they traveled with her to Ardinan.

"She would be the first to tell you not to waste tears on her," Alair said, rubbing Caes's shoulders. He smelled of a rich musk this morning, a far more decadent scent than what was normally used to launder his clothing.

She took a deep breath, leaning against him. "She said something similar when you died."

Alair smiled. "Because she's intelligent. But my message stands—Kerensa wasn't one for grief. She loved her friends, but she'd honor them with a pint and a meal, not sobs. Treasure her memory, but don't use it to bring you pain. She'd be angry if you did."

"She's with Karima now, isn't she?" Caes asked, her voice breaking.

"Yes." Alair's jaw clenched. "That's what awaits all of us. No matter what happens at the Burning Hand. I don't expect that we will ever be released to the fate that awaits all humans."

What would happen to her when she died? Died for good, that is. Caes wasn't a goddess, but she wasn't entirely human, either. Was it her fate to go with the other mortals into the ether and the care of the gods of death? Would she disappear into nothing? Would she age and die? Was she capable of doing so? But something pricked at her mind more than her own mortality.

"Alair?"

"Hmm?" he asked, brushing off the shoulders of her velvet gown.

"Can Reyvern conquer Malithia?"

Alair barked out a laugh. "No. They can barely defend their kingdom, and that's only because of the terrain."

"Then how does Lyritan plan to defeat the empire? I mean, he is a god. But can one god win against hundreds, if not thousands, of Soul Carvers without burning Phelan? Not to mention Karima and Shirla…"

Alair didn't answer and stared at their reflections in the mirror. For this brief moment, Caes was able to picture him as the young prince he used to be, his position and tutoring evident in his bearing. "That is a very good question. I'm not sure how Lyritan—"

Suddenly the door to the main hall opened, and Cylis, Bethrian, and Marva entered the main sitting room, their voices carrying through the walls. When Caes and Alair joined them, they found their faces grim. In other circumstances, Caes would've made some joke about Bethrian and Cylis striding in together wearing eerily matching expressions and clothing—but now was too soon for making jests. Of any sort.

"Well?" Caes asked. "Do you…." Her voice trailed off as she realized what Cylis carried, an object that seemed to sing without sound. "You have it," she said, a statement and not a question.

"Sort of," Cylis said, reaching into his cloak and holding out the piece of metal, carved with familiar etchings. The last time she had seen the sword it was strapped to her father's side before he left Ardinan on his fateful quest. The shard looked so ordinary, too thin to be of service as a weapon. Yet, it was more. The piece seemed to vibrate, sending its energy around the room. The sensation was that of an overcast field before a storm, a mountain lion about to pounce, a dam about to break. The promise of obliteration sang from the metal, in a note that Caes never detected when she saw it last. At that time, the magic was little more than a scent to her, a sense of something that was beyond the physical world. This was as impossible to ignore as wildfire.

"How in the hells are we going to hide *that* from the god?" Alair asked, awed. "I'm assuming you still don't plan on telling him, correct?"

Caes nodded, reaching out a hand. "I think it is best if we keep knowledge of the sword to ourselves."

"Wise," Bethrian said, "considering everything we've seen."

When Cylis passed Caes the metal, at first she felt nothing. And then everything. It was fire and lightning, rage and devotion. Briefly, she saw nothing but blackness, blackness and swirling lights circling a distant star. And then a charge of energy shot through her as her vision took in the room around her, shaking her until she almost dropped the metal. Instead, she held the shard harder. She had to win. She had to. Had to. The metal sliced her hand just enough for a stream of light to break through her skin, followed by drops of blood. The metal was jagged on one side, razor sharp on the other. They had to fashion a hilt...and would the metal even allow such a thing? Would it permit something so trite as wool or leather to contain it?

"Caes," Alair said, holding her upright and gripping her arm. "Let go. Let it go."

"No," she hissed through clenched teeth. "We need this."

"It's not worth it," Alair repeated. His eyes widened as gold light shone out from around her nails.

"We need to be able to use it," Bethrian said. "And hide it. You can't do either."

The sword is made of the gods. As am I.

"Give me a moment," Caes gasped. "I can win."

"Fuck that," Cylis said, taking her other arm and helping Alair guide her to the ground. Marva and Bethrian sat in front of her, watching intently and giving each other wary looks. Of course, they were concerned—Caes was holding a piece of an ancient weapon and was bleeding light and blood. "I don't like it when you get that look," Cylis said. "The last time you did you stabbed yourself in the heart."

"Let me think," Caes spat out. "There is a way to make it obey me. I *know* there is."

"No," Cylis said. "Thinking is bad."

"There's a jest here, but it's not the time," Bethrian said, smirking at Cylis while Alair glared at them both.

"It is made of gods, to be wielded by gods," Caes said. "Let me *think*." *Remember.*

"Let her try," Marva said softly, interrupting whatever feud Bethrian and Cylis were about to enter. "We don't know what awaits us—we need weapons. There isn't a weapon in existence that doesn't have the potential to harm the wielder. This is no exception."

"Alair," Cylis said, "you can't be letting her do this. It will kill her."

"Caes?" Alair asked, his voice layered with fear.

"Trust me," Caes said, meeting Alair's gaze. "I can do this."

After hesitating, Alair nodded and held her. "You're strong," he whispered. "You can do what you need to. You can."

Caes gave Marva a quick nod of thanks and went back to focusing on whatever memories she could dredge up from Liuva, letting Alair hold her upright as she dug into her past.

Some memories were best left forgotten.

Chapter 43

Liuva

Lyritan had left me. Lyritan was gone.

I did not know where. It was better I did not know. He said he had a plan to help me. Save me. One that would let us be together. I trusted him—he was as much a piece of me as my heartbeat, as essential to my being as every breath I took. He told me to be patient and wait—and so I did.

When my mother approached me one morning and asked me to walk with her, I did so with a smile. In that field, on that day, I was able to forget everything in the joy of pretending that everything was as it once was. This was my mother—why would she mean me harm?

And Lyritan, he would not leave me if it meant endangering me. Never.

So, I went with her. Gladly. We walked through a field of dew-kissed flowers that were just opening to greet the dawn. Mother reached out a milky-white arm and grabbed my hand, guiding my steps.

"I have a gift for you, my dearest child," Mother said. "I have not told you what you mean to me, and for that, I am sorry."

"Mother?"

Mother shook her head. Sorrow covered her perfect features, a crime against the beauty of such a being. "You are part mortal," she explained. "You wear their flesh and wield their bones, but your soul is more. It was made from my own." She looked at my eyes, and I stared at her golden ones, which outshone the grandeur of the sun. Was she seeing the same gold in me, her own divinity reflected back to her? Slowly, she reached out a hand and caressed my face. "Someday, you will take your place beside me—you have grown like the flowers of the field. And it has been a joy to watch you through every step of it all." She bent and kissed the top of my head, her love warming me better than the daylight.

"Come." Abruptly she turned and moved me along the path once more.

"Mother?"

"I will teach you something about your nature today—about our nature," my mother said. "When mortals die, their bodies turn to dust, their souls cast elsewhere. But us gods, we don't die. We are transformed."

While we walked, she told me the stories of the earliest gods, the ones who were eaten by their sons and brothers as each generation of divine beings gave birth to the next. The gods eventually settled and ceased their bloody contests, content to wield their power over their pieces of the earth. Though while the practice had ended, the concept remained—the death of a god brought opportunity for those who were willing to seize it.

We were now in a forest, a dark place where the leaves blocked out all but the barest hints of the sun. The trees stood skeletal, their limbs contorted and struggling for light. Little in the way of life lurked on the ground, other than tenacious grasses and weeds. There was nothing like the delicate flowers that carpeted the ground in the forest near our home. I wondered where my mother had taken me, to this place where the sun could not bring itself to shine. And I was afraid.

Soon, we came to a grove where an eerie stillness lurked. Not even the wind blew through the trees and the insects were silent. In the center of the grove laid a young man, his eyes wide and staring at the sky. Though, this was not a mortal man—the light that dripped from his mouth and dropped to the grounds like golden lava, his eyes that still carried a dim glow, indicated that he was more. A god. A dead god.

"How did this happen?" I asked, for there was no visible wound. My hands shook. I had never seen a dead god before, and it was only my experience of witnessing the decay of mortals that told me this god was not asleep.

Mother shrugged, seemingly unconcerned, for both the god and myself. "I cannot say. A thousand things could have befallen him." Memory and hindsight has since told me that there was more meaning to her words, but the fact of the matter was that the god was dead, and the two of us stood before him, staring at his corpse.

"Well, Liuva?" Mother said, taking a silver knife from the sheathe at her side. "Here is power—are you willing to do what it takes to claim it?" She watched me, gauging my reaction.

"What do you mean?" I eyed the knife, a chill seizing my heart. The metal shone in the dim light, a thick blade meant to gouge and butcher. I wondered what it would feel like to have that touch my flesh, to pierce my heart. Would I die? Would I feel pain?

"His power is here, dripping out of him," my mother said, pulling me from the spell cast by the weapon. "Anyone can take it. Anyone." She smiled. "Most of it is in the heart and eyes. I suggest starting there." Holding out the knife, she offered it to me hilt first.

A test. Even as naïve as I was then, I knew there was more than this simple interaction. It was more than a simple gift from a mother to a daughter. Was she weighing if I would be strong enough to challenge her? Was she seeing if I would grasp power as desperately as crows sought death? Or was this simply a gift? If not for Lyritan, I would have taken what my mother offered without question. But I did have Lyritan, and I knew to weigh my words.

"Mother, I do not know if I am ready for such a gift," I said, lowering my gaze to the bare ground.

Her face softened. "Why ever not? You are stronger than you think. You could be stronger yet. Think of what you could do."

"What need have I for power? I have you," I said, keeping my expression honest. She flinched, so fast so as to be a figment of my imagination. Or a wish. "You will protect me," I said softly. "Take it all, Mother. It will serve you better."

My mother nodded and flipped the blade so that she gripped the knife's hilt once more. What she did not tell me then was that the power of the gods faded after death, and while it was true that gods could seize others' power that way, the amount dissipated quickly. She was offering me a gift, yes, but one that had less value than she had indicated. This was a test, and nothing more. One I never learned if I passed.

I have long wondered why she didn't just murder other gods, seize their power, and conquer Karima that way, but that ignored the practical reality of gods—there weren't many, and most were not as defenseless as the man laying in the grove. Shirla could overpower one young god, but she could not handle three or more, if word spread that she was attempting to seize their power for herself. And while Shirla was a powerful goddess, others were more so. Others may have come to stop her, not wanting their own power challenged once her abilities grew too great. It was a delicate balance of power and death.

"If you won't take this offering, then I will tell you a secret, my love," Mother said, approaching the god and holding the knife over him. "There is more than one way to take this god's power. A way for me to change your mind, if this manner proves to be too much for you. Today, you will learn to embrace our nature."

Then she started cutting.

Chapter 44

Caes

Caes opened her eyes, Liuva's memories fading from her like waking from a dream. In their place was left...too much. The good news was that she knew what she had to do to manage the shard. The bad news was *also* that she now knew what she had to do. She was looking forward to what would come next about as much as the time she shoved a knife into her heart. And she had a feeling that what was to come might hurt more than that.

"Whatever I do next," Caes said, looking at each person sitting before her from her position on the floor, "don't move. Don't stop me." She checked to make sure the door was latched shut. It was. Good. Last thing she needed was servants interrupting this.

The fragment of the sword pounded, sending jolts through her hands like a frenzied animal trying to escape. This had to be done. It was the only way to claim the weapon in its raw state, to hide it from Lyritan. Did Shirla realize the lesson she had inadvertently given her, so many centuries ago? Probably not. In the woods, Shirla had shown her how to absorb the gods' power, and what was this sword, but the power of gods?

Though, the sword raised more questions than answers. The sword was never part of Shirla's original plan, from what Caes could tell. Shirla had made Caes to grow a kernel of the goddess's power, enter the Burning Hand, and then sacrifice herself, thereby strengthening Shirla. How did the sword end up near Caes's home, and broken? The sword entering the scene altered Shirla's plans and suddenly gave her a way to destroy Karima at the same time. It seemed to have altered everyone's plans. What had Lyritan told Caes? More importantly, what did she remember? Did it matter what the gods intended? This was a game to them, and they likely viewed such things as little more than a new pawn on the board, one that could be exploited.

But this was not the time to ponder such things. She had a sword to…neutralize.

Alair shook his head. "Caes—"

"Trust me," she said to Alair. "Whatever you see, it will be alright. I know what I'm doing."

"Oh, fuck me," Cylis said, covering his eyes. "I know where this is going."

"I should've never listened to the skull," Bethrian muttered, looking away. Marva stared at the floor.

"I'll be alright. Promise." Taking a deep breath, Caes started to cut.

Using the shard, Caes sliced a line in her arm, bit by bit, near the area that had so recently healed from Bethrian taking her blood in Fyrie. The divine power needed to taste her own essence, and it needed a place within her to hide. Since she wasn't able to eat metal and wanted to avoid slicing her tongue like she did with Shirla, gouging a path was her only option. Would it work? It had to. But what if it didn't?

Too late now.

It took a couple seconds for her mind to register the gore her eyes saw, but when it did it was like her arm was doused in fire. Caes hissed, moving the blade in a line until there was a cut on her forearm as long as the shard. Not deep—thank the fucking gods—but enough to make her bleed. Her blood, that was interspersed with gold flakes, dripped to the floor and spread over her arms. Under her flesh, her skin crackled, like little bits of smothered lightning lurked beneath. Rubbing the flat side of the blade against her skin, Caes used her blood to cover the shard, every single inch.

The worst part was done. Now it was time to finish it.

Just like that. Breathe. It is divine. I am divine. Recognize it.

Divine? Liuva was a lot more comfortable with being part god than Caes. But at that moment, Liuva's delusion came in use.

Like a fire being dampened, the blade cooled to her soul. Caes listened and felt for the part of the blade that was familiar—the divine part that created it—a part that echoed back to her like the continuation of a familiar refrain. It was a weapon, yes, forged metal. But the sword's origins...it was made of the same material as herself. Her divinity was caged in flesh while the shard's was caged in metal. They were the same. The same.

Shard coated with blood, it was now time for the tricky part. She inhaled, imagining the blade as part of her. It *was* a part of her, made from the same substance. She took long, jagged breaths, struggling to stay upright as the room spun around her. Stars burst across her vision. And then...

"What the fuck did you do?" Cylis asked.

Caes opened her eyes. The blade was gone. Her wound was healed. Only the smeared blood on her arms and drops on the floor—how was she going to explain that?—told the tale of her grisly task. Yet, there was more in her now than there was before. If she focused, she could feel the blade, lurking like an animal hidden in the shadows. "It's still here," Caes said, gesturing with her arm. "When I need it, I can find it again."

"You can?" Bethrian asked.

"Caes..." Alair said, uttering a foul curse. Multiple foul curses.

"I'm with him," Cylis said, nodding towards Alair. "You just, what, absorbed a piece of metal?"

"Pretty much."

"That's not normal. You know that, right?" Cylis asked. "Divine metal. Magic metal. You *absorbed* it."

"I agree with Cylis on this one," Bethrian said. "It's bizarre."

"Bizarre?" Cylis asked. "Bethy, it's a fucking curse."

"Bethy?" Caes asked.

"And how, exactly, do you plan on getting it out when we need it?" Cylis's eyes narrowed. "And don't you dare try changing the subject again."

She knew how to get it out, thanks to Shirla telling her tales of what Karima had done with consumed divine bones. And she hoped she'd never have to. For all that it was agony to put the metal into her arm, getting it out would be worse. There was no way it wouldn't be.

"I'll leave it at that I am not calling it forth until it is desperately needed," Caes said.

"Do we truly need this?" Alair asked. "For you to go through this—"

"Alair," Caes said gently, "we don't know what Lyritan has planned. We need our own. My doing this will both hide the weapon and let us use it." She gave him a sad smile. "I am alright. Trust me."

"Can you touch it?" Bethrian asked, eyebrow raised in morbid curiosity. "Is it going to poke out?"

"No," Caes said, rubbing her arm and showing that her flesh was supple and smooth. "It is part of me. For now." She frowned. Shirla had had her absorb something else, once upon a time. A bite of a dead god's heart—a token gift—that she never should've accepted for all that the memory repulsed her. But Liuva had thought she could outwit the gods by playing at their game—Caes was beyond thinking that was a possibility. Though, wasn't that what she was trying to do again? Outwit them?

"What?" Cylis asked. "What insanity are you possibly thinking?"

"Nothing," Caes asked. "I'm just hoping I didn't make a mistake."

A silence settled between them, but then Bethrian snorted. "Well, a bit too late for that, isn't it?"

Chapter 45

Alair

They needed to leave the city of Gilar. Desperately. While Caes was distracted and Lyritan off in his own thoughts and machinations, Alair was focused on the danger that was building around them. Cylis was oblivious, lost in grief over Kerensa, besides the fact that addressing unseen danger was never Cylis's strong point. If Caes noticed—and she likely did—she didn't say. Same with Bethrian. For all his faults, Bethrian could read people. Yet, he said nothing to Alair about how they had all overstayed their welcome.

After Flyntinia's execution, the people at court and in Gilar were tense. Angry. Like an avalanche about to break. While most may have been tolerating them for the sake of their possessed prince, what they saw in the throne room led to fear—which all too easily led to destruction. Hope for their prince had given way to terror. The Reyverni wanted them all gone, no matter how. While it was unlikely that a human mob would be able to kill the god before he could escape, Caes and the Soul Carvers were still far too mortal.

As such, when Lyritan invited Alair to play a game of horsemen in his chambers, he accepted, and found himself in complete agreement with what the god had to say after he banished the curious servants.

"We can leave the day after tomorrow," Lyritan said, moving his footman to vanquish another piece. The game was similar to chess, which was played in the Malithian courts, but horsemen was a more visual version of it, complete with a molded castle and pieces that moved up and down ramparts according to certain rules. It had been in style centuries ago, before chess took over the fashion. How did Lyritan learn it? Fuck if Alair knew. "I know the passageways through the mountains, so that will help us move quickly," Lyritan added. "We will make good time, and hopefully avoid any...complications and foul weather."

"Good." Alair moved his own footman, a sacrificial pawn. It was difficult not to think about how he was a pawn in the god's own game—to pretend to be anything else was foolishness. Caes had mentioned the metaphor once and it was far too apt for their situation. "We've waited too long as it is," Alair said. "Gave our enemies far too much time to plan."

The god raised his eyebrow at the rebuke, but he said nothing and merely stared at the board. His golden eyes smoldered. Alair caught his attention wandering to the god's chest. He didn't care for men that way as a general matter, but it was difficult to ignore such feelings the god stirred in him.

"How many men do you think we should take?" Lyritan asked. "Will the other Soul Carvers come with?"

"They will." Alair paused. "And likely Lord Bethrian."

"Good. The man has a crafty mind. We need that. Yes, it is a good thing he is coming." Lyritan moved his priestess to a tower. Risky. A trap.

"And how many Soul Carvers?" Lyritan asked.

"Two. Cylis and Marva, in addition to myself."

"She came with more than that," Lyritan said, watching him. Did he guess that they had concealed Kerensa's killer from him? While Alair would've had no issue with killing Sabine, he understood that the matter was complicated, and Caes was as justified as any of them to make that determination.

"She did," Alair answered. "They left to go home to Malithia. Caes didn't want to force anyone to go if they were not willing. Not for this."

"Wise. It will be treacherous. Cowardice will be deadly." The god tapped a piece that was already removed from the game against the table while he thought, the rhythm like a heartbeat. "I am debating recruiting a small company," Lyritan finally said. "No more than ten men. We need speed."

"Do you trust the men?" Alair asked. "In the wilds we will be exposed. It wouldn't take much for them to force an accident."

"You're the only one I completely trust with her, because you love her just as much as I do."

Alair nodded. "That is true." As much as? Alair loved her more than the god. She was his soul and desire, the blood in his life's veins, the breath he needed to survive. As for the god, he was a base creature, consumed with his wants. Even now, the god was likely thinking about how a fire and Kerensa's death had ruined his chance at fulfilling his passions. He likely cared more about himself than what the loss of a friend did to Caes, who he claimed to love.

"And her other companions have proven themselves. But the men here?" Lyritan shook his head. "No, you're right. I don't trust them. I know that when I come back to this city, I will have to take it by force. They will bar the gates against me. And I can too easily imagine them trying to kill Caesonia as soon as the opportunity arises. This city will fall, but it will be bloody first." Hmm, apparently Lyritan was more observant than Alair gave him credit for.

"Then I would advise not bringing them," Alair said. He moved a knight into the god's trap. "The challenges we will face will be enough of a concern. No need to bring our own troubles."

"Your point is made. Mortal men are of limited use for what awaits us, anyway." Lyritan brushed his blond hair out of his face. "They're also more bodies to sustain when resources are scarce."

"Do you know what's there at the Hand?" Alair asked, watching the god use the priestess to smite Alair's recently-moved knight. "I've heard all manner of stories, but what *is* there?" He didn't bother asking about the goddesses and Desmin and Damek. They had their own malicious plans, there was no doubt.

Lyritan shrugged. "I haven't been there for over a thousand years and have no way of knowing how it has changed. You must understand—the Burning Hand is not merely a temple. It is a portal. It is one of the places in the world where the true gods broke into this plane when they created it. And other things wander in as well."

"That's how you came to this world?"

"No. But that is how we are able to stay." Lyritan looked at Alair, eternity swirling in his golden eyes. "You call us gods—and we are. We are immortal. We have power beyond mortal understanding. But what is in the Burning Hand makes even us shudder." Lyritan looked back at the board. "And we will have to face it. For her, I will. I will do anything."

"Why does she need to go, then? You said you had a way that wouldn't end in her death."

Lyritan paused. "I promised her over a thousand years ago that I would find a way to free her, to keep her safe, and that is to bind her to me. I'd make her far less appealing to Karima or Shirla or any other god who would seek to use her."

"But the Burning Hand requires death."

"It requires *sacrifice*, and that, Soul Carver, is not always the same thing."

Alair stared at Lyritan, reading his features. "You don't know what to do. You don't know what you'd need to do at the Burning Hand, either. You're guessing. And you're willing to risk Caes's life to do so."

Lyritan's eyes flared. "My thousands of years on this earth are not a mere 'guess.' And do you have a better plan? Caes was placed here by a goddess, and now she has two that will not let her escape. She is their personal game—and we need to take her off the board." He gestured at the table for emphasis. "And what would you suggest—that I leave her *here*? You know that I'm the only reason the goddesses have not killed her already."

Alair did, and he hated it. Hated that Lyritan was right. The goddesses would not ignore her. They never would.

"We will destroy them," Alair prompted. "At the Burning Hand."

Lyritan snorted. "I know that was what she was told. But I have doubts it's as easy as smashing a statue with a weapon. I also have doubts that we want to do that at all, but I know what we will do if needed. No, the best way to save her is to bind her to me, and then I will conquer this empire and eradicate the goddesses down to the root. I will weaken them, and then kill them."

And he planned on doing that...how?

"We don't have the weapon regardless," Alair ventured, to see if he could read any signs of knowledge on the god's face.

There were none.

"No," Lyritan said. "But I have another plan. Trust me, Soul Carver. I want her to live. She *needs* to live. I will do whatever it takes to make this happen. When I remove the goddesses, she will be by my side, sharing in my victory."

That seemed unlikely. And ambitious. And another plot Alair didn't want Caes to be involved in. He had to remember—this was the story Lyritan was telling Alair, which seemed a bit more...convoluted and bare than the story he had been telling Caes. And this was even more complex than the story Lyritan had told her back when she was in Fyrie. Which version was true? Was the god really this confused? Did he truly have Caes's best interests at heart? Or were these little mortals trickier for him to manage than he expected and he was floundering? Of course, it was possible the god changed his mind often, so that every word was the truth as Lyritan saw it. The god had spent a thousand years in a statue, so some confusion was to be expected. But Alair was not about to delve into such philosophical musings about a god's mind.

Instead, Alair nodded and moved another piece across the board, another piece of bait for Lyritan's priestess to attack. When finished, he placed his hands on his lap.

"Your move," Alair said.

It was good that they had their own designs, and it was more important than ever that they keep them hidden from the god.

Chapter 46

Caes

Caes had left many courts before, in very different circumstances.

From Ardinan as a hostage. From Malithia as a princess. And from Ardinan again as a fugitive. But none of those departures had anything in common with how she was leaving Gilar—pretending to be triumphant at a god's side. This was Lyritan's journey to enable him to claim his right over the empire, and so he appeared as a conqueror, leaving for a battle he was sure to win. Was he fooling anyone? What about himself?

Lyritan was never confident without cause.

No, but that didn't mean he understood everything. It didn't mean he was telling them the truth.

At dawn, they prepared to leave the mountainous city on horseback, well-stocked and armed for the journey ahead. The horses wouldn't be able to travel with them for long—soon the path would be far too treacherous—but they would take them while they could. The mountain was not horrendously far away based on distance, but the miles were going to be over slick rocks and deadly ravines, not to mention everything else that waited. Were Desmin and her father lurking outside the city, waiting for them to leave? Or would they be waiting closer to the Burning Hand, once their quarry was spent? Regardless, they would be waiting for her. They were Karima and Shirla's favorite toy to use against her, and there was no doubt the goddesses would hurt her any way they could. If they couldn't use her, they would destroy her.

Caes adjusted her collar, letting some of the winter air strike her skin. Like the others, she wore thick fur coats and cloaks and solid boots—it wouldn't be for lack of equipment if she became cold on this journey. Cylis wore only a light jacket with a thick cloak, and he would've probably been fine even without that. She suspected he brought the cloak in case others needed it, besides him. She asked him once what the cold felt like to him, and after a snarky response of *ice and wind*, he explained that he was perpetually in pain from using his magic. But the cold didn't hurt him permanently, and the cold was better than being too warm. Basically, extra layers just didn't do any good, and the sweating and warmth on his ice-magicked flesh wasn't worth it.

It was time to go.

They were equipped and prepared to depart on the final leg of their quest, one that normally would've warranted a hearty stanza in a ballad. But the company that watched them leave had all the joy of a funeral—and it was, in a sense. They were saying goodbye to their crown prince, and who knew if he would return? From the queen's dour face and the king's unreadable expression, Caes could only assume they were thinking the worst—yes, they were finally losing the god, but they were losing their prince, too. Forever. She tried to give Princess Saryn a small smile, but the princess wouldn't meet her gaze. A stab rent through her heart. The princess had been kind to her, considering the circumstances. They all had.

"Farewell, Your Majesties," Lyritan said from his position standing next to Caes. "I depart for now, but I shall return, and I shall bring Reyvern to glory beyond its comprehension." Unlike when Lyritan gave such speeches before, there were none of the excited listeners in the crowd. What the city witnessed on the day Lyritan killed Flyntinia had quenched any thought that this god was someone they wanted to serve.

"Thank you, Your Majesties, and to the people of Reyvern," Caes said, her voice clear. "I shall not forget your kindness." Few friendly faces looked to her, either, but she had faced more hostile crowds than this. And she was leaving, so who cared what they thought?

"Shall we, my love?" Lyritan asked, holding out an ungloved hand.

Smiling, Caes took it and gave it a little squeeze. "I have been waiting for this, for a very long time."

"As have I."

What exactly did he hope to gain at the Burning Hand? Yes, yes, victory and domination and all, but *how*? Alair told her what the god had revealed to him, and the two of them came to the same conclusion—the god himself was grasping on myths. Or wanted them to think he was.

Lyritan was many things, but never a fool.

No, they were never going to be that lucky.

And then they were gone.

Once they were barely a mile out of Gilar, they encountered terrain that made the mountainous city seem like a gentle park. Unsurprisingly, since the city itself was built into the mountains. Sharp rocks and loose gravel covered the narrow path, making each step treacherous. Lyritan led the company, followed by Cylis, then Caes, Alair, Bethrian, and Marva, each giving their horse comforting words and pets to steady them as they traveled ever higher. Higher they had to go, Lyritan announced, for while the lower path seemed the simplest to reach the Burning Hand, it was apparently a lie that had led many travelers to their deaths.

"What sort of lie?" Caes asked, eying the flat valley beneath them like it was a fluffy bed.

"Pits," Lyritan said. "Unless something has changed in the last millennia, there are sinkholes, hidden in the snow. From what I was told, Reyvern has had little success in marking them for travelers to avoid—snowfalls and avalanches hide all attempts."

"Yeah, let's not go that way," Cylis said. The others nodded and murmured in agreement. That settled the matter—upwards they would go, despite the misery.

Near midday, the first snow of the journey fell, and Caes huddled deeper into her cloak. Closing her eyes, she let the mountain wind bash her face. She couldn't complain now. It was only going to get colder. Harsher. And there was no help for it.

"Are you alright?" Alair asked Caes, his brow wrinkled.

"Perfect," she said. In normal circumstances, she would've admired the snowflakes resting in his dark hair, the way his features echoed the stern and angular beauty of the mountain around them. But this was a circumstance where she was starting to lose feeling in her face, and her ass was sore from plodding against a saddle.

"We should stop soon," Alair called out to Lyritan. "She needs rest."

The god turned around, his brow furrowed. "Caesonia?" Lyritan asked.

"I'm fine," she said to them both. "We just started traveling. It always takes a day or two to get used to the horse again. Right, Bethrian?"

"Yep," Bethrian said bitterly, wrapping his own cloak tighter around him. "Blame the poor horse," he added in barely more than a whisper.

"If you are able to carry on," Lyritan said, "it will be worth it. Just a little further." He surveyed their company, his posture taking on that of a general encouraging his troops. "We need to get higher into the mountain. Trust me. Unless we find a cave, we do not want to rest. And there *are* caves further on. But once we get to one, we will stay there until dawn and out of this wind."

"Let's go," Cylis said, grimacing. His face was the familiar frosted plum color of his magic, his orifices oozing white pus. Once, seeing his magic terrified Caes. Once, he had used his magic against her in the hall of the Malithian palace. Now, she was more concerned he was going to annoy her to death. Oh, how her life had changed. If she could choose only two people to see for the rest of her life, Cylis would be one of them.

Caes nodded, acknowledging Lyritan's plan to trudge on until there was shelter. There was no arguing with the god—what was the point of doing so now?—so they went on their way, following Lyritan higher into the frigid air.

They traveled along the path, Caes's vision dulled by the overcast sky. Wind whipped snow through the air, biting her skin. With Gilar already in the throes of winter, it didn't take long in the mountains before the ferocity of the bitter season hit them in full. Even the few pine trees that still dotted the landscape struggled under the weight of the snow. And it wasn't even the worst of the season—would this route be passable at all in a month or two? Not for the first time—and likely not the last—Caes cursed that their journey couldn't have waited for spring.

"And why couldn't we take the valley?" Cylis asked. "It was flat. All the maps said that way is flat."

Great, not this. Again.

"Weren't you listening?" Marva said. "The ground itself is glass. The animals—"

"Yeah, yeah, 'certain death,' 'impending doom,' 'nightmares incarnate,'" Cylis muttered. "But it's flat. And that stuff sounds like bullshit."

"The sinkholes are not," Caes said.

"Sinkholes are at least out of the wind," Cylis said.

"You can handle the cold," Bethrian snapped. "Stop complaining."

"Nope."

"We've been on the road for less than a day," Alair said. "If you keep this up, I *will* toss you over the edge and be done with it."

"Never." Cylis smiled. "You'd miss me far too much." Alair snorted in reply.

Whatever Lyritan thought of the exchange, he didn't say. His attention never left the Burning Hand that lurked in the distance, towering over the landscape.

"If he doesn't complain," Marva said, "then he has nothing. He'd wither and die. Unfortunately, I have a feeling that we're going to have to get used to this. Unless we *want* him to wither and die."

Caes bit back a grin with her numb lips and Bethrian muttered, "Oh, don't tease me with my heart's desire."

"Please," Cylis said. "I'm only saying what you're all thinking."

No, he was saying the only thing they dared talk about. So much was left unsaid.

Ker's absence rang through their party, a presence that refused to be ignored. They didn't trust the god who led them.

And it was very likely that Caes was not going to live at the end of this. Again.

But they couldn't talk about any of that—which left them with the weather.

After a little more banter their voices faded into silence. The journey dragged on and the winter air slapped their faces, sending bits of snow that felt like being attacked by tiny shards of glass. With each bit of incline the elements became more brutal. The air froze in Caes's nose, stiffening the delicate hairs and making it hard to breathe, and her eyes watered and burned. Each breath made her chest seize, the cold air colliding with her body's warmth. She shook, her teeth chattering, her body spasming.

This was only the beginning. She couldn't be this cold, not this soon.

"We need to stop!" Alair yelled after looking at Caes.

"Soon," Lyritan said.

"She's mortal," Alair said. "She can't handle this. Not like us."

"She's stronger than she thinks." Lyritan flashed her a smile. "Right, Caesonia?"

"I'm with Caes on this one," Bethrian said, his voice muffled under layers of furs.

"My lord," Marva said, "she is strong, but she doesn't recall how to use her powers. Not like yourself. She needs to rest. She needs warmth."

Damn Soul Carvers and their ability to ignore pain and endure everything. Lucky Soul Carvers. At least Bethrian, hunched over his horse and hugging the poor animal, understood her misery.

"We are close," was all Lyritan said.

"You haven't been here in how long, a thousand years?" Alair prodded. "How do you know this cave exists?" Lyritan slowly turned to face him but Alair continued, "She can't go on much longer. None of us can."

Lyritan's lips set in a line. "I know where we're going, Soul Carver. And there is more at stake on this route than just protection from the elements."

"What do you mean?" Caes asked, lips numb.

The god's face softened. "I couldn't tell you until we left the city—too many ears that could ruin it all—but I have a plan. One that will save you. One that will help us bypass this frigid hell." Lyritan shifted on his horse. "I know what we must do. Trust me."

Save her? Trust him? What was he thinking? Fear twisted her gut. What was it that he couldn't tell her in Gilar? Where was he taking them? And did they have any option but to trust him? They'd be all but blind if they tried to navigate this range alone during this season.

"They're right," Caes said to Lyritan. "Please, my love. My body is still weak. I need shelter. And so does Bethrian." With her numb lips the words came out fumbled, but her point was made. Caes didn't have to turn to look behind her to imagine Bethrian nodding his head in agreement.

Lyritan's eyes flashed gold as they locked with hers. "I will take care of you. I promise. Just a little bit further."

A little further. A bit at a time. That was how he hurt me before.

A movement in the distance, on a different mountain's edge, caught Caes's attention. There was a white mound against the snow, lurking. A wolf? A bear?

"What is that?" Caes asked. She pointed in the distance, right as the object stood, revealing itself to be far taller than animal should be. A jolt ran through Caes's body, a sudden desire to both freeze and flee.

Cylis looked. "What—oh, fuck me."

"I never should've listened to the skull," Bethrian said, closing his eyes.

"Oh, gods," Caes said. "Can it get to us?"

"No," Alair said. "See? We will be far from here before it gets to us."

Between them and the creature was a large gulch, one that would be nearly impossible to cross easily, and one that would take their company at least a day to successfully navigate. Besides, the shape didn't seem to see them. It stretched, revealing unnaturally long arms, and then it took off in the opposite direction, crouched against the ground like an animal once more.

"What was that?" Caes asked, horrified.

"That," Lyritan said, "is why we sleep in caves."

Chapter 47

Caes

Somehow, against the odds, the god kept his word. They were safe. And warm. Somewhat.

Soon after Alair's protestations and Caes's prodding they found a cave, one that was a shelter from the wind. More, the cave had wood and coal in addition to other provisions stocked inside. The provisions included lamps and oil, which were lit immediately. There was also old wine, pickles, and preserved meats. These were hardly luxury items, but here in the mountain, who was she to complain? Yes, they had their supplies from Gilar, but they needed every bit of food they could carry to get them to the Burning Hand and back—why would they touch their supplies if they didn't need to?

"I don't understand," Bethrian said, eying the provisions waiting for them in sacks, jars, and crates at the back of the cave. "There's no one around here. We've heard nothing other than how dangerous this route is. And yet there's this?"

Lyritan shrugged. "I made inquiries while in Gilar as to whether Reyvern kept to the old ways. And they do. This is a road to the holiest place for a thousand miles—tradition mandates that the pilgrims be fed, within reason."

"You sent people here, ahead of us?" Alair asked. Here they were, thinking that this was some deserted trail humans did not travel, and the god had arranged for a path of supplies? And didn't think to tell them? Caes was too tired and hungry to be angry. She slouched against a stone wall, just happy that it wasn't a moving horse.

"Sent?" Lyritan asked. "No. This is arranged in the warmer months, when the dangers tend to stay closer to the mountain. The pilgrimages occur in the summer, too. I just ensured that they had been stocked before the end of the season."

"Pilgrimages. Right," Cylis said. "So, we're going to be supplied the whole way?" High-pitched hope crept into Cylis's voice. "And have all this shelter?" He scratched his chin. "This isn't nearly as bad as I thought it would be."

"No." Lyritan crouched and pulled out a rind of cheese from a sack left for the devout. He sniffed it and picked at the wax. "Yes, people come during the summer and supply these, but they don't go much further than this. While tradition says this is for pilgrims, practicality speaks to it supplying ambitious hunters or idiotic adventurers." Caes sure wasn't a pilgrim, and she never hunted in her life. Was she an idiotic traveler, then? She wasn't sure she wanted the answer.

"Then pilgrims aren't common, are they?" Marva asked, shaking out a couple of the bedrolls placed against the wall. Dust and dirt flew out, but it seemed in relatively good shape. Everything here would help their supplies last. It was a good thing they found the caves.

Then Caes noted the scratches on the wall. Shapes? No. It was writing, in a script she hadn't seen in a very long time. Not since...

"Lyritan?" Caes asked.

He raised his head in answer.

"I'm having a memory." The others shifted around her. Whether it was something in her tone or their circumstance, hands were placed on weapons and postures straightened. "This land is cursed."

Lyritan broke into the cheese, peeling back the rind. "You're remembering correctly," he said. "The betrayers are buried here. Close."

"These caves were temples to another god," she whispered. Shirla never spoke of this god. He kept to his part of the earth and never left. Whether he was still alive or not, she couldn't say. Did gods sometimes fade away, scattering like dust on the wind? She closed her eyes. There was another presence here. But was it the old god, or was it the Burning Hand? The earth thrummed, a distant heartbeat that wasn't heard by ears. Whatever it was, they were now in a different world, one where old magics walked and archaic powers still held sway. She shivered, and it wasn't from the cool air.

"Do not worry about him, my love," Lyritan said, taking a bite. "We are far from any danger." She nodded. Even if she didn't believe him, what else could they do? Alair caught her gaze and gave a curt nod. He'd be keeping watch. He would stay by her. No matter what.

"Well, I'm hardly going to complain about any meal and shelter," Bethrian said, helping himself to the provisions. "Damn, riding is thirsty business."

"As you should," Lyritan said. "The travel will only become more taxing. But I understand your mortal frailties. I will protect you. Fear not what hunts these lands at night."

That wasn't comforting.

At least some things they didn't have to worry about. There was grain in the cave for the horses, who ate the windfall cheerfully. And once their makeshift camp was situated and feeling fully returned to her limbs, they surrounded the fire, making idle conversation. Caes pushed back a pang that arose in her heart at seeing Cylis and Marva—Kerensa should've been with them. Joking. Complaining. And now she was...

Oh, gods, she was with Karima. Caes took a slow breath. She *needed* to destroy Karima, if only to protect her friends.

Caes's heart wrenched. If Caes missed Kerensa, there was no doubt Cylis missed her even more. Maybe Flyntinia was right—everyone she loved died. Died, or betrayed her. It was all her fault. If she hadn't been in Malithia, then Beltina, Althain, and Kerensa would still be alive. Tears welled in her eyes. Gods, she must've been tired. She normally contained herself better than this. But...Flyntinia was right.

And even when people didn't die, they still left her.

Like Father.

Damek the Chosen One was her father, no matter who he was now. He raised her. And now he was trying to kill her. The same man who had promised so much to her, who had cherished her, wanted to kill her. She was his *precious one*. His *love*.

His *greatest joy*. He had mused so long about finding the right husband for her, the right position, where she'd be taken care of after he was gone. It tormented him that their prospects in rural Ardinan were so few. His finding the sword and being proclaimed as Shirla's Chosen was a boon neither of them expected, a chance for a better life. And now he wanted her dead.

…Why?

Alair wrapped a comforting arm around her. "It will be alright," he whispered. She gave him a sad smile. "Will it?" she whispered back.

"It will."

She leaned against him. Like she knew her soul, she knew Alair would stay with her. Her friend. Her lover. She, who had lived multiple lives, knew how even the best people changed and moved, like pieces on a board that were there one day and then gone. Even mountains eventually turned to dust and cities fell to ruin. But what she had in Alair, that was something that would linger long after their bodies were scattered on the winds. He had changed her soul forever.

And more, she had Cylis, too. Together, they had already endured against so many trials. They wouldn't abandon her now, not when they were so close to whatever end awaited them.

"Well, this is as good a time as any to tell us your plan," Cylis suddenly said to Lyritan, his face stern. They had been lightly discussing which region of the empire produced the best cheese, but Cylis was not one to shy from unpleasant matters. "Tell us." The others waited to see what Lyritan had to say.

Lyritan wiped the crumbs of a dried apple from the corner of his mouth and let the remainder of the apple rest in his hand on his lap. Though they were in a cave, he sat like a king presiding over his court. "I suppose it is time to tell you," he said, "for we are not going to the Burning Hand. Not right away, at least."

Caes dug her thumbnail into her finger, though she kept her expression even. "Then, where are you leading us?"

"A tomb." When the remaining blood drained from Caes's face, the god continued, picking pieces of dried food from his clothes and tossing them aside. "Well, not exactly a tomb. A receptacle. Like the one you were in for centuries."

"What are you talking about?" Caes asked. "We're finding a corpse? Whose?"

"A child of earth."

"What?" All of them said in various tones, ranging from confused to outraged. Caes was the "child of earth." She was the one referred to in her "father's" prophecy. It was impossible that it referred to someone else—right?

"*I'm* the one who has to go," she said. This entire time, she was the one who had to go to the Burning Hand. She was one of the few who could. And now there was another, close enough to prevent her from needing to go at all? How?

"Tell me," Caes said, forcing the anger from her voice. "Everything."

The god nodded. "You are not the only child of earth."

"Sorry, Caes," Bethrian said. "You're unique in a lot of ways, but not this."

"Wait, how did *you* know this?" Caes asked.

"The skull," Bethrian said. "It was why I had to…" Bethrian held up his arm and pointed at the general area where he had sliced Caes back in Fyrie.

"Ah," Caes said. Her mind swam. Did she know she wasn't the only "child of earth"? The idea sounded familiar, but she couldn't recall if it was from her time as Liuva or not. Though, the idea made sense—there was more than one location like the Burning Hand in the word, so why would she be the only one? Gods, she couldn't remember if Bethrian said something before slicing her, or if Lyritan said something…regardless, it didn't matter. The other "child of earth," wasn't here. She was.

"I told you I had a plan, Caesonia," Lyritan said, looking very satisfied. "Others have the piece of divinity mixed with mortality needed to enter the Burning Hand. This one is merely sleeping. And I will wake him. And bring him to the Burning Hand in your stead."

"Him?"

"Yes. Hanith."

Caes rapidly made eye contact with everyone she could. Everyone seemed as confused as her. Bethrian even gave a dramatic shrug. "But you ate him. Famously 'wore' him in order to hide from the goddesses."

"And a part of him remained afterwards. Come now, Caesonia, I'm not that much of a brute—I wasn't about to completely destroy my son." Caes's stomach revolted. Which part of Hanith wasn't eaten, especially if it allowed him to be restored? Lyritan took another bite, seemingly thinking as he chewed and the others watched, rapt. After he swallowed, he said, "I ate him, but then I bound him to a mortal, and buried him. He became a child of earth."

Memories surged through Caes, of blood and agony, the first sensations of pains ringing through her phantom limbs as they gradually turned to flesh and bone. She was crafted, a piece of Shirla's divinity bound with mortals. And he had done that to Hanith? There was nothing on this earth that could convince her to foist that agony on a child, much less hers.

"Why would Hanith help us?" Caes asked. "I can't imagine that he would be happy to see you." *Not after undergoing that by your hand*, she left unsaid. When Shirla made Liuva, she didn't have any other experience, and she didn't even exist until Shirla crafted her. Liuva had never questioned the necessity of the brutality that had brought her into the world. But Hanith had been a god, and he was forced to go through *that*?

"No, he won't," Lyritan admitted. "But as much as he hates me, he wants this to end. He wants freedom, and this is the only way to get it. He will be more than happy to go to the Burning Hand and destroy the goddesses. What do you think Karima was like as a mother?"

Caes didn't know. Shirla was a kind, loving guardian, so long as Liuva did what she wanted. If even Shirla had acted in such a contradictory manner, what would Karima have been like?

Karima would have made it known that he was nothing but a tool. By killing him, Lyritan may have saved him.

The Liuva part of her mind had a point—but did Hanith think of it that way?

Still, Caes doubted Hanith was going to be as accommodating as Lyritan thought, but that was his concern, not hers. Was Hanith even Hanith any longer? After what happened to Liuva after undergoing a similar process, it was doubtful there was much left of the being he once was.

Caes stared at the god's perfect face. Unreadable. Unchallengeable. "So," she said, "Hanith can also enter the Burning Hand and destroy the goddesses. I'm guessing he has a weapon to do so?"

"Indeed." Lyritan took a deep breath. "To enter the Burning Hand, you cannot come out. Not as you were."

"You die," Cylis said.

Lyritan shrugged. "Depends on what you consider to be death."

"When your body stops breathing," Cylis said.

"What a quaint definition," the god said. And that was all he said on the matter.

Yes, Caes knew that the Burning Hand required sacrifice and death, no matter how Lyritan tried to repackage it. It was why she had believed Lyritan wanted to use her, to trick her into entering the Burning Hand and sacrificing herself for him. But Hanith changed things.

"Hanith will be glad to manage the Burning Hand," Lyritan said. "And he has the means to do what needs to be done. So, you see, Caesonia, you will be with me in victory—and you won't need to risk yourself." He smiled. "I told you I would keep you safe."

"Why not tell us earlier?" Alair asked. "Why make her think that you needed her this entire time, and make her face such dangers?"

"And risk letting those fools in Gilar know that my child is buried somewhere near their reach? Did you want me to risk your safety further by leaving you with them?" Lyritan wiped his mouth. "Think—they learn that Hanith is buried here, and they will start to wonder what else is undiscovered in these mountains. Things that should stay there."

"This area has already been notorious for treasure hunting," Bethrian said. "Go into the Glynnith market on any day and there will be a vendor selling pottery, stones, and blades claiming to be from the Burning Hand."

"Fools and opportunists," Lyritan said. "It's all fakes. The real hunters find nothing. Or never return. But with the might and planning of Reyvern's royal family behind a search..." He didn't need to finish that thought. If the king and queen of Reyvern wanted to send an expedition into the Burning Hand, odds were they'd be more successful than some desperate treasure seekers.

Caes smiled back. Despite Lyritan's convoluted plan, the main point remained that he had an answer for her to live.

To live.

He wants to save me. Protect me.

A pang entered her heart. For her to live, Hanith would be reborn, only to die once more. Someone would suffer and die. And that was if Lyritan's plan worked at all.

Caes couldn't sleep and it wasn't from the cold, for she was wedged between Lyritan and Alair, both men cocooning her under layers of blankets and the warmth from their bodies. No, it was an eerie sense of discomfort, the kind that comes from knowing that a momentous event was about to occur, and that one was powerless to stop it. The night before a battle. The day before a wedding. The eve before a trial. The same foreboding wracked through her, unending.

Not to mention everything else that weighed on her.

Caes sat up and gingerly crept over Alair, careful not to wake him. It didn't do any good. His mirrored eyes instantly flickered open and followed her movements. Did he truly sleep at all? In turn he stood and followed her to a back corner of the cave, where they wedged themselves in a little niche, a place where they could attempt to be alone. The others slept soundly, trusting the horses at the entrance to alert them to anyone or anything approaching.

"What's wrong?" Alair asked in a whisper, pushing the hair out of her face. He placed a kiss on her forehead.

She debated saying it was nothing, that she just needed some time to herself. But she had to tell someone about the storm of emotions threatening to shatter her, or they would break at the worst time. She needed him, more than she could ever say.

"Everything." Caes sighed. "My life hasn't been a life. I've been a tool. Even when I was 'happy,' when I was with my father" –Caes choked back a cry– "that life was hard. We had our moments of joy, but I never fit in with the others. I was always an outsider. I had my life planned without knowing how I was going to manage without Father. And then, in Ardinan...I never got to be me. I never had a real choice. I never—"

Alair leaned forward and wrapped her in his arms, his solid chest pressed against her. His rough and calloused hands covered hers, holding them steady. She inhaled his scent, leather and smoke, and let herself forget where she was. What was to come. There was only him and her, a single star against the coming night.

"I gave myself to the Soul Carvers to obtain the life I thought I wanted," Alair said gently, "and I lost everything. My home. My family. My position. All that was left after I awoke was pain and loss. Until you, I never thought I'd find something to make all this, all this *shit* worthwhile." He took a single finger and lifted her chin so that she looked him in the eyes, the dying embers reflecting in his mirrored gaze. "I don't know what is waiting for us, but I do know that we will be together. That is all I want. I don't care where or how, but I want you. Only you."

Worry flickered across his fine features. "There's more, isn't there?"

"I haven't been able to care about dying," Caes admitted, keeping her voice low.

A raised eyebrow was the only answer.

"No, I mean, I don't want to. I want to live, especially since I don't know what is to come for me after death. But how I feel now, it wasn't like I felt when trying to break Lyritan's curse. I can't seem to..."

"Fear it?" Alair offered.

Caes nodded. "What's wrong with me? I'm afraid, but I'm...not." Her voice lowered to barely more than a breath.

For a long moment Alair held her, softly caressing her face. "I died twice," he finally said. "In an odd way, so did you. It stops carrying the same dread, after time. Not when you know there are worse things." That was true. She had died. And death was preferable to reliving certain days in her life.

She wanted him to keep holding her. She wanted to talk and grieve and worry together with her friend. But their time uninterrupted could end at any moment. Anyone could wake and wonder what they were doing together. Lyritan could wake. "Do you trust that he will be able to awaken Hanith?" Caes asked, listening to make sure no one was stirring. "That I won't be asked to go into the Burning Hand at all?"

"No." Alair shook his head. "I don't believe it at all. If he was so confident in Hanith, why bring and risk you? Why tell us this story?" He gripped her hand reassuringly. "I would've been able to protect you in Gilar, and he knows it."

"But we are going to the Burning Hand already and willingly," Caes said. "Why does he need to lie to us? He's told me so many conflicting things, now that I've had a chance to think about them."

"It's easier to manage us if we believe him," Alair said. "He's not showing it, but he is afraid."

"What?"

Alair nodded. "He has to be. His entire existence on this plane depends on you doing exactly what he needs you to do. There is a lot that can go wrong between here and getting you inside that mountain. And he's not used to mortals challenging him—he probably didn't think he needed to watch his words."

"I'm not mortal."

"But Liuva loved him." That was true. Liuva would've believed everything that he told her. *Did* believe everything he told her. "Only a fool believes a desperate god," Alair added, his voice little louder than a breath. "We can hope that he has a plan to save you, but we need to be prepared that his plan will fail. Or that there is something else at play."

Caes frowned. Alair's words triggered something in her memory, something about the Burning Hand. There *was* something more about the mountain. Fuck...what was it? Sacrifice? Yes. But there was more than just death. Something...

"I hate this," Caes said. "Being pushed and pulled, with no say in my fate."

"You've said it yourself—this is a game to the gods, one in which they play with the ultimate stakes. What else are the pawns supposed to do?"

Chapter 48

Cylis

Thanks to the cursed deal he had made with Karima to become a Soul Carver, Cylis was more than capable of handling frigid weather. Though what his merry companions liked to forget was that while Cylis would survive the cold, that didn't mean he wasn't immune from the pain it caused. Sure, he'd keep his limbs, and had a satisfying amount of power as a result, but he still fought the burning pain taking over his fingers and other more sensitive appendages. It was like Kerensa's gift—sure, she could survive a bonfire, and despised the cold with the hatred of a cat for a bathtub, but that didn't mean she didn't feel the pain of the flames, even as her magic preserved her.

So yes, Cylis was cranky. He was in pain. His ass was sore from riding on the stupid horse—and it really was a stupid horse that kept trying to walk off cliffs—and his best friend was dead. He was allowed to be pissed.

It also didn't help that he had to deal with Bethrian's grinning face each time they caught a glimpse of each other. No mortal should've been this happy in these conditions. Cylis had thought that at the very least this journey would allow him to see Bethrian in pain, and nope—Bethrian was here, riding along on the stallion like a cheery little child bobbing along on his pony. It was the third morning of travel, and Bethrian seemed to have adjusted from being miserable to considering this a grand adventure.

He truly was a fuckwit.

The sun was setting over the mountain range once more when Lyritan guided them to another cave, the third one they had stayed in. Once inside, he realized that some things were left to be desired.

"Is it just me, or is this getting…worse?" Cylis asked, holding up a dried apple that was little more than a brown blob.

"The further we travel from the city, the less these will be maintained," Lyritan said. The god frowned, until he discovered a bottle of something liquid under a moldy blanket.

"Be glad the cave is here at all," Caes said. "Though you can stay outside if you're so inclined."

Cylis rolled his eyes. "We've been over this, Caes. Just because I can survive out there doesn't mean I want to."

"You were outside plenty the last time we ran through wintery woods. You liked it."

"Hardly." That's what he got for trying to preserve his image as an impressive magical warrior. And frankly, warm rooms after the cold were often excruciating to the point that staying outside was a better alternative—it was choosing between pain and debilitating pain.

"What if I want you to like the outdoors?" Bethrian asked, then chuckled when Cylis gave him a half-hearted rude gesture.

While Cylis would never admit this to them, the cave was what he considered to be perfect weather. Cool, but not cold. He didn't have to deal with the pain using his magic caused like he did in the deeper winter weather, but he also avoided the blistering itch and burn that came with being exposed to heat. In short, Cylis loved caves. When this adventure was done, perhaps he would buy one somewhere. Somewhere far away from Fuckwit.

"How many more days do you think we will have supplies in these caves at all?" Alair asked.

"I do not know," Lyritan said. "The caves themselves are going to be scarce soon, but I have another plan."

"You do?" Caes asked.

"Yes." The god took a seat against the wall, prying the cork off the bottle. "I didn't want to tell you in case it's no longer there, but we are getting close to a larger cave, one that will let us bypass most of this mountain."

"We're going to tunnel our way there?" Cylis asked, taking his own seat against the wall.

"No. Not the whole way." The god took a deep breath. "It will just help us get past the part where we are most likely to freeze to death. That is all."

"Oh," Caes said, taking her place at Alair's side on the ground.

"I'll take it," Bethrian said. "Anything."

"Careful what you wish for, Bethy," Cylis muttered. At this point, he had learned that when it came to anything with gods and royals—or Caes—nothing was easy. There was a catch. There had to be.

"We haven't had any sign of the Ardinani prince," Marva observed.

"They wouldn't wait for us here," Lyritan said. "It isn't impossible, I suppose, but they have mortal bodies—they will be someplace more hospitable."

"More hospitable for killing us," Cylis quipped.

"Quite," Lyritan said, not catching Cylis's sarcasm. "Shall we eat?"

After digging through what supplies were in this cave, they ate another meal of pickled beets, dried fruit, and bitter wine. Caes chatted solemnly with both Lyritan and Alair, somehow managing to keep both men content in her presence. How in the hells did she manage that? Especially since the god was still lusting after her. Cylis knew the look of lust. It was nauseating.

Though, there was one thing to be grateful for, and that was Bethrian's silence. And then there was Marva—Marva wouldn't stop staring at him. That wasn't good. It was making Cylis very aware that he hadn't had a proper bath for days, while Marva...it wasn't right that someone so messy could look so good. He caught himself glancing at the curve of her smooth neck, where her dark hair caressed it. Imagining—*remembering*—what it would be like for him to touch it. For her to—

"Cylis," Caes said, "are you alright?"

Cylis felt his cheeks burn. He was hardly the one to be mocking Lyritan about lust. If it wasn't for losing his best friend, who knew what would've happened between him and Marva by now? "I need to sleep," he said. Alair cocked his head, but if he had any misgivings, Alair kept them to himself. One of Alair's better traits.

Caes nodded, relieved. "I understand. Rest, please."

Yup, it was time to take some time to himself. After saying a grudging farewell to the others, he left the group and covered himself with blankets in a back corner of the cave. Caes had often teased him that he could fall asleep at a moment's notice, and Cylis wasn't about to disappoint her now.

Unfortunately, just as he fell asleep, he heard an etherial voice say, *Don't think I've forgotten you.*

Karima.

A hand gently nudged him awake. "Cylis," Marva whispered. "Cylis!" she hissed.

"Wha—" He barely formed the word before her lips crashed into his, at first harsh and then gently coaxing his mouth onto hers. Heat roared in Cylis's body, answering her fervor, and before he could think, he gripped her shoulders and tugged her down to him. She nibbled on his bottom lip and he groaned, only to be interrupted by a finger over his lips, silencing him. Leaving him gasping for breath. Alright, this wasn't a bad way to wake up.

She hovered over him, her delicate features bathed in the dim light of the dying fire, her eyes looking at him with an emotion he knew all too well—want.

"Not here," she whispered. "There's more space further back. The cave keeps going."

There was? It did?

Cylis wasn't in the mood for thinking. He was in the mood for following. Moments later, he matched Marva step by step through the cave, away from the fire and the sleeping company. No one bothered to keep watch. Alair and the god slept closest to the entrance, and Alair was a notoriously light sleeper. In fact, he probably knew what Marva and Cylis were doing. Well, it was too bad for Alair that Cylis owed him multiple times in that regard.

Once they were away from the others, down a path of twists and turns and in darkness so complete even he couldn't see, Marva pressed her lips against his and pushed him against the stone wall. This time Cylis was ready. He grabbed her shoulders, his hands echoing her movements as she explored his body over his clothes. And then under. Her skin was soft and smooth and eagerly responded to Cylis's movements. And then her breasts, perfect and round, filled his hands as he flicked the peaks back and forth. He smiled when he was rewarded with a moan, and his own arousal pushed against her stomach.

"I wish I could see you," Cylis said. "I didn't expect this to happen. Not now."

"Why not?"

"Because we're in a cave. On a death mission."

"Exactly. When will we have a better chance?"

"When we're not on a death mission?"

"I'm not asking you to marry me, Cylis. Or even love me. We both could use this. Unless you don't want to?"

Cylis chuckled. "I didn't say that."

Stop? Ha. Hardly. Had Cylis ever turned down women before? Yes. More than Bethrian would probably think. Ha! Probably more women than Bethrian even had in his life. But as for beautiful Soul Carvers? Cylis didn't turn them down often.

Marva giggled softly. "I all but begged you to take me to bed in Gilar."

Cylis frowned. "You did not."

"Yes, I did. I went to your room. I kissed you. I tried flirting with you—"

"No. Impossible. I mean, yes, you kissed me. But that was it. You had us stop."

"Cylis?" Marva asked.

"Yes?"

"Do you want to argue about whether I was trying to seduce you, or whether I was a fool and I've since changed my mind, or would you rather..." With that, Marva slid a hand in and down the front of his breeches, gripping him firmly and immediately doing a slick up and down movement that made him bite his lip.

Point made.

Cylis tugged his breeches down and then off, not noticing the cave rock now scraping against his bare skin. If only he could see as Marva took him into her mouth. No matter what he imagined, seeing her mouth on him had to be even better. Her hot, perfect mouth that gripped him, sucking and teasing until release threatened to arrive far too soon. Damn Soul Carvers—they knew all too easily what their partners liked.

There was only one way to stop that.

Gently, Cylis moved Marva away from him and proceeded to remove her breeches. "Ouch!" she said, giggling. "Careful."

"I can't see."

"Neither can I. But that was my hair."

"Sorry. I'm trying to—"

She caught the hint and joined in, moving in a mess of tangled limbs to take off her breeches. Another movement and his hand touched bare, hot flesh. She gripped his hand and pulled it towards her core, saying without words what she wanted.

That was all the invitation he needed. Gods, she was so soft. And wet. And soft…She moaned as soon as he touched her. Moaned louder as he worked his way into her.

The two of them laid on the ground and Cylis crouched between her legs, using his fingers and mouth to tease her until her hips jutted against his face and she covered her mouth, stifling her cries. She tugged off her tunic and then he did the same, for once not caring that another person could see his bare and damaged skin. Because she couldn't.

The cave's rocks made it difficult to move, his tender skin complicating his actions, but the two of them found their way around the challenge, laughing and guiding each other in the boulders and the dark. Was this his smoothest coupling? No. But it was definitely one of the most memorable.

In more ways than one.

She was delicious, she tasted like…no. He wasn't going to think about what she tasted like. Because this was Marva. And that was the only thing that mattered.

Soon he was going to be inside the same place he was touching and tasting, and his member strained at the injustice of having to wait. But wait he would. He sucked on her harder, noting which movements in particular made that breathy rasp followed immediately by a pleasure-laden sigh.

"No more," Marva gasped once he repeated the same movement for the third time—one she seemed to particularly enjoy. "Too soon. I want—you. First."

Good. Because he was really getting impatient.

Using his hands to lift her ass, he positioned himself against her opening, using her slick wetness to prepare himself. And then, after moving in slowly—once, twice—he plunged all the way in, making Marva grip his shoulders. "Cylis," she hissed, "you're too much."

"No woman says that, Marv," Cylis said, kissing her neck. "Though I appreciate the compliment."

"Not that, you ass. There's too much weight on my hip. The rocks."

"Oh, sorry." Laughing softly, they readjusted themselves, until Cylis was able to move without protest.

Though, what if she was still uncomfortable? Cylis froze. "Are you alright? Want me to stop?"

"Never." She gripped his ass for emphasis, pulling him in deeper. He smiled.

Slowly, Cylis thrusted, only going faster once she relaxed around him and little cries of pleasure escaped her lips. She was so warm, and the way she gripped him made him lose all sense. Thank fuck Karima let his member be unscathed from the perpetual frostbite. Maybe Karima did have some mercy in her after all. Thank fuck he was able to enjoy Marva, clamped around him, softly uttering his name, using her hand to pleasure herself while Cylis rammed into her, harder and harder until her back arched and she let out a long, punctuated sigh that could've only been one thing.

A moment later, Cylis followed, his release spilling into her. There was nothing but Marva. Nothing but him and her and *this*.

Afterward he pulled out of her and clumsily wiped himself while Marva did the same, and then he laid next to her, holding her in the small section of the cave. Their breaths slowed and their fingers entwined, together in the darkness.

"Well, that was a surprise," Cylis said softly.

"Oh, not that again," Marva said. "I'm just happy I finally decided to do something."

"Me too."

Marva snorted. "Yes, your happiness is in me as we speak."

The image of Marva, filled with him, made him harden once again. "You know, we could..."

She turned towards him, covering his mouth with hers and softly dancing her lips over his. "Not tonight. I think I heard people stirring, and even I have limits for privacy. But we will again. Soon."

"Promise?"

"Definitely. The rumors didn't lie."

Cylis's heart stilled. "What rumors?"

"Oh, that you're a better lover than you'd think."

"...I don't know if that's a good thing."

Marva trailed her hands over Cylis's body, gently massaging as she went. Despite her insistence there would be no more tonight, he stiffened even further. "Don't worry. Coming from me, that was very much a compliment."

Chapter 49

Bethrian

Bethrian was an admirer of the romantic arts. Hells, he made a decent income from selling his wildest inventions regarding such arts. Soul Carver trifectas, princesses and priestesses, a peasant/princess and a demon, a fairy prince making a fleet of mortal women battle over him— there was little Bethrian didn't attempt to craft into his literary endeavors. And he usually succeeded.

But that didn't mean he liked hearing evidence of the real thing. Especially when it involved Cylis.

Oh, sure, he could tell they tried to be quiet, but sound carried. And there was only one thing that people skulked off deep into a cave to do in the middle of the night. Bethrian pretended that Marva was giving Cylis an intense foot rub. It was better that way.

"You're awake," Bethrian said, noting Lyritan sitting by the fire, gently feeding it. The god's face flickered in the light, accenting his handsome angular face with its perfect nose. Bethrian didn't find men attractive as a rule, but exceptions could always be made—exceptions *had* been made—especially ones that would serve as inspiration for his next novel.

"Sleep is a necessity of this body, but that doesn't mean it's pleasant," Lyritan said. Did gods dream? What of? Bethrian wasn't about to ask.

Since it would've been rude to leave or lay down to sleep, Bethrian sat at the fire, clasping his hands on his lap. Here he was, alone with a god. An actual god. There were legions of clergy, philosophers, and scholars who would've murdered their favorite baker for a chance to have this—the ability to talk to someone who had been alive since the world was formed. A being of endless power and mystery.

And all Bethrian could think to do was ask, "Do you think the next cave will have any food? It seems like the supplies are becoming less."

Was he afraid of the god? Yes. But Bethrian was a lord, and lords were adept with dealing with beings of power. As a rule, groveling only got one so far, and Lyritan didn't seem to be one to indulge in it, as far as their company was concerned. Thus, he would pretend that Lyritan was just another companion. A companion with glowing eyes who could smite someone with lighting.

"I do not know." The god poked at the fire with a stick, his posture somehow both refined, arrogant, and relaxed. Bethrian needed to learn that trick. "We have supplies enough to make it to the Burning Hand. Even if we receive no other aid."

"Truly? It feels as if we've been in the mountains forever." Bethrian paused. "But what about returning? Are there supplies enough for that?"

"By the time we are done at the Burning Hand, supplies will not be my concern."

Well, wasn't that just what he wanted to hear…

Instead of voicing displeasure, Bethrian rubbed his feet, trying to get some feeling back into the limbs. His socks were hanging out, drying by the fire with the others'. He wasn't necessarily too cold, but he hadn't been properly warm in…oh, since Malithia?

"Concern yourself not, mortal. Our journey is progressing as it should."

Bethrian nodded. Not like his arguing would've done any good. "While I would have loved to see a valley of sinkholes, I'm alright not having that experience. The mountain is fine enough for me."

The god looked at Bethrian, his gold eyes as brilliant as embers. "You will see plenty to astound you, before the end."

Wonderful. That was just what any mortal wanted to have a god tell him in the middle of the night.

"You are a lord, are you not?" Lyritan asked.

"I am. In Malithia." Bethrian sat up straighter.

"And you are not with your lands?"

"No. I...the emperor and I were never friendly." Bethrian moved his feet so that he sat on them. He grabbed a nearby bedroll, one of the ones from the cave, and placed it under him. Much better. Warmer, at least. And being occupied with his feet let him ignore the god's stare.

"What does being a lord mean to you?" Lyritan asked. "I know what rulership is to me—it is in my nature, but I never understood why mortals fight so hard for something so temporary."

Gods, it was too late in the night for that question. "I...it is who I am," Bethrian said. "I am my father's son, and my place is at our home. With our people."

"You care for these people?"

"I do." He did. Bethrian never had much of a mind for governing, but he was great at reading people and appointed those who were efficient and fair. Bethrian checked on their work regularly. "They're my responsibility."

"Interesting." Lyritan watched him some more. "Your sense of self is based on what others gave to you."

"No." Bethrian shook his head. "My father gave me my title. But it takes more than a name to make a lord. I've seen many lords squander their fortune and lands into ruin. I may not have been perfect, but I do my best. I do what needs to be done. And thus far, my lands have prospered. I have fulfilled the name I was given, and I have done it well."

Slowly, Lyritan's lips curled. "I see." Whatever Lyritan was looking for, Bethrian's little speech accomplished it. He didn't lie to the god, but he wasn't an accomplished courtier for nothing. Being an accomplished courtier meant being able to turn a pig turd into a cake. And not mentioning the mistakes he had made in his youth. Gambling ones.

When the god was seemingly lost in his thoughts again, Bethrian cleared his throat. "May I ask, why Seda? I've since guessed that you're the one who brought her back to life, such as it was. But why? Why her?"

Lyritan blinked hard, seemingly attempting to remember what Bethrian was talking about. "Seda...Seda...the mortal princess. Yes. Usually we can't resurrect the dead, but she wasn't truly alive, by the time I was done. So, I found a way around that problem. She had a purpose for me, and that was her reward. The only thing I could do for her."

"She's gone now. Her skull was shattered." Bethrian didn't mention that he had swallowed her tooth. That was disgusting. And not the god's concern.

"Oh." Lyritan rubbed his chin, the news of Seda's death seemingly an inconvenience at most.

"She said you had plans for her. That you wanted her," Bethrian pressed. "Didn't you need her for something at the Burning Hand?"

"Her?" Lyritan scoffed. "No. You. I needed you."

"*Me?*"

"Yes. I determined that she was the best way to get you to the Burning Hand. Where you are needed, Child of Sky."

"Um…Your Godliness, can you please explain to me, uh, what is going on?" A Child of Sky. Seda had said as much, back when she was "resurrected." But Bethrian was still confused. He didn't like being confused. Nor did he like the cold sweat that erupted all over him.

Lyritan shrugged. "Along with a sacrifice, the Burning Hand needs to be opened by two—Children of Earth and Sky. One made of both mortal and divine, the other of earth and the heavens. Long ago, a goddess used your home to ascend from this plane, connecting it—and you—forever. That magic she used to leave stayed. In your blood."

"Those ruins? That was real?" Bethrian thought back to all the hours on his estate he had spent on the crumbling stone. In fact, Bethrian had visited there shortly after receiving the summons from the emperor that he was to return to the Malithian court. The goddess had really ascended to the heavens there? Clovild, one of his intense childhood tutors who still gave him nightmares, was *right* about that?

"It was." The god nodded. "This all occurred after I was trapped, but the gods did leave the mortal plane, and they each chose their places to do so. So, yes, there are others in the kingdoms who have the same claim as you, based on being tied to different locations, but you were available and in Malithia. And with your knowledge of Caesonia, I determined you would be most likely to help."

"Wonderful." Bethrian's brows knit together. "Wait, so you needed a lord? A lord of my lands?"

"Yes." Lyritan raised a knee and draped his hand over it, resting his foot on the ground. Was he...happy about getting a chance to lecture Bethrian about this? That his master plan came to fruition? "To your point, a deity leaving the planes like that changes things. Your family carries an echo of that action, being tied to the land as you are. So, yes, you can help open the door. You're the only one here who can."

"But what if someone else's family took over as lord after Karima left?" Bethrian asked. "Would they be the...Sky Child?" Sky Child. He had teased Seda with that name, and now it was his. Fuck. Him.

Lyritan shrugged. "What is on the mortal plane echoes to the next. It would probably just follow the next lord. I cannot say I've had a chance to test it."

Well, here was hoping that no one in his family had found a handsome soldier in a wood pile, thus creating a non-legitimate Bethrian. Though Bethrian's coloring *was* a bit bright for a Malithian. Oh, no...

Meh. Oh, well. Too late to worry about that now.

"Cylis's family is religious," Bethrian pointed out. "Are you sure that he couldn't help you?"

"He doesn't smell right," Lyritan said. "He does not have the correct blood."

The fuck?

Smell?

Cylis?

No.

Bethrian shuddered. So, Seda was nothing but a tool to get Bethrian to journey from Malithia, to Ardinan and Caes, and ultimately to the Burning Hand. Everything that he had done—including to Caes—was just one step of the god's plans. The fact that he had managed this...how deep did this god's plans go?

"Why didn't you just ask me to go?" Bethrian asked. "I probably would have."

The god shook his head. "No. At that time I did not have a body. And what person, after dreaming of a god and being asked *that*, would have listened?" The god frowned. "I could not take the chance."

Well, that explained Seda. Poor Seda. Where was her soul now? He could only hope that she found peace in the afterlife—or his chamber pot—and that he would see her there again someday. In the afterlife, not the chamber pot. And hopefully that meeting was a very long time from now, for Bethrian's sake.

But that didn't explain why he had swallowed her tooth, why he had felt the urge to do so. Maybe it was just the action of a grieving mind. Grieving minds were capable of bizarre things. And yet, Bethrian was so logical in every other respect, swallowing bony body parts wasn't typical behavior for him. Or anyone.

"Your guess worked," Bethrian said. "I'm here—and I'm committed until the end."

The god nodded, pleased. If also a bit smug.

Bastard.

Bethrian folded his hands on his lap. "While I have your attention, Your Divineness, have you ever heard anything about the royal family of Malithia? If they might have some...powers?"

"Powers?" The god chuckled. "Not that I have heard of. They're mortals, correct?" Bethrian hesitatingly nodded. "Yes," the god said, "magic can sometimes be hereditary, but I thought such things were rare in the empire at this time." Rare? Practically unheard of, unless one was a Soul Carver or some other odd exception. "All I know of the royal family," the god continued, "is that it is truly a miracle that they managed to hold onto their power for so long, sworn to Karima as they are."

So, Bethrian didn't suddenly gain the ability to fly when he swallowed that tooth. Damn. No matter—his secret cannibalism was still safe with him. He wasn't going to tell the god what he had done, because knowing his luck it meant absolutely nothing and Cylis would walk in and hear and then that would entirely ruin everything.

That was enough divine talk for one night.

Bethrian did his best to give the god a sincere smile as he bowed his head. "Thank you, God. I'm honored to serve." Really, what else was he supposed to say?

It wasn't until Bethrian was tucked back into his bedroll and he heard Cylis and Marva turn up from wherever they scampered off to that he realized that the god had mentioned a sacrifice. The god never deigned to explain what that sacrifice would consist of. Would it be as simple as giving a bit of blood, like Seda believed? After all, that was why she insisted he drain Caes in Fyrie.

But knowing Bethrian's luck, it wasn't going to be so easy.

Chapter 50

Caes

More traveling. More snow. More cold. More caves—some were spacious, and some were not. None were provisioned anymore.

How much longer would they have to contend with the wintery mountain? The rest of the journey promised to be flat. Ish. Caes would've given anything for the terrain to be flat. She would never taste honey and cheese again if it meant that the terrain would be flat. Anything.

"Courage," Lyritan called out from horseback. "Today is the last day we will have to endure this cold."

"What?" Caes asked, looking around her. All she could see were mountains, trees, and snow. All a wintery hell. There was no way to avoid it.

"I promised that I had a way for us to get over the mountain safely." Lyritan turned to face her, the surrounding snow and ice setting off his sharp cheeks and blond hair. "And today, I make good on that promise." He turned forward again, facing the untouched path before them. "Though this is our last day with the horses. They cannot go further."

"Lovely," Cylis muttered. Caes shared the sentiment. Would the horses manage to return to Gilar on their own, in this terrain? Caes chose to believe they would, and that they had a flock of attendants watching for them, waiting with warm blankets and fresh oats. The alternative was far too depressing.

"A tunnel is better than falling off a cliff," Bethrian said. "He has some sort of tunnel, right?"

"I think so," Caes said, gripping her horse's reins. What else could it be? She made eye contact with Alair, who shrugged. Whatever was next, they were entirely at the mercy of the god.

"So, not to change the subject, but are you sure that's the Burning Hand?" Cylis asked, apparently admiring the same rainbow flares that Caes had noticed around the mountain. "It looks a little too...happy. At first I thought it was something from the weather, but nope. No storm does that."

"What do you mean?" Lyritan looked at the mountain. "Oh, the rainbows. Yes, that happens."

"I expected the Burning Hand to be more, I don't know, burning," Bethrian said.

"Well, poisonous fumes are what causes the color, if that's any consolation," Lyritan said. "I imagine it burns if one breathes it in."

Caes sighed. "You had to ask."

"So, it's like a volcano?" Bethrian asked.

"It's a portal connecting the worlds," Lyritan said, his voice strained. "Sometimes things come through—and come out. And yes, the Burning Hand didn't earn its name for no reason."

"Really," Caes said to Cylis, "I could've done with not knowing that."

"What?" Cylis asked, indignant. "You'd rather not know about the fumes that will burn your lungs out? It's not like my asking suddenly made it an awful death mountain."

"No," Caes agreed, "but I could have pretended for a few more days. I'm the one who will have to go in there." She waited to see if Lyritan would correct her. He didn't. Darn.

Though, Cylis was a little prickly. Caes thought of making a quip that she would've thought Marva had put Cylis in a better mood and then decided against it—no point in potentially angering Marva just to heckle Cylis. There was more than enough to heckle him about already.

And there was more than enough on this journey to make her miserable. Damn, when this was done, she was never traveling again. Anywhere.

Near midday, they neared an area where the ground decidedly leveled out and the mountain they had crossed in the first days towered behind them, while before them lay a network of chasms and ledges. An unseen weight pressed on Caes's chest, like the air itself was laden with foreboding. Yet, nothing about the scenery seemed amiss. That was what worried her most of all. What if that creature from the first day came back? What if something worse came instead? There was always something worse.

"We can take the horses no further," Lyritan said, dismounting with a heavy thud into the snow.

"What?" Caes and the others asked in surprise. "Now?"

"Yes," the god said. "They were useful for supplies over the mountain, and we needed speed, such as it was. I would bring them further if we could. But they will be a hazard on this terrain, and far too tempting for predators."

"But they'll die here," Bethrian said, repeating Caes's earlier fear, for both the horses and herself. This was coming. She knew it was coming, their having to toil along on foot. But she thought they'd have at least the rest of the day before they had to say goodbye to their four-legged companions.

"Possibly." Lyritan worked at unpacking his saddle bags, tugging out the travel sacks that would securely attach to his back. Everyone had one with them for this part of the journey. "But if they stay with us, they absolutely will die."

"They'll be fine," Marva said, patting her horse. "They'll just wander off and take care of themselves. They always do."

Grumbling, the rest of the party dismounted and worked at unpacking the saddlebags and readjusting their provisions. How much food were they able to bring with? As much as possible. The weight would slow them, but starvation would slow them even more. Caes eyed the great mountain in the distance. The Soul Carvers could carry more than Bethrian or herself, but they needed their strength as well. How much further did they have to go? A week? Maybe? Lyritan gave no more than vague answers for how much time was left to travel, and as such, she steeled herself to the fact that it would possibly take weeks. Weeks of misery.

"Ride over the mountain," Cylis mumbled. "Get a sore ass. Abandon the horse. Get sore feet. Die. Sounds about right."

"Oh, come now," Caes said. "It's not that bad. Yet."

"I disagree." Cylis said, twisting the reins around his hands. "It's been that bad for some time now."

Kerensa, he likely meant. Her absence lurked between them. And always would.

Caes watched the others, who were distracted, unpacking their own horses and sorting through their supplies. Alair and Lyritan were discussing something seemingly grim, while Bethrian said something that made Marva laugh. Caes stepped closer to Cylis, putting her hand on his arm. "I'm sorry," she said softly.

"Stop that," Cylis said. "You crying isn't going to bring her back."

"No. But are you angry at me for how I handled it? With Sabine?"

Cylis paused at untying the pack straps. His mirrored eyes danced with light reflected from the snow. His face was a blotchy purple, and he had ooze in the corners of his eyes, but overall, he didn't look too horrendous. "At first I was upset. And then I realized that this whole situation is a pile of shit we all got caught in. And you were right—Sabine did save your life." Cylis shrugged. "Kerensa didn't like Sabine, and she had a thing for vengeance, but she would've known who was really at fault."

"Flyntinia," they both said. Caes's stomach twisted at the name. She deserved to suffer more than she did.

"What's wrong?" Cylis asked after a pause. "I mean, you somehow got even paler."

"I was just thinking of what Flyntinia said, before Lyritan killed her." She rubbed her eyes. "About how people keep dying for me. And how she was right."

"Caes?"

"Yes?"

"Stop. You're sounding like a distraught princess in some novel and it's not you."

"I'm not—"

"You are." Cylis's voice raised an octave. "Oh, everyone I love dies and suffers, all because I'm so pretty and kind and my burps smell like roses. And all these men love me for some reason."

"That's not—"

"Look." Cylis's voice lowered to normal. "Kerensa? That was an accident. A fucked-up accident, but one nonetheless. Beltina? That was Seda. Not you. Your father? I don't know what happened with him, but again, I'd blame Shirla, and not you. Althain? Again, Desmin. Not you. It's not you—it's because you have the misfortune of being someone shoved around power-hungry goose gizzards."

"But if it wasn't for me—"

Cylis rolled his eyes. "Let me finish. Are people in the midst of inter-kingdom politics known for living long lives? No. Are people squeezed between feuding gods known for living long lives? Again, no. You didn't ask for any of this, and frankly, the amount of death surrounding you is singularly mediocre, considering. Yes, I'm including the butchered Malithians. And Bethrian's men. Sorry," Cylis called out to Bethrian, who raised his head upon hearing his name. Bethrian shook his head and went back to talking to Marva. With a slight huff, Cylis re-focused his attention on Caes. "My point is—stop dragging your mind through the gutter for this. It wasn't you. None of it. And by the time this is done, hopefully you'll be saving more lives by stopping this."

"But you're *here*," Caes said. "You're in danger. And Marva."

"Eh, what's the point of being a Soul Carver if I don't risk my life epically now and then?" Cylis grinned. "I'll need something to entice the ladies once we get back to Malithia."

Ladies? What about Marva? Caes had heard more than enough of their physical encounter to know there was something between them. But this was not the time or place to pester Cylis about his relationship, and Cylis...was Cylis. He was oddly private about some matters.

"Back to Malithia?" Caes asked instead. "Is that what you will do when this is done?"

"I'm not sure, yet," Cylis admitted. "Probably. I need to get things together before I find my sister. Though it will depend on what you and Alair are doing, too. If I'm remembering right, you owe me a Tithran estate."

Caes smiled. "At this point, it will be a sandcastle estate. I no longer have royal funds."

"Good enough." He grinned with his deep purple lips. "See, Caes? Don't worry. I'm not dying yet." He stretched, raising his arms to the sun, like he was getting ready to race. It was then his turn to shake his head, his face suddenly crestfallen.

"What is it?" Caes asked. "Tell me," she added in a whisper.

"You."

Her eyes narrowed.

"No, not like that," Cylis said. "It's just, you talk about all these people dying, with all the pain and misery surrounding it. Loss eats at a person—always. How have you not become the villain?"

"I don't follow." Caes crossed her arms, watching the others out of the corner of her eye.

"You have power," he whispered. "You have the ear and love of a god. And you have more than enough fuckers who betrayed you and deserve to be wiped from this earth. How have you not decided 'to hell with it all' and destroyed everything? Again, how are you not the villain?"

"How do you know that I'm not?"

Cylis stared. "Well, *that* took an unexpected turn."

Caes let out a long breath and slowly shook her head. "*We* know we are saving lives, Cylis. *We* know what the goddesses will do to people if they are allowed to continue waging their war unchecked." Caes paused and watched a sole bird fly overhead, one of the few forms of life she had seen in days. "But others don't. What do you think the people of Malithia would do if they knew I was trying to destroy their goddess? What about Ardinan and their love for Shirla? I was surprised the Reyverni didn't rip me apart." She nodded to Lyritan. "He is the only reason they didn't try."

Cylis opened his mouth, but whatever he was going to say was interrupted as Lyritan pointed at a nearby cliff. "There it is," Lyritan called out. "Follow me. We can finally get out of this blasted cold for a few days."

"The tunnels go, how far?" Caes asked. Granted, she didn't want to traverse the labyrinth of rock and ice that lurked above, but the cave—their new road—wasn't dark. And caves were supposed to be dark. This one was something else entirely. An eerie glow emanated from the rock, making various stones illuminate a muted silver light. It was dim, but it allowed them to see.

"Two days?" Lyritan said. "Maybe just one? But the tunnels end in the valley, where things should get a little easier."

"Alright," Bethrian said. "One night in here, in the eerie hole. We can do it. Disturbing, bizarre tunnels. I can do this."

"Shut up, Bethy," Cylis said from his place at the back of the party.

Caes stopped, inspecting the stones. "Why is it bright in here?"

"Lit ash," Marva answered. "A feature of the Burning Hand."

"She is correct," Lyritan said. "We are coming to the place where the rules of our world are going to bend. These stones still bear the markings of the world's creation. A little light is to be expected."

"As long as it keeps to only light. Light I can handle," Cylis said.

"Speak for yourself," Bethrian said.

"I always do."

"Will you two stop, just for once?" Marva asked. "You're both practically yelling in my ears."

The three of them bickered while Caes followed Lyritan and took stock of their new "road." They maneuvered down the tunnel in a single line, Caes nestled between Lyritan at the front and Alair right behind her. At least it was warmer in the tunnels than on the surface, though the air was still reminiscent of a cool spring night. But there was no wind here, which also improved matters considerably. The ground itself was covered in a fine gravel, making the steps easy and sure. Thus far, the tunnel seemed to be a massive improvement.

Caes rubbed her eyes. She thought she saw the stones shift. How long had it been since she slept through the night? Too long. She desperately needed a full night of sleep.

"Uh, did you hear that?" Cylis asked.

"Hear what?" Caes asked.

All of them stopped. The Soul Carvers looked around the tunnel. "Something is moving," Alair said.

"It doesn't sound like an animal," Marva said.

"Oh, I was worried about that," Lyritan said, and resumed his walking.

"Worried about—" An old man's face appeared in the stone, complete with white, fleshy eyes that blinked at Caes in wonderment. And then Caes's words were changed into a scream as a stone hand reached out to grab her.

"The fuck!" Cylis said. The Soul Carvers pulled out their swords and magic, moving to attack the stone specter. But then the face and arm disappeared, leaving them all alone in the illuminated cave.

Were they actually alone?

"No point in attacking them," Lyritan said, now a fair distance ahead. "Even if you catch them, it won't harm them."

"What are they?" Alair asked, a hand protectively on Caes's shoulder. "Stay close to him," he said to her. She didn't need to be told twice. She scampered up to the god, and after hesitating, the rest of their party followed, staying as far from the walls as possible. "Magic?" Alair asked louder. "Did magic do this?"

"In a way," Lyritan said, rubbing a finger over the walls. "Places like this carry memories. Sometimes they carry a bit more than that." He turned around and gave Alair a smirk. Alair didn't return the gesture. "Think of this place as a jar of honey. And these are the flies."

"They're...people?" Alair asked.

"Used to be. They were old when I first saw them, thousands of years ago. I imagine they're little more than shells now, condemned to these halls." His voice drifted off listlessly. "Creation is a messy business, Soul Carver. It requires some destruction in the process."

That was potentially the worst thing Lyritan could have said to comfort them. "Won't they hurt us?" Caes asked.

Lyritan shrugged. "Probably not. I think they're just curious. Though, I wouldn't sleep too close to a wall if I were you."

Wonderful.

It was difficult to sleep. They took turns keeping watch, two at a time to keep each other company and awake. Lyritan insisted that they were safe, for the most part. However, there were multiple heads and arms and other body parts that periodically pushed in and out of the stone and reached for them, occasionally clutching on a cloak or hair that got too close. Some of the faces snarled, others had their mouths open in a silent cry—all of them struggled to escape and could not. It was unsettling. It was like the stone was a pregnant stomach and the bodies were infants testing the limits of space. It made Caes suddenly glad she likely wasn't able to have children, even if she lived long enough to try.

Her watch that night was with Lyritan.

"Do you remember the last time we came through here?" Lyritan asked, resting next to her and reclining against the stone. He was the only one who felt comfortable enough to do so. So strange. She didn't trust the god and was depending solely on his needing her as much as she needed him, but for this exchange she was able to forget about that. She *needed* to forget that.

We enjoyed each other, despite everything. Before everything.

Caes frowned. "This tunnel? I don't remember it."

"No. We never came here. The mountains."

"Ah." She thought for a moment, and then answered. "Some. Pieces. It's like an old dream."

"Probably for the best," Lyritan said. He shifted, wrapping his cloak tighter around himself. "Last time nothing went like I planned."

"I don't think anyone could've planned for it," Caes said. The two of them sat there in an awkward silence.

He broke my heart.

But it was a misunderstanding. A trick to fool the other gods, or so he had told her. And she had believed him. As for the Caes of now, it was easier to believe him, back when they were in Reyvern with a million other distractions, including their survival at court. It was more convenient to believe him, then. Here, there was nothing but the wilderness and her memories.

But she had believed him before, when she was Liuva.

What would happen if she told him what she suspected? What if she told him that she had a piece of the Sword of Might buried in her arm? What if she was being too harsh on him? What if...

"It wasn't fair," Lyritan suddenly said. "None of it was fair. After everything, the fact that you went to sleep believing that I had..." Lyritan sighed. "But things had started to fall apart long before that. I wasn't able to protect you before, but I will now. I promise."

The urge to believe him again, to trust him, rose within her. It would be so easy and comforting to let him take care of her again. Be protected by him.

He shifted. "Are you sure you don't want to sit next to me?" he asked, his voice carrying more than just a question about seating—with his tone, he meant so much more. Her stomach jumped. He was handsome. It was flattering. It was...

"I think I'll avoid sitting anywhere near that wall, thank you," she said.

When the god opened his mouth she interrupted and asked, "How far away are we from Hanith?" She was desperate to change the conversation. So far, Lyritan had enough manners to let his physical lust lay dormant in her grief over Kerensa's death, but that apparently was at an end. As for her, after everything, some part of her still stirred whenever she looked at Lyritan, and heated whenever his eyes locked with hers. A buried part of her urged her to run into his arms and forget everything that had happened and would happen. But that part would get her killed.

Alair shifted on his bedroll and she bit back a smile. Of course, he was awake. He wouldn't leave her to deal with Lyritan alone. Thank goodness for the hubris of gods—a mortal man would've felt jealous of Alair long ago, with potentially disastrous consequences to their goal. Lyritan likely attributed her avoidance of his body to grief, exhaustion, Ardinani prudishness—literally anything other than that she didn't want him.

Why would he think that I don't want him? What mortal could resist a god? What mortal would prefer another to him?

Well, Caes wasn't mortal. And gods were well-versed in hatred.

Lyritan's jaw clenched at Caes's question about Hanith. He focused on the tunnels, the silvery paths that would lead them closer to their fate. "It will be a few days, at the least," he said. "Things are different now than what they were before, but the essential mountains are the same. We aren't far from his tomb."

"And then how far is that from the Burning Hand?"

"A week after that? Maybe two?" Lyritan reached for her hand. She let him take it, let herself relax at his touch. "Do not worry. We will be victorious, my love. We will."

They had to find Hanith. Then make it to the mountain. Then have Hanith gain entrance to the mountain where he would destroy the goddesses, after which Hanith would likely die. And then...?

"And then what?" she asked. "What happens when Hanith is done?" Lyritan still never explained his purpose in bringing Caes. She was unnecessary, if Hanith was truly his goal. There had to be more. There was always more.

"Once we are done, then I will assume my throne in Reyvern," he announced. "Without their goddesses, the kingdoms will be desperate. I will conquer them—with you at my side."

"Will Reyvern have enough military might to do so?" Caes said, fumbling with the fabric of her cloak. "I don't know much about armies, but I thought theirs was small."

"Do not fear. I know how to manage *that* easily enough. I made it through the ages in stone in order to be with you again. I will not squander our sacrifice."

Caes made herself give him a small smile. These proclamations always made war sound much simpler than it was, even for a god.

First things first. Before anything else, she had to handle whatever was at the Burning Hand. Once there, maybe she would find some way to convince Lyritan not to conquer the world, to abandon his body, and be content with being a god. She had to. Her fate and that of those she loved depended upon it.

The two of them spoke in hushed murmurs a little longer, and Lyritan told her forgotten tales and songs, memories held by no one else walking the earth. It was soothing, like hearing a favorite childhood story, and for a short time it let her ignore reality.

When she finally went to sleep, curled up next to Alair, it was to the sound of a female voice near her ear. A whisper. A promise.

We are watching you, little one, Karima's voice said. *And we are waiting.*

By that point she was too far into sleep, and decided it was nothing but the onset of a dream.

Chapter 51

Alair

I made it through the ages in stone in order to be with you again. I will not squander our sacrifice.

Lyritan's words rang in Alair's head, even though they had been spoken hours ago. Even now, they were louder to him than the rustling of the beings moving in the stone. It was his turn to watch with Bethrian, and the two of them sat in silence in the gloomy hall. Was it jealousy that was making him replay the words? Was that why he was stewing?

Yes. Alair wasn't so obtuse as to think he was above such emotions. But there was more than that. Did the god mean what he said? Or were there multiple layers, pieces that would become painfully evident only when it was too late?

"You seem tortured," Bethrian said, from his place sitting cross-legged nearby. "I mean, more than normal." A head belonging to an old woman with a bent nose and sparse hair popped out of the stone next to Bethrian.

"Consider where we are, my lord," Alair said. He sat next to Caes, close enough that he brushed her hair while she slept. Close enough that he heard each breath of the god lying next to her.

"True," Bethrian said softly, "but I fear it is more than that."

"You fear?" Alair asked. "I saw you at court for years—you know what I have done. What I was expected to do. All you did was your own schemes and plots. And now you want to discuss my fear?"

"Damn," Bethrian said, looking at his hands. "If you're looking for me to say that I've reformed, I haven't. I'm still a lord, and I still do what needs to be done."

"What's best for you, you mean."

"Come now, we can't deny that it's convenient when what's best for me and what needs to be done is the same thing." Bethrian flashed Alair a winsome smile, but that was pointless. And irritating. What was there to smile about?

"I think it's best if we continue our watch in silence," Alair said, clenching his jaw.

"Noted. Regardless, I'd like to say that I do have regrets," Bethrian said softly. "Many of them." He nodded towards Caes, whose gentle snores broke the silence. Truly, this man picked a horrible time to remind Alair that he had sliced his love and stolen her blood, all on the orders of the woman who had tried to murder her when she was helpless. Cylis was right—he *was* a fuckwit.

"Is Seda one of your regrets?" Alair asked. Seda was the woman who kept Bethrian away from his home, the one who sparked rumor after rumor that Bethrian would be the future empress's consort. The one who seemed to bring out the brightest and boldest in Bethrian—nothing like the tired and ragged lord who sat before him now.

"Never, Alair," Bethrian said. "I'd sooner regret my life entirely than regret having had her."

Yes, he was a fuckwit.

There was a movement in the wall. A familiar tall figure moved in the stone, facing him. This one wasn't like the other figures. Golden eyes, dulled under the rock, met his own. Familiar skulls adorned her hair and garments. A cold sweat broke out on his back.

"Karima," Alair whispered.

"What?" Bethrian asked, looking back and forth between Alair and the wall. "What is it?"

"You are my creation," Karima said, her voice ringing through the hall, unmuffled by the stone. But from how Bethrian didn't react, Alair assumed he was the only one who could hear. "I gave you life. Twice. A true life. And this is how you repay your mother?"

"My mother is dead," Alair said.

"Alair," Bethrian said, "you're scaring me. Should I wake Caes?"

"All this," Karima said, "because a young prince couldn't be content with what he had." A dreadful smile broke out on her face. "You always craved more."

"I was a fool."

"I could give you more now," Karima said after a short pause. "I am willing to help you still. I *will* forget everything. Do you not wonder why the worlds are weakening around you, how you hear the voices of those long turned to dust? I can guide you. I can perfect you." She cocked her head and reached out a bony hand. "Join me, and you will want for nothing again."

Alair hesitated. Moments passed, an eternity in the space of heartbeats. "I think you know what my answer is."

He had spent centuries in Karima's realm, and she had spent that time studying him. They knew each other too well. She should have known it was not worth her time to ask.

The figure faded back into the stone. "I had to try," she said, her voice fading. "Now you cannot blame me when you lose everything."

Bethrian stood, his movements making everyone stir. "What in the hells was that?" Bethrian asked. "Alair, are you alright?"

"No."

Chapter 52

Caes

Alair had seen something in the night. He wouldn't say what—not even to Caes. To make matters more confusing, when she asked Bethrian, he only said something about how Alair didn't know how to accept an apology. Alair was silent, Bethrian was confused, and Caes gave up trying to parse it out. There were souls in the wall, trapped spirits—Alair could've seen literally anything.

But more importantly, they were free of the cavern. Lyritan had guided them out of the tunnels, right as the sun began its descent to the west. They were not happy about being back in the cold, but considering how the tunnel contained haunted stone, the cold was preferable.

"Caves will be hard to find, from now on," Lyritan said, pointing at the wasteland before them. The ground was flatter than it was before, for the tunnels had taken them on a gentle slope that brought them to the canyon floor. In fact, if Caes looked carefully, she was willing to bet she was able to see the spot above them where they had entered the possessed tunnels the previous day. But being on the floor meant they were exposed, for there was little in the way of trees.

"After last night, I'm alright with that," Cylis said. "I never want to see a cave again."

"For once, you and I are in agreement," Bethrian said.

"What are we to do for shelter?" Marva asked Lyritan.

"Whatever we must. Alcoves and boulders are going to be our only option, for the most part."

Alair brushed against Caes and rubbed her arm reassuringly. Caes blinked hard against the brilliant winter sun, and then followed Lyritan, trudging through the snow. The Burning Hand wasn't going to walk to itself. It was a piece of irony, that she would work harder than she ever had before to get to where there was a good chance she was going to die. And while the mountain may have been closer than it had ever been, they still had a ways to go.

"Here," Lyritan said, pointing to an outcrop of stone that connected to a larger ridge. The forbidding rock was nothing like the enclosed shelters they had access to so far, but it was enough that it would block most of the wind, which was the important part. Now that they were at a lower altitude the temperatures were generally bearable, if they were out of the wind.

"Already?" Cylis said, craning his neck to look at the sun. "We have time—"

"Come, Cylis," Marva said, moving next to him. "Better to take the shelter too soon than not have it at all." Thank goodness Marva was there—she had worked miracles in having Cylis keep most of his complaints to himself. Caes would know that it was normally worse. Caes had traveled through a wintery snowscape with Cylis before.

"She's right," Alair said, and then frowned, turning to look behind them. In fact, all of the Soul Carvers did so.

"Animal?" Marva muttered.

"A little big for that," Cylis said.

Bethrian unwound his pack and dropped it at his feet and removed his heaviest coverings. He nodded at Caes. Point made. Caes would prepare to run too. She could grab everything else later. Lyritan moved towards them, his eyes trained on what had the Soul Carvers' attention. Could he see anything? His eyes were apparently mortal—what could he hope to discover?

Caes strained her ears. Nothing. Nothing other than wind and...more wind.

Maybe they were mistaken?

"What do you think—" Her words were interrupted by rustling overhead. Fear swept through Caes's body, pausing her breath, making her startle towards the sound. Lyritan turned to where she looked, pulling out his sword.

"Caes," Lyritan said between deep breaths, "get back."

"Wha—"

A roar echoed through the valley.

"Get back!" Alair yelled, yanking off his heavy cloak and pulling out his sword. Marva and Cylis did the same.

At that moment, Caes finally had a chance to appreciate the weapon Lyritan had given Cylis when they arrived in Gilar, for it was not a normal blade. The steel sword glowed blue through cracks, like the weapon itself was made of an unnatural frost. The hilt was now a brilliant blue that emitted a light that encircled Cylis's hand and up his arm, like it was an ice vambrace. Was it the sword that caused the onslaught of Cylis's magic, or was it merely that it enhanced it? Whatever it was, Cylis now appeared like a vengeful ice elemental, horrifying and dangerous. All beauty was gone from her friend's face—instead there was a grotesque man, whose frostbitten skin oozed the very substance that caused his death, wielding a weapon of nightmares.

Unfortunately, her time to appreciate the weapon was short.

Caes was suddenly jerked back by a yank to her wrist. She whipped her head around, finding Bethrian. The lord had his sword extended, but one hand was still on her, pulling her along. "Come," Bethrian yelled. "We'll only be in their way." Caes followed. He was right. Alair didn't need to be distracted worrying about her. None of them did.

A short rush on foot brought the two of them to large boulders, a place to take shelter while the Soul Carvers and the god fought what attacked them. They had left not a moment too soon, for the creature made itself known, lunging at their companions with unnatural speed.

"What the ever-fucking gods it *that*?" Bethrian asked. Caes shared the sentiment.

The white, hairy creature that was attacking her friends stood twice as tall as the Soul Carvers, and was easily four times as wide. Its arms spread, revealing long claws. No...not claws. Not entirely. The end of each arm pointed outward, revealing hands that had bi-folded palms that opened and shut like clams. Each of those palms had several fingers with long, black claws that glistened in the fading light.

The creature roared, and Caes's attention was drawn to its head. The monster's head was like a bear's, but worse, with a long forked tongue that tasted the air. Whatever it was, it seemed to like what it tasted, for it turned to the Soul Carvers and licked its lips, revealing at least four rows of jagged teeth.

"This land is cursed," Caes said, hugging herself and leaning against Bethrian.

"What in the hells is he doing?" Bethrian asked, pointing at Lyritan.

The god's eyes glowed gold as he moved to stand next to the Soul Carvers, who gave him an acknowledging nod. Cylis, Marva, and Alair moved, signaling to each other with abrupt gestures. Whether they were using a Soul Carver language or one common to all fighters, Caes didn't know. She never thought to ask. But at an unspoken word, the three of them separated, maneuvering around the creature. Their movements were smooth and controlled, each step and positioning of their blades evidencing practiced skill. Sometimes it was easy to forget that Soul Carvers were fighters, forged and trained in Karima's realm, created to serve her. These were her friends. Her lover. But at that moment they were something other—weapons made to destroy.

Crebalys, Caes named the monster. "Cursed," in old Malithian. For what other existence could a creature such as this have? How old was this being? If Caes was told that it had been there when Liuva had walked these lands, she would've believed it.

Before she could gather another thought, the Soul Carvers struck. Marva's flesh ripped, sending rivets of blood down her face. She lifted her sword and rushed at the crebalys from the side, ducking at the last moment when it swiped one of its arms at her. Faster than any human had the right to be, Marva bolted, dodging the creature's swipes, bending with an unnatural balance.

She didn't fight alone. Cylis joined her, attacking the creature's back, rushing at it with his blade of ice. The monster howled. Did Cylis hurt it? Did Marva make contact? It was hard to see what happened. There was already so much blood from Marva's Soul Carver magic. A moment after Cylis moved, Alair struck from the front. He hesitated, but then charged towards the crebalys, attacking it. Blade high, he feinted at the creature before sidestepping a blow and striking its back from behind, grazing it. Did he try to use his magic and control it? Was he not able to?

"What is that insane man doing?" Bethrian asked. Lyritan joined the Soul Carvers, the sole "human," slashing at the creature. He had a mortal man's movements and limitations, but every gesture was as if crafted from a lifetime of skill. It *was* a lifetime. Several of them, in fact.

Though the seconds of terror where her friends' and lover's lives were at risk rang through her, a long note on the instrument of time, it wasn't a long battle. It was only one minute, maybe two, when one of the Soul Carvers—Cylis?—stabbed the monster. Once it was distracted, Marva grabbed hold of the monster's arm. And then there was blood. So much blood. Marva cried out and collapsed on the ground, the sanguine liquid pooling around her.

"Marva!" Caes cried, shaking off Bethrian and running towards the Soul Carver. The crebalys was strewn apart on the snow, white bone and sinew glistening on the formerly pristine landscape. There was no danger to her. Not anymore.

Cylis crouched next to Marva, holding her on his lap. "You didn't need to do that, Marv," he said, wiping the blood off her torn face. Already her wounds were showing the early signs of knitting together, the effect of her magic fading. "We would've won regardless." Cylis was tender with her, more gentle than Caes had ever seen him with anyone. A stab rent through her heart—he never had much of a chance before. At least he had someone now. At least now he had a place he could safely do so, such as it was.

"Is she alright?" Caes asked, hovering near them. She glanced at Alair, who was speaking with Lyritan and Bethrian and gesturing towards the slaughtered creature.

"She will be," Cylis said. "Our magic demands a heavy price."

"And I'd pay it a thousand times to keep you safe," Marva said to Cylis. "Otherwise, what good is it for?"

Caes slowly backed away. This was not her place. She let the two of them stay alone together. Soul Carvers healed fast, and Cylis would know what needed to be done—there was nothing she could help with.

Instead, she approached Alair, who, other than having the sheen of fresh sweat on his face and drying blood—the creature's?—seemed to have escaped the battle unscathed. His jaw was clenched in determination, his brilliant eyes focused on taking stock of the battle's effects. He cleaned off his sword on the monster's fur and then on snow before wiping it dry and shoving it back in the scabbard. For now she resisted rushing to hold him—there would be time, and he needed a chance to catch his breath.

"What was this thing?" Caes asked, looking at the slaughtered monster.

"Welcome to the Burning Hand," Lyritan said as he approached. "This is, unfortunately, just one example of what I expected us to find. Are you alright, Caesonia?"

Alright? How could she be alright? This was just the first of the monsters they would encounter here. There would be more—she could feel it like she felt the cold slapping her face.

"Yes," Caes said. "I'm fine. I was far from the conflict."

"Good," Lyritan said. "I am afraid I cannot guarantee that will always be the case."

No, it wouldn't be. She would have to face one more conflict. Her father and Desmin lurked somewhere, and it was only a matter of time before the goddesses made their intent known.

Suddenly Bethrian coughed, interrupting them. "So,'" he said, "any chance this is a creature worth eating?"

Chapter 53

Cylis

"I never want to see snow again," Cylis said, stepping over a snow-covered rock. He barely caught his footing and avoided careering into the ice. That would've been a piece of irony—death by ice. Again. It would have been a fitting end to this rotten pumpkin of a journey.

Furry demon? Check. Haunted cavern? Check. A god who was getting more and more sullen, but Cylis seemed to be the only one who noticed it? Extra check.

They had killed the snowy fur beast the night before—and didn't eat it, since apparently there was a chance it was poisonous—and today they were back on their merry way to the mountain. And with each mile, Lyritan seemed to be extra sullen and kept giving Caes these lingering glances that were eerily reminiscent of how someone would look at a sick dog. For someone who claimed to have a grand plan to save Caes, something was off. But good luck talking with the others about it without the god hearing.

Cylis wasn't keen on dying from ice, but dying from a delusional god was somehow even worse.

"I don't think you have a choice," Alair said to Cylis. "Snow is going to follow you. Your magic is ice. That may be difficult."

"Excellent observation, Your Augustness. I am, in fact, a creature of ice."

Alair glared at Cylis's use of the title. Did Cylis remember to tell Caes that Alair was technically the rightful Malithian emperor? No, he didn't. Oh, that was going to be fun. Though, Alair should've thanked him for doing the research—glaring made Alair look extra dignified, and Alair could use more dignity. Alair, Cylis, and Bethrian hadn't had access to a decent razor since they left, and now they were all starting to be rather bristly. However, in Cylis's case, the bristling was due to more than hair.

Cylis picked at his sleeve, which was still crusted with the dead creature's smelly blood and had a few more holes than it did at the start of the journey, both from the fight and the travels. What in the hells *was* that thing? Yes, that monster was dead, but it was likely there were more lurking. Waiting. And probably hungry.

"When are we stopping to eat?" Cylis asked.

"Not yet," Alair said.

"Sounds delicious."

"What?"

"Never mind." Cylis shook his head, unsure of what he was trying to say himself, of what joke he was attempting to make.

There was pause in the company's banter, the only sounds the wind and the crunching snow. By this point, most were too tired to engage in small talk. That, and they probably wanted to keep their ears open for more furry claw monsters.

"No one made you come along," Alair finally said to Cylis.

"Like I'd leave you to do this alone. You'd be dead already."

"No one would have blamed you if you did." Alair turned his attention ahead, where Caes was now talking softly with Marva, their expressions solemn. Marva, too, had dried blood on her clothes, and odds were there would be more before this ended. She had healed well, as was to be expected, but it was never easy to see someone you love rip themselves apart, even in the name of magic.

Love? Did Cylis love her?

No, not yet, but there were certainly the beginnings of it. He recognized the feeling, the sensation of someone consuming your thoughts, pulling you towards them with every movement. He had never been with someone long enough to experience it in its entirety. But if this was love, this was the last place Cylis wanted either of them to be.

"Well," Cylis said slowly, "sometimes I don't make the smartest decisions."

Alair nodded. "Yes. But I'm glad you made Marva one of them."

Cylis swiveled his head towards Alair. "What in the hells is that supposed to mean?"

A shrug was the only answer he got. Silvery bastard. All mysterious. And muscular. And somehow, he didn't get heckled by the women in Gilar. How did he manage that?

"Well, we'll see what happens," Cylis said, mostly to get Alair to stop talking.

Alair smiled. "I'm sure we will."

That night's dinner ended up being nothing more than cold salted meat and hard bread, which threatened to crack Cylis's beautiful teeth. He sat next to Marva, trying not to focus on her thigh rubbing against his own. They were in the wilderness. They were eating one of the worst meals he had ever had. But he sure as hell wasn't about to move away from her. She was the only thing that made this evening tolerable. Hells knew it wasn't the rest of the company. The evening's talk was stilted—there was little they hadn't talked about by this point. And as the mountain moved closer with each mile, it was far too easy to remember that this journey would end, and it was unlikely that everyone would be making their way back.

"We are close to Hanith," the god finally said from his place in their little circle, where they huddled together before taking shelter for the night. "The closer we get to the Burning Hand, the more things will change. While the Burning Hand has its own dangers, the climate is not one of them. We won't be in this cold forever." Everyone nodded, happy. Even Cylis was pleased, as he was more than sick and tired of having to use his magic to stay somewhat comfortable. It was only because he was literally surrounded by ice that he was able to keep himself from being at risk of burning through his magic—and his life.

"Good," Caes said. "How long until we find Hanith? Do you think we will find him tomorrow?"

The god nodded. "I think so. I can feel his presence. It grows stronger with each step."

"What is he buried in?" Cylis asked. "A casket? A robe?"

"In a mountain tomb."

Cylis frowned. "You think you can recognize it?"

"No need," Lyritan said. "I can feel it."

"What's he buried in?" he asked.

"Cylis," Caes said, rubbing her temples, "does it matter?"

"I'm just curious," Cylis said.

"Maybe be curious about silence," Alair said. Cylis glared and resisted the urge to make a colorful gesture.

"Can't blame me for wanting some details," Cylis said. That, and something seemed off about the god's story. Was it so bad he wanted answers? Marva rubbed his back, moving in soothing circles. Alright, that was nice.

"I understand your fears," Lyritan said. His pensive face looked at the mountain range, where there was still a strange haze around the Burning Hand. "The end of our journey approaches, and this is unfamiliar to you."

"That's an understatement," Cylis said.

"Do not fear and sleep soundly, Soul Carver. But…" The god then turned looked at the direction they had traveled from, at something they could not see. That was never good. "Keep watch tonight," the god finally said. "Hanith isn't the only thing of the divine near us."

Chapter 54

Caes

Dawn broke over the mountains, rosy and brilliant against the world of gray and white. Caes stretched from where she laid next to Alair, absorbing every bit of warmth from him that she could. The stony outcrop had protected them from the wind, so they were comfortable as they slept.

She rolled over and kissed him, just as he started to stir. "I love you," she said softly.

"I love you too," he answered, his voice catching in his throat. He gently pushed a strand of hair out of her face. "Did you sleep well?"

"Well enough. Watch was quiet. Cylis and I didn't feel like talking."

"I gathered as much." The others stirred around them, and Bethrian let out a muttered slew of curses as he emerged from his bedroll. "Ready to go?" Alair asked.

Caes sighed. "Not really. But there isn't another choice."

"Truer words have not been uttered on this journey."

With that, it was time to go. Once they ate another bland breakfast of dried meats, fruit, and bread washed down by watered-down wine, they were on their way once more. After several minutes of walking, Caes pulled up her hood, tucking away as much of her face as she could. The wind whipped through the valley, and despite the cold, the wind and sun wrecked havoc on her skin. Her face was burned, her skin dry and flaking. The fact that this was a brilliant, tolerable winter day was the only thing that kept her spirits high. Yes, the sun had been burning her skin as viciously as in the height of summer, but it also kept them warm. So...a literal bright side?

A weight wouldn't leave Caes's stomach, and it had nothing to do with their dried diet. Something was going to happen today, she could feel it. Perhaps she was reading too much into things like Lyritan's body language, but *something* was going to happen. Were they going to find Hanith? And when they did find Hanith, would he really sacrifice himself in the Burning Hand, and thus let Caes avoid that fate?

Gods of the hells, this was a mess. Liuva was created to be a sacrifice in the Burning Hand and thus let Shirla, her mother take her power. But the weapon permitting destruction of the other gods—the Sword of Might and whatever other weapon Lyritan had—complicated things. If Caes did go into the Burning Hand and kill the other goddesses, what was going to happen to her power if she did so? She frowned. What *would* happen afterward? How did it work? Would it be like when she sacrificed herself to break "Hanith's" curse and thus basically had to meditate on who she wanted to receive her power? Did something else decide where it went? Liuva hadn't known—Shirla hadn't had a chance to tell her. And as for Lyritan...memories were budding, but Lyritan had left out a few explanations on the process when they were here last. Did Lyritan even know?

"We're awfully silent," Bethrian muttered, trudging along behind Caes.

"We're tired," she replied, wading through snow that went halfway to her knee. "Hardly the time for conversation." Caes took as many steps and possible in the path Lyritan made, and Bethrian and the others largely did the same, walking in lines.

"I just think that, truthfully, we should consider—"

A cracking sound interrupted them. The noise was like dry branches snapping, except there were no trees. Then what had caused it? The company paused and looked at each other, Alair motioning Caes to get closer to him. She obeyed.

"Oh, fuck," Cylis said, "not again."

"I say the word, you run," Alair whispered. Caes nodded, shedding the pack and layers that would impede her. They had been through this before—there was nothing she could do for them in a fight. The Soul Carvers and Lyritan again tugged off their packs, cloaks, and coats and pulled out their weapons, Marva's skin already taking on the etchings of blood-red lines.

"You, too, Fuckwit," Cylis said, revealing his blue sword and looking around. "I don't need to trip on you."

"I can fight," Bethrian said.

"Not as good as us." Cylis sneered. "And someone needs to keep her" –Cylis gestured at Caes– "from falling off a ledge."

"Aww," Bethrian said, "you're worried about me. Admit it."

"Now's not the time," Marva snapped. She gestured at the Soul Carvers and again they went into some seemingly predesigned formation.

"I don't see anything," Caes said anxiously. Indeed, she didn't. The sky was clear, a brilliant blue that only came on clear winter days. A soft breeze carried the snow through the air, dancing around her in a brilliant whirl. The world was calm. Pristine. There was no danger.

Other than the ominous cracking, which grew ever louder. She grimaced. It was like...bones shattering? Oh, that was unpleasant.

"You can hear it," Alair said, stretching his arms, sword in hand. "It's here."

"Yes. I wish I couldn't."

"Caes," Bethrian said, walking up to her, eyes darting around them, "maybe we should—"

That was as far as Bethrian got before the ground cracked and split in two.

A gash the length of a cottage opened in the earth, sending mounds of snow into the opening mere yards from them. A terrible grating sound rent through the air, as if the ground itself were screaming in protest. Caes and the others stumbled back, gathering their footing while the ground shook and then stilled.

She took a heavy, rushed breath. And another. And another. Everyone stared at the gash, frozen in place.

What was happening?

Suddenly, two sets of hands burst out of the snow, pushing themselves up with unnatural speed and strength, revealing their torsos.

Desmin. And her father.

It finally happened—Desmin and her father had found them.

Chapter 55

Alair

Alair had never cared overmuch for Bethrian. He never exactly hated him, but at the same time he wouldn't have been disappointed if their paths never crossed again.

But at that moment, when Bethrian was guiding Caes away from the fight, away from the abominations that broke through the earth, Bethrian was his new favorite friend. Caes would be safe and away from the battle. Bethrian was capable enough. Bethrian would keep her safe.

And Alair had a demon to kill, for that was the only explanation of what was in front of them, the monsters Desmin and Damek had become.

Damek was taller now than he had been as the mortal Chosen One—Alair would've heard if it was otherwise—he now towered over the Soul Carvers at a height no man could naturally achieve. Damek's skin hung loose from his body, puffed and draped around him like an overlarge set of clothing. All he wore around his waist was a tight cloth, nothing that had a place in a fight. Yet, Alair had read the legends—if they were true, Damek's skin was as hard as iron, impenetrable due to the will of the goddess. Goddess*es*. Worse than Damek's draping skin were the dozens of eyes that were placed over his body where they did not belong. On his forehead. His cheeks. His neck. His arms. Eyes that looked in every direction, moving of their own accord. Through them, Damek would see everything.

Possessed by whatever foul magic the goddesses gave him, Caes's father was no longer a man. Whatever kindness he may have once held in his gaze was gone. Whatever love he ever had for Caes was gone.

And Desmin? That bastard was already a demon. Now, bizarrely twisted like Damek, he was just one on the outside, too.

Alair's gaze drifted downward. In addition to their twisted forms, both of them wielded jagged knives in each hand, no doubt enchanted with some foul magic. Or poisoned.

"Fuck this to the hells," Cylis said, letting his magic consume him, made stronger by the cold and the god-touched sword. His sword shone, calling extra ice to his arms and body. He snarled, muffling sounds of pain from his powers overtaking him. "They're *ocul d'carn,*" Cylis said in disbelief. "They shouldn't be alive." Since when did Cylis use such terms? But after a second's thought, Alair realized that Cylis was right.

Ocul d'carn. Roughly translated—"eyes of flesh."

Ocul d'carn. Creatures born of the goddesses' nightmares, built to serve and destroy. Unlike Soul Carvers, who retained their personalities, the essence of who they were after magic changed their bodies, these creatures' minds were gone. In exchange for power, and what they considered divine favor, they surrendered everything of who they were to the goddesses. This would be a battle that tested everything the Soul Carvers were. A nightmare of legend made flesh.

Why would someone choose to become *this*?

Easy—someone who was willing to do anything for power.

The irony that similar things could've been said about Soul Carvers wasn't lost on Alair. That was what happened when one tangled with goddesses. Those who sought their power paid with more than their lives—they bartered with their souls.

"No, they shouldn't be alive," Alair said, swinging his sword. "But they are." He checked behind him one last time. Caes and Bethrian were making their way from the fight. Far from here. Caes stumbled and Bethrian immediately lifted her, helping her regain her footing. Alair didn't have to worry about them right now. A good thing, too, for the fight was about to begin, and he no longer had time to worry.

With an unholy cry, Damek and Desmin lunged towards them, their jagged knives raised high.

And so, the battle began.

First, Alair attempted to use his magic, but it instantly hit a block—he had nowhere to send it to. It was like their minds didn't exist. Shrugging, he abandoned it—his magic was of no use against these creatures. He had his other weapons—his sword and his Soul Carver strength.

Ducking a well-aimed blow, Alair swung at Damek, making contact with his arm. The skin bubbled in waves, but Alair didn't make a dent in the translucent flesh. Damek gave Alair a feline smile as Alair backed away, repositioning himself next to the other Soul Carvers. The legend that the *ocul d'carn's* skin was impenetrable by weapons was true.

Fuck...how were they going to kill them?

Before Alair could gather his thoughts, Marva attempted to use her own magic, gashes appearing on her face as she did so, deep rivets that spilled blood down her face and seeped from under her sleeves. While Alair distracted Damek with another blow, Marva seized his arm, screaming as her magic poured into him and her wounds deepened. Her only reward was the tiniest gash on Damek's arm, while her face became shredded, white bone appearing under the mangled flesh. Alair risked a glance at Cylis, who attacked Desmin along with Lyritan. Cylis's magic was faring little better—Desmin seemed to withstand his ice, and it did little other than distract him. But Cylis's blade—*that* seemed to have an effect. A weak one, but Cylis was at least able to slice the monster's skin, leaving fine lines like paper cuts.

Were Damek and Desmin immune to all of their magics? Was it because they were made by Karima, and now they were being attacked by another created by her? Cylis's sword was imbued with Lyritan's magic—did that make a difference, why his worked?

Alair couldn't think—he was too busy countering Damek's blows. The creature's jagged blades shone in the sun, the edges as fine as a razor's. Damek swung towards Alair, but he twisted away, the blade coming close enough that a chunk of his hair was sliced. It floated to the ground, twisting in the breeze.

"Move faster!" Marva yelled.

"Obviously," Alair muttered. This time Damek only cut his hair. The next time it could be his neck.

Marva lunged toward Damek, ducking and flipping out of the creature's way, using the monster's arm as her leverage. Meanwhile, Alair moved to Damek's other side, striking blows that went nowhere and pierced nothing. Suddenly, Marva screamed—a new slice had appeared on Marva's arm, and not from her magic. The cut fabric already stuck to her skin from the blood. Another close call. They couldn't do this forever—but they couldn't stop. If Alair and Marva didn't stop Damek, he would kill Caes.

They moved in a fluid dance, Alair and Marva against Damek, two Soul Carvers against a monster. The Chosen One had allegedly been granted the ability to fight when he found the Sword of Might, but this—the barrage of limbs and blows—was beyond that. This was skill that could only have been granted after a lifetime of devotion. Or gifted by a goddess.

There was a sudden flash of gold, and Alair allowed himself the briefest turn and found Lyritan. A god in a mortal's body, he glowed with gold light as he attacked, his skin blistering and smoking as his magic emerged. While against the last monster he had showed himself to be adept with a blade, it was in line with a mortal's skill. Now, it was as if in facing divine power, he let his own shine through. He wasn't going to let himself be bested by the goddesses, even if he burned. Not here. Not like this.

Lyritan alone was seemingly able to make a notable blow against these foes—Desmin had a couple lines on his arm from where Lyritan and Cylis sliced him. But even a god and a magic blade wasn't enough. Was it because this was the power of one god against two? Was it that Lyritan was trapped in flesh, even as that flesh crackled and burned from his power?

Alair didn't know. All he could do was fight, and hopefully distract their foes. For all his strength, Alair was able to do nothing—he and Marva were only buying time for Lyritan and Cylis to destroy Desmin. Then they could all work together on Damek. They had to—it was their only chance.

Suddenly, Damek let out a scream, a high-pitched whine that knocked the Soul Carvers and Lyritan to the ground, desperately covering their ears without dropping their weapons. The world shook, and whether it was in Alair's head or it was the ground actually trembling was impossible to say. All Alair wanted was for the sound to end. For everything to end. His head rattled, his brain feeling like it would burst his skull. Not even in the strongest depths of his magic and torment did his head feel this pressure, the urge for the bones to break. For the desire for relief, even if it killed him.

My child, if only you let me spare you this suffering.

Karima could damn herself to the hells.

Then the sound stopped.

Thank the hells. Warm and wet liquid ran out of Alair's ears. He reached a hand to feel the substance. His hand came away red and sticky. Blood. Blood that, for once, had nothing to do with his magic.

"The fuck?" Marva asked, looking at her own bloody hand. Even Damek the monster sat on the ground, stunned by his own actions.

Alair shook himself off, bracing for the fight to continue as Damek grabbed his weapons and stood.

It was then, when Lyritan and Cylis stumbled towards them, that he realized someone was absent.

Desmin.

Chapter 56

Bethrian

"How much further?" Caes asked, clutching her stomach. Bethrian's breath burned in his lungs and sweat gathered under his jacket. Surely, they had gone far enough. They could barely hear the fighting any longer. Surely, it was enough. And if Bethrian was feeling like this, Caes was probably feeling just as awful. Maybe worse.

"I don't know. I haven't exactly ran from many battles," Bethrian said. "There." He nodded towards a rock formation that was only around a hundred paces away. "Shelter. We can catch our breath there."

If those monsters could run as fast as they fought, this formation wasn't nearly far enough away. But their lungs were spent. It took the last bit of his energy to make it to the rocks and boulders he had spotted. Would Alair want them to keep going? Probably. But Bethrian was mortal. Bethrian had limits. Bethrian was…Bethrian's limbs shook. Black specks dotted his vision when he looked over the white landscape. He needed to catch his breath. Desperately, he unbuttoned his shirt, fanning it to let the cool air in.

"They're going to come for me," Caes said once they reached the rock, panting and shaking her head. "They always come for me."

"Yeah, that seems to be a habit with you," Bethrian said, gently helping Caes up a stone ledge and to the little shelter. It wasn't much, but it would keep the wind off them while they gathered their bearings, especially since they probably had to run again, soon. The last time Bethrian had been this exhausted, it was a lot more pleasant. And involved a woman. This was worse in every respect.

"You should keep going," Caes said, looking behind them. They couldn't see the fight, other than bursts of light and magic that shot up in the distance. Now and then he heard a scream that wrenched his manly heart. Was it Marva? Cylis? Alair? It was too much to hope those were the dying cries of Damek or Desmin. As for Lyritan, Bethrian wasn't in a position to worry about the god—if the god couldn't take care of himself, he wasn't worth worshipping.

Caes turned to Bethrian. Suddenly, he was aware of how sweat ran in rivets down his face, his hair plastered to his scalp. After all this time of travel, he must've seemed positively rustic, with his beard growing on its own accord. Nothing like the stylish lord she knew in Malithia. "I mean it," she said. "Go. There's two of them. *Only* two of them. They want me. You'll be safer away from me."

"Isn't that the goddess's truth," Bethrian said softly, motioning to Caes to sit next to him on the rocky ledge and she did. The lord dangled his legs, rubbing them and trying to slap feeling back into them, all while staring in the direction of the fight. Could he run much further? All this time in the snow, with excessive physical activity and poor diet, made it so that he was no longer a prime specimen of masculinity. "Sorry, Caes. I'm staying here. Against my better judgment."

"Why?"

"Beyond that your lover would skewer me on his sword if I left you alone?"

"He wouldn't."

Bethrian snorted. "You're right. There's worse things he can do."

Caes stared at Bethrian, obviously still expecting an answer. So Bethrian thought—why *was* he staying? Damn, that was far too deep of a question considering the circumstances. "I'm stubborn," was all he said. Was she expecting some speech about how he was truly a loyal soldier at heart and would never let a woman suffer while he was around? Hopefully not—Bethrian didn't feel like spending what was likely his last minutes on this earth lying.

"This is beyond stubbornness," Caes said.

"Is it believable that I figured accompanying you is my only chance of being a lord again? If I save the land from the goddesses, I was hoping for better connections. Divine ones."

Caes paused. "That I believe. But I also know you could've stayed in Gilar and still counted on those things. There's more."

Bethrian rubbed his face with both his hands and groaned. When he lowered his hands, he looked at Caes. Her skin was somehow both a blistered red and unnaturally white, and there were dark shadows that normally weren't there. She needed a nap, a long one. Despite everything, her golden eyes shone, marking her as inhuman. "Whatever happens," Bethrian said slowly, "this is history. A legend—they will be writing sagas and ballads about this for generations. I wasn't about to miss it." The last month of this adventure alone could keep him full of Passionflower stories for years. "And" –Bethrian squirmed– "I feel like I owe you."

"You don't."

"If I had been bolder with Seda, if I hadn't been so keen on trying to use you in my own way, I could've saved us both a lot of trouble. Hells, maybe you wouldn't have been forced to take up that curse in the first place."

Caes nodded. "And you did slice my arm."

"That too."

She hesitated and then said, "For what it's worth, I'm glad you're here."

"You are?"

"Yes. I need all the friends I can get, apparently." Her lips set in a line. Was she thinking about how even now her father was attacking her friends? Caes never spoke about Damek, about what his betrayal had done to her, but from his own experience with his father, he guessed it burned deep. Even if she never spoke about it.

"I never thought to see them," Bethrian said, changing the topic. "Those things. When the people at Gilar spoke of monsters at the Burning Hand, I didn't think they meant this."

"Me neither," she said softly. "I don't think anyone could have expected them."

Fuck. Those men were more than just monsters. They were her father. Her former betrothed. There were a million puns about evil former lovers he could've crafted, and he left them all unuttered. This was neither the time nor place.

Damn. Caes didn't deserve this. Bethrian certainly knew some people who did—Lord Seltyn, who loved holding children ransom when their parents were overdue on rent, for one—but Caes wasn't one of them.

Not that Bethrian didn't have his own experience with awful fathers.

"You know," Bethrian said, "my father once made me travel a week in the mountains from our hunting lodge back to the estate. No food. No supplies, other than a small knife. He claimed that if I was worthy of stewarding the lands, I would be able to obtain my sustenance from them." Bethrian picked off a piece of ice from the rock, flicking it to the ground. "It wasn't a mountain tradition either. It was just him being a brute."

Caes frowned. "Why are you telling me this?"

"Your father isn't you. He may have been responsible for you when you were a child, but what you are is not tied up with him." Bethrian took a deep breath. Damn, he was trying to find the right words, and every thought he had was more scrambled than the last. "What I'm trying to say is that sometimes people need to find their own family. Blood may be thicker than water, but it's also messier."

Caes smiled. "That's true."

A massive screech that made Bethrian's heart leap into his mouth rang over the landscape, followed by an eerie cracking that echoed over the sudden din of the distant battle. Shit. That was Bethrian's cue.

"Should we run?" Caes asked, pushing herself up.

"I think it's too late for that." Bethrian stood, divesting himself of the remainder of the voluminous winter gear and pulled out his sword. He hopped down and tested the terrain immediately around him with a cautious foot. The snow in this area was shallow, the ground relatively flat, permitting him to use decent legwork. Bracing for the monster, he posed, one foot on a stone, sword held high, his hair blowing dramatically in the wind.

If he was going to die, he wasn't going to waste his last chance to look good.

Chapter 57

Cylis

"Stupid. Fucking. Wraith." With each word Cylis swung his sword, the gift from Lyritan. Damn, it was an excellent weapon. At its peak of utilizing Cylis's power—once Cylis figured out what he was doing—it was able to pierce through Damek's flesh. Well, the eyes. An eye on Damek's arm popped, emitting a stream of white liquid that sizzled and steamed when it hit the snow. Damek cried out in pain. That was a beautiful sound.

"Where's Desmin?" Alair yelled.

"Fuck if I know," Cylis yelled, reaching into himself for the power to make another strike. Cylis didn't ask questions—Cylis attacked what was right in front of him, and now, it was Damek. He didn't care where Prince Pig Penis went. "Alair—"

But Alair was already gone, running in the direction of Caes and Bethrian. Would he find them? The snow would help with tracking, but they've had a decent head start. Unfortunately, due to the second set of prints that was more like a ditch, Piggy was now a better runner than either of them.

Fuck—he wasn't about to leave Marva alone with Lyritan. Alair would have to be enough.

Unfortunately, rather than making Damek cower, piercing one of the eyes only seemed to have made him more vicious—now he was lunging at greater speeds. Luckily, Cylis was a Soul Carver. Faster than any mortal fighter, Cylis flipped and ducked, right before Damek's sword rang over his head. He caught himself when landing, raising his sword once more and bracing for the next attack. At least the magic sword was able to attack eyeballs. That gave them hope. Cylis had never been so happy to see eyeballs pop before.

Lunging back, Cylis prepared for another attack when a white hand gripped Damek's arm and a gash appeared underneath, stemming from the hand and reaching another eye. And popping it. Damek screamed, doubling over once more. The white pus splattered in the air, like a cloudy rain that smelled like skunk and iron.

A beautiful sight, but a dangerous one. "Marva, don't! Stop!" Cylis cried, once Marva backed away from Damek. "It's not worth it." Her face was a bloody horror, gashes and rents that spread from her dangling lips to her sliced ears. Her hands were slick and sanguine, and blood coated her teeth.

"It's the only way we're hurting it," Marva yelled. "The eyes."

"My sword can do it."

She shook her head, splattering blood on the pristine snow. She held out her sword, swinging and ducking when Damek went for her. "It's not enough!" she called out.

It was. It had to be. Cylis gave up using his magic alone for attacking—there was no point when the sword was doing the work for him. But Marva...Marva was expending herself, too fast. Too soon.

Suddenly, there was a flash of gold. Lyritan moved behind the creature and pressed a golden hand onto Damek's back, his sword following, stabbing. The sword only made a slight cut, a dent in the creature's flapping skin, even though Damek howled in agony. Even a god was nearly helpless against the creature.

Cylis prepared to attack when suddenly Damek bent over, and a red mist surrounded him as he crouched. Marva, Cylis, and Lyritan looked at each other in confusion. What was Damek doing? A light feminine laugh rang through the air, sending a chill down Cylis's spine. He knew that laugh. He knew there was no point searching for it.

And he knew that nothing good ever came from it.

And then Damek erupted, contorting and changing as his flesh inflated, the eyes now little pinpricks in the waxy skin. There were thick veins the size of nightcrawlers under the skin, pulsating and making the eyes quiver with each beat. And then, holding out his daggers, he moved. He had turned into a whirlwind of flesh and blades. His eyes—the ones that were where eyes belonged—narrowed and focused on Cylis with seething hatred. Did Damek hate Cylis in particular for popping his eyes? Or did he hate all Soul Carvers? Or was it something else? Regardless, Damek had to die. Somehow.

While Damek was inhumanly fast before, that was nothing compared to now. Damek swung his daggers, making Marva and Cylis contort and maneuver in ways that tested their abilities. Using techniques that were rarely utilized, Marva and Cylis worked off each other, using each other to best guard and attack. Cylis shot ice at Damek, aiming for his head. While he was distracted, Marva lunged, attacking an eye. Her point was not to destroy it—she couldn't—but to give Cylis the chance to land a precise blow. Even this, their deadly dance, was barely enough. The Soul Carvers may have been brought back from death, but the creature they fought now brought rampant death in its wake.

They could not keep this up forever. Blood pounded in Cylis's ears, his hands long numb and frozen from his magic. His breath burned in his lungs, twisted as it turned to frost that ripped his insides. He had reserved his magic, he was surrounded by ice and had the sword, but even he was becoming spent.

Damek turned to Cylis, lunging with his blades. Holding his head high, Cylis met the challenge, darting and attacking, until Cylis tripped on a rock, sending him landing on his back in the snow. And the next sight was Damek's blade careening toward him.

"No!" Marva cried. A new wave of blood poured from her as she lunged towards Damek, grabbing his arm and holding on. She held on. And on.

"Marva!" Cylis called, pushing himself up.

Marva didn't let go of Damek. She screamed as she bled, her fingers now raw bone and gristle. Simultaneously, new wounds appeared on Damek's skin. Rupturing the eyes, tearing his flesh.

"Enough! Marva, stop!" Cylis cried out. Finding a fresh burst of energy, Cylis attacked, infusing the sword with new power. With all of Cylis's strength behind it, the magic reared into the creature's flesh as it punctured another eye.

Damek roared, attempting to throw Marva and Cylis off him, but it did no good. She latched on, pouring her magic into him. Gouging him.

"Marva, let go!" Cylis called out.

For a long moment, Marva caught his gaze, her face brutalized beyond any recognition. She smiled. And screamed.

And then Marva started to shift into mist. Mist and dust.

Pieces of Marva flaked into the air and drifted away. Dried. She was reaching the end of her magic and turning into a husk. Like Soul Carvers had always been warned, their magic had limits. Pushed too far, and they would shrivel and fade. Marva had pushed herself too far.

"Stop!" Cylis screamed, his voice hoarse.

Marva didn't answer. She screamed until her throat disintegrated, leaving one last gash on Damek's neck and one last eye popped. Damek stood there, his hand on his throat, staring at the blood from both him and Marva. Suddenly, a blast of light shot through Damek, and the edge of a blade emerged from his chest. With a loud thud, he fell to his knees, the sound shifting the stones of the mountains around them.

Was it the sound that made the mountain tremble? Or was it the end of the goddesses' power, escaping in one last blast? Regardless, snow poured off the mountains around them, shaking at the death of the creature.

Marva was gone. Marva was gone. Marva was gone.

And the creature was still there.

At the end of all the chaos, Lyritan stood behind him, holding his sword through Damek's body, light pouring from him. Light that burned the body he possessed, leaving his hair singed and skin blistered.

Cylis didn't wait and stare. He dove forward, using the distraction Marva paid for with her life, driving his sword into Damek's chest. Cylis's own magic was exhausted. His body was nearing the end of its endurance. But it was enough. With the god-blessed sword, this final bit of effort was enough.

Damek slowly exhaled, and with his breath a black mist poured from his mouth and into the air. The extra eyeballs popped out of his skin, landing in the snow, staring at nothing. His skin fused to his body, turning back to the man he used to be. An ordinary man. Now Cylis could see what he had been, before he succumbed to this. The brutalized man who was Caes's father.

But at the same moment Damek gave himself up to death, Lyritan collapsed, the divine light fading, the body sizzling.

"Shit," Cylis said, running over to the god. He knelt by Lyritan, gripping his hand. Red and gold blood poured from his mouth and ears. "Not you too."

"No," Lyritan said, closing his eyes, his chest moving rapidly. "This will not fell me. But the game has changed once more."

Chapter 58

Caes

Too soon, "Desmin" caught up to where Caes and Bethrian waited, his unnaturally long legs rushing through the snow. And once he did, a battle Bethrian surely never intended to be in resulted. Bethrian alone, against a monster forged by the gods. As he was now, Desmin *had* to have been forged by the goddesses—he had been a passable swordsman, but he was never known for having great skill. In fact, Caes suspected that the opponents he had bested during court tournaments in Ardinan were either threatened or bribed. There was nothing in Desmin's history that accounted for his new talents, nor the inhuman speed that attended it.

But where Desmin of Ardinan had been all show, Bethrian had skill, as demonstrated by the fact that he lived through the first exchange of blows. With surprising agility, Bethrian fought, parrying Desmin's strikes, showcasing expertise that was honed by the finest trainers over a lifetime. But it was no good. Desmin was a man possessed by divine power, while Bethrian was merely a man. A mortal man.

One strike. Two.

Desmin sliced Bethrian's legs, sending him careening to the ground. The ground quickly soaked red and Bethrian cried out, slapping the ground with his fist as he thrashed in agony.

"Bethrian!" Caes screamed, grabbing a rock. She had a couple small daggers, but they were in her bags, discarded in the snow. She would be facing Desmin with nothing but a single stone.

Desmin raised his head from where he watched Bethrian fall, and then he locked eyes with her. A smile peeled back from his face, the puffy skin scrunching together. All of his eyes focused on her.

Her.

Caes took a deep breath. She was going to access her divine power, even if it destroyed her. It was better to burn than to be killed by him, even if her power wasn't enough to defeat him. If she was going to leave this world, Desmin wasn't going to be the one to do it. Was she strong enough to kill him? Could she take him with her in death?

Only one way to find out.

Did Desmin know what she could do? Doubtful. But then again, Lyritan himself struggled against Desmin and her father. Maybe Desmin *did* know about her powers and didn't care. Maybe he was enjoying the moment too much to let such a thing cross his mind. Maybe Desmin the demon was just like Desmin the prince, assuming that the world would bow to his wishes—because it always did.

Like a cat avoiding a puddle, Desmin stepped over Bethrian, slowly approaching her. But right when Desmin's bare foot landed on the ground, Bethrian pushed himself up, grabbed Desmin's ankle, and bit him on the leg, snagging on the monster's bunched skin.

Caes shrieked, half in surprise, half to beg Bethrian to stop. Desmin may have left Bethrian alone if he got what he wanted from her. Biting would do nothing but anger him.

From the way Desmin glanced down at Bethrian, a hearty laugh emitting from his throat, Desmin agreed. He reached out a single finger, shaking it back and forth like he was scolding a child. Like they were foolish for trying to stop him.

But then Desmin started to deflate.

Bit by bit his skin fused together, each extra eyeball popping out of its socket. His remaining eyes widened in fear as, suddenly, he couldn't wield his daggers. He cried out in surprise, gripping his leg, grappling with Bethrian, who had reached up to pull the prince to the bloody ground. Desmin stumbled, his voice returning to the throaty screech Caes recognized. Mortal—Desmin was now a mere mortal. He slumped under Bethrian's strength, all fight gone from him along with the magic. Was he really weakened? Was it over?

Fuck this.

Caes ran towards Desmin, rock in hand, her fingers slipping into the grooves.

As Bethrian held him down, Desmin's eyes widened in terror when he saw her approach. He must've seen something in her face that he knew better than to ignore. It was likely the most accurate observation Desmin ever made in his life. During the last few steps she relived every callous laugh. Every jeer. Every betrayal. Every bit of pain.

Althain.

The other Malithians.

The young woman she used to be.

"Caes," Desmin said, "you're not cruel. Don't do this. I didn't mean—" Desmin raised his hands over his face.

Caes struck him in the head anyway. A sickening crunch resulted and Desmin squealed. She raised her hand and struck him again. And again. Blood splattered from his head and over Bethrian, followed by chunks of bone.

Another strike.

Another.

Another.

Another.

Caes screamed, her howls matched only by her strikes. Soon the rock collided with a mass that was more soft tissue than bone, Desmin's teeth and brains splattered on the snow. The sharp bone and gelatinous tissue glistened, ruining what was left of the landscape's beauty.

Meanwhile, wincing, Bethrian had ripped off the bottom of his tunic and tied it around his legs, all while giving Caes concerned looks. But he didn't interfere.

She didn't care what Bethrian thought.

Desmin assaulted her.

He betrayed her.

He tortured her.

He—

"Caes," Bethrian said gently as Caes's hands reared for another blow. "It's done. He's dead. Caes!"

Caes wiped her eyes with the back of her bloody hand. "He...he..."

"He can't do a thing now." That was true, Desmin would never do anything again. Bethrian let out a hiss as he crawled over and kneeled next to her. Slowly, he moved his hand down her wrist, coaxing the rock from her hands. It dropped to the ground with a soft thunk, barely noticeable amidst Desmin's smashed corpse.

Desmin was gone.

She was free.

She smiled.

Chapter 59

Bethrian

What the hells happened?

Seriously, what had happened?

Well, Bethrian took a bite out of a demon/creature/possessed nightmare.

To be honest, Bethrian had wanted to bite Desmin for some time. That urge was easily explainable. Who wouldn't have wanted to take a chunk out of Desmin when presented with the opportunity?

But what the hells happened after that? Since when did Bethrian's bite have the power to negate magic? Could he do that to anyone? What would happen if he bit Cylis? Was he some sort of vampyr? Ooh, that would be a delightful turn of events, one that would certainly be an excellent plot for a story. But Bethrian was out in the sunlight and didn't have a general compulsion to drink blood, so he likely wasn't a vampyr. And there was also the small issue that Bethrian was very real and not a figment of an idle imagination.

Thankfully, the two of them weren't alone for even a minute after Desmin's grisly slaughter. All Bethrian could think of was that it was going to be a long time before he ate any sort of sausage. But Alair's dark shape quickly careened over a nearby hill, took stock of the scene once he reached them, and then worked at tying up Bethrian's legs after ensuring that Caes was alright. Turned out Bethrian did a half-assed job with that.

"How bad?" Bethrian asked Alair as he re-tied Bethrian's knots with a Soul Carver's strength and skill.

"If you haven't bled out by now, probably not awful," Alair said. "But this is a shitty place to have a wound."

"Yep," Bethrian said, grimacing while Alair tied the bandages even tighter.

"We'll take a better look once we get back and have our supplies," Alair said.

"Just promise me Cylis won't be the one to stitch me up," Bethrian said.

Alair smiled. "I can make no such promises."

Bethrian watched Alair all but carry Caes back to the others, slowly, so that Bethrian could waddle next to them, his weight shifted onto Alair. His legs burned, hot blood dripping out of his bandages and then freezing in the cold. They had supplies for healing in their packs, and hopefully everyone else survived the battle and weren't buried in that series of distant avalanches Bethrian thought he saw. Could've been the blood loss. At least Marva was good at tending battle wounds, so she could help him, and not Cylis. Please, never Cylis. He took a deep breath, ignoring the pain in his ribs.

For now, the members of their little company were distracted and counting their blessing that they were alive. Though all too soon they would have questions for Bethrian about how he bested Desmin. Ones he wasn't sure how he was going to answer.

Chapter 60

Liuva

*T*ime. What was time to me?

After the encounter with my mother, during which she cannibalized a god and made me taste a few precious bites, I knew in my heart that something was stirring in her. It was something dark that did not bode well for me. The golden mother of my youth was gone, replaced with someone who still said the correct things and made the correct gestures, but the light behind them was extinguished. Her gaze no longer softened when she looked at me. She no longer sought my company to the extent she used to. I had the impression I had become a chore to her, something she visited only out of duty.

My time with Lyritan was the only thing that brought me joy and hope. His return was the sweet air after a turbulent storm, the warm hearth after a cold journey. I could wax poetic about how he was my breath, my heartbeat, my soul—I fear I already have before—and what would be the point of saying it all again? There is no point in repeating all of that merely to say that Lyritan was not merely my love—he was everything.

He told me we had to bide our time and be patient, for the time for us to be together would come soon enough. All I had to do was wait, and be careful that my mother did not discover our plans too soon.

And then the day we long feared arrived.

"Liuva, my delight," Lyritan said, bowing his head and kissing my hand. His face wore more lines of late, even for a god. And no surprise—he was balancing a delicate act between Shirla and Karima, one that he kept me innocent of. To save me, he said. To protect me, he said. Shirla's little pet would not have been expected to know the affairs of the wider world—who would tell her?—so he kept me ignorant in order to make it easier for me. And I agreed to be naive. It was hard enough for me to pretend around my mother as it was. What would it be like if I knew everything that was transpiring? It was tricky enough to act as Shirla's beloved daughter, though I knew that everything she did was for herself.

I did not matter to her. I never did. I never would.

"I did not expect to see you," I replied, frantically glancing around the riverbank. We were alone—my companions were distracted with a dance held a short distance away. Lyritan had always seemed deft at avoiding them, at visiting me in the brief windows I was unattended. "You were just here," I said. It was true—he had visited me two nights before.

"And now we are leaving," he said. "Together."

I shivered. "Now?"

He nodded. "We have to. Shirla has changed. I think she will make a move against you soon. I refuse to risk you any longer. We need to go."

"To the Burning Hand?"

"Yes," he said. "There, I have a plan. One that will free you from this forever." He leaned toward me, his hot breath tickling my ear. "I finally have the tool that will free us all." A chill settled in my heart, though whether from his tone or from fear, I could not say.

I should have questioned him more—what made him decide it was time for us to flee? But I was consumed by my love for him, to the loss of all sense and reason. Instead, I was focused on another word he had uttered.

Forever. For gods, forever was now. It was not some abstract thing, a term cast around to imply sincerity. When a god said "forever," they meant it.

"Will you come with me?" he asked.

If I went with him, there was no going back. I could never return to my mother. She would know that I knew the truth and I would be caged until she needed me. If she let me live at all.

While Lyritan, he would set me free...

"Yes," I said. Smiling, he took my hand and guided me into the wood, away from everything I knew.

I did not say goodbye to my companions. I left with Lyritan that very moment without so much as a backwards glance.

We traveled, bringing me to parts of the world I only imagined. We were gods and did not tire as mortals, but we still took time to traverse the great world. Valleys, forests, and mountains were a blur to us as we moved, stopping only when we desired rest. To enjoy each other. To seize a breath of peace in the chaos to come. It would be difficult, he warned me. The Burning Hand, a source of all power in and behind this world, did not do things for free. It created. It gifted. But all creation meant change, and change meant pain.

Too soon, though months had passed, we came to the foothills of the great mountain. It loomed over us, its aura setting itself apart from the surrounding range. It was brilliant and majestic.

It was deadly.

We camped that night, resting one last time before the day that would decide our fates forever. "I have a plan," he had told me over and over during our journey, even as he left me at times. "It's best you don't know details," he said. "I'll be able to tell you everything soon. Soon, it won't be dangerous for you to know everything."

I trusted him.

He never told me anything else about the tool he had mentioned when we left, claiming he didn't want to bother me with such things. That they didn't matter.

I trusted him.

That night he took me while I braced myself on a rock, the roaring mountain behind us. Frenzied, he devoured me. There was nothing gentle in what we did, for fear laid behind every word and movement. What was to come? He was a god, and even he did not know.

We rested in a small cave after, his cloak covering me, his body pressed against mine. I woke in the middle of the night, the stars shining bright overhead, and reached for him. I was alone.

I sat, rubbing the sleep from my eyes. Lyritan had left before, but he had always told me beforehand. What was it this time?

Unease rippled in my chest. I laid back down, but my mind would no longer grant me rest. I sat up again and stared, waiting for Lyritan to return. And when he didn't, I decided I was not going to let my mind get the best of me any longer.

Slowly, I crept away from our camp, searching for the god. He wasn't hard to find—by now I knew how to look and listen for the subtle signs that indicated a god had passed through. Curious, I crouched and crept over to where he sat, conversing with a stone nymph, one of the minor beings who governed their homes of rock. At first I was not alarmed at finding my lover speaking to a beautiful woman—all of us divine creatures had unnatural beauty, and more than once we had to placate those whose lands we traveled through. It was easier, that way. Hidden by a boulder, I breathed softly, and listened.

Their conversation was boring. Talk of weather. Common friends. Travel. I was just about to crawl back to our bed when my heart stopped.

"Are the rumors true?" the nymph asked. "You have Shirla's child?"

Lyritan shifted. "What do you think?"

"I think you'd be a fool to go to the Burning Hand without a way to appease it. You need her."

"Well, let's just say don't worry about me in that regard."

"So, you are going to use her."

"I'll do whatever I need."

A pause. "You've always been a crafty one, Lyritan. I'll give you that. But what about the weapon? She dies now, her power goes to who—Shirla?"

"Unless she has the will to choose otherwise. But I have a weapon. As if I would go through all this trouble without having a plan." Shifting. "I'll have her destroy the goddesses, and then choose me to take her power when the Hand takes its price. And it always takes its price."

"What if she won't kill Shirla?"

"As long as she enters the mountain, I will win regardless. I know what I'm doing."

"You'd sacrifice her?"

"Why not?"

A light laughter rang out. "You always knew what to do."

"You know me so well," Lyritan said.

My heart snapped.

My life ended.

I had heard enough. I crouched and moved away, away from our camp. Away from the mountain. Away from our life.

He would do whatever he needed. He didn't deny it. He was going to use me, just like everyone else.

That's all I was. A way for him to get power. A way for my mother to get power. Karima was probably trying to find a way to use me as well.

That's all I was.

Before I left Lyritan for good, I rushed back to our camp. With gold tears streaming down my face, I found the sword in Lyritan's pack, the only weapon in our possession. I had ignored it prior to this—who was I to care if he had a weapon of the gods? He was a god. I held the sword in my hands, and swore that no one would use it again.

See, here is a little thing about divine weapons. They can still break, with the right force.

With the sword in hand, I fled our camp and faded into the night.

Tears were flowing in earnest by the time the dawn rose. The tears still flowed by the time the sun set. And then, by the time the moon rose again, the tears were replaced by heaving sobs. I traveled through fields and forests, over mountains and canyons. Running. Always running. I had nowhere to go. Who would shelter me with at least two deities hunting me? When I stopped running I'd have to face the truth that I belonged nowhere. I tossed shards of the sword as I went, not caring that the weapon itself cursed my name as I shattered it. The sword promised that I would pay for its suffering. I cared not. What could a sword do to me now?

Was Lyritan trying to find me? Of course he was. He needed me. He said so himself. I was his tool.

The pain in my heart threatened to break me.

I just wanted it to end.

And then, when I had only the sword's hilt still in hand, I found my mother.

When I had pictured my mother finding Lyritan and me together in the woods, I imagined fury wrought on her face, her brilliant features burning like lighting. What happened instead was that Shirla and I met in a forest like we had thousands of times before. The trees and birds were the only creatures that would bear witness to our meeting. Instead of anger, her face was sorrowful, for she had obviously cried tears of her own.

"Liuva," she said, "how could you?"

"You are going to kill me," I said. There was no point in pretending any longer. Yet, there was no expression of surprise. She had likely guessed that Lyritan told me everything.

"Plants are born to die. Humans raise cows for the slaughter. How are they any different from you, my love?"

"Love?" I hissed. "This is not love." Could the gods truly love? I was part mortal—perhaps that was why I so easily loved and was betrayed. Was there anyone I loved who hadn't betrayed me?

"I regret what I will have to do," Shirla admitted. "I thought I wouldn't care for you, but I found that the pain of losing you…" Shirla sighed, looking at the ground. "I have let this go on too long. And you let yourself be used by him. I see it now—how you both have used me like a fool."

"What now?" I asked, wiping my eyes. "Are you going to kill me? I will never go into the Burning Hand for you."

"No," Shirla said, clenching her fists. "I am going to make you rest. And when you wake, you will have forgotten all of this. And then, perhaps, there will be a way to make this right after all."

"Wake?" I dropped the hilt on the ground, which opened and swallowed the metal, hiding it from sight. It would not be found again until it wanted to be.

The goddesses strode over to me, hand raised high. The vengeful goddess of my imagination had appeared, making me cower before her. I did not beg for mercy. There was no point. "If this is how Lyritan wants to play the game," Shirla said, her voice rumbling like thunder, "let us see what happens when his favorite pawn is off the board."

Shirla, my mother, lowered her hand.

And then I forgot everything.

Chapter 61

Caes

"My love," Lyritan said, rushing towards Caes as they made their way back to the scene of the battle. His face was blistered, his golden hair burned, but he was alive. He was whole. Caes stiffened at the sight of him—she now remembered just how badly he betrayed her. What had been faint memories was now vivid, the ache in her heart as fresh as if the betrayal was only yesterday.

He loved me as much as he knew how.

Whatever Liuva needed to tell herself. Caes had more pressing issues.

"I'm alright," Caes said, keeping her arms crossed and avoiding the chance to run into his open arms. The god flinched when he saw that she wasn't coming any closer, but recovered fast, moving his arms to his sides. Who cared about the god's feelings? Her friend was bleeding. She gestured to Bethrian. "He needs help. He—" Then Caes caught sight of the husk on the snow. "Marva!" She ran towards it, where Cylis crouched, his purple face streaked with frozen tears.

"No..." Caes's throat caught. Another friend was dead and strewn on the ground before her. "How...?"

Cylis shrugged, though it was laden with defeat. "We are warned not to use too much of our magic. This is why." Cylis's face was grief set in stone. As much as she wanted to hold and comfort him, he wouldn't thank her for it. He needed to be alone.

Caes bit her hand, grimacing at the taste of dried blood. Crying out wouldn't help anyone right now, no matter how much she wanted to. Tears never brought back the dead.

Marva. Another person, another friend, was dead—for her.

Bethrian, bleeding into the snow. He was injured—for her.

"Why?" Caes whispered to no one. She sat on the snow, not caring that the melting ice seeped into her pants. The bright sun, now sinking towards the horizon, mocked her. It was too brilliant a day for so much loss. Cylis looked up briefly, but he was lost in his own grief and immediately went back to staring at what was left of Marva. "I did everything I was supposed to," Caes muttered. "And it is never enough. And this...how much longer will I have to see my friends die?" Her throat caught, barely able to utter the words.

Alair looked up from where he was attending to Bethrian and gestured to her to join them. She obeyed, though she had no recollection of deciding to move. For his part, Lyritan was off walking into the distance, his attention on something no one else could see. Whatever he was doing, he'd get no objection from her. He needed to get Caes to the Burning Hand—she had to trust that he wouldn't do anything that would harm them before then. But beyond that, who knew what he had planned?

She sat next to Alair on the snowy ground, watching as he sewed the wounds in Bethrian's legs. They were a few inches long and parted the flesh like a bloody clam, though the bleeding had slowed. While Alair worked, Bethrian's eyes squeezed closed and his fists clenched. He groaned with each stab, but his breathing was deep. His color was healthy. Both good signs.

"Is he alright?" Caes asked.

"He will be. Nothing critical is hurt, but he's going to have nasty scars." Alair reached for a vial out of the pack. "And his healing will be complicated by how much we have to move."

"Just wonderful," Bethrian hissed.

"Be grateful," Alair chided. "This could've been much worse." He lowered his head to Caes. "Talk to me," he whispered.

Caes leaned against Alair and pressed herself close to him, his warmth seeping into her, even through all their layers. Still, she was careful to give him room to work. "Marva—" she whispered.

"—fought well and died honorably," Alair said. "But she will be missed. Terribly." Caes nodded in agreement, right as Bethrian let out another series of groans.

"It's just...to the gods we are nothing but pawns," she said. "And pawns are sacrificed." Soon, she needed to explain to Alair what she remembered today from her time as Liuva, but now was not the time. Not when Bethrian was writhing on the snow while Alair was driving a needle into his flesh.

"You are only a pawn if you decide you are," Alair said, tying off a knot and then trimming it with a little scissors. "What happens next is your choice and yours alone."

What happened next...

Lyritan, their guide to the Burning Hand, was gone. And who knew what he would do once he returned?

Karima and Shirla, though no doubt distracted by the loss of Desmin and Damek, would come for them again. The goddesses would not give up so easily.

The others didn't have to stay here. They could run and try to evade the goddesses. She had to meet her fate at the Burning Hand, but that didn't mean everyone else did too.

"I can't ask everyone to go any further," Caes whispered. "They've already suffered too much."

"That is their choice whether or not they go. We aren't holding them prisoner." Alair rubbed the contents of the vial over Bethrian's freshly-sewn wounds. Bethrian shrieked and bit his hand, muttering a series of expletives they ignored. "But no matter what," Alair said, looking at her with his mirrored eyes, "I will go with you."

The surviving members of their company camped far enough away from the fight that they did not have to see the blood-covered snow or Damek's corpse, but close enough that they could return and lay their friend to rest. Once the camp was set and they caught their breath, Alair, Caes, and Cylis moved Marva's body to a little overhang of stone. What remained of Marva was wrapped in her cloak, and more rocks were placed around her body, blocking it from the elements as best they could. All the while they said nothing. What would they say? Who would they pray to? Even now, Marva was in Karima's realm, with Kerensa.

Karima was not known for kindness.

The only prayer Caes said in her heart was that hopefully Marva wouldn't be tormented for long. Karima had to be destroyed—it was Caes's only hope of saving her friends from an afterlife of suffering.

But what would happen to the Soul Carvers once their goddess was gone? None of the Soul Carvers expressed any concern on the matter, and they knew the plan was to kill Karima long before this. She would trust that they knew what they were doing.

While the three of them worked at doing what they could to bury Marva, Caes watched Cylis, who had stayed silent, other than the most essential mutterings. What was he thinking? Her poor friend. He had lost Kerensa. And now Marva. He didn't cry. He didn't complain, for once. Seemingly he just worked, attempting to bury his lover.

Bethrian stayed at their little makeshift camp that was against another outcropping of rock, resting his injured legs and suckling on a flask of liquor. It wasn't the worst injury, but Bethrian would have to be careful, using Alair and Cylis as a crutch to help him make the rest of the journey. How would he ever make it home, even if he didn't get blood poisoning? They were just about to return to where Bethrian waited when a familiar blond shape walked over a nearby hill, trudging in the snow.

"Figures," Cylis said.

"We would be dead without him and Marva's sacrifice would have been for nothing," Alair said. "Remember that before saying something we regret."

Caes's heart stilled. Lyritan.

Had she ever meant anything to him, other than what she could do for him? Impossible to say. Yet, she couldn't help the sigh of relief that escaped her at the sight of the god. Without him, they would have little chance of making it to the Burning Hand, of evading the goddesses. They were closer to the mountain now than ever, yes, but there were still dangers.

But right before Caes called out her forced greetings, she noticed a bloodstain on Lyritan's arm, soaking through his coat. The god looked alright, maybe a little pale, but his eyes golden eyes were resolute. Was he injured in the attack? Or did his injury happen after he left? Lyritan was wordless and solemn, and merely greeted them with a nod and took his place near Bethrian on the ground, staring at the last of the sun fading over the horizon. There still wasn't timber for a fire, so they sat in a circle, staring at each other. At first no one spoke, the sounds of their bodies crushing snow and the wind blowing in the mountains thundering in the immense silence of the wilderness.

"What now?" Cylis asked dourly.

"We keep going," Caes said softly. "Though, please, do not come just for my sake. You can go back to Gilar. To Malithia."

Cylis snorted. "Yeah, like that's happening. Let's find Hanith and get this nightmare over with."

"I'm afraid that will be a problem," Lyritan finally said. "After the avalanche that occurred when the *Ocul* fell, I went to see if I could find Hanith's tomb. It was as I feared." He closed his eyes, as if gathering his strength. "It was buried." He opened his eyes and let out a long sigh of dejection.

"What?" Caes asked. There went her hope of using Hanith to end this. She would have to face the Burning Hand after all. Good thing she didn't let herself hope much anymore.

"Explain," Alair said, his voice uncharacteristically deep.

"What can I say, Soul Carver?" Lyritan said. "We cannot get to his tomb. We would need hundreds of men and many months to find it now."

"What will we do?" Bethrian asked. "There's no point in sending Caes into the mountain without the weapon to kill the goddesses. Is there?" Caes held back a smile—good on Bethrian for remembering that Lyritan had no knowledge of the sword shard hidden in her arm. And for reminding the rest of them to keep up the charade. The gods were playing their game, and they didn't know that the game pieces had planned their own moves. For the entire time Caes had been aware of the divine plots, the deities pretended that they had intended her to use a weapon to destroy each other all along, instead of the sword being something Lyritan unexpectedly inserted in their game.

It was time to return the favor.

"Indeed, there is not," Lyritan said, "which is why I was gone for so long. I made this." He reached into his tunic and pulled out a dagger.

Being that a god was sitting in front of her it was hard to tell at first, but once she noticed the sensation it was impossible to ignore. The weapon glistened a deep gold, and it made the air around it vibrate, singing a song of magic and death. Lyritan had another weapon like the Sword of Might. One that could destroy the gods.

...How?

Lyritan smiled, as if presenting her with a treat. "For you, my love. I told you I had a plan. I'm only sorry I did not tell you sooner. I did not know if I could manage this." He sighed, pushing his hair behind his ears. "That is, altering my weapon drained me."

Caes thanked whatever fates that spun the threads of her life that she had years of practice at courts. She returned his smile, reaching into Liuva's hopeful love for Lyritan to push emotion into her eyes. Yearning and love. All she felt was yearning and love.

Though, what Lyritan did was good, right? There was another weapon. Now she didn't have to pull the shard out of her arm. The shard would be painful and difficult to use, to say the least.

Lyritan held out the dagger and she took it, relishing its power. She knew how to handle a divine weapon now without letting it overpower her, though from the flicker of Lyritan's eyebrow, maybe she handled it too well. Was she supposed to struggle wielding it, like she did at first with the shard? Liuva didn't struggle, not like Caes had.

Too late.

"Thank you," Caes said. "We can end this."

End this, and leave Lyritan master of the world, for they had no other choice. A Karima left in charge would wreck havoc on the empire and torture Kerensa and

Marva for eternity. Shirla would exact vengeance on the Soul Carvers and anyone else who she felt slighted her over the last thousand years. And if Caes killed them all, she would be leaving the lands empty for other gods and invite the potential for ruin—malicious gods who consumed humans for sport.

She couldn't think about what Lyritan would do. Whether she liked it or not, he was the only choice.

He will be fair. He cared for mortals.

That was before he had the potential of gaining her power, too. She, who was only part divine, would still have to sacrifice herself at the Burning Hand—what else was she going to do? From how Lyritan talked to the nymph, she could focus on her power while she died and send it to someone of her choosing. Who would she send it to? Did she have to choose?

Caes huddled closer to Alair, who had his arm wrapped around her. She breathed in his scent, letting it relax her.

"So, we continue on," Bethrian said, nodding and rubbing his legs. "We have the means, now."

"Yes," Lyritan said. "The goddesses are regaining their strength and no doubt planning their next move. We must move quickly." He looked at Bethrian, and a flicker of concern wrapped over his features. "As quickly as we can."

"I will keep up," Bethrian said. "You will not suffer on my account."

Suffering—they had all suffered enough already.

"There's no reason to stay here," Alair said softly. "Even though we are leaving a piece of ourselves."

"We can't do anything else for her," Bethrian said, wiping his face. "You did the best you could. And we have precious little time before our supplies run out."

"What about Damek's corpse?" Cylis asked. "We haven't touched his body. I'm assuming we're leaving Piggy where he is."

Yes, they were leaving him. Desmin did not deserve a grave, though her father was a trickier matter.

Cylis and Bethrian turned to Caes, while even Alair stiffened. What should they do with Damek's body? He was her father, but he…

"Leave him," she said. "I don't know how it happened that he came to be corrupted by Shirla, but he was. And even before that..."

"What if it was Shirla's influence all along?" Alair said, hinting at how Caes had told him that Damek was different once he—*she*—found the first part of the sword. "It might not be him."

"There's no way to know." And that was the truth. She would never knew if her father was a victim, and regardless, she had to live with the consequences. Not everything in this life was going to give her a neat answer. Did her father love her and care for her? Or did he abandon her for the chance at power? The Damek who raised her was not the Damek who brought her to court, and he especially was not the monster that attacked them. "I...can't..." she said. "I can't do any more with him."

The others nodded. They wouldn't force her to see his corrupted face. Caes wiped away a tear and took a deep breath. She could mourn what she had lost, or she could treasure what she still had.

Lyritan coughed. "Caesonia, I didn't want to tell you sooner, but I know what likely happened to your father."

Caes felt as if she swallowed all the snow on the mountainside. Alair gripped her harder. "What? How—"

"When a mortal takes a weapon such as the Sword of Might," Lyritan said, "they taste the divine. They feel the first brushes of creation. And in some people, such weapons overwhelm their senses. They lose themselves in the power and the promise of more. A promise that will never be fulfilled.

"What I suspect is that your father took the sword and had the ability to...absorb its power. Which he did. And it grew as he found the remaining pieces." Lyritan gestured at the mountain. "But when he decided to go to the Burning Hand on his quest, Shirla couldn't allow that. He wasn't *you*. He would've been useless at the Hand. And who knew what he would have done with his magic and the sword?"

"So," Caes said, "one of them attacked him, to deter him from going further."

Lyritan nodded. "And it also set you in motion to do what you were made to do. You would've been useless to Shirla as a lesser princess. All those silly restrictions."

"I was a hostage in Malithia."

"Yes."

"I almost died. Several times."

"Yes."

"I was tortured." Cylis and Bethrian looked at the ground in front of them. However, Lyritan didn't shy from her gaze. "Yes."

"All to get me where they wanted me." Scoffing, Caes shook her head. Was Lyritan right? It made sense. It explained so much. All of her life, her suffering, all of it was this...*thing*. This amusement. This was all a ploy for someone else to gain power. She meant nothing. She was nothing. Her father loved her, and then he became lost in power. It became more important than her. Her throat clenched.

"Breathe," Alair whispered in her ear. "I have you. Always."

She did have him. Whatever messed with her fate, it had given her him. He wouldn't leave her. He stayed with her and protected her in Malithia. He came back from the dead for her. Even now, he fended off a god for her. He would go with her, to whatever end awaited them. To whatever hells lurked in the Burning Hand's depths.

No, not him, too. There had to be a way to protect him. Lyritan would win, Karima and Shirla wouldn't, and Alair would live. She was forced to play this game and lose pieces of herself in the process. Now she would do whatever it took to win, and she would protect what remained of her friends.

"I'm going to the Burning Hand," Caes said, gripping Alair's hand under their cloaks.

"Well, obviously," Cylis said, ignoring the conversation's morbid tone. "What else are we going to do? Go back to Malithia and let the goddesses twiddle our lives to fuck all?"

"If we want this to end, we need to go," Bethrian said.

Caes shook her head. "You don't—"

"Yes, I do." Bethrian's shoulders slumped. "You heard Lyritan—you need me. I'm your Child of Sky. That's the most ridiculous name for this, by the way. Though I suppose it conveys the meaning." The god huffed in agreement. Poor Bethrian—he, too, had wanted power, and ended up in a cold mountain camp with her.

"All this talking of the divine shit raises a good question," Cylis said to Bethrian, narrowing his eyes. Cylis seemed more wane than normal, and only by knowing him well did Caes notice the extra weight behind his gaze. "How exactly did you manage to banish Prince Pig Penis? Un-magic him."

"He bit him," Caes said. "And it made Desmin...shrink. I've never seen anything like it."

"How?" Cylis asked.

"I, too, am interested in this," Lyritan said, his brow furrowing.

Bethrian squirmed. "I'm not really sure..."

"Bethrian," Alair said, "I've had a miserable last few weeks and lost more close friends than I ever wanted to experience. Tell me how you did it. Now. I really don't want to have to force it from you. But I will."

Bethrian gulped, giving all of them one last frantic glance before resigning himself to answering. "I...ate Seda's tooth."

"What?" All of them asked at once, though Cylis's question included, "Fuckwit, why?"

"I don't know," Bethrian said, and then delved into the story of how he witnessed Seda's skull being smashed, managed to save one tooth, and then ate it once outside of Fyrie. "I was so distraught, I thought for sure I was next, I...I wasn't thinking."

"No shit," Cylis said.

"Lyritan?" Caes asked. "Could that explain it?"

"Possibly," Lyritan said. "Unless the mortal is hiding some other abilities" –Bethrian shook his head vigorously– "the Malithian royal family is sworn to Karima. It is possible some of that magic protected—negated—what the goddesses did."

"Yes, let's go with that," Bethrian said. "Seda was a magical tooth princess."

"Oh, for fuck's sake," Cylis said. "He's such a fuckwit, I believe him."

"He is," Alair said. "That's a story someone would come up with only if it were true."

Caes shrugged. "Sorry, Bethrian. I agree with Cylis." She paused. "Though I don't share the extent of his sentiment."

"Understandable," Bethrian said.

"Did you know Seda was capable of this?" Alair asked Lyritan. That was a good question—was Seda part of his longer game?

"No," the god answered. "I assumed there was some sort of blessing in her family's blood, but to be perfectly frank, Malithia's rulership has changed so drastically over the centuries I wasn't sure if—or what—remained."

"That's a lot to assume," Caes said. "Isn't it?"

Lyritan shrugged. "I forget you were spared most of this, but in the earliest days, we had to stoop to severe lengths to gain mortals' favor. Luckily, those days are done."

"Luckily," Cylis echoed. Luckily for them, the god seemed too distracted to notice Cylis's sarcasm. Or he had just gotten very good at ignoring Cylis. Or decided that Cylis was permanently beneath his notice.

"She saved me," Bethrian said, a hint of reverence in his voice. "Seda. After everything, she saved my life."

"In the most disturbing way possible," Caes said. What would possess someone to swallow a tooth? Caes looked at Alair, at his jaw, imagining the rows of teeth inside. What would it be like to swallow one of those? What would it take for her to get that idea? He caught her staring at his mouth and smirked, as if he guessed what she was thinking.

"Let's discuss something else," Cylis said. "I can't think of Bethrian swallowing anything right now. I know—let's talk about how we're all going to die."

"You won't die there," Lyritan said. "You have no future in the Burning Hand. And I will get you back to the mortal lands."

"Thank you," Caes said sincerely. At least one of her friends would live. Would Lyritan keep his word? Impossible to say. There were ways gods could be bound by their oaths, but from what Liuva knew—and what Caes remembered—there was always a way to break them.

"Still," Cylis said, "after what we've just seen, I don't like our chances. What's next? Poison? Razors?"

"There are plants near the Burning Hand that can melt skin," Lyritan said. "I suggest not touching them."

While Lyritan and Cylis gently conversed on the various ways to blister human skin, Caes faded into her thoughts.

Caes turned to look at the stones behind them, where even now her friend lay dead, fated to rest hidden in rocks. Her father was dead—now in body, as well as in spirit. Kerensa was dead. And despite Bethrian's flippant tone, it was only a matter of time before he joined them. Her heart wrenched and she blinked back fresh tears. Why would she expect Bethrian to live through this? He was injured. He was mortal. And there was still more to come.

The conversation lapsed, and Cylis focused on the snow in front of his boots, absentmindedly kicking it. Lyritan's golden eyes dimmed, seemingly watching something the rest of them could not see. Even Alair took extra deep breaths, possibly thinking of how their demise lurked before them. Even if the goddesses left them alone, they still had to make it to the mountain and satisfy whatever was within.

Something that would demand her willing death.

So many beings had prodded her to the mountain, and no one told her what she would have to do once inside, or what she would face. It was because they likely didn't know. The gods were made there, in a way, but this was a place where even the gods balked before powers greater than them.

"I have a confession," Bethrian suddenly said, breaking their musings. "There's something I need to tell you before we go any further."

"What now?" Cylis asked. "You swallowed Seda's toe?"

"No. Worse." Bethrian took a deep breath. "I am Lady Peony Passionflower."

Gods, it had been a long day.

Caes erupted in manic laughter, stilted and sharp. Alair seemed torn between laughing and worried about her sanity. She let the laughter roll out of her, not caring who or what was around to hear. The members of her party stared at her, Lyritan's expression borderline amused. "I'm sorry," she said, catching her breath when she was finished. "I thought you said you were Peony—"

"Passionflower," Bethrian said, gesturing at himself. "All me."

"What?" Cylis's eyes widened and he pointed at Bethrian. "You mean to tell me that *you* were the reason I was harassed in Gilar, and called Fenrick?"

"…Yes."

"They asked if I had a knot."

Bethrian grimaced. "Well, yes. I'm sorry about that."

"Do you know what a *knot* is?" Cylis asked the company. Everyone pretended not to know, including Caes. "*You* were the reason the Gilar courtiers were in a frenzy. You were the one writing the most perverted love novels I have ever—"

"Ever what?" Bethrian asked, a twinkle in his eye. "You read them?"

"No." Cylis reddened, as much as possible for someone with skin splotched dark purple.

Alair let out a soft chuckle. "That's amazing. I never would've guessed."

"We should've known," Caes said, mostly to rankle Cylis.

"But you wrote the stuff with the—" Cylis gestured dramatically. And rather obscenely.

"Again," Bethrian asked, "how would you know?"

Cylis's jaw clenched. "After so many women mentioned it to me, I finally had to sit down with a few pages," he admitted.

"I'm surprised you stopped at a few," Caes said.

"You read it?" Cylis asked Caes. *"You?"*

"A little," Caes admitted. "Marva told me—" Caes stopped when Cylis's expression darkened. The levity was banished from the conversation as deftly as wind thrashing snow. Silence descended on the party, a sudden awkwardness as they remembered the friend they had lost just hours before and didn't have time to grieve.

"Marva cared for you. All of us," Caes said. "She would want us to smile at her memory."

"How do you know?" Cylis asked with a little sneer.

"Because she comforted me after I lost Alair." Caes looked at each of them in turn. "She told me to share the happy memories. The good ones. The ones that make the grief worth it."

Cylis rested his fists on his lap. "That's Marva."

"Caes is right," Alair said. "Marva wouldn't want us to grieve. Not now. Not when we are so close to the end. After we are done here, we can do whatever you think she would like to be remembered by. I promise."

Cylis nodded slowly and wrapped his arms around his knees. Did he believe them? Caes would do whatever it took to help Cylis mourn. Whatever he asked.

"Hold on to the good memories," Bethrian gently said, "because if these tales are true, our world is about to turn to absolute shit."

Chapter 62

Alair

Shit, Bethrian had said. They were about to face shit. His language was vulgar, but conveyed a valid point. How much worse could it get, truly? They had faced harsh winter cold, demonic creatures, and had lost their friend. Moreover, they were trapped into staying with a god, one that Alair trusted less and less the closer they got to the Burning Hand.

Damn the fates that there was no other option, no other choice for a deity to govern the lands. Their choices were this pompous divine lord—or murderous Karima and Shirla. It was choosing between a snake and tigers. Each one dangerous. Each vicious. But which was the best of the bad options?

Lyritan. Lyritan would at least protect the Soul Carvers, and the realities of war would keep his worldly ambitions in check. Lyritan's body had limits. His power had limits. And people never liked doing what they were told. The mortals would stop him before his power became too much. They would have to. Or so Alair told himself.

At least the god kept to himself more and more, growing morose as they approached the Hand. If one couldn't avoid someone's company, silence was the next best thing.

Alair watched Caes trudge through the snow. The depths were lessening and the chill was fading—thank the gods—but the journey still wore on her, in more ways than one. Her head was bowed lower than normal, her eyes rimmed in red. She didn't mention Marva. She didn't mention her father, though that was a wound that would never heal. Caes was strong, but some things…some things would rip at a person, nag at them bit by bit until they broke. But Caes could likely learn to manage it. She was strong. But whether she would live long enough to do so was another matter.

"At least the snow is going away," Cylis said, strutting along beside Alair. "We'll be faster."

"Indeed," Alair said, shielding his eyes from the brilliant sun. The mountain was close. Two days, three at most. Three days and his world would end. Caes would have to face the mountain and her fate. But he'd be beside her, no matter what she said. She was fated to die, and so was he. He wouldn't leave her to face this alone. They had both died once or twice before—what was another time? Alair didn't think about the afterlife that awaited them. Anticipating what came after death never did one any good. It was always wrong.

"These are really odd rocks," Caes suddenly said, breaking the silence and pointing to the tall stone spires sticking out of the ground. Almost like pillars, the smallest was more than twice Caes's height.

"They are," Bethrian said. "You know, if you look at the tips at the right angle, they almost look like nails." He looked around them. "All of these things are in batches of five, too."

Caes paled. "We need to go. Now." She took off, pushing through the snow.

"What's wrong?" Alair asked, hand on his sword's hilt, the others trailing behind her.

"Probably nothing," Caes said, shuffling along. "They're dead. They've been dead a long time."

"What?" Alair asked. "The stones?"

"Those aren't stones," Caes said.

"She's right," Lyritan said, speaking up for the first time all morning. "Those are from the first creatures, the giants." The god seemed oddly weary, lost more and more in thoughts he did not design to name. "Gods weren't the first things to walk this earth." He nodded towards the mountain. "And we are getting close to where they came from."

"But they're dead," Cylis said, rushing to keep up with Caes. "Why are we running? They're dead, right?"

"Yes," the god replied. "There are many things to fear on this earth, but this is not one of them, Soul Carver."

Well, at least some good news.

Chapter 63

Cylis

Cylis was miserable. Kill him. Roast him. Pickle him. Cylis didn't care about how his misery ended, so long as it did.

What was the point of caring? Caring led to disappointment, and he was beyond the ability to handle more disappointment.

His ass hurt. His feet hurt. Not to mention the agony caused by his Soul Carver magic. The snow was now barely over their ankles, but the terrain was getting more treacherous as they began the ascent. They were near the base of the Burning Hand, right? They had to be. Now Cylis smelled a strange mix of smoke and frankincense that wafted through the air whenever the sky shimmered with the eerie rainbows. At least that was something to distract him. He couldn't count on anything else. The travelers barely spoke amongst each other anymore. Who had the energy? What was there to say?

And all this, for what? To see the remains of some creatures that would've considered Cylis nothing more than a piece of meat stuck between their teeth? A pain shot through his heart—Marva would've loved to see this. She loved unique things. Marva *should* have been there to see this.

I told you not to betray me, Karima's voice said, echoing in his head. Again. *Her death was your fault. Even now, she is paying the price of your betrayal.*

Cylis bit his lip until it bled, his lips and cheeks now scarred and bloodied. He took a deep breath, shaking. Karima was trying to get him to snap, to get him to do something he'd regret. She may have Marva and Kerensa, but he'd be fucked before he'd give her anything else.

He couldn't afford feelings. Feelings were a luxury.

"Fuck!" Bethrian suddenly screamed, moving back a step. For how injured he was, Bethrian was admirably sturdy. Though he had to have been in agony—those were nasty slices on his legs—he didn't complain. Well, he muttered curses under his breath. But he didn't whine. Turned out that Bethrian was capable of more than writing Cylis into a romance novel.

"Oh, hells, what now, Fuckwit?" Cylis asked.

"Stop!" Bethrian held up a hand. Cylis listened. They all listened. "Don't move!"

Cylis adjusted his pack. "What in the hells—"

"The ground," Caes said in awe, pointing at where the snow was gone. Instead of snow, there were now rocks, honed to razor-sharp curved edges. Cylis was surprised Caes noted what was wrong so fast—Caes was certainly worse for wear after their journey. She had a giant bruise on her cheek from where she fell and cut herself on a rock, and her eyes had a vacant look that Cylis hadn't seen since the first journey from Ardinan, when she was tossed into the back of a cart. Careful not to move, Cylis took in every bit of the ground he could see. The rocks were all jagged. All sharp. There was no avoiding them. Cylis grimaced. Turned out things did get worse.

"I thought we avoided most of this," Caes said. "I didn't think—"

"—that the mountain emitting poisonous gas wouldn't also have razor shards around it? How could we ever have guessed?" Cylis shook his head. "Now, what are these? Giant hairs?"

"No," Caes said. "My guess is teeth. Or scales."

"Scales?" Alair asked.

Bethrian coughed, stifling laughter. Cylis whirled to him. "Bethy, if this ends up in one of your books, I swear—"

"An artist takes inspiration from whatever life provides," Bethrian replied, a smile still somehow slapped across his face.

"I don't know what they are," Caes said. "The giants were dead long before I was born. The first time," Caes added, almost as an afterthought. "I only heard rumors that when this world was made, things broke through at the Hand and, well, sometimes it takes worlds time to settle. Like setting a pudding."

"Pudding," Cylis said. "Caes, you've lost it."

"Lyritan," Alair said, "do you know what they are?"

"It doesn't matter," Lyritan said. "I'm only surprised they're still here." Lyritan resumed walking, somehow stepping on the correct stones with a skill he didn't explain to anyone else.

"Lyritan, how do we cross?" Caes asked. Lyritan walked on, ignoring her.

Damn, he was useless, though at least they now knew there was a way forward. What was wrong with Lyritan? He couldn't claim that he was grieving Marva. Or anyone. He should've been happy. He was about to be the big god—king god—or whatever they were called.

"I never thought I'd be glad for snow," Bethrian said, looking mournfully behind him and then at the path ahead. "The packed ice probably saved us."

"How's your foot?" Alair asked.

"Fine," Bethrian said. "Just grazed it. Though now my boot has seen better days."

Cylis carefully walked over to some exposed stones and crouched. The stone in front of him had a glistening edge, sharp even after thousands of years of being exposed to the elements. Maybe they *were* scales of some sort. But what sort of creature had scales bigger than Cylis's head? This was going to be difficult, trying to cross this without slicing themselves. But if Lyritan could do it, they could. He reached out and touched a few of the rocks, feeling the different textures under his fingers. There was something different between the areas on the rocks' surface. It was a slight difference that maybe, just maybe—

"Is it just me," Cylis asked, "or are the razor rocks textured differently?"

"What do you mean?" Caes asked, carefully moving towards him, Alair hovering over her.

"The one Fuckwit stepped on. See—it has those bumps on the side. Ridges." Carefully he took a step on the stones, making a point to set his feet only on a smooth surface. Maybe these were scales, and the razor depended on what direction they were facing. That was a creature Cylis hoped they would never see. "See? Avoid the ridges."

"Avoid the ridges," Bethrian echoed. "Avoid the ridges in a sea of stone. This will be fun."

"What do you think happened to that one?" Bethrian asked, pointing at yet another skeleton. Well, a skeleton's foot. Human, based on the shape and size. These bones were bleached a brilliant white from sitting under the mountain sun for...who knew how long.

"Same thing that happened to all the others," Cylis snapped. "Died."

"Why, yes, my most unimaginative friend—but *how* is the question."

"You're one to talk about imagination, aren't you, Peony?"

"That's Lady Passionflower to you," Bethrian said, holding his head extra high. "And I specialize in the physical act of love. Not death in a wasteland."

Cylis paused and took in their latest surroundings. More travel, slower now than before because of the fact that a wrong-placed foot could easily result in a very damaged foot. As much as he hated to admit that Bethrian was right about anything, they were definitely in a wintery wasteland. The Burning Hand towered over them, the sunset illuminating its peak to the point that it was difficult to tell if they were on the mountain itself, or merely some other foothill. It was hard to tell such things, when navigating around a landscape of razor rock. While the dangerous rocks hadn't disappeared, a rather voluminous amount of human remains *had* appeared. Whether from lost travelers, misguided adventurers, or peoples of a civilization long gone, Cylis didn't know. And he was too tired to care. How long could a skeleton sit here, anyway, without crumbling to dust? Judging from the way some of the skeletons were strewn about and missing pieces, something helped itself to the travelers' flesh. Hopefully after death.

Caes and Alair walked in the front of their company, huddled together and speaking quietly. Good thing she had Alair. Alair would know the right things to say to her. She lost her father, and while it would've been ideal for Cylis to have croaked off some redemptive story to raise her spirits, life wasn't that tidy. He had his own losses to deal with, and he would. Eventually.

But for now, he had a fuckwit.

And his own likely imminent death. But what else was new?

"Come on," Cylis said, moving forward once more. "They're getting too far ahead of us."

"He's awfully quiet," Bethrian said, whispering so low only a Soul Carver could hear him. Bethrian had to be talking about Lyritan, who led their company across the landscape from around fifty paces ahead. Cylis clenched his fist. The bastard could've been leading them in a merry loop for all Cylis knew.

"Yes," Cylis said.

"That's not good."

"None of this is good." Cylis took a wide step, avoiding one of the scales that still littered their path.

"Well," Bethrian said with a wince, "I managed to survive Barlas Tuncer's court, for the most part—I've picked up on these things. Trust me, whatever he's thinking isn't good."

Bethrian was right—the god had changed. He had long stopped mooning after Caes, his earlier love for her seemingly forgotten to the point of ignoring her existence. "Do you think it's guilt?" Cylis asked. "No, that's ridiculous."

"Normally I'd say your first hunch is right, considering he *is* sending his former lover—whom he apparently still loves—to die. But I doubt gods feel such things."

"So, what can we do?" Cylis asked. "I can't exactly push him off a cliff. Yet."

Bethrian shrugged. "Watch. I don't know about you, but I don't trust him to keep his word to take us back when this is done. I've been remembering the path as well as I can."

"Good." Cylis hadn't been paying attention at all.

"Don't worry," Bethrian said, "we each have our skills. Mine is my mind and yours is...other things."

Cylis scoffed. "Be happy they need you."

"Oh, I am," Bethrian said, flashing a toothy grin. Apparently, a path of razor stones, skeletons, and an injury to his legs couldn't keep him from smiling. It was infuriating.

"Now, what's your plan for when this is done?" Bethrian asked in a more conversational tone, carefully stepping around a rock, grunting as he did so. His legs had to have bothered him—once in awhile Cylis smelled blood and that ointment Alair used—and again, Cylis marveled at how he had made no complaints, other than moaning like a cow with burrs between its legs.

"I don't know," Cylis said. "I have to get out of here first. And then find my sister, and Kerensa's."

"More journeys."

"Lots more."

Cylis looked at Caes again. She wasn't going to be going with him, wherever he went. And neither was Alair. The three of them hadn't talked about what it meant, but she'd be going into the Burning Hand. And she wouldn't be coming out.

Fuck...what was Alair going to do? He was going in with her—or so Cylis assumed. But then what?

"She'll be alright," Bethrian said. He stumbled, and before he impaled himself on a rock, Cylis caught him, straightening him back up.

"You're not dying yet, Fuckwit. We need you."

"I mean it," Bethrian said, ignoring Cylis's comment. "This is Caes. She'll be alright."

Cylis huffed. "Well, considering I just lost two good friends, trust me when I say I'm not optimistic."

"*I* am," Bethrian said with a smirk. "One of us has to be."

Chapter 64

Caes

Midmorning, three days after they defeated Desmin and Damek—and lost Marva—something shifted in the air around Caes. That "something" was a pressure of foreboding that darted into her body, both heavy and charged. She looked to the bright blue sky, and then at the rainbow-patterned gusts that emitted from the mountain seemingly on a schedule—nothing had changed where either of those things were concerned. The current best guess remained that the fumes were caused by some sort of volcanic gas from deep within the earth. A simple explanation, but considering where they were, it wasn't that simple. Nothing was. Caes turned around, facing the valleys and mountains below them, now noticeably smaller than they had ever been, while the Burning Hand rose above them, towering and ageless.

"What's wrong?" Bethrian asked, dropping his pack next to him. He could only carry some garments in his condition. A couple hours ago they had seemingly left the razor rocks behind for good. Now, as the razor rocks were becoming more sparse the further they walked, they were left to navigate the normal dangers of hiking up a mountain in their fatigued state.

Alair stepped next to her and placed a reassuring hand on her upper arm, though his eyes were marked with concern. A small dot in the distance was all she could see of Lyritan. He had left the party behind and was now looking for...something. He had all but stopped speaking to them by now, and barely looked at her. Did the unease from the mountain's presence strike him earlier, because he was fully divine?

Lyritan has his moods.

That was true. She just had never known them to be directed at her.

"I think we're here," she said, dropping her bags. They landed on the ground with a thud. If she was right, she wasn't going to need them again. Her throat constricted. She had imagined this moment hundreds, if not thousands of times. And now that she was here, it felt like everything was happening to someone else. Someone else was going to die here. Someone else was going to go into the mountain, never to see the sun again.

Her mind hadn't quite comprehended that this time, she wasn't coming back to life.

Dropping his own bags, Cylis looked around them. "This? But this is...just rocks. Isn't there supposed to be some door or portal or something? You're the writer, Fuckwit. Where's the guardian? Where's the trials? Where's the...opening?"

"You really need to stop asking me these things," Bethrian grumbled. "I write romance. I deal with entirely different sorts of openings."

Caes squirmed and stifled a smirk, despite her fears. "That's not what I need to think about." Bethrian exchanged a series of looks with Cylis that were more reminiscent of schoolboys bickering than a Soul Carver and a lord. Their journey back was going to be something else. If only she was going to be around to see it.

"You'll have time for this later," Alair snapped at them. He turned to her. "You're sure? This is it?"

"I am." She sighed.

"Lyritan!" she suddenly yelled. "Where're you going?" Her voice was mostly caught on the wind, but the god had to have heard her. Yes, he did, for he flinched as she called for him. But he didn't stop. He kept walking, refusing to look back. Shit—she needed him to know what to do next.

"Well," Cylis said, "there goes asking him for help. What's wrong with him? Shouldn't he be gloating?"

"Gods aren't like humans," Caes answered.

"Yeah, that's a given," Cylis replied.

"No. It's...it could be nerves. It could be guilt. Or fear. Or—"

"Maybe he is having his conscience tickled?" Cylis asked.

"I don't think it's nearly so innocent," Alair said.

"He still needs us," Caes pointed out.

"Unfortunately," Bethrian said, "unless you feel like chasing him, we're going to have to let him go."

"I'd like to stop here and rest, if it's alright, instead of trying to get inside the mountain now," Caes said. The weight of her journey descended on her. She didn't want to go forward and into the mountain, but she didn't have a choice. She was at her end, much like she had been when she stood before Lyritan's statue a lifetime ago. "Maybe the memory of how to get inside will occur to me later."

The others nodded in agreement and worked at unpacking their things while Cylis said, "You're the one risking your ass to save us all. The least we can do is let you take a nap first."

Caes dreamt of darkness. Darkness that blocked out the chaos of the world. Darkness that let her feel safe and loved. It was quiet. Serene.

And then a voice broke through, like something smashed the windows of her consciousness.

This was not how I wanted things to occur, my dearest child.

Shirla.

"Tell me," Caes said, not bothering to keep the sting from her voice, "what did you want, then?"

I wanted you.

"Me? You had me."

I never expected to love you. I was weak. I let things go for too long and gave you the ability to feel hurt. And that caused so much suffering. I'm sorry.

"You're a fool if you think I'm going to believe you. After what you did to me, to my father—"

You remember him with a child's memory and love, Caesonia. Did you never wonder why he was alone? Why he never tried to remarry? Where the rest of his family was?

No, she hadn't. He had told her that the rest of his family had either died or weren't worth speaking to. He had told her that she was all the family he needed.

"He loved me more than you did," she said, her voice threatening to break.

He was a mortal, and more, he only raised you. Meanwhile, I made your very soul. And neither of these things changes the fact that Damek lusted for position. For power. And he hated that life made him the poor farmer he was. There was so much he never told you. How he prayed to me for wealth and respect. The things he whispered when he thought no one would hear.

"And he will never whisper anything else. He's dead. You sent my own father to kill me."

The world is at stake. Do you really think I can worry about your heart? Everything I did, from guiding you to court, to stopping his journey. All of it was to bring you here, where you can save millions.

Shirla was why her father failed? Lyritan was right. All of this, all this shit in her life, was the goddess's attempt to get Caes where she wanted her.

"You're desperate and changing your tale. What is it? Tell me what you want. I know this is nothing but a game to you. Stop insulting me by thinking you can appeal to my feelings."

A single white hand emerged from the darkness, caressing her face.

Alright. I shall speak plainly. The kingdoms need a goddess. You need to make one of us complete, or the world will suffer, whether Karima and I choose to fight each other or not. Lyritan is gone. And as you will see in the Burning Hand, your options for filling the void with better than me are slim. Choose me, and I promise I will leave your loved ones alone. More, I will guide them from here myself, easing their paths. I will aid them and protect them.

"And if I don't?"

A pause. *I joined with my sister, for now, because we are afraid of Lyritan. Yes, I can admit that now. And we were willing to sacrifice you in the process if it couldn't be avoided. This is far bigger than your life. But what do you think Karima is going to do to the Soul Carvers who betrayed her? The only reason they still draw breath, that she hasn't taken back the life she gave them, is because we both needed to get you here in one piece, and she can't afford to anger you. What do you think she is going to do to the kingdoms who rejected her worship? I, however, promise mercy to those who followed my sister, so long as they choose me, in time.*

They needed her in one piece? So, keeping the Soul Carvers alive was a move that Karima kept aside in case her plan needed them. The Soul Carvers had died in her service, suffered because of her magic, and that was all they were to her. Nothing but something to be used and discarded. Anger prickled under her skin. This whole fucking journey was nothing but another game.

"Wait—she *can* kill them? Even now?"

They are part of her, crafted from her magic much as you were from mine. She gave life—she can take it back on a whim.

Caes stilled. Hells, what was she going to do? Now Shirla promised hope for her friends, but Karima...but Shirla could've been lying about everything. But Shirla...but Karima...

"Lyritan is here and is an option. He will come back. Why *wouldn't* I want to choose him?"

You never saw what Lyritan was like with power. If he had one of the gods' weapons, and he had you destroy us in addition to gaining your power, do you know what he would do to the world?

Memories flooded Caes's mind. Not her memories. Shirla's.

It was a full moon, the last one before the snows were due to come. The landscape was harsh, with the once-brilliant leaves now blanketing the ground. Shirla loved this time of year, no matter that it didn't have the sweet blossoms of spring or the intoxicating happiness of summer. And she wasn't the only one, for the mortals were having a festival tonight, celebrating the fruits of their harvest. A harvest she had given them.

"Goddess!" The people cried out when they saw her. She nodded in acknowledgement. It was nice to be appreciated like this. Worshipped. Maybe next year she would take Liuva to one of these festivals—it would do her child good to see what it was like when the mortals were content. How the mortals would do so much to keep them happy. It was too bad mortals had such short lives—Shirla would do great things for one village, and before she knew it they were all dead and threatened to forget about her until she reminded them. Tedious.

She stayed back, nodding graciously when children brought her dried flowers and laid them at her feet. A few maidens stood at the edges of the crowd, their eyes wide and faces smooth. Were they trying to decide whether to approach her for a favor? She was in an excellent mood—if they approached, she would be inclined to grant a prayer or two. As long as it wasn't anything too difficult. Flowers were one thing, while bringing back the dead was another matter entirely.

"I'm surprised you're here," Lyritan said, stepping from the woods.

Shirla straightened, watching the villagers. "These are my lands. Of course I'm with them."

Lyritan let out a soft chuckle that reverberated through her. She had to make up her mind on what to do with him one of these days. It was dangerous to have a god wandering her lands, no matter how distracting she found his company.

"What are you doing here?" she asked.

"Looking for you."

"You have found me," Shirla said. "What is it you wish?"

"Oh, nothing." A shy grin crossed the god's face. Shirla wasn't fooled. "I just have an idea for how to fix a problem of yours."

"And what problem is that?"

"Karima."

The god took his place next to her. The villagers eyed the newcomer, but no one came to interfere. Wise, on their part.

"Who says my sister is a problem?"

"Everyone."

"I have the matter in hand." The burning pain of guilt stinged her. The time would come when she had to tell Liuva why she made her, but that day was not today. It did not need to happen for a long time. Thousands of years, even. And maybe a different solution would present itself in the meantime.

"Oh? And what if I told you I had a way to help that would take care of the matter with minimal difficulty...or bloodshed? Well, except to Karima. But that's a given."

Shirla stilled. Did he know about Liuva? It was possible—the girl wasn't a secret. Others could have told Lyritan about her. But did Lyritan know about her role, what Shirla had planned for her? No, he couldn't. Right?

She forced a smile. She would figure out what he knew later, and his plans, but for now, she needed to please him. *"I'm listening."*

"Tomorrow," he said. *"I—"*

"Divine one," a mortal man called out, his words slurred. *"You honor us."* Beaming, the man turned away and back to the festivities.

Shirla smiled and gave a gentle wave, but Lyritan crossed his arms. *"There's more than one god here."*

"Apologies," the man said, stumbling around and holding his tankard high.

"No." Lyritan stood and strode over to the man, right when golden ropes shot out from the earth, wrapping the man's arms. The man cried out, tugging against his bonds, while the other villagers backed away, their merriment now replaced with fear. Writhing on the ground, the man begged for mercy, praying for Lyritan to forgive him.

He had taken no more than three steps before Shirla stood, overwhelmed from the silent prayers of her worshippers reaching her. As much as she wanted to interfere, she couldn't—Lyritan had something she wanted, and she was not going to offend him. But this...the mortal had acknowledged her, and she was the man's goddess...

"When a god grants you attention, you reciprocate appropriately, understand?" Lyritan said, reaching into the fire and pulling out a burning branch. The man begged, his words no more than cries. Suddenly, Lyritan thrust the burning flames against the man's side, burning through the clothing and searing the flesh. Long

moments passed—too long—and then Lyritan removed his torment and placed the end back in the fire.

"Have you learned your lesson?" Lyritan asked.

"Ye-yes," the man sobbed.

"I don't think you did." Again, Lyritan pulled out the branch and pressed it against the man's groin, laughing at how the man screamed. "Look, he's wiggling so much!"

Shirla's heart stopped beating. This wasn't what was supposed to happen.

A dog's barking interrupted them, a small puppy that ran up and growled at Lyritan, nipping at his legs.

"No, Balthor, no!" A little boy cried out, running to the small animal and stopping before the god. With the ferocity of lightning about to strike, Lyritan turned his fury on the puppy and the boy.

Enough.

"Lyritan," Shirla called out while the god's golden light flared, "let's find better amusement than this."

The god paused, turning to the boy and the dog, the burned man, and then her.

And then he smiled, casting aside the branch, and said, "I agree. Let us go."

"My lady," a nymph said to Shirla, "I—I can't speak of this."

Shirla sat on a wooden chair in her home in the woods, the one she shared with Liuva and her attendants. This nymph in particular had been with her for some time. Her name was Isilia, and she was one of Liuva's closest companions.

"Speak," Shirla said. "I have heard nothing but that you are in pain. Tell me—what happened?"

The woman bowed her head, her dark brown hair cascading over her shoulders. Nymphs were close to human, but if one looked at the details, they were not. Their skin was lined as bark, their hair formed like branches. And their eyes were ringed in green and black. And now Isilia's stared at her, tears welling.

"Tell me," Shirla said.

"It...Lyritan," Isilia said. "He...forced himself on me."

Shirla took a few deep breaths. "Are you saying what I think you are?"

"Yes, my lady." The nymph sobbed. "I'm sorry. I was caring for Liuva—"

"Did he touch her?" Shirla snapped.

"No." Isilia shook her head violently. "He didn't go near her." Relief tinged with guilt rang through Shirla's chest. "But the rest of us, we're afraid."

Lyritan. Was it true? Her nymphs never lied to her before, and they wouldn't now. Not for this. She believed Isilia. But what was she supposed to do? Lyritan had a way for her to achieve her goals, and with time she would be able to manage him. She was older than him and had managed far trickier gods than he.

But what else could he possibly do? What other behavior would she have to manage?

That was just the start.

Lyritan demanding offerings from Shirla's worshippers, and killing or maiming them when they did not comply. As the memories progressed, he became crueler. He turned from using burns, to removing nails, to committing atrocities that made Caes gag to witness. Even to children. How could he envision such things, much less smile as he did them?

But were these actually Shirla's memories, or were they something Shirla created to trick her?

What Lyritan loved most about mortals was their capacity for worship, Liuva echoed in her mind. Liuva was sadder now than she had been before, the god she had loved nothing but a lie. Oh, hells, what would have happened if Caes had met Lyritan without Alair's love consuming her? Would she have fallen under the god's spell once more? Caes didn't want the answer.

At least, not that one.

"Why didn't any of you tell me that I was never created to destroy another god?" Caes asked her mother, referencing how the Sword of Might's appearance, thanks to Lyritan, changed everything. "Why didn't you tell me that instead I was made to empower you with my death?"

What did it matter? By that point the weapon was in play.

"You could've asked what I thought."

Oh, my love. You are mine. In more ways than one. But it's irrelevant—the weapon is gone. You will be empowering someone, and that one will have to manage the other gods on their own. Choose me, grant me your power, and I will banish Lyritan. I will protect your friends. I will not take out my vengeance on those who worshipped my sister. Choosing who will gain your power is the last act you will do in this game—the last thing you can do to change the fate of this world.

Damn, Shirla had gotten very good at lying. Though, she did have a point...maybe Lyritan wasn't the best choice for a god after all. Lyritan was selfish, and he had already lied so many times to get what he wanted.

"Alright. I will think on what you said," Caes said.

I know you will, my child. That's all I ask...

And one more thing—here is a gift. This mountain doesn't have a door, but I remember the way inside.

Chapter 65

Bethrian

An hour after sunset, Caes awoke in a fit. Groaning, she sat up, rubbing her eyes. Bethrian found the whole thing delightfully ordinary, considering that was likely the last time she would ever sleep. She blinked and found her companions—minus Lyritan. He still hadn't returned.

"We didn't want to wake you," Alair said from his place near her. "And I think we've all needed to think."

"Speak for yourself," Cylis muttered. Bethrian elbowed him gently in the ribs, though he silently agreed. Thinking got one into trouble.

"It was probably a good thing you didn't wake me," she said grimly. "I needed the dreams."

Bethrian hadn't been much of a military adventurer, preferring instead battles of wits, but he had seen more than his share of executed criminals, ill patients, and students facing impending exams to recognize the even face and blank stare of someone facing their own mortality. That same empty expression was plastered on Caes's pale and weather-beaten face.

"Anything you want to talk about?" Cylis asked. "Please, anything to distract me from Fuckwit."

"Oh, come now," Bethrian said. "You've enjoyed our chats." Cylis glared in response. Bethrian knew that Cylis may not have wanted to admit it, but he liked talking to Bethrian. He just hated that he liked it. That was alright. It would change soon enough, and then Cylis would learn what thousands of courtiers had before him—Bethrian was a delight.

"Stop," Alair said to Bethrian and Cylis. "For the sake of whatever gods we still worship, stop."

Caes flicked her wrist. "Let them bicker. I still need to think. I'm so close to figuring out how we can get in. I know it."

For once—maybe it was something in her voice—Bethrian didn't feel like talking when Cylis was so ready to be verbally prodded. Instead, he admired the soft night sky, filled with more stars than he even contemplated the existence of. Was it just because he was away from a bright city and it was night? Or was it something else about being near the Burning Hand? Or had his cuts become putrid and they were now infesting his brain, making him see things that weren't there?

"Bethrian?" Caes asked softly. "Remember how you sliced my arm in Fyrie?"

Bethrian squirmed. "Unfortunately, yes."

"Well, lucky me," Caes said, "I get to repay the favor."

"...What?"

"To get into the Burning Hand. I know what we need to do."

"Come on, Sky Child," Cylis said, cracking his knuckles. "Sounds like you get to have some fun."

An hour later found Bethrian and Caes standing and facing each other over one of the stones, a boulder that went up to their waists with a convenient flat top. Cylis and Alair stood a few paces back, arms crossed and watching. Still, the god was nowhere in sight. What was this? Lyritan had brought them to this mountain and now he couldn't be bothered to be here? Probably for the best—he was getting unsettling.

"You're sure this is the right place?" Bethrian asked. "This is just a rock." It wasn't any different from the thousands of others that dotted the mountainside.

"You sure I can't be the one to cut Fuckwit?" Cylis interjected. "I'd be more than happy to."

"It doesn't matter exactly where we do this," Caes said, ignoring Cylis. "I can feel...trust me. This will work." She held out a dagger, nodding towards Bethrian. "You're first."

"No. You're not cutting me with that." Bethrian reached into his coat and passed her one of his own blades, the one with diamonds inserted within a brilliant interlay pattern on the metal. "Use this. Please." If he was going to be cut, it was going to be in style.

"Fine." Caes took the weapon and Bethrian held out his hand. His poor calloused and scraped hand.

"Wait," Lyritan suddenly called out, coming over a ridge. "Stop." Caes lowered the weapon to her side as their attention was consumed by the returning god. "There's something I need to tell you."

"Better late than never," Cylis said. Everyone ignored him.

Lyritan jogged toward them, and Bethrian was given a surprise when the god got close—he was transformed. Like the last leg of the journey had not happened, Lyritan was refreshed. Yes, his burns were still there, he was once again the Lyritan from Gilar, the one who was a courtier. The one who was obsessed with Caes. All exhaustion was gone from his posture, and his eyes radiated a brilliant gold. Where in the hells had the god gone that *this* happened? Bethrian peered behind him, at the cliffs in the distance. He couldn't wait to leave this mountain. It was full of too many old things that had no place in a civilized society.

"Where were you?" Caes asked once the god rejoined them.

"I'm sorry, my love." Lyritan brushed what was left of his long blond hair out of his face. Did he somehow manage to wash it? "I was worried I was failing you at the last moment, when you need me the most. I've been overwhelmed by my failure, how I couldn't save you. I couldn't stand it. I needed to think. To remember. To break myself out of my misery."

...What? Something wasn't right.

"It's alright," Caes said, giving Lyritan a coy smile. "This journey was hard on us all, and you were bearing the weight of all our fates."

"And I was afraid. So afraid." Lyritan took a deep breath and surveyed the company. "It seems you remember part of the way to enter the Hand, but there is more. In addition to blood, the Hand requires sacrifice. Each entrant will have to provide an offering. Pain, but not of the body."

"What sort of sacrifice?" Alair asked warily.

"Whatever you treasure most," Lyritan said. "You're about to walk before the one who made this world. It was never going to come for free. The Hand has the power to remove memories, lives, and kingdoms. Remember that before you commit."

Caes looked at Alair nervously. "Oh," she said. Shit. That was what the Hand would take from her, the price of her entry—Alair. He was what she treasured most, and what it would take from her.

"Caes—" Alair said.

She shook. "No."

It didn't pass Bethrian's notice that the god seemed oddly pleased by this turn of events. Lyritan needed to learn that petty jealously was never a good look on a man, even a divine one. But poor Caes, if only there was something that could be done...

"The blood isn't enough?" Bethrian asked. "Seda never mentioned this to me."

"Because I never told her," Lyritan said. "Tell me—do you think blood is all it would take to see the source of creation?"

"But asking this of her—"

"The magic triggering entry is driven by need. And need has to be proved."

Caes was biting her hand, choking back sobs. By now Alair's arms were around her, holding her as she trembled. Hells, she didn't deserve to have to do this, too. The poor woman had been used by almost everyone in her life, and now she was going to forget the one person she loved most? Was the universe really that cruel?

Yes, it was.

Lucky for her, Bethrian was never able to abandon a woman in need. And unlucky for him, he had an idea.

Bethrian coughed. "Does the one who enters the Hand need to be the one to make the sacrifice?" he asked. "What I mean is, can I give the offering in Caes's place?"

Caes shook her head. "Bethrian—"

He smiled. "Consider it payment for what I did to you in Fyrie."

"Yes, mortal," Lyritan said. "You may. The Hand requires sacrifice. In this matter, it isn't picky as to whose." Bethrian couldn't help but notice Lyritan wasn't volunteering, even though the woman he claimed to love was about to literally die to secure his power. He would have let her go to her death with no memory of her lover. Yes, he probably preferred it that way.

Cylis groaned. "I'll do the other one."

"Cylis," both Caes and Alair said. Then Caes turned to Alair, "You're not coming with me. I can't let you—"

"Cylis," Alair said, pulling Caes closer to him. "You're not doing this—"

"Stop. Both of you," Cylis said, the scowl deeper than Bethrian had ever seen it. "We know what's going to happen if either of you do this—you'll lose the other, right?"

Lyritan shrugged. "That's a possibility. Either through death or a removal of love. Or memory."

"Yeah," Cylis said. "Sorry. I went through too much to have either of you give up now because the other is gone. Which would happen."

Alair broke away from Caes placed a hand on Cylis's shoulder. "Thank you," he said. Tears streamed down Caes's cheeks. Hells, even Bethrian's eyes were a little misty. They were all so fortunate to have each other.

Yep, he was definitely dying from putrid blood.

"Then let us begin, if you are in agreement," Lyritan said.

"Yes, let's," Cylis said sarcastically.

What was Bethrian going to lose? His knowledge of Peony Passionflower? The best horse at his estate? One of his nieces or nephews? No, not that—that wasn't what the Hand would take. He loved the children, but from a distance. A great distance. Damn, Bethrian's life was sad. Without Seda, there was very little in his life he could claim to truly love. Maybe he really was the best one to be making this sacrifice.

Lyritan gave them curt instructions on how to make the sacrifices—a lot of thinking, wishing, and bleeding—and then Caes and Bethrian stood facing each other over the same rock that they were hovering at before Lyritan decided to appear and give his dire pronouncement. Once again, Caes held Bethrian's dagger over his outstretched hand.

And then she sliced his palm.

It wasn't deep, as far as slices to the hand went. And while a cut to the palm was painful, it wasn't likely anything was going to be permanently damaged. It wasn't that painful.

Alright. It was extremely painful.

Too painful.

"Holy tits ground in ass," Bethrian cursed, not caring that the vulgar words made no sense. He left the blood drip onto the stone, and once there was a little puddle he sucked on his palm, digging for the bandage in his coat pocket with his uninjured hand.

"My turn." Caes handed him back the dagger and Bethrian quickly sliced her proffered palm. She winced, letting her blood drop to mingle with his. At least this time they were both suffering, and Bethrian wasn't getting wheedled by a talking skull.

"You alright?" Alair asked, holding out a bandage.

"Fine," she ground out, letting him wrap her hand.

A Child of Earth and a Child of Sky, their essence mixed on the stone, payment given to the Hand in blood.

Nothing happened.

More moments passed, and still nothing happened.

And then, once Bethrian opened his mouth to ask what they did wrong, the stone cracked, revealing a hole in the earth the size of a well. Lyritan perked up at seeing the opening, like an excited puppy. The god was pleased. Beyond pleased. It didn't take a mind reader to guess that much. He was also the only one to indulge in enthusiasm.

"That...was not what I expected," Bethrian said, eying the hole that seemingly fell straight into the earth. Forever. He pressed his bandaged palm against his cloak, feeling the urge to press it against fabric. It still stung, but the pain was fading. At least the physical part of his day was likely done. He didn't have to deal with *that*. "You'll die," Bethrian said. "You can't survive the fall."

"Once you enter the Hand, you don't return," Caes said. "It doesn't need stairs."

"I'm going with you," Alair said.

"What?" she whipped her head to him. "Alair. You can't. Even if I agree, the Hand won't let you."

"What, so if I stepped in it, would it stop me from falling to my death?" Bethrian asked, suddenly morbidly curious. Cylis's arms were crossed, watching them debate and muse, while Lyritan stood there, observing like he was patiently waiting for them to end this. The bastard could wait a bit—he would only gain today, while everyone else stood to lose.

"Don't test the Hand," Caes warned Bethrian. "With anything."

She turned her attention back to Alair. "You're not like me. It won't let you enter."

"I think it will," Alair said. "I told you several times before this that I was going with you—to whatever fate awaits. That wasn't an empty boast. Remember how Karima is bonded to her Soul Carvers? How we carry a bit of her divinity? Well, she brought me back twice. The second time required more of her divinity to be tied into me. I'm enough like you that I can do this."

"So you've said, but you can't risk it. Please. Please don't risk it." She shook her head. "I was hoping you would change your mind."

Would Alair's plan work? Or was Alair merely desperate not to let his lover face her doom alone? Even if he was just desperate, Bethrian couldn't blame him. Lyritan should've taken notes—*this* was how a lover acted in extremis.

"Lyritan," Caes begged, "tell him he can't do this."

Lyritan shrugged. "The Soul Carver has a point. The Hand would likely accept him. Maybe."

"I'm going too," Cylis said.

"No," everyone said at once. Cylis frowned as everyone listed their reasons.

"You're not like Alair," Caes said. "He's taking a risk as it is. Please. I need one of my friends to live."

"No," Alair said to Cylis, and left his argument at that.

"You're not leaving me on the side of this fucking mountain alone," Bethrian said, ignoring that the god was right there. "I'm injured and you're my only chance."

"The Hand would only be irritated if you try to enter it," Lyritan said. "I assume Karima has already tried to send a Soul Carver inside and failed."

"Fine," Cylis said with a huff. "I'm only staying back for Caes. Not you, Fuckwit." He pointed at Bethrian. Bethrian didn't care why Cylis decided to stay, only that he did it. He really didn't want to be left alone.

Silence fell over them. At this point they were just delaying the inevitable.

"It is time for your sacrifices," Lyritan said. "Touch the hole."

Despite the gravity of the situation, Bethrian couldn't restrain all of his giggle, and received glowers and glares from the others. "I'm about to make a great sacrifice," Bethrian said. "Let me have my levity."

"As you please," the god said. Was this the god's attempt to sweet talk him so that Bethrian helped him—and consequently Caes? If so, he needed some lessons.

"How do we do this?" Bethrian asked, his palm stinging from the last sacrifice he made.

"Approach the Hand," Lyritan said. "It will tell you what it wants."

"Great. Well, I guess I'll go first," Bethrian said. Waiting wasn't going to make this any easier. After several hesitant steps, Bethrian crouched in front of the hole, staring at the black abyss. There was nothing in there. No movement. No sounds. Nothing. It was a portal into the very depths of the earth from which no light would ever escape.

I see you.

The words didn't ring through his head, so much as the knowledge of their meaning. Somehow, Bethrian knew that the being who had spoken to him was so old that it was from a time before words. A time from before this world was anything other than a dream in the consciousness of something greater.

Something that was pointless to try to comprehend, much like how an ant had no understanding of human lives and deaths. Bethrian shivered and had to forcibly fortify his bladder. *That* was what waited in the Burning Hand? Poor Caes. Poor Alair.

Fuck...

"Here goes," he said, and placed his hand inside the hole. He could still see his hand, though it was mired in darkness, and the temperature plummeted, as if a cavern of ice waited underneath.

I accept your offering.

A sudden jolt rang through Bethrian's body, pushing him into the air and making him land on his back with a thud. His legs cried out in agony since they attempted to brace against the impact, and the cut on his hand reopened.

"Bethrian!" Caes cried out, running towards him. Cylis and Alair helped him sit up, checking his head and the rest of him over. He was fine. Winded, and he would need his bandages re-wrapped sooner rather than later, but fine.

"Are you alright?" Alair asked. My, he sure was asking that a lot today.

Wait, Bethrian was fine?

He was alive.

Alive.

"I think so," Bethrian looked over his body. He still had his member. He was intact. He was still Peony Passionflower. He was still in possession of all his faculties. He was—

Bethrian's chest felt like it was gripped in a vice. "I'm no longer a lord," he said.

"What?" Caes asked.

"I'm not a lord. It's...it's like I never existed in that role. Was never named as heir."

Fuck. So that's what he truly loved—being a lord. And now he was...just a lady. The irony. Lyritan nodded, as if he expected as much. No wonder Lyritan didn't volunteer himself—if he was eligible, there was a good chance that he would no longer be a god after paying the Hand's price.

"How can you know this?" Caes asked.

"I...just do." Like remembering a dream, his memories were now tinted with something of the ether. His family would remember him, but they would have no memory of his being named. His birth order had been re-worked, so that he was no longer the eldest son. He existed, but as far as the world was concerned, he lost what little power he had left. He never had it at all. Was that really possible? Yes. After what Bethrian encountered from his slight brush with the Hand, absolutely yes.

"Damn," Cylis said and let out a low whistle. "Watch—I'll come away from this no longer a Soul Carver."

"Would that be such an awful thing?" Alair asked.

"No. But it would be an adjustment," Cylis said. He clapped his hands. "Let's get this over with." Without looking back he left the group, striding towards the hole. Much like Bethrian did, Cylis crouched down and shoved in his hand.

He, too, was blown back moments later. Caes and Alair went to him, and when he sat up, his eyes were wider than normal and his skin was somehow paler than it had ever been.

"What happened?" Alair asked.

"...I...I don't know where Cecilia is." Cylis said once he regained his breath.

"Who?" Bethrian asked.

"My sister," Cylis said. "I don't know where she is."

"I can just tell you again—" Alair said.

"It would do no good, Soul Carver," Lyritan said. "The Burning Hand can't be so easily circumvented. And I would suggest not testing it, lest something happen to her."

"You have a sister?"

"Yes, Fuckwit," Cylis snapped. "I have a sister."

That was right—Cylis's family was from that intense Karima cult. How could he have forgotten that? And Cylis did have a sister that disappeared from the temple, caused quite the scandal and, oh, gods, *that* was how she escaped, wasn't it? Cylis and Alair, the Mind Melder. That was a scandal the temple would likely not forget for another century or two.

Though if Cylis was worried about Bethrian, he needn't have been—Cylis's secret was safe. One, Bethrian wasn't cruel. Two, Bethrian didn't care overmuch for the temple. And three, no one cared who Bethrian was anymore.

While they were physically intact, both Cylis and Bethrian had each paid a great price at the Hand. A price that would only become known once they tried to live their lives once more.

Chapter 66

Cylis

When was the first time Cylis saw Caes? Was it when she was brought out to the cart that would haul her to Malithia? No, it was a little before that, in the Ardinani throne room. The Soul Carvers had been told to behave at the Ardinani court—including no threats or murders—and had Cylis ever listened? No. So, he snooped. He wanted to see exactly who had made them travel across kingdoms.

The daughter of Shirla's Chosen. Gifted with strange magic. Hated Soul Carvers and likely had the means to destroy them.

Why not kill her right away? They had asked. *Why did they have to bring someone so dangerous to their home?* Caes was a threat and a curse, a woman whose reputation swelled with rumor.

Orders, they were told. The emperor wanted to take the Chosen One's daughter's measure for himself. It had made no sense, but Cylis wasn't hired for that journey to ask questions. He was hired to obey.

So, he went into the palace, expecting to see this monstrous witch, and instead he saw Caes. Beaten, subdued, disgusting, unbathed Caes. Still, her appearance—and how she had obviously been treated—did nothing to evoke his pity. How she looked was an act, a way to make them let their guard down so she could strike when they least expected it. Yes, that was it. Clever of the Ardinani to arrange such a ruse. So, the Soul Carvers watched. And waited. And watched. And provoked, hoping to get her rumored magic to bud sooner rather than later and finally give them an excuse to execute her before they reached the city. And they were ultimately disappointed.

That same degraded little mouse had become one of his closest friends and was preparing to step into a hole in the earth forever. And he now had to say goodbye. That hole was going to consume the last two people he cared about on this earth, and they weren't coming back. He had lost Kerensa, Marva, and Cecilia—he was going to lose Caes and Alair too. The world didn't appreciate that these two were sacrificing themselves to save it. The world didn't deserve their gift. Or his pain. The world could burn if it meant that his friends were safe.

"Cylis," Caes said, wrapping him in her arms, "I'm so sorry," she said, a sob catching in her throat. "Cecilia—I never would've—I shouldn't have—"

"Caes, stop," Cylis said, pushing her to arm's length so they could look at each other. Her face was rough from travel and blotchy and red from tears, but she was still the same Caes. The same woman who bored him to death in the library, who brought Alair so much happiness, and who was prepared to give up everything for others. "I knew what I was doing. I knew there would be a price."

"But *this*?" Caes asked.

Cylis swallowed and felt Caes's small frame under his hands. "Look, you needed it. And you will be sacrificing your life. The least I could do was give knowledge." *And let you keep Alair*, he left unsaid.

"But Cecilia..."

"I know she exits," Cylis said. "And that she is safe. That is enough." Was it enough? No. But it would have to be. He was not about to send Caes and Alair to their deaths with this on their conscience. He did not want this to be the last memory he had of Caes—the last gift he would give her was the peace that everything was going to be alright. He didn't know what waited for her in the Hand, but somehow he knew that the hardest part was yet ahead of her.

Cylis took one of his fingers and lifted Caes's chin, much like he used to do with Cecilia when they were children. "Look, you were a farmer who became a princess, who became a hostage, who became victorious. And now, you're playing a game against the gods" –he leaned forward to whisper in her ear– "and you will win. You can do this."

She nodded, face smeared with tears. Gods, this was horrendous. He lost Marva and Kerensa, yes, but Caes...this was Caes. And he was never going to see her again. In some ways, it was easier when one didn't know that the person they cared about was going to die.

"Thank you," Caes said to Cylis, finality in her tone.

"My pleasure," Cylis said. "All of it." It was. This wasn't the time for a snarky remark.

Caes stepped away to speak to Bethrian, and the two of them proceeded to converse in hushed tones. Meanwhile, Alair approached, his stoic face grim. "This is farewell," he said.

"Yep."

"You were a good friend," Alair said.

"Same." Alair was. Alair had helped him when he could trust no one else, and Cylis had done the same. While Soul Carvers protected each other, Alair did more than that. Was more than that. Cylis couldn't believe that after today, he was never going to see the gray-haired bastard again.

"I wish I could tell you more," Alair said. "About Cecilia."

"I know," Cylis said. He wasn't about to pry Alair for answers. If Lyritan warned them that the Hand wouldn't appreciate them trying to work around their sacrifice, Alair needed to respect that. He wouldn't endanger Cecilia.

Another nod and Alair stepped away, and then Caes and Alair approached Lyritan, who stood like a Soul Carver officiating a wedding. Damn, maybe Cylis would try to marry people at some point. That power was part of their status as a member of Karima's clergy, though this was not the time or place to stew on his potential future hobbies.

"Your destiny awaits, my love." Lyritan bent down and grabbed Caes's hand, and then planted a solemn kiss that made Cylis squirm. "I am so proud of you."

"Thank you."

"This has been thousands of years in the making," Lyritan said, not hiding the hint of joy around his eyes. "It is time to end this once and for all."

"I am honored, dearest one," Caes said affectionately. "I only wish I could see you when you take your rightful place." Damn, Caes was a good actress. If Cylis didn't know better, he would've believed she was actually flattering the god.

"My only regret is that I didn't have a chance to know you physically," Lyritan said. At that, Cylis's bowels threatened to become watery. "But after the loss of your friend…"

"This journey did not provide much opportunity for such things," Caes quickly said. "I will forever wonder what it would've been like to lay with you."

"It seems our story is destined to have regret."

"Unfortunately, it will."

It was painful to watch the exchange, but as much as Cylis was wishing death would smite him, the vein in Alair's neck was throbbing. He was furious.

But then it was over. The god let go of her hand and gestured to the mountain and its snow-crested peak. "It is too late for such things. This is our destiny—it is time to meet it. Just make sure that when the time comes, you think of me. No one else. Me, and my love for you."

Caes nodded, gripping Alair's hand. Alair whispered something in her ear that made her take on an expression that Cylis would've normally referred to as "sickening," but for now he was glad that Caes seemed to take comfort from Alair's presence. At least they wouldn't be alone.

That was it. The farewells were said.

It was now time for his friends to die.

With Lyritan's dagger in hand—at least Caes wouldn't have to peel the shard out of her skin—she walked over to the hole and hesitated, looking at each of them one last time. The wind blew through the rocks and cliffs, and though he heard no words, the quiver of Caes's lip made Cylis suspect that she was hearing the same bodiless voice from the hole that haunted him before his sacrifice.

Caes. Alair. They were going to one last battle, and there was nothing he could do. Nothing.

"Fuck," Cylis whispered at the same moment Caes smiled sadly and said, "Thank you." Then she jumped into the hole. Not even a heartbeat later Alair followed her. The mountain seemed to accept him without complaint, for he disappeared. Thank goodness for small blessings.

Moments later the hole in the earth sealed, turning into nothing but rocks once more.

Caes and Alair were gone.

They were dead, or as good as dead.

The two of them had gone to the doom that would save them all.

Chapter 67

Caes

The Burning Hand. The home of the Source. The place where the true creator of their world resided. This—this place—was what she was created for and suffered for. All of her existence was one long road to come here.

And die.

Caes expected fire in the Burning Hand. Pain. Noise. An instant thrusting into agony and death.

What she did not expect was to find herself and Alair in a dim tunnel, hearing a voice. No, "voice" wasn't the right word for what she experienced, rather, it was a sensation. Images. An intense urge to take one path over another darted into her mind, pushing her on the road she knew they'd have to tread. Guiding them. It was a voice that rang through her soul, piercing and prickling, diving into every piece of her. Judging as it prodded. What lived in the Hand knew they were here, and it wanted to see them. Soon.

The narrow tunnels were illuminated with some unearthly silver light that seemed to seep from the stones, identical to the haunted tunnels they had encountered. At least this time the walls were not filled with the dead, staring and reaching for them as they passed. Still, they were silent, careful not to touch the stone. Alair walked behind Caes, holding her hand, his steady breaths easing her own. After several moments her panic subsided and her stomach stopped threatening to attack her throat, letting her focus on her surroundings with a sounder mind.

"This is not what I expected," Caes said, keeping her voice low. "It's like the haunted tunnel Lyritan dragged us through."

"It is," Alair agreed. "But let's hope nothing lives in these walls."

"Doesn't look like it." Caes briefly squeezed her eyes closed. "I never want to see that again."

They walked in silence for some time, and Caes spent the first few minutes cursing Shirla for not warning her about the second sacrifice. What was Caes going to do once she got to where the Hand led her? Despite the "guidance" Lyritan gave her, and her own memories, the actions she would have to take were uncertain. No one knew for sure what she would face. What the Hand would demand. Or do.

Lyritan had given her the dagger, so at least she didn't have to dig the shard out of her arm. But that would still leave Lyritan as the master of the world, with her power. The idea left a rancid taste on her tongue. Hells, maybe Shirla did have a point that she would be the best option...

As for Karima—Karima was still the last choice. She was not going to give sovereignty to someone who harmed her friends.

"You didn't have to come with me," Caes said once they arrived at a split in the tunnels. By her best guess they had been walking for close to a half hour. It seemed that their destination in the Hand was going to take some time to get to.

"I promised, more than once, that I would be with you, to whatever end," Alair said. "I meant it."

She stopped and faced him, and slowly wrapped her arms around him. Taking a deep breath, she relished the feel of his familiar body pressed against her own and blinked back tears. He was with her. He not only claimed he loved her—he showed it. Everyone else she had ever loved wanted to use her, and ultimately betrayed her. Not Alair. He kept his promises. He was here.

"I love you," she said, filling her words with all the emotion she could. "I just wish I could go to my death knowing that you were safe."

"No, none of that." Alair wiped a tear from her cheek and held her. "I could never forgive myself if I were not with you at the end. What sort of partner would I be if I left you when you needed me the most?"

She rested her head on his chest. She inhaled his scent, the leather and something that was uniquely Alair. If only they had more time together, a lifetime. If only she could make this moment last for eternity. She never had the chance to experience a life with him, and now she never would. "How did I get so lucky as to have you?" she asked, voice breaking.

"Sometimes, the fates are kind. Our bodies are fated to be ashes and dust, but what we have will never fade from the earth. I'm yours. Through our demise and devastation, I'm yours."

"I led you to death."

"No. Never. You have given me a life." Then he kissed her, slowly and deeply, as if by doing so he could bind her to him forever. And she wanted nothing else, nothing other than him. She didn't know what fate had destined for her after her true death, but she begged the being in the mountain that she could be with Alair. That was all she wanted. Not power, not accolades—just him. Even if he was sent to the Hells, she would follow. There was no suffering greater than being apart from him again.

Reluctantly, Caes broke away from their kiss. "I think I'm going to choose Shirla," Caes said softly.

"What?" Alair's brows knit together, searching her face. "Why?"

"I feel like I have no other choice. Lyritan is…you've seen him. And Shirla showed me more, when I was sleeping—what he was like to the mortals. I can't choose someone who tortured for pride."

"You didn't mention this earlier."

"And risk Lyritan hearing? We need him to keep Cylis and Bethrian safe."

Alair ran a hand through his hair and let out an exasperated sigh. "Fuck. Caes, Shirla could be lying."

"I know."

"The goddesses are unbalanced. It was why you were made—left as they are they *will* destroy the world if they are not foisted from power. They cannot stay as they are. I understand your hesitation with Lyritan, but Shirla, after what she did to you…" Alair's jaw clenched. "I cannot. I cannot condone her having that much power. Please, choose someone else."

"And if I kill Karima, *when* that happens, what will happen to you, being bound to her?"

"I don't know," Alair admitted after hesitating. "But you cannot let what might happen to me or the other Soul Carvers sway you. Millions of people are going to be affected by your choice. We are few in comparison to so many. Who you choose will likely be the divine ruler of these lands for thousands of years, long after the Soul Carvers are dead. Don't think about me."

He could say that all he wanted. And it was true—the Soul Carvers numbered few in comparison to the rest of humanity. But there was no possibility she was going to ignore what this could do to him. To all of her friends.

Though, did she *have* to pick a god to have her power? Could she just send it into the ether, unused? Lyritan was a complete god. He'd have to abandon Phelan's body, but he could take Karima and Shirla's place without her gift. And thus, he would be limited in what he could do to the mortal realm. Yes, she could kill Karima and Shirla, give her power to no one, and let Lyritan take over. She smiled, gripping Lyritan's dagger. If that could be done, that was the best solution. It was a way to handle the problem of the unbalanced goddesses, and keep Lyritan from being a tyrant.

There was a sudden pressure in her mind, squeezing her head like a gentle vice. It was an urge pushing her onward.

"Can you hear that?" Caes asked. "Feel it, I mean."

"Yes. We need to go." Alair bent down and kissed her gently on the lips, savoring her. When they separated, he said, "I promised that you would never be alone again. I meant it. I'm yours until my soul has faded to nothing, until there is nothing of me left to love you."

"Alair—"

"I know." He rubbed his fingers over her hands. There was so much to say and not enough time.

"Come," he said, placing a hand on her shoulder and guiding her forward. "Whatever is here, it wants us now."

They walked through endless halls, through passageways that led them deeper and deeper into the heart of the mountain. They talked aimlessly, trying to distract themselves as best they could, mostly about how Cylis and Bethrian would fare on the journey back. Anything to avoid thinking about what waited for them. Caes was just starting to wonder if they would have to spend the night in the stone tunnels when the passageways opened to a massive cavern. It was larger than the throne rooms in Malithia and Ardinan combined, and just as majestic. Caes trembled and had to fight not to fall to her knees.

"Oh goddess," Alair whispered from beside her, his hand holding hers. Huddled against him, she took in where the end of their journey waited.

The cavern was hewn from stone, the walls smooth and etched with runes from a language long forgotten. The words themselves shone with some strange fire, illuminating the script and dancing in endless lines of an intricate web. Along the walls, evenly spaced apart, were small stone alcoves, each around the side of a loaf of bread, that held a white figure inside. Dozens—hundreds—of these alcoves filled the halls. When Caes and Alair entered the room, every one of the figure's heads turned to look at them, watching them.

"The other gods," Caes said. That was what they were—the other gods who were bound to a physical plane by the Hand. "This whole time the gods could see in here?"

"Maybe. But something tells me they can't do much other than watch." Caes understood why he thought that—the figures didn't talk or move their legs. They merely gestured, seemingly bound to their spots.

"Do you think these gods are all from our world?"

"I do not know," Alair said, his voice barely above a whisper. "Our world is vast, much larger than you or I could contemplate." Seeing all of the gods in this hall, it was easier than ever to imagine the size of a world she had barely dreamed of. Just how much was there that she didn't understand, and now she never would?

She was so taken in by the walls of gods and goddesses that at first she didn't see the massive crater in the middle of the room, which was large enough to hold several farmhouses. From what she could see, what lurked within was complete and utter blackness, similar to the one that led them into the mountain. Seeing the crater jolted something within her, something primal that told her to *run*.

"What's that?" she asked. She didn't have to specify the "that."

"Get behind me," Alair said, taking hesitant steps towards the crater, hand on his sword. Caes obliged and kept behind him—his balance was better than hers, his senses keener, his usable magic stronger. If there was any danger, he would know first.

Her heart pounded in her ears and her stomach churned, despite having barely eaten in more than a day. Since they entered the room that prodding presence had stopped pressing on her head, but that didn't help the dread she felt in her core as they peered over the edge. Straight down was nothing but blackness, a dark that absorbed all light.

"What is down there?" she asked. Her voice didn't echo like she expected. It was like the hole led to...nothing. Existence as she knew it ended where the dark began.

"Part of me thinks I should drop a rock," Alair said, "but a larger part of me thinks that's a horrible idea."

Caes nodded in agreement and moved away.

Without turning her back on the hole until she was several paces away, she approached one of the walls, where dozens of gods and goddesses stared at her. Young gods, old gods, ones dressed in breaches and wearing bizarre hats and others wearing draping garments—and some wearing nothing at all—watched. Curiosity was written on their faces, and when they caught sight of the weapon in Caes's hand, several of them shook their heads frantically. Considering what the weapon was, they knew what it could do to them. But these gods didn't need to worry—they were safe. They weren't who Caes was here for.

What a piece of irony. She was once a hostage, a prisoner. And now gods feared her.

"Well, shall we?" she asked Alair. They had to find the goddesses before they could go any further, but after that...well, she'd have to hope that something from her time as Liuva would help her know what to do. Was she supposed to just stay here in the cavern and wait to die of starvation? Was some awful monster going to come and make their deaths quick? Lyritan had his prompts for what she would need to do, but Caes had the feeling he was guessing.

Then Caes realized a major difficulty. "Uh, where's our gods? There's hundreds. At least."

"That is a complication. Unfortunately, I think we are just going to have to start looking."

"That will take forever."

"I think it will be too much to expect them to wave to us. You start on that end," Alair said, pointing at one wall. "I'll start on the other. Don't worry. We'll find them."

With Alair's help, it didn't take nearly as long as she expected to find Karima and Shirla's statues—part of her was pulled to them. After all this time, she finally witnessed the thing that Shirla created and molded her to do—she was to kill Karima by destroying her statue, and then gift her innate power to Shirla so that Shirla could rule. While Caes was dead.

Shirla's statue was a perfect replica of the goddess, the same curve to her lips. The same satisfied expression. Her mother's image stood before her, and an unexpected pain stirred. Things could have been so different. So different, if only the goddess wanted to love her instead of use her.

"Is this really it?" Caes asked. Lyritan's weapon was suddenly heavy in her hand. "Am I really here?"

"I'm afraid so," Alair said softly.

"Where's Lyritan's statue?"

"He can't be far," Alair said. "The gods seem to be grouped together by domain." That made sense. She wanted to keep talking to him, do anything other than what she had to. But it would only delay the inevitable.

"Is that him?" Caes asked, pointing to a statue a few paces away. It was him—she would have recognized that face anywhere. Lyritan's statue watched her, a confident hand on his hip and a pleased smile on his face. Caes didn't return it.

"What's going to happen to me once I die?" she asked Alair, turning away from Lyritan. Now that she faced it, fear ran through her. She was very mortal indeed. "I'm not human. I—"

Make your choice. Whatever you came to do, do it.

The voice pressed against her awareness, clearer this time, yet it reverberated through her, much like the string of an instrument being plucked. Despite how they were alone in the room, they were very much not so. Something—besides the gods—was watching them. And waiting.

Alright. She may as well start with the goddess she knew she *wasn't* going to pick.

Caes walked over to Karima's statue, the goddess haughtily holding her head high.

With Alair holding her other hand, she raised her weapon.

And then her world went black.

You didn't think it would be that easy, did you, little mortal one? Karima hissed. *Let's see if you make the same decisions again. And again. And again.*

Chapter 68

Cylis

For some time after Caes and Alair disappeared, Cylis stared at the ground, at the very spot where they entered the Burning Hand. How long did he wait there staring at dirt, rocks, and his filthy boots? Minutes? Hours? It didn't matter. Gravel was better than his reality. He was now alone with Fuckwit and a god.

A god who seemed oddly pleased.

Disturbingly pleased.

"I promised Caesonia that I would take you back to the kingdoms," Lyritan said. Cylis finally dragged his focus away from his misery. "And I will keep my word."

Cylis nodded and kicked his boot against the rocky ground, sending pebbles scattering. They could make it. Now that Alair, Caes, and Marva were gone there were less mouths to feed with their meager supplies, but they would have to be careful on their return journey. Especially with Bethrian, who was in no position to sprint anywhere. Fucking hells, if they encountered more monsters on the way back, there was no way Bethrian would be able to fight. Or run. Or protect himself. It would fall on Cylis and Lyritan to keep Bethrian alive.

Cylis really *was* desperate and alone. Here he was, caring about Fuckwit.

"You think we'll actually get back safely?" Bethrian asked. "It's a long journey. In the heart of winter."

"Oh," Lyritan said, flicking a wrist. "I have no intention of making us walk."

Cylis's forehead scrunched. "We're flying?"

"No," Lyritan said. "Time and distance won't matter to me once Caesonia completes her task. I will have the power to take you wherever you wish to go. And to honor her, I will—you will be safe."

"Her death will give you *that* much power?" Cylis asked, restraining a frown. He couldn't anger the god—not now, and probably not ever.

"Not her power alone. But once she kills the other goddesses, why, I'll be able to do anything." Lyritan cracked his knuckles, his golden hair catching the first rays of the budding dawn. Poor Phelan's body was cracked and burned, his former handsomeness worn away from the brutalities of the journey and a god who consumed him from within. Hopefully Lyritan had a plan for handling things once Phelan's body gave out—there was no way it would be able to function much longer.

"How would killing the other goddesses affect your power?" Bethrian asked. "I didn't realize that mattered."

"Normally it wouldn't," Lyritan said. "Or it required a *very* concentrated action on the part of the slayer to direct it. But with my weapon—forged from my being—Caesonia won't have a choice. Their power will come to me when she kills them. It would be a shame if it all went to waste."

Ice ran through Cylis's chest, and it wasn't from his magic. "Does she know that?" he asked.

"No. What will it matter?" Lyritan said. "She will be dead."

"She deserves to know what her actions will do," Cylis said, anger rising. "She deserves to know that killing the goddesses will just give more power to your over-powered ass."

Lyritan frowned and irritation flashed across his features. "Careful, mortal. I gave her my word, and I don't want a reason to break it."

Cylis pointed at the god, his hand shaking. "You *knew* that if you told her what your dagger would do, that she wouldn't agree. That's why you left that out."

"Doesn't matter."

"Yes, it does," Cylis said, pulling out his sword, the blue sword that this god gave him. Rage bubbled through him, sending his magic to the surface, a familiar burning and numbness at once. He leaned into it, embracing his power, fueled by rage. "My friends went to die—they *did* die—and for what? You?" Cylis sneered. "A pathetic god who needs to lie to get his way. Who needs to lie in order to have any real power." A smart Cylis would've attacked the god immediately, but he wanted to give Bethrian time to scurry away from the battle that his fury wouldn't let him avoid. An opportunity Bethrian took, ultimately hiding behind some very large boulders the size of a horse. Bethrian was smart, when it suited him.

Lyritan's golden eyes darkened. "Your last chance, mortal. Apologize and I will consider this an act of grief."

"No," Cylis said, ice spittle flying out as he spoke. "This is *your* last chance. See, you made a big mistake. One—Caes has part of the original Sword of Might." He grinned as the god's eyes widened. "Yes, *that* one. Caes had some secrets of her own, but you'd have known that if you bothered to try to know her. And two—just in case Caes doesn't realize your little game in time, I'm going to stop you now. While you are very, very vulnerable." Cylis lifted his sword, which glowed blue with his power. "While this may not be one of the god-killing swords, I'm going to guess this will hurt like hell, right? Slow your plans down a *lot*. And Phelan isn't looking the best as it is. You should have taken better care of your host."

Lyritan pulled out his sword and faced him, his eyes glowing bright, his magic pulsating under his skin. "Alright, mortal. I tried. Shall we?"

Chapter 69

Caes

"Smile, Caes," her father said from his seat across from her. His graying brown hair was cropped next to his head and he looked at her from under a creased brow. The carriage hit a bump, making them jostle. "You're going to be a princess. A real princess." He raised his arm for emphasis, showing the sleeve of the embroidered doublet he wore, a new marker of their new life.

Caes tried to smile. She really did, if only to make Father happy. But all she managed was a pained grimace as she smoothed out her skirts. The gentle satin fabric caught on her calloused hands. Hands that were never meant to wear things such as this. The carriage—sent by Ardinan's king—shook yet again from the rough road, making her gasp. They had been traveling for hours, and they had days, if not weeks of this journey ahead of them. Outside the carriage the guards bantered, their laughter carrying mirth that Caes did not—could not—feel.

"You will need to work on your manners," Father said. "Princesses can't show their emotions, especially so plainly. You're not happy."

"What if they don't like me?" Caes asked, her voice strained. Barely any of the girls back home at their farm tolerated her, much less were friends with her. *Weird*, they called her. But she wasn't weird. Not in any way she could tell. Why didn't anyone want to be her friend?

Beyond not wanting to be her friend, many of the other farmers downright despised her. The dress's fabric irritated the still-healing burns on her shoulder—a gift from a farmer's wife, who was supposed to care for her while Father was gone. Caes had thought for sure the wife was going to ultimately kill her, until Father swooped in one day with a completed Sword of Might, claiming that she was going to marry Ardinan's prince and become a princess.

That moment changed everything. Caes went from not fitting in with anyone to being royalty. Now her life had purpose. Hope.

But what if something went wrong? What if court was just like home?

"They will like you." Father pursed his lips. "I'll make them."

"What if I don't like the prince?"

At that, her father's gaze finally softened, and he was—for now—more like the man who had raised her. He was tired, the weight of the kingdom on his shoulders. It was to be expected that he would be short tempered now and then. "You will. He's a prince, and he is handsome. Remember, I have met him. And if you don't like the man—who is pleasant—I'm sure you will like everything else that comes with the position. Respect. Fine dresses." He smiled. "Worry not, Caesonia—I would never leave you some place where you'd be unhappy."

Caes decided not to mention that he had already done so by leaving her with the woman who burned her. Father might decide to run back and kill them, not to mention whatever else he could decide to do. Instead, she took a deep breath and said, "I'm just nervous, Father. Court? I've never left our village."

"It will be alright, darling," Father said, his hand gripping his sword's hilt. "And if it isn't alright, I'll make it be so."

That was true. Father had power now. People respected him. Caes let her shoulders relax and gave a true smile. People would have to be nice to her. People would have to like her. And she'd never have to pull a weed again.

Being a princess was going to be wonderful. There was no other possibility.

Chapter 70

Alair

"You can't let them bother you so," Iva said to Alair. They were huddled in a desolate corner of Glynnith's palace, near the library. As such, few were likely to surprise them, tucked away as they were. Father was off meeting with some lord or another with his brothers, the ones who mattered. Thus, no one was paying attention to Alair. No one but Iva.

"How can I not?" Alair said. "They're right—I'm not important to the family."

"No, they're wrong. You do matter. To me. You're the best of them." Iva gently caressed Alair's face. Queen of Blood and Queen of Bone, she was beautiful. Her black hair glistened, even in this dim light. Her features were both delicate and sharp, just like Iva. She was a court beauty, but she was known first and foremost for her wit. Iva was a lady who was already being sought by various men at court. She had everything—birth, intelligence, and beauty. A prize many desired. It was surprising she wasn't already betrothed.

However, Iva had eyes for no one. No one except him, who had nothing of worth to offer her.

"It isn't fair," Alair said. "I have nothing. I have too many brothers to matter to the family. And your family will never let me marry you. No matter how we beg."

Iva's lips trembled. She didn't contradict him, because he was right. In families like theirs, what they wanted was the least important thing of all.

"There's nothing that can be done," Iva said. "We can't change your birth order. And I can't change who my parents are. We will have to beg and hope they change their minds."

"That won't matter."

"We will make it work," Iva insisted. "I refuse to live without you."

She was right—there was nothing that could be done. Alair knew that despite what Iva hoped, they were never going to be allowed to be together. If he was the eldest of his brothers, would that be enough for Iva's family? Probably not even then. The next emperor of Malithia itself was a possibility for Iva's husband—her family was wealthy and well-connected enough that she was destined for royalty, not someone like him, who barely had the title of prince. Their love and hopes of a future were nothing but dreams that would fade once reality foisted itself upon them.

Instead of arguing, Alair pulled Iva close to him, relishing the feel of her body against his. While he still could.

"Watch it!" a burly man called out, followed by a stream of rough curses. Alair ignored him and kept running. Besides, what was anyone doing in the streets of Glynnith at this time of night? Nothing good. There was no one worth stopping for. Nothing he *would* stop for.

One after another, Alair's footsteps slammed against the cobblestone streets. *Go away, Alair*, his brother had said. *You're nothing. I'm going to inherit, and your job is to serve me.*

While his brothers weren't the kindest of siblings, their mockery tonight was extra vicious, because someone at court had seen him with Iva, when they had been hiding in a garden. And then told his brothers.

Ha—the idea someone like Iva would be with you. Pathetic.

His heart thudded in his ears. Sweat had broken out on his back and chest several blocks ago. He would run. His lungs burned, screaming for air. He would keep running, no matter what it took. He had only one chance to change everything. After this—*if* he survived—he still may not be worthy of Iva, but it was his best chance. But at least he wouldn't have to serve his brothers when this was done. With this act, *that* course of his future would be dashed aside for good. No, he'd be a servant of someone worthier. His life would have power and possibilities that had never been there before, a chance to craft his own future.

The temple spire rose in the distance, the outline of its ominous stone jagged against the black night. Within the stone walls resided the goddess, and his fate.

He was going to become a Soul Carver, or die in the endeavor.

Chapter 71

Caes

"What should we do next?" The guard asked his companions. Guard? More like torturer. His companions laughed, passing a flask amongst themselves as they sat on the stone ground in the dark cell that was lit by a few torches. There were dark brown stains on the walls, especially next to hanging chains that had curled and dried pieces of flesh attached.

Caes sat in the middle of the cell's floor, her hands bound in front of her, cut and bleeding around her bonds. These were now old wounds that had been opened many times. She wore nothing but a thread-bare shift, her feet unshod and scraping against the soiled floor, bloodied and bruised. She hadn't had a bath in months. Months. Not since father died.

"Too bad she's filthy," one of the guards said. "I can think of something she'd be good for."

"Prince said that's off limits," another guard said.

The others nodded in agreement. "Remember the last time? Bastard's missing a hand."

Caes's eyes stung. That guard was missing a hand, but she'd carry the memories with her forever. And it wasn't out of the kindness of his heart that Desmin banned the guards from doing such things—it was because he knew that after time, adding such violations would just blend into the other miseries of her life, and became yet another thing she endured. And he liked her being afraid that he would change his mind.

Caes adjusted her hands, where the ropes sliced into the skin around her wrists and fresh red blood saturated the ropes. She shivered. The damp cold of the cell was nothing like she had ever experienced before. Water dripped in the corner, pooling on the floor where it would nourish rats later, once the guards were gone. She hadn't been given anything to eat in...a day? Maybe two? It was impossible to tell in the dungeon. Her urge for sleep was her only marker of the passage of time, and she liked to sleep. Sleep was where she was able to forget.

"I know," one of the guards suddenly said, clapping his hands, "we can make her dance."

"What?" the others asked.

"Dance for us," the guard said to Caes, a feline grin on his face. He turned to the others, who gave him encouraging nods and gestures. "We'll feed you if we're happy with your performance. We have bread. A little old, but" –his face contorted to a smirk that highlighted a hairy mole in the corner of his mouth– "you're not in a position to be picky."

Food. Caes didn't care what the food consisted of. It was food.

Restraining a groan, she stood, ignoring the way the guards leered at her. She had dealt with much worse during the last few months. Her feet cried out in agony—it was likely that a toe or two was broken. She had to dance—had to—if she wanted to eat. Gently, she started swaying, moving to some music she couldn't bring herself to pretend to hear.

"Faster," the guard said. "Act happy about it."

Caes forced a smile and lifted her feet, dancing bolder. Faster. She bit her tongue, refusing to cry out at the jabbing pain in her feet. The guards laughed and congratulated the instigating one on the "brilliant" idea. Hot tears stung Caes's eyes. Her father had promised she would become a princess, and now she was this. She was nothing but a thing to be used and hurt.

She was alone.

She was alone.

This was all she would ever be.

Chapter 72

Alair

"Let's do this again, shall we?" a replica of Alair said to him. Or was Alair speaking to himself? After all this time, he wasn't sure how to regard his constant companion, his clone that was the source of his misery. Did it matter? Alair was in Karima's trial, he knew that much, and his mind was his own tormentor. Unfortunately, "his mind was his tormenter" was literal.

"You wanted power," he said to himself. "Now get cutting." Alair looked at the clone, the one with his body. His face. The one who decided what his torments would be and made him undergo them. Over and over again. Brandings. Amputations. Disembowlments—he had done all of these things to himself.

How long had he been in Karima's realm? Was Iva worried about him? Did his family know where he went? Did they care, or were they happy to get rid of an excess son? His mother cared, he knew that, but she was one heart among many. Did his brothers think of him at all?

On the table in front of the two Alairs was a third Alair, tied down and mouth gagged. The tied-down Alair's eyes widened as he stepped forward, scalpel in hand, the edge glistening in the unnatural white light.

"Please," Alair said to his instigator. "I cannot."

"Then you die," his voice replied. "The goddess does not accept failure. Or weakness. Slice, or die."

Alair's hand shook as he approached himself on the table. Simultaneously, he saw himself through those same eyes, watching the scalpel hover over his face.

When Alair sliced himself between the eyes, both versions of himself felt the pain. Both versions of himself howled in agony. Alair cut again, deeper, in a different direction, and then began peeling off the skin, even as his fingers became coated in the hot blood.

He would have to do the entire body, remove every bit of flesh before the instigator would be satisfied.

And he would feel every sensation, every bit of pain.

He was flaying himself alive, like he had a thousand times before. And would a thousand times more.

This was Karima's realm, but it was his hell, and he was never going to escape.

Chapter 73

Bethrian

Anyone who lived in Malithia likely imagined what it was like when gods fought—a consequence of the extensive ballads and tales circulated by the temple. Grand and deadly, the stories spoke of magic duels and powers that mortals would be honored to see.

The tales were nothing like reality.

Like a cat hiding under a bed, Bethrian crouched behind the rocks, watching the god fight the Soul Carver. With the god limited by his human body and Cylis fueled by the goddess's magic and Lyritan's sword, they were rather evenly matched. Damn, they were fast. Too fast.

The god swung, aiming for Cylis's head, and his strike was blocked by Cylis's weapon, which spewed blue sparks. Before the god could recover, Cylis ducked and struck the god from behind, a blow that Lyritan barely staved off with a reflex no human could have managed. The magic from Cylis's sword wrapped around his arm, his body charged with power from two gods.

There was a good chance Lyritan was regretting giving Cylis that weapon.

Bethrian winced when the god managed to get past Cylis's defenses and slice his cheek. It didn't slow the Soul Carver—it barely made him flinch—but it showed that the god could yet win.

Why did Cylis have to pick a fight with the god? If Cylis lost, Bethrian was never getting off this mountain. He was injured. His only hope was that Cylis won and...

Using his magic to summon a ball of ice, Cylis threw it at the god. It made contact with the god's head, sending him careening to the ground. Just when Cylis lunged, the ground shook, and the air around them became hot. Too hot.

Shit. Heat was the last thing Cylis could tolerate with his magic. Flecks of ash fell from the sky like snow. Bethrian covered his mouth and coughed.

Really, Cylis had to pick a fight with a god?

Alright, Bethrian understood why—in the event Caes fell for Lyritan's trap, Cylis killing him now was the only chance to prevent an all-powerful Lyritan from being unleashed on the world. With his host gone, Lyritan might have trouble finding another, especially if Reyvern's tale spread. Bethrian had lived through the reign of one conquering and despotic emperor. There was no possibility that an emperor with divine power was going to be a good thing.

Damn...

There was a very good chance they were both going to die.

Chapter 74

Caes

Today she was going to be given to Malithia. The guards had informed her of her fate, and there was nothing she could do to avoid it. She was going to be given to the empire that conquered her kingdom, the empire that worshipped the goddess responsible for her father's death. And there was nothing she could do to change it.

Forcing her trembling legs to keep her upright, Caes walked to where the royal family and the Malithian delegates waited in the throne room. Caes stood before the royals, like a beggar before their brilliant figures. Was it truly only six months ago she believed she would be standing with them? The grim king and queen sat on their golden thrones, while to one side of the king and queen stood Caes's old friends, Princess Melonie...and Prince Desmin.

Desmin. Seething, Caes clenched her fist and forced herself to turn away from Desmin. There was nothing she could do, and after today she'd never see him again.

Their exchange was not missed. A finely-dressed middle-aged man walked up to Caes, glanced at Desmin, and then peered at her with a distinctive mix of disgust and fascination. "You were to be married to this one, correct, Your Highness?"

"That is correct, Your Excellence," the king said bitterly, like he was admitting Desmin had been engaged to a tavern whore.

"Hmmm, no great loss there," the Malithian representative said. The courtiers chuckled. Burning tears rose to Caes's eyes and she blinked them back. She wasn't going to cry—not now.

The representative clapped. "Well, is there anything further?" he asked, and then said something Caes had trouble understanding.

"Take her," the queen said. "May Malithia do with her as it wishes. From this day forward, she is Ardinan's subject no longer. She is no longer divine Shirla's own."

The crowd murmured and Caes's heart sunk in a downward spiral. Would she be Malithian now? Would she be alive long enough for it to matter?

As for the goddess, hopefully the darkest hell would take that bitch too.

The representative and monarchs exchanged final forced pleasantries before the representative turned to walk down the hall, the courtiers parting before him. Caes followed him out of the palace to where several black carriages waited, along with one fully enclosed wooden wagon. The winter air darted through Caes's clothes like thousands of needles. She wrapped her threadbare cloak around her, though it would do no good in this wind.

Near the carriages stood six black-haired men and women. At first, it was the way the men and women were attired that caught Caes's attention—they were dressed for battle in black metal armor and bore an array of swords and daggers. They wore no silks or brocades, but the craftsmanship of their weapons and armor were excellent, the level of detail down to the artwork on the sheaths and blades spoke to wealth. Whoever they were, these people were no mere foot soldiers.

Then Caes saw their faces. Each of them was eerily beautiful, unnaturally so, and the eldest seemed no more than fifteen years older than Caes. Not a single blemish marked their alabaster skin. And then they turned to her. Caes gasped when the day's light caught and flickered in their eyes, making a brilliant reflection like mirrors reflecting bits of sunlight.

She admired them, like a child distracted by a new wonder, until the realization of what they were hit her.

Soul Carvers. Servants of Malithia's goddess, twisted by her vile magic. They were the ones her father had set out to weaken and destroy. And here, six had been sent to fetch her.

Should she be afraid, or flattered?

The representative turned to look back at Caes and then at the Soul Carvers, understanding dawning on his puffy face. "Ah. I see you haven't yet had the pleasure." The representative motioned Caes forward. "Don't worry. They won't harm you. Yet. There are orders. And despite what you may have heard, Soul Carvers are very good at obeying orders."

Caes nodded and remained silent—what was one more veiled threat? For their part, the Soul Carvers looked at her with curiosity and smirked.

One Soul Carver, a young shaggy-haired man, sneered at Caes and said, "This is who was supposed to destroy us? No wonder they failed." Suddenly, a green and brown syrup erupted from his skin like water rising on a peat bog. The gelatinous substance spread across his face, his skin folding and crinkling under the ooze as his eyes turned mustard yellow. The scent of sulfur and skunk wafted over the air. In an instant, the strikingly handsome man had disappeared and was replaced by a monster of corruption and rot.

Caes's heart leapt and her eyes darted in panic. She clenched her fists—she couldn't run. The Soul Carvers would catch her. And then…

"Stop, Fer," the representative said with a dismissive wave of his hand. "She isn't the only one witnessing your little display. And this is not helping our…diplomatic measures."

The representative muttered something to the Soul Carvers, and one left the line to walk up to Caes and lightly grab her upper arm with a gloved hand while the others went to their carriages. "This way, Caesonia," the Soul Carver quietly said, his accent drawing out the first syllable of her name so that it fully rhymed with "ice." Caes's eyes darted upward. This Soul Carver, as breathtaking as the others, was near her age, despite the silver streaking through his shoulder-length black hair. The Soul Carver's eyes met hers and her heart stilled. His mirrored eyes carried no emotion or reaction—they were as empty as a dried well and as dark as a vat of ink.

He was familiar.

She knew him.

From where? She had never seen a Soul Carver before.

Her lips mouthed words, but no sound came out. The Soul Carver frowned.

Moments stretched. The Soul Carvers chattered around them, a couple had noticed their exchange.

"Come on, Alair," a Soul Carver with short black hair said. "We need to go."

The two of them did not separate.

"Caesonia..." Alair muttered.

"Alair," she said.

Alair.

Alair.

"Caes," he said, as if the word suddenly came to him. Recognition suddenly flooded into his expression. Whatever spell was cast on them, seeing each other, knowing each other, apparently shattered the illusion.

They had passed the test.

"Caes..."

Caes broke down, sobbing against his chest. "You're here. You're real."

"I am," he said, holding her against him. He glared at the other Soul Carvers. "Unless you want a really bad day, you are going to wait."

"What is the meaning of this?" the representative asked, stomping back from around the wagon. "She's supposed to be inside."

"You're supposed to be inside." A trickle of blood worked its way down Alair's ear while the representative climbed into the wagon and clanged the door shut behind him. Caes let out a smothered laugh—it was about time the man realized what it was like being trapped there.

"How do we get out of here?" Caes asked softly. "What are we supposed to do? Are we going to have to re-live it all? The rest of it? *Again*?" She had to live through torture and betrayal—some of the worst memories of her life—twice. How could she bear it another time? Though...how did she know she hadn't gone through this multiple times, her memory cruelly altered just when she learned the truth?

"No," Alair said, pointing at the palace. "I don't think so. The illusion is breaking. None of this is real. Look."

Caes turned. The tops of the palace glistened in the sun, just like she remembered. But something was different—the tops were bent, like wax under a candle's flame. She watched as more and more of the palace melted, leaving behind a brilliant white light. As the melting advanced, it picked up speed, rushing towards them. By this point, the others in their world were frozen, like children's toys ready to be snatched. Cylis's arm was outstretched, pointing at them, his mouth open mid-sneer.

"I'm never letting you go," Alair said in her ear. "We are staying together. Even if I have to live my life a thousand more times to do so."

"Always," she said.

The white light spread around the castle and courtyard, consuming everything. Consuming them.

And then Caes and Alair awoke in the Burning Hand, just in time for Caes to pull back Lyritan's dagger, right before it shattered Karima.

Caes pulled back her killing blow, her heart threatening to escape her chest. Lyritan's dagger was still in her hand, the weight suddenly heavy. Lyritan's statue nodded at her, urging her to continue, while the other gods watched, waiting for what would come next. Sweat trickled down her back. Was her hesitation, this unease, a remnant from the dream Karima sent, or something more?

Something more?

She looked at Alair, and he at her.

From the moment her father gained his powers, his calling was to kill Karima. All the misery that had happened to her in Ardinan and Malithia was because he failed to do so. Now she was here, set to do the very task at which he had failed. But the goal of killing Karima was to weaken the Soul Carvers, to destroy them. She had to kill Karima, but what would the goddess's death do to her friends?

"What is it?" Alair asked.

"When she dies, you might…"

Alair nodded slowly. "I cannot claim to know what will happen. But we know the alternative if you don't kill her. We all do. It is a price that must be paid." He searched her face. "There's something more. What is it?"

"Something feels wrong." An understatement. The feeling was like a crack running through ice, a branch creaking under weight, leaves crunching in the woods, made by a creature unseen. "Something…" She dropped Lyritan's dagger, the metal ringing through the cavern as it made contact with the stones. "Something isn't right."

"Caes—"

"No. If I'm doing this, I'm doing it my way," she said. There was no other choice. She had lost too much. Suffered too much. This was going to end the way her father had initially intended it, with the blade she had found.

The way her story was originally meant to be.

Lyritan had lied to her, in both of her lives. During this entire journey he had twisted the truth, telling stories and spinning false hopes, such as with Hanith. Hanith was probably not even buried anywhere. Lyritan probably never intended for her to survive, never wanted her to rule with him. After he plied her with so many tales, why should she use the dagger that Lyritan provided for her? There was only one way to be sure he wasn't going to trick her again, and that was by doing the one thing he didn't expect.

Alair's lips set in a line. He obviously wasn't pleased, but what about this was something he'd be happy about? They were in a cavern near the true creator of the world. They weren't going to leave this cavern alive. What was a little more blood and pain? Instead, he moved behind her and held her steady.

"Are you sure?" he asked.

"Yes."

Time to get this over with. Caes held up her arm and willed for the weapon she had concealed to come forth. A heartbeat later and a hard line emerged under her skin, working its way out of her arm with each breath. Screaming, Caes watched the blade push against her flesh, turning it translucent. And then it sliced through, its exit both a relief and agony. Fire replaced the sensation of ripping skin, and blood dripped down her arm in dark rivets, staining her tunic and pooling on the floor. She grabbed the blade, tugging it out, leaving a gaping wound in her arm that did not heal. Quickly, Alair tied a cloth around her arm, staunching the blood, while Caes stared at the blood-covered shard in her other hand, the secret they had managed to keep from Lyritan.

Alair buried his head in her neck while Caes tried to stop shaking. "Steady. Steady. It's done," he said between her gasping breaths. "It's done." It was. Even now the pain dulled and she could think again. She didn't worry about tending to the wound or getting blood poisoning—she wouldn't be alive long enough for that to matter.

Instead, Caes gripped the sharp blade, not caring that it sliced her fingers. Who cared about blood when one was about to kill a goddess? With Alair standing behind her, bracing her, she turned back to her task.

Alright. She could do this.

One last time she stared at the statues of the two goddesses—and one god—proud and smirking in their poses. Was it her, or did Lyritan look...concerned? Caes ground her teeth. Bastard. He had nothing to be concerned about. He was a god. He chose to play this game, such as it was. He had no *right* to be concerned. She was the one who suffered, while these beings acted without any care other than their own power. What about the ones who worshipped them? Did deities care about mortals beyond what they could gain from them? Probably not.

Too bad she couldn't destroy all of the gods here, but even she wasn't that reckless. Who knew what that would do to the world? Her decision would have to be confined to the three deities in front of her.

Now, who was she going to choose? She had to act quickly, in case the goddesses were able to send her and Alair back into the hells that was their past again. Or worse.

Shirla.

Karima.

Lyritan.

Shirla.

Karima.

Lyritan.

Shirla...

All of them toyed with her. Tortured her. Used her. She was their pawn, expendable in their eternal game. She had lost so many that she loved. She never had the chance to just *live*. She was made to be used, and then destroyed.

I loved them.

Yes, she did. And look at what they did to her.

"Whatever you choose, I'm here," Alair said. He frowned at her bleeding hands, freshly sliced from the shard. Gently, he moved one of her hands and gripped one side of the blade, his fingers intertwined with hers. "We do this together."

"Thank you," she said, her breath ragged. "I couldn't have done this alone."

"Yes, you could have, because you're strong. But that doesn't mean you should have to. I'm here because I *want* to be, Caes. Remember that, whatever you decide."

Whatever she decided.

A moment of clarity hit her, an idea she didn't dare say.

"Do you trust me?" Caes asked. She had made her decision, and she was going to see it through.

"Yes," he said without hesitation.

"I'll hold you to that."

Biting her lip and moving as quickly as she could, she raised their hands and smashed the weapon into Karima's statue, grinning as her light faded. The shards faded into the air, changing first into a stream of what looked like chunks of bone and drops of blood, and then, finally, into a current of glowing dust that entered the sword's shard.

"What *was* that?" Caes asked. Whatever she expected the statue to do when it was destroyed, she didn't anticipate blood, bone, and something like diamonds.

Though she didn't care about the goddess. Hopefully Karima enjoyed her new existence of meaningless oblivion.

Most importantly—Alair was still here. He was still *here*. Did he still have his magic, with the goddess gone?

"Keep going," Alair said, not giving her time to ask or even look at him. The earth shook, threatening to rock her off her feet. The world felt what she had done by destroying a divine being tied to the earth. Karima was gone, the goddess now nothing more than a memory and prayers uttered to the void.

That was just one divinity gone.

Caes had to keep going.

Chapter 75

Cylis

The world shook, throwing both Lyritan and Cylis off balance. The entire range trembled, snow clouds flying into the air as far as Cylis could see from sudden avalanches that set off along the range. There was no doubt that the shaking was felt throughout the empire.

Cylis caught himself, but not before slamming his knee into a rock, while Lyritan fell to the ground. Crying out in pain, Cylis called his magic, the ice power from the sword the only thing keeping him intact in the heated ashy inferno the god had summoned.

He couldn't do this much longer. He was tired, so tired, forced to use his magic to levels he never had before in order to simply exist.

And then...

"Fuck," Cylis said. His magic faded. He wasn't dying. He had energy left. But he was...it was...

"Having an issue, mortal?" Lyritan asked, pushing himself upright. The god's eyes glowed brighter, a sickening grin on his face. "Looks like Karima has lost."

Karima was dead.

Dead.

A goddess was dead.

And his magic was gone.

"Well," Cylis said, brushing himself off, "looks like you shouldn't be gloating yet. If you had Karima's powers, I'd be dead by now. Seems like Caes outsmarted you."

A slight frown was the only indication Cylis had that he was right. Good for Caes. He should've known that he could trust that suspicious mind of hers.

Instead of attacking, he could have waited for the god to find out that he wasn't gaining all that power after all, and then deal with him sulking all the way back to Malithia. That's what Cylis got for taking the initiative.

Whatever he was feeling, the god did not glower for long. Slowly he lifted his head and his sword, his eyes glowing bright, the skin on his face blistered and charred. "That may be," Lyritan said, "but you have not seen what I am capable of." The god lifted his hand and the air itself shimmered with fire. Another wave of ash, seemingly from nowhere, rained down on them, while the god's skin crisped and burned, peeling away and revealing muscle and bone. The god didn't bleed—any blood charred and smoked and blew away on the wind.

"This would be a great time to make up your mind, Caes!" Cylis yelled, knowing that she couldn't hear him. His powers were gone, both his ice and his strength, but he still had knowledge of how to fight. He wouldn't just roll over and let the god kill him.

That wasn't his style.

Chapter 76
Caes

"One more choice," Alair said. "You only need to choose one more deity. Then we can be done here."

"Yes," Caes said solemnly, "and I have made my decision."

Shirla and Lyritan were the only two deities left, the goddess and god seemingly smirking at what Caes had done to Karima. Of course they were smirking—her death meant that they had a better chance of winning overall. They both fully expected that Caes would choose them in mere moments. The earth had stopped trembling—the statues would've no doubt already crashed to the floor if they weren't fused to their spots. It was time to make the last decision. The decision that would decide everything.

What if she picked wrong?

Too late to go back now. Any other path was futile.

"Here we go," Caes said. Together, they attacked Shirla's statue, sending more blood and bone into the air, the goddess's essence seemingly being consumed by the shard as Karima's had been. Caes's hand screamed with pain, her flesh a bloody mess. Alair hissed, the shard cutting his hand as well. The dozens of other nearby gods and goddesses stared at them, mouths and eyes wide with horror.

It was done. It was done. She had destroyed her creator, she had done the exact opposite of what she was made to do.

Things could have been so different, if only Shirla was honest with her. Loved her. And now she would never know what could have been.

But she wasn't done with her tasks in the Hand yet.

Lyritan was now the only remaining god. Lyritan.

Again, the earth shook at Shirla's death, sending Caes and Alair careening to the ground. The goddesses were bound to the earth—it was unsurprising that it cried out when they were torn from it.

Caes pushed herself up, rubbing her skinned knees. Once she was upright she faced Lyritan—the god's statue seemingly couldn't contain his glee.

He had survived. What he had worked for for over a thousand years had come to fruition. He was now the god of these lands.

Caes felt sick, her stomach threatening to expel what few contents it had. She had set the stage for this monster to rule the world.

"It's over," Alair said, letting go of his side of the shard and helping her stand steady. "Now you need to just—"

"Fuck this," she cried out. Before he could stop her, Caes smashed her weapon against Lyritan's statue. There was barely a moment to take in his surprised glance before the shard sent the god's statue to blood and dust, sending what remained careening to the ground with the remains of the two goddesses. The other statues in the room practically jumped with surprise, watching what was occurring with rapt attention. Were they worried that Caes was going to destroy them too?

Good. They deserved to be afraid.

"What have you done?" Alair asked, breathless. "We need a god—"

Case didn't turn away from what remained of Lyritan. "We did not need one of *them*."

"We went over this. Over and over, Caes. We would've picked another. And now—Caes—"

While Alair ranted, more frantic than she had ever seen him, Caes let a sense of calm wash over her. She was made to be destroyed—it was in her nature that she would bring chaos with her.

"Why, Caes?" Alair asked, his breaths loud.

"You forget where we are," Caes said. "This is where the world was made. Here, anything is possible." She turned to him, his mirrored eyes now returned to those of a normal human with Karima gone. Were his powers gone too? What about the other Soul Carvers? "They forced me to come here—what they did not expect was that I would wipe the board clean."

Bring me the shard.

Caes rubbed her temples, ignoring the blood sticking to her hair. The being within the Hand knew what she had done. Somehow, she sensed they only had moments to themselves before it would ask for the shard again—and it would not be as polite when it did.

"You just killed two goddesses," Alair said. "And a god. What else could be done?"

"Didn't you hear that?"

Alair stilled. He had to have felt it too. "What is going on?"

"Trust me," Caes said, reaching for Alair's bloody hand. She took it gently, holding the shard in the hand that was already sliced. She was in pain. So much pain. But they weren't going to leave this cavern alive—that much hadn't changed. She wouldn't be able to feel pain much longer as one needed to be alive for that to happen. "There's always a choice. The deities were the ones who told me that I had to select one of them. But they weren't the ones who wrote the rules. *That* did." She nodded to the blackness in the center of the room.

Alair smiled grimly. "You're right. There is. But let's just hope this choice somehow doesn't make things worse."

"Only one way to find out."

Her plan was simple—the Hand created the world. She would give it her power, and the shard, and ask it to choose a new god, one who would be worthy. Would the Hand be just in its choice?

There, that sense of calm came over her heart again, the steadiness telling her yes, *yes* she was making the right choice. That sense hadn't lead her astray so far—she would trust it now.

Slowly, she approached the opening in the ground, the one that seemingly led to oblivion. At the edge of the hole, with Alair's undamaged hand still holding hers, Caes screamed, "Use us. Give us to someone worthy, anyone, to take their place. Some other god." The two of them huddled together, waiting for an answer.

No.

...And there went that plan.

Though the Hand was not done with them yet.

At the bottom of the crater an inferno emerged. The flames burned orange and green, their light far was beyond what should have been lit in this cavern, and it rushed up the depths, towards them. Alair stepped behind her, gently nudging her backward with him. "Caes—"

"Wait."

"We'll burn!" he yelled.

"Wait." There was no point in running. If whatever was in that cavern wanted to burn them, there was no place to run. There was no place within this mountain where they could hope to hide from that power. "We can't run."

Alair pressed her into him, shielding her as best he could. And they watched their death approach.

The fire crept upwards, a gushing blast that shot up and up, beyond the surface of the cavern floor. But the blaze was more than fire alone—Caes's attention was caught by a...hand? A literal burning hand. She smiled. This whole time she thought the Hand was a metaphor—no, it was very real. This hand did not belong to a human, no, it was large enough to make the ones on the mountainside—the ones that seemingly belonged to giants—appear like little children. A hand that was larger than houses. Trees. It moved towards them, bringing a brilliant heat and light that made Caes and Alair step back. A gravity entered her heart, a urge to prostrate herself on the ground in both respect and terror.

This, she knew, was a true god, one of the beings who had made the earth, the true master of their existence. The one who charted the course of their lives. And the other gods here only survived and received worship at its pleasure.

She bowed her head before the Hand and held out the shards. "Anyone. Please."

Would it answer? Would it accept? Did it know what she was asking? Humans couldn't understand the language of rats, why would they hope that this creature understood mortal thoughts? Shit, this was why they did not choose this plan to begin with—attempting to do anything other than select a god from the three options. The Burning Hand—

Come forward and receive your fate. Costs must be paid. Above all, balance must be maintained.

Caes looked at Alair, his face brilliant in the light. Sweat beaded on his skin and his mirrored eyes were brilliant in the god's fire.

"*Our* fate?" she asked.

Yes. Both.

It was time. At least they would be together.

Caes gripped Alair's hand and they nodded to each other. He had heard the voice too. Their death was what was always going to happen in the Hand. They expected nothing less. It could have been worse. How many could say they were killed directly by the true creator of the world?

But whatever happened, they were together.

"I love you," she said, tears blurring her vision, "until our end and ruin."

"Always," Alair said, kissing her one last time.

Together, they stepped off the edge and into the Burning Hand's fire.

Together, they met their fate.

Chapter 77

Bethrian

It turned out that when a god died in the Burning Hand, it was rather anticlimactic. Other than the earthquake.

The god's body was another matter.

Lyritan was standing there one moment, ready to slice Cylis to bits. The next, Phelan was dead on the ground, burned beyond recognition, the golden light gone from his eyes. The poor bastard's empty gaze stared at a sky he would never see again, his hair long burned away, leaving a charred bald head. At the same moment of Lyritan's demise, all of the god's fire magic left the earth, leaving behind a thin layer of ash that Bethrian wished he could bottle and then sell as a souvenir. He needed some sort of income, since he was no longer a lord. There had to be a market for god ashes, right?

This was not the time. He had to look after the one who fought to save their lives.

"Are you alright?" Bethrian asked the Soul Carver.

Cylis laid on the ground, huffing with his eyes closed. Sweat, ash, and blood made a smeared paste all over his pale skin, his dark hair coated in something resembling mud. His complexion was oddly pale—at this point, Bethrian barely recognized Cylis without the dark purple skin and mirrored eyes.

"Fine enough," Cylis slurred. "Let me lay here for a bit."

Bethrian was more than happy to oblige.

The night had turned to morning, a bright red dawn breaking the horizon. The mountain was eerily still and not even the wind crept over the rocks, though clouds of avalanches in the distance still sent mounds of snow darting into the air. Fortunately, the area directly above them was devoid of snow, though they would have to be careful while walking for some time. While waiting for Cylis to regain strength or a desire to leave the mountain—it was impossible to say which—Bethrian stared at the rocks that had reappeared once Caes and Alair entered the Burning Hand, and the dried blood that was still splattered across the boulder. That was all that remained of the former princess and the Soul Carver, who sacrificed themselves for a world that largely despised them.

He also stared at Phelan's corpse, but that was more out of grim curiosity than anything else.

As a result, Bethrian had more than enough time to ponder what he and the former Soul Carver should do next.

With Lyritan now gone they suddenly had more than enough provisions to last them a journey back, if they were prudent. Bethrian's legs would slow them down, but he would manage. So, seeing no reason to keep his stomach miserable, Bethrian carefully chewed on a hard biscuit, waiting for Cylis to do…something. Anything. Caes and Alair weren't coming back, so what were they waiting for? It wasn't like they could expect their friends to appear and tell them that the quest was done and it was time to leave. Though, of all the ways Bethrian expected this journey to end, it wasn't with him being alone in the middle of the wilderness with Cylis.

Cylis. Cylis, who barely showed signs of life.

Though, the poor man did fight a god without magic and lose his friends in a single night. He deserved rest for a bit. No matter how impatient Bethrian was getting. The last place he wanted to be was near Phelan's corpse and the bloodstained rock.

Suddenly, Cylis rolled over and crouched, cursing as he held his stomach. The curses soon turned into howls and threats.

Fuck.

Bethrian darted and helped Cylis sit up, and placed a wad of fabric in Cylis's mouth as he screamed. No point in Cylis losing his tongue while he was at it—the blood loss could kill him. Cylis needed to calm down before he hurt himself.

What was wrong with the man? Wound poison? Magic shit? Bethrian was just about to truly panic when then, as suddenly as it started, the screams faded.

"What in the hells was that?" Bethrian asked when Cylis spit out the former wad of cloak.

"I'm not sure," Cylis said, panting. His eyes were mirrored once again. "But Karima is dead, and I'm pretty sure something else just happened. Everything is going to change."

Chapter 78

Cylis

He had fought a god and lived. He had lost his friends and his magic. And now he was stuck on a mountain with Fuckwit. This was somehow the grandest and worst day of his life.

"Can I do anything?" Bethrian asked Cylis.

"Nothing." There wasn't anything Bethrian could do to help him. He felt weird, like he had drank too much tea and lost control of his limbs. Shock from the battle? Blood loss? It could've been anything. Everything.

"You're sure?" Bethrian winced, digging through his pack and passing Cylis a flask of water. Gratefully, he sipped, ignoring how the water jolted his stomach.

"I need to sleep," Cylis said. He leaned back against the stone and closed his eyes, trying to stop shaking. "Let me rest."

"Alright." There were shuffling sounds as Bethrian made himself comfortable, throwing a blanket over Cylis first. "After the day you had, you could use some rest. And there's no way I can get off this mountain without you." A pause and then, "You better not be dying. You look...worse than normal."

"Shut up, Fuckwit."

Chapter 79

Caes

After they jumped there was fire. Then there was darkness. And then there was gray.

Let's see what happens when the powerless have power—if they make a more fitting choice.

And then the world came into focus, one bit at a time.

She was in a garden in a stone courtyard. Roses, orange trees, and lilacs all grew in the space and bloomed at the same time, something that would've been impossible in the mortal world. For they were not in the mortal world—they were dead. They had to be. Despite the flowers, the world was gray. And they had jumped into a literal pit of fire. She had felt the air scorch her lungs, her body become wrapped in the blaze. Her skin sizzled and peeled, her muscles and tendons became scorched and shriveled in the flames. Her eyes boiled and erupted in her skull.

The pain lasted only a moment, but it was all-consuming. There was no life after something like that.

How was it that she existed at all? That was something she did not expect, because of how her soul was created by and for a goddess who was now dead.

"Caes," Alair said. She turned to him.

"Alair," she said. Tears of happiness clouded her sight. They were together. The fates had let them be together. Alair stood before her, as handsome and healthy as he was at the Maltihian court. He shone, the color in his body the only thing that wasn't gray in this cold world. Wait, they both shone. Well, they were dead. It was to be expected that could make strange things happen.

But his eyes were golden, not mirrored. That was new.

"We're dead," Caes said. "The last time you were dead you were gray. But how am I with you? Where are we? And—" she held up her hand, gesturing with the golden light that seeped through the edges of her fingernails.

"We're not dead," Alair said softly, wrapping his arms around her. "I've been dead before. Feel. Listen."

Resting her head against his chest she did as bid, closing her eyes to this new strange world around her. "What am I listening for?"

"Shhh."

Caes focused, listening for anything. She heard his heartbeat, yes, but there was more. The echoes of a million voices. If she tried she could pick one or two out from the chaos—she was able to choose who to listen to. And see them.

She thought of Sabine, and realized that she could see Janell, Fer, and Sabine walking through the woods, talking with an ease she had not expected from them. Whatever had happened with the three of them, they had come to an understanding and kept their word to her.

Another thought and Caes saw Emperor Barlas sitting at a table in his study, pouring over correspondence, and then was instantly pulled to Malithia's armies massing near the border it shared with Cyvid. There would be bloodshed and chaos in the empire, but such was the fate of men—all peace was temporary.

Eventually, all empires fell.

Her eyes opened. "We're not dead."

"No," Alair said. "We're gods."

Chapter 80

Alair

Caes and Alair walked through the garden—Karima's garden, for Alair recognized it from his time there.

"How long have we been here?" Caes asked. "I feel like we've been walking for hours."

Alair shrugged. "Time does not move here like it does in the mortal realm." The two of them were sitting on the grass, each surface they touched turning to color, because they willed it so. They were gods and this was their realm—it would obey them. If he so wished he could banish the gold, like Karima often did, but he wouldn't.

He reached his hand out and touched a peony, watching the light pinks sink back into the flower, the floral scent wafting over them. Every few moments his mind was hit with a sensation that was something other, like someone calling his name. Were they mortals, issuing prayers? If they were in Karima's realm, it seemed that the Hand gave them Karima's power, at the very least. There were so many questions, so much they had to do to find out how to navigate their new existence. But that would all come with time. For now, he would smile that fate gave him what he wanted—Caes.

She was leaning back on the grass, running her hands over the green blades. Coyly, she smiled at him, and his heart leapt—at the same moment he remembered how much he had lost in order to get here.

I'll miss you, Iva, he thought. *Rest in peace.*

Somehow, he knew she heard him. He didn't know the exact limits of his power over the realm of the dead, and he intended to find out. There were a lot of people he wanted to see again. And a few he wanted to ensure entered the harshest hells.

"What are we supposed to do?" Caes suddenly asked. "We can't be expected to just sit here forever, are we?"

"No. Maybe we should—"

"There you are," Kerensa said from behind him. "I've been looking all over for you." He turned and there was his friend, just as he remembered her, even down to her mirrored eyes. Her arms were crossed, but she didn't bother to hide her smirk. "Now, how did you two pull this off?"

Chapter 81

Cylis

That night, Cylis fell asleep and dreamed he was in a garden with Kerensa. It was a strange garden, as such things went. He liked oranges, but he never saw them on any tree in Malithia. And he surely never saw them next to lilac bushes. And this place reeked like peonies. He must've hit his head during that battle with Lyritan. That was the only explanation. And it was a very possible—that was the hardest battle he had ever been in.

"Took you long enough," Kerensa said, hands on her hips. Most of her black hair was tied in a neat braid, and she looked as she had when Cylis saw her last. Which meant she was more than ready to torment him.

"Ker." Cylis crossed his arms. "You lost. You died first. I won our bet."

"That's what you have to say to me? Not, 'I miss you,'" Kerensa said, brushing a curly strand away from her face.

"Well, considering this is a dream, there's no point."

"Is it a dream?" Kerensa asked, motioning around. "You've been here before."

"Alright, not a dream. I'm hallucinating."

"Let's call it 'having a vision.'" Then Kerensa abruptly pointed at him. "Now, we're going to try this again. Say, 'I miss you, Kerensa. I'm so happy to see you.'"

"Why state the obvious?" Cylis looked around at the garden some more, the vibrant colors standing out even in the night. She was right—he had been here before. They all did. "So, if this isn't a dream, there's been some redecorating. It's a lot more colorful than it used to be."

"Yes, well, with Karima dead and all there's been a change." Kerensa nodded towards the entrance. In walked Caes and Alair, both glowing gold like Lyritan.

And Karima. Though, Karima was very good at keeping her light muted in her realm. Karima wasn't a fan of brilliant light.

Wait, Caes and Alair were glowing like a god.

A god.

No...seriously? *That's* what happened to them?

"No. No. No. I'm *not* worshiping you," Cylis said, crossing his arms harder. "You can't make me."

Caes laughed. "Well, we do technically own your soul, so maybe you should reconsider..."

Then Marva walked in behind them, giving him a wave and a smile. Alair grinned too, not bothering to hold back his budding laughter.

"Fuck this," Cylis said. "So, Shirla's gone too? And Lyritan? And instead we have you two?"

"Yes," Alair said. "And while I'm not going to tell you to worship us, we need someone to start if you want us to keep your area of the empire safe."

"Say that again, but simpler," Cylis said.

"Gods need to be worshipped," Marva said. "They need people to start worshipping them. Unless we want bad things to happen. Simple enough?"

Cylis stared. "Yes." Marva was just as beautiful as she always was. He swallowed hard. They couldn't be together—not for a long time—but at least she was happy here. At least, it looked that way.

Alair nodded in agreement. "We still don't understand everything, but we have reason to think that since we're new, older gods might test us. There's other gods that will be more than happy to try to encroach. We need you to tell the Soul Carvers that we are Karima's replacement. We will try to tell them ourselves, but there are limitations."

"It's tiring to talk to you like this," Caes said. "You're not supposed to be here. Not yet. Your soul is fighting us."

"What?" Cylis asked. "No. Wait, first things—if Karima's gone, what happens to Soul Carvers?"

"Do you still have your magic?" Caes asked.

"I...fell asleep." The three of them stared at him. "Hey, I had a rough day. I fought Lyritan—"

Caes's eyes widened. "Cylis, you fool—"

"We don't have time for this, as much as I want to hear your tale," Alair said. "You should have your magic. We can feel it. Our power is inside you."

Cylis would have normally made some sort of inappropriate joke, but there was a time and place. This was neither.

"We're keeping things as they are," Caes said. "At least for now."

"What about the Soul Carvers still in their trials?" Cylis asked. "So the poor bastards that come through the portal—"

"We are going to give them a chance to go back before the trial starts, if we can," Alair said, "but we're not undoing the magic that has been done. Or try too. There's too many Soul Carver souls here. And we're not sure what would happen if we change the process."

"We don't want to risk anything happening to them," Caes said. "Any of them. But we will make sure that whoever volunteers understands the exact price of such magic."

Fair enough. Well, having Caes and Alair as the Soul Carver gods would probably make the experience...better? Maybe? But they were trapped in a bit of a soggy pickle, especially if they didn't want to risk harming the other spirits of the Soul Carvers who were now trapped in this realm. Magic could be like a tapestry—snip the wrong thread and the entire thing could crumble apart.

"Alright," Cylis said, "so you're the new Karima. Now what's this about worship?"

"Gods grow from worship," Caes said. "And we'd like to keep our lands *ours*."

"Alright," Cylis said. "Got it. Any particular style?"

Alair rubbed his eyes. "Use your best judgment. We don't have time for this."

"Nude dancing it is."

"Cylis," Caes warned.

"The empire is going to fall to pieces," Marva said. "If it hasn't already, losing Karima is going to be the final push. I'll be shocked if it can hold on to more than a few kingdoms after this."

"Well, empires have to end sometime," Cylis said. "Good thing I wasn't planning on going back to the Malithian court."

"To Marva's point," Caes said, "we will protect this land as best we can. And keep peace in nature. But we can't do that without support. And that starts with you."

Cylis blinked. And blinked again. Harder. "I have to worship Alair. And Caes." Cylis sighed dramatically. "This is the worst day of my life."

"Well," Caes said, "look at it this way—with us helping you, you'll have divine assistance getting wherever you need to go. At least away from the mountain."

Cylis raised an eyebrow. "Just how powerful are you?"

"We don't know yet," Alair said. "We're practicing on you."

"Wonderful, *Your Augustness*." Cylis was rewarded with Caes turning to Alair, obviously very confused.

"I'll explain later," Alair muttered. Cylis smiled. Too bad he was going to miss that conversation, but at least he knew that it would be occurring. That was all he wanted.

"So," Marva asked him, "what are you going to do—"

"—now that all my friends are dead?" Cylis finished.

"I was going to say," Marva continued, "now that you have life to live as you wish. But you've always had such a way with words."

Cylis paused. What *was* he going to do? Well, he did have a plan. One from before Alair turned into a god. Alair. A god.

Alair.

Cylis turned to Kerensa. "I'll find your sister. I promise. That is where I am going next."

She nodded. "I know you will. Thank you."

"Like I said, speaking with you like this is harder than you'd think," Caes said, "since you're very much alive. So, this is goodbye for now. But know that we're always listening."

Alair locked eyes with Cylis creepily. "Always."

"Wake up," Bethrian said, shaking Cylis awake. "You're having a nightmare."

"No, I wasn't."

"You were moaning 'all my friends are dead.'"

"Shut up, Fuckwit." Cylis sat up and watched the sun slink over the horizon. Groaning, he pushed himself up. How long did he sleep? That wasn't a dream, unfortunately. No, it was fortunate. His friends were fine, and he would see them again. Someday. Even if their new state was a complication for his self-esteem.

"I was worried you were never going to wake." Bethrian had very dark circles under his bloodshot eyes, and his hair was a mangled mess.

"You're not that lucky. Look, there's something I need to tell you, and I think that everything will be best explained by watching me in silence for the next few minutes."

"Must I?"

"Yes."

Slowly, Cylis moved to his knees, ignoring that they were swollen from the fight, and saluted the rising sun. "Hail, glorious Alair, great god of the world. Savior of shit and stuff. I honor you, great one. You truly are great."

Fucking Alair, the only person alive who somehow managed to fuck his way to godhood. This really was the worst day of his life.

And Cylis wasn't done yet.

"Hail, glorious Caes, great goddess and stuff. You're so majestic and goddess-y. I am your...servant."

When he was done he sat back on his heels and looked at Bethrian.

"So," Bethrian said, picking at his beard, "they took both goddesses' and the god's places," he said.

"Yep, pretty much. You managed to figure out what happened fast. Oddly fast."

"Your eyes are back to normal and your skin is that purple color again. It wasn't hard to put the pieces together."

That explained a lot—his magic underwent a shift after Karima's death. That was why he was so sick after the battle. A fight for his life, losing his magic, and then having it forced back into his body again. That all left one feeling a bit unsettled. But based on Caes and Alair's new home, his magic was never destroyed—it simply changed hands. Hence why he was still a Soul Carver. That was his best guess.

Bethrian leaned back and stretched out a leg, gently rubbing where his bandage was. "Are they...happy?" Caes and Alair, he meant.

"I think so. They have each other."

Bethrian nodded. "I'd say this ended about as best as could be expected for them."

"Of course it did—they literally get to torment me for the rest of my life and all of eternity."

"Please. You know you wouldn't have it any other way."

No, Cylis wouldn't. But he would never admit that. Instead, he stared at Fuckwit until the man sighed. "Well," Bethrian said, "if you're feeling better, there's no point in hanging around here any longer, then."

"Nope."

"I was thinking..."

"Yes, Fuckwit?"

"It won't be smart for me to go back to Malithia quite yet, what with the conflicts and all—and the emperor hates me. At least, not by the most direct route from here. And I'm not a lord, so what do I have to go back to? Do you...mind if I go with you?"

"Whatever." Maybe it wouldn't be the worst thing to have some company on his next journey.

Cylis stood and he and Bethrian groaned and packed what few bags they had. His magic had returned, his strength rushing back into his limbs, but even Soul Carvers needed time to heal. While they worked, they discussed the finer points of their plan, including where they were going after they were done with the mountain range, and just how often they were going to have to worship Caes and Alair.

"Do you have anything to offer me for bringing you along?" Cylis said. "Or am I protecting you due to my generous heart?"

"Anything? Why, I have funds."

"You're not a lord."

"No, but I *am* a lady—Lady Peony Passionflower. And she kept her money in separate account under her own name. Accounts that I fully expect are untouched."

"...Oh." Damn, Bethrian was clever, and the separate accounts were necessary if he didn't want anyone at court finding out who he really was.

Bethrian bent over to inspect one of his legs, poking at it dramatically. "So, are we going to try to find your sister too? Once we find Kerensa's."

"We can't. I don't know where she is."

"I wouldn't be so hasty," Bethrian said. "Think—when Alair first told you where she was, how did you feel?"

"Um...relieved?"

"Did you think about visiting her?"

"...Yes?"

"And what did you feel about that?"

"Hopeful. Like it was a possibility."

"Alright—that's two clues. She's someplace safe and relatively accessible."

"You really think we can find my sister off my...feelings?"

Bethrian stood, straightening out his breeches. "I think we're going to have a long journey, and you will be surprised what I'm able to parse out."

"Lovely." A long journey, alone with Bethrian, while Alair was literally being worshipped.

That was just Cylis's luck.

"I wonder, do you think we could become their saints or prophets or something?" Bethrian asked. "Think about it—Caes and Alair became deities. Surely, there's room in the myths for someone like us."

"That's what you're thinking about? You want to be Caes's prophet?"

The former lord shrugged. "Why not? I could use a new title."

Cylis looked at the mountains ahead, at the journey that awaited them, knowing that once he stepped off this mountain a part of his life was going to be over for good. Caes and Alair had their fate, and Cylis had his. It was time he took his own steps to meet it.

"Come on, Fuckwit. We have a long way to go."

Chapter 82

Caes

That night, or whatever passed as night, Caes and Alair were laying in their new rooms. While Karima's palace—or whatever it was—was stone, it was stone that embraced the garden, and even in their room, roses, foxglove, and ivy lined the walls.

"For such a dreadful goddess, she sure had taste," Caes said, biting Alair's bottom lip. Caes's legs were wrapped around Alair's bare waist, the thin fabric of her shift the only thing between them. And from the familiar glint in Alair's eyes, it wasn't going to be there for long.

"It wasn't like this when she was here," Alair said. "The skulls are gone. From the palace, that is."

"That's good. I don't like skulls."

He nuzzled her neck, moving her hair away from her ears. "This is our realm now. Our home. We can make it look however we want."

The look of the realm was one thing. So far they spent the "day" meeting the Soul Carvers who lived in their palace and getting accustomed to where everything was, all while managing their new bodies. It would take time, but they had time. They had forever. Even though the other gods were a concern, gods did not move quickly. Cylis would probably have joined them by the time it became a pressing issue.

Something more insistent than worries about gods pressed against her. "Hmm...the decoration can wait," Caes said.

"Oh?" Alair guided her hand down to his member, where she stroked it gently. This part of their bodies had not changed. If anything, she felt every sensation more. The burning in her core turned into need. She needed him, now.

"You know exactly what I'm talking about," Caes said with a grin.

"You want me. Admit it."

"Always."

With that, the two of them fell into each other, the world outside forgotten.

Caes did not belong at court. She did not belong to any kingdom. But she belonged here, with him.

She was home.

Acknowledgements

Book three. An entire trilogy and a book of companion stories. Since I first drafted *Serpent* in 2019, I moved across the country, had a baby, bought and sold a home, experienced COVID, and adopted a fourth cat. Not in that order. A lot of life has happened while I worked on and published this series, and I am both proud and saddened to be bringing Caes's story to a close.

And once again, there is a long list of people I need to thank for helping me make this happen.

Elizabeth S. Tralfagar—The literary delight of my life. Thank you for everything, including extensive edits. And I will get you to try cheese curd pizza someday, or tatertot hotdish—your choice.

To Parker and Wilson—The two of you have been an inspiration and motivation. It has been a pleasure and privilege to observe the dedication you bring to your own life and work.

Samantha—Your love for my stories and characters has been a constant and greatly appreciated motivation. Thank you so much for all of your beta reads and brainstorming—and your friendship.

Emily Almanza—Sorry I killed everyone. But it ended up ok, right? See? Soul Carvers *are* happy here.

Beth—Thank you so much for the beta reads and last-minute typo catching. Oh, and the swag ideas. Cylis is shown in his best light because of you :)

To Dewi Hargreaves and Ivy—Thank you so much for your artwork and design which has made all of my books absolutely gorgeous.

My ARC readers—Thank you for taking the time to read my books to help me get reviews in place before publication. Indie books live and die by their ARC reviews, and I am so grateful that you have taken the time to leave ratings to help *Serpent* find its audience.

My husband—Thank you for giving me time to write, constant support, and not saying a word when I announced I commissioned more art. Or bought more books. Or decided to take up amateur leatherworking. Or when I turned the basement into a greenhouse. Or when I turned what remained of the basement into a library. There's more, but I think I made my point.

And to my readers, thank you so much. Your messages, comments, and love for my books are what keeps me going. Thank you.

Final Note

Thank you so much for reading this book and very likely the whole *Serpent* series! With all of the amazing authors available to readers, I am humbled each time someone chooses my books.

As an indie author, reviews from readers are critical, including that reviews influence how sales platforms display and recommend our books to others. Indies don't have marketing teams or corporate funding—instead, our books live because of our readers. If you're willing to leave a review for my books, or even just a rating, it means so much to me, and it helps me continue to bring more books into the world.

Thank you again for choosing to spend time with my characters, and I hope to see you again on later adventures.

-Scarlett

About the Author

Scarlett D. Vine is the author of *The Twice-Cursed Serpent* series and the forthcoming *Twisted Worlds*. When she isn't reading or writing, she spends her time gardening and tending to her clowder of cats. She lives in Minnesota with her husband and son.

Printed in Great Britain
by Amazon